THE MAN WHO FORGOT HIS WIFE

www.transworldbooks.co.uk

THE MAN WHO FORGOT HIS WIFE

John O'Farrell

Doubleday

LONDON • TORONTO • SYDNEY • AUCKLAND • JOHANNESBURG

TRANSWORLD PUBLISHERS
61–63 Uxbridge Road, London W5 5SA
A Random House Group Company
www.transworldbooks.co.uk

First published in Great Britain
in 2012 by Doubleday
an imprint of Transworld Publishers

A CIP catalogue record for this book
is available from the British Library.

ISBNs 9780385606103 (cased)
9780385606110 (tpb)

Addresses for Random House Group Ltd companies outside the UK
can be found at: www.randomhouse.co.uk
The Random House Group Ltd Reg. No. 954009

The Random House Group Limited supports the Forest Stewardship Council (FSC®), the
leading international forest-certification organization. Our books carrying the FSC label are
printed on FSC®-certified paper. FSC is the only forest-certification scheme endorsed by
the leading environmental organizations, including Greenpeace. Our paper procurement
policy can be found at www.randomhouse.co.uk/environment.

Typeset in 12/14.5pt Ehrhardt by
Falcon Oast Graphic Art Ltd.
Printed and bound in Great Britain by
Clays Ltd, St Ives plc

2 4 6 8 10 9 7 5 3 1

For Lily

Chapter 1

I remember when I was a child I used to watch *Mr & Mrs*. We all did; it seemed like the only option available, so everyone just put up with it. A bit like all those marriages on the programme, now I think about it. Obviously *Mr & Mrs* wasn't the cultural high-light of our week; we didn't all rush to school next morning and share our outrage that Geoff from Coventry didn't know that Julie's favourite foreign food was spaghetti. But unquestioningly we just watched the procession of unglamorous couples go through the minor embarrassment of revealing all the little things that they didn't know about each other. Or, worse still, that there weren't any.

If ITV had wanted to increase the ratings a bit, perhaps they should have done a little more covert research about the big stuff the partners really didn't know. 'So, Geoff, for tonight's star prize, do you think that Julie's favourite way to spend a Saturday night is: (a) Watching television? (b) Going to the cinema? Or (c) Secretly meeting her illicit lover Gerald, who at least asks her about her day occasionally?'

But the subtext of *Mr & Mrs* was that this was all there was to marriage: just knowing each other very well. Being very familiar with one another. The giant heart-covered cards of Valentine's Day should say '*I'm really used to you*' or '*Love is . . . knowing every single thing you're going to say before you even bloody say it.*' Like two lifers sharing a prison cell, you just spend so much time in each other's company that there really shouldn't be anything left that might surprise either of you.

My marriage was not like that.

Lots of husbands forget things. They forget that their wives have an important meeting that morning, they forget to pick up the dry cleaning, or they forget to buy their wife a birthday present until they are passing the Texaco mini-mart the night before. It drives their partners mad that men can be so self-obsessed as to overlook a major event in the life of their other half or a key date in the marriage calendar.

I didn't suffer from this careless absent-mindedness. I just completely forgot who my wife was. Her name, her face, our history together, everything she had ever told me, everything I had said to her – it was all wiped, leaving me with no knowledge that she even existed. I would not have done very well on *Mr & Mrs*. When the glamorous hostess escorted my wife out of the sound-proof box, I would have been losing points already for optimistically asking which one I was married to. Apparently women hate that.

In my defence, it wasn't just my wife I forgot, it was everything else as well. When I say, 'I remember watching *Mr & Mrs*', that is actually quite a momentous statement for me. The phrase 'I remember' was not always in my vocabulary. There was a period in my life when I might have been aware of the TV show but would have had no personal memory of ever having seen it. I was very even-handed during the dark ages of my amnesia: I had no idea who *I* was either. I had no memory of friends, family, personal experience or identity; I didn't even know what my own name was. When it first happened, I actually checked to see if there was a name tag on the inside of my jacket. It just said 'Gap'.

My bizarre reawakening occurred on a London underground train at some point after it had emerged into the daylight, stopping pointlessly at nowhere places that seemed unsure whether they were the outskirts of London or suburbs of Heathrow Airport.

It was a drizzly afternoon in what I vaguely still understood was the autumn. There was no blinding flash or euphoric energy surge; just a creeping confusion about where I was. The humming tube carriage started up again and then I became aware that I had no idea why I was on this journey. 'Hounslow East' said the sign outside the grimy window as the train came to a halt, but no one got on or off. Perhaps this was just a momentary blackout; perhaps this blank nothingness was what everyone felt as they reached Hounslow East.

But then I realized that not only did I not know where I was going, but I couldn't remember where I had come from either. Am I going to work? What is my work? I don't know. Now the panic was rising inside me. I'm not well; I need to go home and go to bed. Where is home? I don't know where I live. Think! Think – it will come back to me!

'Come on—' I said out loud, intending to address myself by my own name. But the end of the sentence wasn't there; it was like a missing rung on a ladder. I searched for a wallet, a diary, a mobile phone, anything that might make it all fall back into place. My pockets were empty – just a ticket and a bit of money. There was a small red paint stain on my jeans. 'I wonder how that got there?' I thought. My brain had rebooted, but all the old files had been wiped.

There were loose pages from free newspapers scattered around the floor. I saw the tear in the fabric of the seat opposite. My mind was processing new input at great speed now, devouring advertising slogans and signs telling people to look out for suspicious packages. But staring at the tube map in front of me, I found all these new lines of thought were unable to link up with anything else on the network. The synapses in my head were closed for essential refurbishment; the neurons were being held at King's Cross due to signalling problems.

The fear made me want to run away, but this was an affliction that followed me around. I was pacing up the empty carriage now, bewildered as to what to do next. Should I get off at the next deserted station and try to get help? Should I pull the emergency lever in the hope that the sudden stop would jolt my memory? 'It's just a temporary blip,' I told myself. I sat and squeezed my eyes closed, pressing my hands against my temples as if I could force some sense out of my head.

Then, to my relief, I was no longer completely alone. An attractive-looking woman boarded the train and sat diagonally opposite me without making eye contact.

'Excuse me,' I said quickly. 'I think I might be going a bit mad!' and I may have emitted a slightly manic laugh. Before the doors even had time to think about closing, she got straight up and left the carriage.

I noticed on the map that the train would do a loop at Heathrow. If I travelled back in the direction in which I had come, maybe a station or some visual prompt might help me relocate myself? And more people were bound to get on the train at the airport; surely then I would find someone who could help me? But at Heathrow Terminal 2 I went from travelling alone on an empty train to being trapped in a jam-packed carriage, with luggage-laden travellers squashed up against one another, talking a hundred different languages, none of them mine. I noticed every button on every shirt, heard all the different voices at once – everything was louder, colours too bright, smells too strong. I was on a tube train with maps clearly stating the route, with thousands of people travelling there with me, and yet I felt as lost and lonely as it is possible to be.

*

Half an hour later, as the only person standing still in a teeming railway terminal, I scanned the boards for some route back to my previous life. Arrows pointed to platforms and numbered zones; dozens of signs told hurrying travellers where they might go, as ceaseless information scrolled across screens and distorted announcements filled my ears. There was a short queue at a stall offering 'Information', but I was guessing they wouldn't be able to tell me my identity. I ventured into a public toilet just to stare into a mirror and was shocked by the age of the bearded stranger I saw frowning back at me. I guessed I was around forty, maybe more, greying at the temples and thinning on top. It was impossible to know whether it was the years or the mileage. Without even think-ing about it, I'd presumed I was somewhere in my early twenties, but now I could see that I was actually two decades older than that. I learned later that this was nothing to do with my particular neurological condition – that's just how everyone feels in middle age.

'Sorry – can you help me? I'm lost . . .' I said to a young man in a smart suit.

'Where do you want to go?'

'I don't know, I can't remember.'

'Oh, yeah, I know where that is. You want the Northern Line; change at Wanker Street.'

Other passers-by just ignored my requests for help: eye contact was avoided, wired-up ears were deaf to my pleas.

'Excuse me – I don't know who I am!' I said to a sympathetic-looking vicar pulling a suitcase on wheels.

'Ah, yes . . . well, I don't think any of us knows who we really are, do we?'

'No, I mean I really don't know who I am. I've forgotten everything.'

His body language suggested he was already keen to be on his way. 'Well, we may all sometimes feel as though we don't know if there is any meaning to it all, but in fact each of us really is very special indeed . . . Now *I*'m forgetting that I'm already late for my train!'

Seeing the clergyman made me wonder if I had actually died and was on the way to Heaven. It seemed unlikely that God's sense of humour was so warped that he would make us travel to Heaven on the London underground during the rush hour. 'Paradise plc would like to apologize for the delay for those travelling to the afterlife. Customers destined for Hell are advised to alight at Boston Manor, where a replacement bus service is in operation.' In fact, this experience did feel like a kind of death. Trapped as I was in some dream-like suspended state, I knew of no one who cared if I lived or died. I had no character witnesses who could vouch for my existence. I think I learned then that that is the most basic primeval human need of all – that simple reassurance that you are alive and will be acknowledged by other human beings. 'I exist!' declare all those Stone Age cave paintings. 'I exist!' say the graffiti tags on the underground walls. That's the whole point of the internet – it's given everyone the chance to proclaim their existence to the world. Friends Reunited: 'Here I am! Look over here! Yes, you had forgotten me but now you remember me again!' Facebook: 'This is me. Look, I have photos, friends, interests. No one can say I was never born – here is the proof for all to see.' That is the central tenet of twenty-first-century Western philosophy: 'I tweet, therefore I am.'

But I was trapped in something worse than solitary confinement. Even the individual travellers around me, thousands of miles from their homes, would still have their friends and family with them, efficiently packed away in their heads. My mental vacuum had physical symptoms; I was shaking and felt short of breath. Part of me wanted to go back to the underground platform and throw myself in front of the next train. Instead I watched a rushing commuter aim an empty coffee cup at the trolley of a litter-collector, but then continue on her way when it missed and fell to the floor. I bent down, picked it up and added it to the other rubbish that was being slowly collected by the elderly Asian man in his ill-fitting luminous suit.

'Thank you,' he said.

'Um, excuse me, I think I've had some sort of stroke or something . . .' I said, as I began to explain my predicament. It sounded so implausible, I thought, as I heard myself describing it, that I felt an enormous gratitude to this man for appearing genuinely concerned.

'You need the hospital! King Edward's is a mile up the road,' he said, pointing in the general direction. 'I would take you there, but . . . I'd lose my job.'

It was the first compassion anyone had shown me and suddenly I felt like crying. 'Of course – medical help!' I thought. 'That's what I need.'

'Thank you! Thank you!' I gushed to my best friend in the whole world. The location of the hospital was confirmed by a map on the side of a bus shelter; you just went straight up the road and turned left at the giant lump of chewing gum. Now I was going somewhere; just this mission gave me a fragment of hope. And so I strode up the busy main road like an amazed time traveller or an alien from another planet, trying to take it all in, some of it strangely familiar, some of it completely bizarre. There was a brief moment of hope when I saw a sign on a lamp post with the headline 'MISSING'. Underneath was a photocopied picture of an overweight cat. And then the towering concrete block ahead turned into the hospital and I felt my pace quicken, as if the people in there might somehow immediately make everything better.

'Excuse me – I really need to see a doctor,' I gabbled at the front desk of Accident and Emergency. 'I think I've had a sort of brain freeze or something. I can't remember who I am or anything about myself. It's like my memory's been completely wiped.'

'Right. Could I take your name, please?'

There was a split second when I actually went to answer this question in the casual manner in which it had been posed.

'That's what I'm saying – I can't even remember my own name! It's like, all personal information has suddenly been erased . . .'

'I see. Well, could I take your address then, please?'

'Um – sorry – I don't think I'm making myself clear. I've got this extreme amnesia – I can't remember a single thing about myself.'

The hospital receptionist managed to look harassed and bored at the same time.

'Right. Who's your registered doctor?'

'Well, *I don't know*, obviously. I was on a train, and then I suddenly realized I didn't know why I was on it, where I was going or anything. And now I can't remember where I live, where I work, what my name is, or even if this has ever happened to me before.'

She glanced up at me as if I was being particularly un-cooperative. 'NHS number?' Her exasperated tone at least conceded that this was a long shot. The phone rang and she left me there in limbo while she dealt with someone more amenable. I stared at a poster asking me if I had remembered to examine my testicles. I didn't know, but felt this probably wasn't the moment.

'I'm sorry, but we're not allowed to process you without asking these questions,' she said, when she returned her attention to me. 'Are you currently on any prescriptions or regular medications?'

'I don't know!'

'Do you have any allergies or follow any special diet?'

'No idea.'

'And could you please provide the name and contact details for your spouse or next of kin?'

That's when I first noticed it. The indented ring of white flesh on my fourth finger. The ghostly scar where a wedding ring had been. All the fingertips were crowned with badly bitten nails, red raw around the edges.

'Yes, next of kin! I have a wife maybe?' I said excitedly. The ring could have been stolen, along with my wallet and phone. Perhaps I had been robbed and concussed and maybe my dear wife was looking for me right now. The shadow of a wedding ring filled me with hope. 'Maybe my wife is at this moment ringing round all the hospitals, trying to find me,' I said.

A week later I was still in the hospital waiting for her call.

Chapter 2

My fingernails had grown back and the skin was no longer gnawed away until it bled. I had a label on my wrist that said 'UNKNOWN WHITE MALE', though the hospital porters had dubbed me 'Jason' after the fictional amnesiac in *The Bourne Identity*. However, it turned out that knowing absolutely nothing about yourself was not quite as exciting and eventful as it appeared in Hollywood blockbusters. My status seemed to have evolved from emergency in-patient to layabout lodger at King Edward's Hospital in West London. Already I found myself feeling sufficiently established to refer to the place as 'Teddy's'; the fundraising posters featured a friendly teddy-bear character that had presumably been chosen ahead of the image of a 1950s Teddy Boy or an item of lady's lingerie.

I had no illness as such. I had been examined on the first day for a possible blow to the head, but there was no such logical explanation for why on Tuesday, 22 October, my brain had suddenly decided to restore factory settings. Each day I had woken up hoping that I might have woken up. But the split second of disorientation that you experience on stirring in a strange bed had now lasted an entire week. I kept reaching in vain for my missing past life, but it was like the ghostly sensation when you imagine your phone just vibrated in your pocket and then check to find that no one called.

I had been seen by a regular stream of doctors, neurologists and attendant students, for whom I was paraded as something of an interesting novelty. They were all united in their diagnosis. None of them had the faintest idea what had happened to me. One medical student asked me rather accusingly, 'If you've forgotten everything, how come you can still remember how to talk?'

One of the neurologists, on the other hand, was particularly focused on my claim that I hadn't lost memories of general current affairs or the wider world. 'So would you remember, for example, the publication of *The Computer Under Your Cranium* by Dr Kevin Hoddy?'

'Er, Kevin, lots of people might not remember that . . .' interjected one of the other doctors.

'Okay, what about the BBC Four series *The Brain Explorers*, co-presented by Dr Kevin Hoddy?'

'No – I don't recall that.'

'Hmm, fascinating . . .' said Dr Hoddy. 'Absolutely fascinating.'

It only compounded my depression to realize that, at the moment, my very best friend in the whole world was Annoying Bernard in the next bed. In one way Bernard provided a valuable service to me during those first seven days. On the inside I was almost crippled with anxiety about what had happened to me, who I was and whether I would ever recover the rest of my life. But it never seemed like I had much time to dwell on this, due to being in a constant state of mild irritation at the man in the next bed congratulating me for remembering what I had for breakfast.

'No, that's not a symptom of my condition, Bernard. Remember, you were there when the consultant explained it all.'

'Sorry, I forgot! It must be infectious!'

Bernard meant well; he wasn't an unpleasant person – in fact, he was unremittingly jolly. I just found it a bit wearing to have to spend twenty-four hours a day with someone who seemed to think that my neurological disorder could be overcome if I was just upbeat and cheerful about the whole 'bloomin' business'.

'I tell you what, there's a few embarrassing things in my past that I wouldn't mind forgetting, I can tell you!' He chuckled. 'New Year's Eve 1999 – know what I mean?!' and he mimed drinking as he rolled his eyes. 'Oh yes, I wouldn't mind forgetting that one! And a certain lady from the Swindon Salsa Dance Club . . . oh yes, I wouldn't mind that episode being struck from the official record please, Mr Chairman!'

Eventually one doctor in particular seemed to take the lead on my case. Dr Anne Lewington was a slightly mad-looking consultant neurologist in her fifties who was supposed to be at this hospital only two days a week, but was so perplexed by my condition that she made a point of seeing me every day. Under her supervision I had a brain scan, I had wires attached to my head, I had audio-visual stimuli tests; but in every case the activity in my brain was apparently 'completely normal'. It was a shame my brain had no button just to switch it off and then switch it back on again.

It took me a day or two to work out that Dr Lewington's excitement at examining my results bore no relation whatsoever to any progress or understanding of what had happened to me.

'Oooh, that's interesting!'

'What? What?' I asked optimistically.

'Both hippocampi are normal, the volumes of both entorhinal cortices and temporal lobes are normal.'

'Right – so does that explain anything?'

'Nothing at all. That's what's so interesting! No bilateral damage to the medial temporal lobe or diencephalic midline. It would appear that your extra-personal memories have been consolidated in the neocortex independently of the medial temporal lobe.'

'Is that good or bad?'

'Well, there's no discernible logic or pattern to any of it. But then that's typical of brain scans as a whole – such a mystery!' she said, clapping her hands together in delight. 'That's what makes it so utterly compelling!'

I felt my body slumping back in the chair again.

'And as for how memories are processed and stored – that is one of the most baffling areas of all. It's such a thrilling subject to be researching!'

'Hmmm, great . . .' I nodded blankly. It was like having open-heart surgery and hearing, 'Wow – what's this big muscle in here pumping away of its own accord?!'

It was quite a few days before Dr Lewington had reached her conclusion and came and sat by my bed to explain what she thought had happened. She talked so quietly that Bernard was forced to turn off his radio on the other side of the curtain.

'From cases similar to your own in the United States and elsewhere, it seems that you have experienced a "psychogenic fugue"; literally a "flight" from your previous life, possibly triggered by extreme stress or an inability to cope with whatever was happening.'

'A fugue?'

'Yes, this only happens to a handful of people every year in the whole world, though no two cases seem to be identical. The loss of personal items such as your phone or wallet was probably deliberate on your part as you slipped into the "fugue state", and it's usual to have no recall of consciously abandoning all traces of your former life. Clearly you have not forgotten everything or you would be like a newborn infant, but typically with "retrograde amnesia", the patient would know, say, who Princess Diana was, but might not know that she had died.'

'Paris. 1998,' I said, showing off a little.

'1997!' came Bernard's voice from the other side of the curtain.

'Your recall of these *extra-personal* memories suggests you stand a good chance of getting your *personal* memories back and returning to your old life.'

'But when exactly?'

'Thirty-first of August,' said Bernard. 'She was pronounced dead around four a.m.'

Dr Lewington was reluctant to make any promises, and had to concede that there was no guarantee that I would definitely recover. And so I was left alone with this frightening thought, staring at the green curtains around my bed, wondering if I would ever make contact with my previous life again.

'Maybe you're a serial killer?' said Bernard's nonchalant voice.

'Sorry, Bernard, are you talking to me?'

'Well, she said it might have been caused by a need to shut out your past; perhaps it's because you couldn't stand the torment of being the undetected murderer of homeless vagrants whose bodies are stored in freezer cabinets in your basement.'

'That's a lovely thought. Thank you.'

'It's possible. Or perhaps you're a terrorist.'

'Well, let's hope not, eh?'

'A drug dealer. On the run from the Chinese triads!'

I resolved to say nothing in the hope that the speculation might peter out.

'A pimp . . . A compulsive arsonist . . .'

There were some headphones somewhere. I looked under my bedside table for a way to block out the list of appalling crimes that might have precipitated my breakdown, most notably 'paedophile', 'vivisectionist' and 'banker'.

I dismissed Bernard's speculation as completely ridiculous, and then later that afternoon felt a flush of fear and guilt as I was informed that there were two policemen waiting for me in the ward sister's office. In fact, they had not come to arrest me for war crimes against the people of Bosnia, as Bernard suggested. It turned out that they had come with a large file of 'Missing Persons' which they now went through very slowly, staring carefully at each photo before looking studiously at me.

'Well, that one's clearly not me,' I found myself interjecting, desperate to see if I was on any of the later pages.

'We have to give due consideration to every single file, sir.'

'Yes, but I'm not that fat. Or black. Or a woman.'

They looked at me suspiciously to see if I might have attempted to cover up my African, feminine features and then reluctantly turned the page.

'Hmmm, what do you think?' said the officer, looking between my face and the photo of a wizened old pensioner.

'He's about eighty!' I objected.

'A lot of these people look older than they actually are, sir – they might have been on drugs or living on the street. How long have you had that beard?'

'Er, well – since before I can remember . . .'

'Just roughly speaking. A month, a year, ten years?'

'I don't know! Like the nurse said, I am suffering from retrograde amnesia, so my mind is a blank about everything prior to last Tuesday.'

They looked at each other, gently shook their heads in exasperation, then continued looking for any similarities between my appearance and the photos of a teenage girl, a Sikh, and a Jack Russell terrier, which at least they conceded had been put in the wrong file.

The fact that no one had reported me missing seemed to tell a story of its own. There had been no urgent reports on the news, no tearful appeals from a loving family, no full-page adverts in the newspaper for this dearly missed husband, father or work colleague. Had I been this lonely before my fugue, I wondered; had that been the stress that provoked my mental Etch-a-Sketch into shaking the screen clear to start again?

Whatever my past, all I could think about was being rescued from this desert island in a city of eight million people. I wanted to build a big fire on the beach, put a message in a bottle, spell out giant letters for passing aircraft.

'Could we get something in the newspaper?' I kept suggesting to the ward sister. 'A sort of "Do you know this man?" feature next to my photo?' Despite her general air of never having enough time or appreciation, she eventually agreed that this might be a good idea, and I sat in her tiny office while she nervously rang the news desk at the *London Evening Standard*. She explained my situation, but I only heard her side of the conversation, as she covered the mouthpiece and relayed their questions about me.

'They want to know if you are really brilliant at the piano or anything like that?'

'Well – I don't know . . . I can't remember. Maybe I should speak to them?'

'He doesn't know.' Another pause. 'Are you, like, an incredible linguist or a maths genius or anything?'

'I don't think so. I can only do the easy puzzles in Bernard's Sudoku book . . . Should I speak to them?'

'Er, he can do easy Sudoku puzzles. Does that help at all?'

Apparently the paper didn't have the staff to send anyone round to the hospital, but said they might run the story if we sent over all the details with an up-to-date photo. The next day in the centre pages there was a huge double spread headed 'Who's the Mystery Man?' Beneath it was a picture of a well-groomed young man standing beside Pippa Middleton at a charity polo match. I went through the paper twice, but there was nothing about me. It transpired that they had been intending to run my story, but then the scoop about the mystery companion of Prince William's sister-in-law had broken, and the editor had ruled that they couldn't have two 'mystery man' stories in the same edition. The journalist who had taken our initial call was now on holiday, so the potential story was now assigned to another reporter. 'Tell me,' she asked, 'are you, like, really brilliant at the piano or anything?'

I found it hard to sleep at night, and sometimes slipped away to the dark and empty Day Room, which boasted a great view of the hypnotic London skyline. It was on the fourth night, staring out at the million tiny lights of the city, that it hit me that this was my life now; that this syndrome wasn't some temporary blip. Someone was called to investigate the loud thumping noise coming from the tenth floor. It was there that one of the orderlies found me, banging my head against the glass over and over again. 'Hey, mate, don't do that!' he said. 'You'll break the glass.'

Sometimes I would pass a few hours in the television room. It was on one of these visits that I discovered *Mr & Mrs*, which had been reinvented featuring celebrities and their good-looking spouses. This programme became something of an obsession with me. I just loved how these couples could remember so much about one another, and I laughed along with every marital faux-pas and basked in the couples' easy familiarity.

'Ah, found you!' declared Bernard in his unmistakable high-pitched nasal whine, just as the second half of the programme was about to begin. 'Look, I got a couple of books for you from the newsagent's in the lobby: *How to Improve Your Memory in Just Fifteen Minutes a Day*! I don't know why we didn't think of this ages ago!'

'That's very kind of you, Bernard, but I'm guessing that's more for general forgetfulness than retrograde amnesia.'

'Well, it's all degrees of the same thing, isn't it?'

'Er, no.'

'Believe me, I know what you're going through because I can never remember where I've put my keys.'

'See, I don't suffer from that, actually. I can remember

everything I've done since coming to this hospital. But I just can't remember a single thing about my life before that day.'

'Yes, yes, I see what you're saying. So you might need to do more than fifteen minutes a day,' he conceded, opening the book at random. '*When you are introduced to a new person for the first time . . . try repeating their name out loud to lodge it in your memory. So instead of just "Hello" you say "Hello, Simon".* Well, you could try doing that for a start!'

'Yeah, but you see, I don't think that's going to unlock the first forty years of my life . . .'

'Scissors is the other one. I can never remember where I left the scissors. Sometimes I think they must be deliberately avoiding me! Ooh, this is a good one: "*If you have problems remembering telephone numbers, try making associations. For example, if a friend's number is 2012 1066, then just remember it by thinking, London Olympics and the Battle of Hastings.*"'

'Okay – great. If that particular number comes up, I'll definitely remember it like that.'

'You see!' said Bernard, gratified that he'd been such a help. 'And it's only fifteen minutes a day. Ooh, *All-Star Mr & Mrs*!' I'd love to go on that programme. You know, like, if I was famous . . . and had a wife.'

When my favourite TV show was over for another day, I announced I was heading back to my bed, but Bernard jumped up 'to keep me company', triumphantly revealing the other book he had bought on the ground floor. He had decided that one way to trigger a memory of my own identity might be to read out every single male name in the worryingly thick tome entitled *Name Your Baby*. Part of me wanted to scream in frustration, but I knew that in his uniquely unhelpful way, Bernard was only trying to be helpful.

During the course of that long afternoon it became clear why *Name Your Baby* has never been a huge hit as an audiobook. Sure there are lots of characters, but none of them is ever particularly developed. 'Aaron', for example, has a walk-on part right at the beginning but then we never hear from him again. The same was true with 'Abdullah', who also failed to offer up any clues as to whether that might be the sort of name my parents had given me.

'I'm not sure you should lie down like that,' said Bernard. 'You're still really concentrating, aren't you?'

'Definitely. I'm just closing my eyes so I can be sure there's nothing else to distract me . . .'

I eventually woke up to the alliterative poetry of 'Francis? Frank? Frankie? Franklin?' Even though Bernard had been going for several hours, he still declared every name with extraordinary gusto and optimism. I had just had the same dream I'd experienced a couple of times now: a snapshot of a moment sharing laughter with a woman. I couldn't remember a face or a name, but she seemed to love me as I loved her. The sensation was pure happiness, the only colour in a black-and-white world, and I was crushed when I awoke to the huge void that was my life right now. Had it not been for the gripping narrative of Bernard's book, I might have allowed myself to be quite depressed.

'Gabriel? Gael? Galvin? Ganesh?'

'Hmmm,' I thought, 'I don't think I look much like a "Ganesh". I haven't got four arms and the head of an elephant, for a start.' Maybe I could ask him to stop now; perhaps claim that after several hours of intense concentration I was tiring a little.

'Gareth? Garfield? Garrison?' An unspecified electronic buzz was coming from the ward reception desk. 'Garth? Garvin? Gary?'

And then something extraordinary happened. On hearing the word 'Gary', I just heard myself mumble '07700 . . .'

'What was that?' said Bernard.

'I don't know,' I said, sitting up. 'It just came out when you said "Gary".'

'Is that it? Is that you? Are you *Gary*?'

'I don't think so. Say it again.'

'Gary!'

'07700 . . .' There was more. '900 . . . 913.'

It was like an involuntary spasm; there was no context or meaning to it – it just felt natural that those numbers followed that name.

'That's a telephone number!' said Bernard excitedly, writing it down.

'Yeah, but whose?'

Bernard looked at me as if I was being particularly stupid. 'I mean, someone called Gary, probably, but I wonder who he is?'

We had discovered a fragment of DNA from my past life. Bernard had successfully shown the way to my hinterland. I'd been sceptical and negative and he had proved me wrong. I might have actually congratulated him on his tenacity and initiative if I hadn't noticed that these very qualities had caused him to reach for his mobile phone and start dialling.

'What are you doing?' I screamed.

'Ringing Gary. Was it "913" at the end?'

'No, don't! I'm not ready! We should talk to the doctor! You're not allowed to use that in here—'

'It's ringing!' and he threw the handset over to me.

Slowly I raised it to my ear. 'There's no one there. It's probably just a random number. I can't believe I'm even listening to this . . .' Then a distant electronic crackle. And after a whole week, the first faint sound heard by rescue teams digging in the rubble.

'Hello?' said a male voice, on a weak, distorted signal.

'Um . . . hello? Is that . . . er, Gary, by any chance?' I stammered.

'Yeah. Vaughan! Is that you? Where the hell have you been? It's like you suddenly disappeared off the face of the earth!'

In a panic I dropped the call and threw the handset back to Bernard.

'Did you recognize his voice?'

'Er, no. No, I ... It's probably just some random bloke,' I stammered. But the stranger was ringing straight back. And soon they were having quite an animated chat about me.

'Not any more,' said Bernard. 'I think *I*'m his best friend now ...'

Chapter 3

Gary hugged me meaningfully while I just stood there, enduring the physical contact like some teenage boy cuddled by his aunt at Christmas.

'Vaughan! I was so worried about you. I love you, man!'

'You love me?' I stammered. 'So am I your . . . ? Are we, like, *homosexuals*?'

The meaningful embrace ended very suddenly as Gary glanced across at Bernard. 'No, I don't love you like *that*. I mean I love you like a brother, you know . . .'

'You're my brother?'

'No, not literally your brother – I mean we're like brothers, you and me. Gazoody-baby!'

'What?'

'Gazoody-baby! That's what we used to say, isn't it? Gazooooooody-baby! Remember?' and he gave me a little playful punch on the arm which actually hurt slightly.

This was my visitor being reserved and unassuming after he'd been given a little talk by the doctor. She had warned him on the phone that I was unlikely to know who he was, and might react nervously if he was too presumptuous or over-familiar. It was good that he had taken so much of this on board. Despite the solitude I'd felt up to this point, the sudden friendliness of this stranger felt inappropriate. Some primal defence mechanism kicked in; clearly early hunter-gatherers had learned that total strangers were only this friendly when trying to get you to come to an Alpha Course meeting.

'Look, I know this is going to sound a bit rude, but I'm afraid I really don't know who you are. Until you called me "Vaughan" I didn't even know that was my Christian name.'

'Actually it's your surname. That's just what everybody calls you.'

'See? I didn't know that! I don't know anything. Do I have a mother, for example? I don't know.'

The man paused and placed his hand on my shoulder. 'I'm sorry, mate. Your old mum kicked the bucket about five years ago.'

'Oh, okay.' I shrugged. 'Well, I don't remember her anyway . . .'

And he laughed as if I was making a joke.

'Yeah, the nurse said you've lost your memory or something? She's hot, isn't she? Has she seen you naked?'

'Er, no.'

'Well, that's probably just as well. Do you want to go and get a pint or two? I really fancy a pickled gherkin.'

And then I found myself emitting an unexpected laugh. It was the first time I had laughed since Day Zero, and my visitor hadn't even been trying to be funny. Just the randomness of his thought processes felt comical and refreshing. My own personality had been a mystery to me when I walked into the hospital; the various darkened rooms just needed the right people to open the doors to show me the way around. Bernard had lit up my irritable, slightly intolerant side; Gary had shown me what made me laugh.

'So, Vaughan, put some clothes on, for Christ's sake, 'cos you can't go to the pub in your fucking pyjamas!'

'He's not allowed to leave the hospital!' interjected Bernard, looking a little put out by this interloper's arrival. 'In fact, the doctor said she wanted to be here when you two first met.'

'Yeah, but I got fed up of waiting, didn't I? I've been sitting out there twenty minutes. I don't need an appointment to see my best friend!'

I tried not to look too smugly towards Bernard at this description of myself. After a week in an institution, my friend's disregard for rules was infectious and part of me was tempted to jump at this opportunity for a trip into the outside world. I might have remained in two minds, had Bernard not explicitly forbidden me to leave the ward.

Walking out of the hospital with Gary felt both exhilarating and terrifying. I had almost forgotten what fresh air smelt like and here was someone who knew all the secrets of my past life. I jumped slightly at the noise of a passing motorbike and felt intimidated by the other hurrying pedestrians, who all seemed to be so sure about where they were going.

Gary was a tall, spindly man about my age who dressed in the clothes of someone twenty years younger. He wore a leather motorcycle jacket, though it turned out there was no motorbike. His sideburns came slightly too low for someone whose hairline was creeping that far back, and he exuded an air of easy confidence and a powerful reek of nicotine. But although I was a little thrown by his overly casual manner, it was refreshing to be talked to as if I was normal. It made me like him – this was my friend 'Gary'. I had a friend and we were off to the pub together.

'So we might as well get this out of the way . . .' he said, look-ing a little awkward as we got to the street corner '. . . but you do remember you owe me two grand?'

'Do I? Sorry, I don't have any money . . . I . . . if you could just hang on a bit?' and then I caught the glint in his eye and he burst out laughing.

'Ha ha ha – yeah, 's all right!' He laughed. 'I'm just pissing with you!'

'Yeah, *obviously*!' I said, doing my best to laugh along.

'I should've made it a bit more, shouldn't I? Can you really not remember anything?'

'No. I have no idea what I've been doing for the past forty years.'

'Yeah, well, I know how you feel.'

Forty years had been a good guess. It turned out I was thirty-nine, and according to Gary, my fugue state was just 'a typical bloody mid-life crisis'. I got the impression that he didn't consider my medical condition to be a particularly big deal – as if he'd done so many drugs down the years that this was just one of many altered states on the spectrum. I found it a little disarming that this man casually addressed me as 'Wanker' and 'Dingbat', as if these were my actual names. Although I quickly understood that these must be ironic terms of matey affection between two old friends, when someone you have just met says, 'It's this pub here, Shit-for-brains,' you have to fight an instinct that finds this a tiny bit rude.

The pub was filling up with lunchtime customers so we grabbed the last booth. Now I had free rein to ask him whatever I wanted. It would be like my own private edition of *This Is Your Life*, except in this version the host recounted the incredible life story to the star for the very first time: 'You won't remember this voice,' or, 'And here tonight is that teacher who inspired you all those years ago, although you'll have to take our word for it; it could just be the old lady who runs the tea bar downstairs.'

I had chosen a pint of Guinness because Gary told me that's what I usually had. The infinite possibilities felt overwhelming; I might like bitter, lager or a mineral water with a dash of lime. I might be twice married, a father of seven, an Olympic sailing champion or a bankrupt criminal.

I resolved to ask the questions in some sort of chronological

---

order, so that we didn't jump about all over the place and miss out any important details. Perhaps at some level I wanted the news broken to me slowly: if I was a total loser, I might feel better if I understood how I ended up that way. But my attempt to pin down some basics about my early years did not start well.

'So. Have I got any brothers and sisters?'

'Nope. You're an only child. Oh, I forgot to get anything to eat—'

'Okay. Where am I from?'

'Nowhere really. Everywhere. You're from all over the place. Your dad was in the forces, so you moved constantly as a kid. You lived in West Germany, Cyprus, Malaysia, er ... Yorkshire. Where else did you mention? Hong Kong, I think. Shangri-La maybe?'

'That's not a real place.'

'Isn't it? Oh well, not Shangri-La then. Shanghai maybe? But I remember you saying that you were never in the same school for more than a year.'

'Blimey. So I'm a very adaptable sort of person, I expect?'

'Er, if you want ... I wish I'd got some pork scratchings or something—'

'Well travelled.'

'Well travelled. Rootless, yeah.'

'The son of a soldier!'

'Air force. He was quite high ranking, though I think he only did the accounts or something. Yeah, poor bloke had a heart attack soon after your mum died.'

'Oh.'

'But I remember your parents from when we were younger. They were a lovely couple, God bless them. Very powerful home-made wine.'

With no memory of them whatsoever, my mother and father felt like abstract concepts – just names on a family tree. Everything he told me about myself might as well have happened to another person, in some made-up story. In fact, Gary knew very little about my early years and was vague on any specifics before the two of us had actually met. 'How do I know what grades you got in your bloody GCSEs?' he protested.

'Sorry, I just feel a bit nervous about getting my exam results. I feel nervous about all of it. So did I go to university?'

'Ah, right, yeah, now this is where we met,' he recalled, with more enthusiasm. 'I was doing English and American Studies. I switched from doing straight English—'

'Sorry, where was this? Oxford? Cambridge?'

'Bangor. I chose there because this gorgeous girl at my school had put it down, although she ended up in East Anglia so it didn't really work out . . .'

Over the next ten minutes I learned that Gary and I had shared a student house in North Wales, that I had been in a college football team with Gary, and that I had done the same degree as Gary, though I had not copied my entire dissertation off a student from Aberystwyth like Gary. Frankly, it was fascinating to find out so much about myself.

He came back from the bar with another pint, despite me requesting just a half, and a greying pickled egg, which I think he chose because it was the least fresh thing they had. There was one question that I had been desperate to ask, and the whole time he'd been at the bar I had found myself staring down at the white shadow where the ring had been. I was almost too nervous to broach the subject. If there was a wife out there, I wanted to understand the context in which I had come to meet her. I wanted to know who I was when I got married.

'So you don't remember this pub at all?' said Gary, sitting down.

'No. Why? Have we been here before?'

'Yeah – you used to sell crack in here before all that shit with the Russian Mafia kicked off—'

'Oh, yeah, of course, the Russian Mafia. They left a beetroot head in my bed, didn't they?' I felt a shiver of pride at succeeding in making Gary chuckle. 'It's weird. I don't know who I am or what I did. But I know I wasn't a crack dealer.'

'No, hard drugs were never really your scene. You fret about whether it's acceptable to give your kids a bloody Lemsip.'

That was how I discovered I was a father. 'Your *kids*' Gary had said, in the plural. I had children.

'Oh, right, yeah – your kids!' said Gary, when I pressed him for more information. 'Yeah, you've got two nippers. Boy and a girl, Jamie who's about fifteen or twelve or something, and then there's Dillie who's younger, like ten maybe. Actually, she must be eleven, 'cos they're both at secondary school. Though not at your school.'

'What do you mean "my school"?'

'Your school where you teach.'

'So I'm a teacher? Look, just slow down a minute, will you? See, this is why I wanted to do everything chronologically. Tell me about my children first,' I said, while filing away a bizarre image of myself wearing a gown in front of an old-fashioned blackboard.

'Well, they're just kids, you know. They're cute. I'm actually godfather to Jamie. Or is it Dillie? I can't remember, but I'm sure I'm godfather to one of them. But, yeah, great kids. You can be really proud of them.'

But I couldn't be really proud of them. I dearly wanted to be proud of them, but they were just a cold, historical fact.

'Mind if we sit here?' interjected a woman carrying bags of shopping, and without waiting for an answer she slumped into one of the two spare places at our table. 'Over here, Meg! Got two seats here!'

I was a parent to two strangers. But not like some passing ship's captain who'd unknowingly fathered a child in a distant port. These children would know me; hopefully, they would love me.

'Get a menu!' shouted the lady to her companion, her daughter maybe. 'I can't read the blackboard without my glasses, and they never put menus on the table.' This woman's face was now imprinted on my mind, yet I had no idea what my own children looked like.

'So what are they like?'

'What do you mean?

'My kids? What are they like?'

The woman did a poor job of pretending not to listen.

'Well, Jamie looks just like you, actually, poor bastard. He doesn't say a great deal, but that's probably his age.'

I nodded, but inside I was shrugging. I was a father and teacher with no experience of children whatsoever.

'He's getting quite tall now, trendy, into music. Don't think he has a girlfriend, but he might be keeping it quiet, I suppose.'

'What about my daughter – Dillie? Is that her real name or is it short for something?'

'Don't think so – you've always just called her Dillie.'

'Could be Dilys,' said the woman at our table.

'Sorry?'

'Your daughter's name? Dillie could be short for Dilys. Or "Dillwyn" is a name. Welsh, I think. You're not Welsh, are you?'

'I dunno. Am I Welsh?'

'Nah, don't think so.'

'Well, it could be that.'

'Thank you. That's very helpful.'

The detail of my own parenthood suddenly recast everything in an even more serious light. Now my mental breakdown was not just something that had happened to me, but to a whole family.

'So what else would you like to know about them?' Gary asked me, though the lady might have thought he was addressing both of us.

'Er, it's okay,' I mumbled, 'it can wait.'

'Been in prison, have you?' enquired the woman, nonchalantly.

'Er, something like that,' I smiled.

'Murder,' added Gary, in the hope of scaring her off, but she didn't seem thrown by this detail.

'My husband walked out on us when Meg was two. We never heard from him again. He wouldn't recognize her if he passed her in the street.'

'Right . . .'

'Er, so what other news can I tell you?' Gary said. 'Er, the Tories are back in power. And everyone has mobile phones and home computers and Woolworth's went out of business and, er, Elton John came out; that was a big shock obviously—'

'Yeah, yeah, I know all that stuff. It's just everything about *my life* that's been forgotten. I can remember who won the FA Cup all through the eighties and nineties; I know every Christmas Number One. But I just can't remember anyone's name or anything about them.'

'Ha! That's just being a bloke, isn't it?' said the woman, with a sigh.

After that we talked in hushed mumbles, which suggested that Gary was divulging information that was somehow classified. Now that we seemed to have abandoned any idea of doing my life in chronological order, I jumped to the question that had been gnawing away at me since my mind had first pressed the reset button.

'So, Gary, I'm father to two children,' I whispered. 'Tell me about their mother.'

There was a pause, punctured by a food order being called out from the bar.

'Er – she's cool, yeah. God, actually, this egg is disgusting. I might get something else. I wonder if they sell peperamis—'

'No, no – hang on. I just want to get my head round this. Let's start at the beginning. What's her name?'

'Her name? Maddy.'

'Maddy?'

'Madeleine, yeah.'

'My wife is called Madeleine! That's a nice name, isn't it? Madeleine and Vaughan!' I rolled the name about in my head, feeling how it fitted with my own. 'Vaughan and Maddy.'

'You know Vaughan, don't you? He's Madeleine's husband!'

Just this fragment of information felt enormously reassuring to me; this would surely be the foundation stone on which my life would be rebuilt.

'So where did I meet her? And don't say she was mail order from Thailand.'

'You hooked up in your first term at university, didn't you? It was like "Bye-bye, Mummy, hello, Wifey!" Know what I mean?'

'No.'

'Well, you were like so totally into one another, it was actually quite annoying for the rest of us.'

'Thanks.'

'So, yeah, anyway, after college you both spent a few years bumming around doing nothing. And 'cos you didn't have the faintest bloody idea what to do, you decided you might as well train to be a teacher.'

'Yeah, so I'm a teacher! Wow! That's not just a job, is it? That's a vocation! A teacher . . .' I stroked my beard as I pictured myself as Robin Williams in *Dead Poets' Society*, as Sidney Poitier in *To Sir, with Love*.

'Yeah, some god-awful comprehensive next to the Wandsworth one-way system,' he said. 'I think you said your school specializes in Business and Enterprise, so you don't produce drug addicts – your kids learn to be the dealers—'

'A teacher. I like that. What do I teach? Tell me it's not metal-work.'

'You teach history – and sometimes "citizenship", whatever the fuck that is.'

'A history teacher? Ha! The historian with no history of his own.'

'Yeah, I suppose that is quite ironic. You don't know anything whatsoever about the past, but then neither do any of your pupils, so it makes no odds really . . .'

Another food order was called out from the bar and Gary

looked forlornly at the plate of fish and chips being handed out.

'But hang on, we hadn't finished talking about Madeleine and the kids. We need to tell them I'm okay, don't we? I've been missing for over a week. Were they worried about me?'

'I dunno, mate. I haven't spoken to her.'

'I was missing for a week and she didn't call you?'

'Well, it wasn't really like that . . . Do you fancy sharing a plate of chips or something?'

'Wasn't like what? Is Madeleine away, or ill or something?'

'Maybe I'll just eat a sachet of ketchup to get rid of that disgusting egg flavour. At least they're free.'

The woman gave Gary a disbelieving look.

'What do you mean, "it wasn't really like that"? What's wrong?'

'Well, you and Maddy have been through a bit of a tough time of it recently.' He was tugging wildly at the ketchup sachet, failing to rip it open. 'When I spoke to that doctor on the phone she asked if you'd experienced any stress or pressure prior to your memory-wipe thing, and I said, 'Well, yeah, he's just split up with his wife, hasn't he?''

At this point the sachet suddenly ripped open, and ketchup splattered everywhere on me and on the mother and daughter sharing our booth. The two of them jumped up and made an enormous fuss, while I was still trying to digest the crippling news that the wife I had only just learned about had, seconds later, split up with me. It must have been the shortest marriage in history.

'Oh, sorry about that,' said Gary to the woman, without sounding particularly sorry. 'Here – have some of these napkins. Or you could always lick it off your blouse. It's nice ketchup—'

'*You* might do that—'

'I'm not licking ketchup off your blouse, love – that's crossing the line. Vaughan, mate – you got sauce on your shirt there . . .'

'Gary,' I said quietly, 'I think I want to go back to the hospital.'

I found myself squinting at the bright sunshine as we stepped out of the dingy pub. Gary lit a cigarette and offered me one.

'No, thanks.'

'No? You normally smoke like a fucking beagle.'

'Really?'

'Yeah, you tried everything to give up – gum, patches, reading that book by that smug bloke, but you were completely addicted.'

'Right.' I nodded, watching him inhale with no desire or craving whatsoever. 'Until I forgot I was.'

So far Gary had told me that I was a chain-smoking teacher, in a sink school, whose marriage was on the rocks. Normally one would discover this about oneself over a period of decades.

'Are you all right, mate? You look kinda weird.'

'Can I just go back to the hospital, please?'

'Listen, you can't stay there for ever. You know, you can always shack up at my place. You stayed for a while when things started to go a bit wrong on the marriage front.'

'When things started to go a bit wrong?'

'Yeah.' He chuckled incredulously at the memory of it. 'You turned up at my place with this blood-soaked bandage on your hand, saying that was it – the marriage was over.'

Then the penny dropped. 'Oh, I get it!' I laughed. 'This is another one of your stupid jokes, isn't it? Maddy and I aren't separated at all, are we?'

Gary winced as he took a deep toke of his cigarette, as if it was the strongest skunk on the market.

'No joke, mate. You and Maddy can't stand each other no more. Oh, and that's the other reason you can't stay in the hospital. You're divorcing her on Thursday.'

'I'm divorcing her on Thursday!?'

'Oh, hang on, no, I've got that wrong—'

'What? So it *is* a joke?'

'It's not Thursday. It's Friday. When's the second of November? That's Friday, isn't it? Yeah, you're divorcing her on Friday. Is there a snack machine at the hospital?'

Chapter 4

Google Images had revealed that there was more than one person in the world called 'Madeleine Vaughan'. Now I could see why the marriage hadn't worked out. She was either nine years old, a Labradoodle puppy or a very tanned porn actress.

That night I had gone upstairs to spend some time on the computer terminal 'provided by the Friends of Teddy's', which for a moment I had thought must be a pre-school children's TV show. The only time you could get on it was late at night, but this added to the shady sense of espionage I felt. 'Maybe my wife had kept her maiden name,' I thought, in which case it was just a question of scrolling through every picture on the internet tagged with any version of her name and seeing if any of them looked remotely likely.

Researching details about myself had been no easier. Facebook wouldn't let me log in; it seemed to be really strict about the level of personal information it demanded. I couldn't believe I hadn't asked Gary what my first name actually was. But with the little knowledge I had so far and a bit of detective work, it had eventually been possible to track a man down who quite possibly could have been me. I found a secondary school in the exact location Gary had described and there on a list of staff members at 'Wandle Academy' was 'Jack Vaughan–History'. It was either an unusual double-barrelled name, confirmation of my subject area or a description of my personal status.

Without pausing to reflect on what I felt about my full name, I continued my investigation, narrowing the search by adding 'teacher' and 'uk', and found that there were a couple of references to 'Jack Vaughan' at an education conference in Kettering at which I'd spoken a year earlier. On the school website I scanned photographs of students and other members of staff – people I must have known. Then in one rather low-quality photo I finally spotted myself, grinning inanely on the edge of a staff group shot. So I did exist before 22 October! I shifted uncomfortably in my seat. I felt as if some identity thief had been freely walking around pretending to be me: teaching history, talking at conferences, alienating my wife.

It was nearly dawn by the time I forced myself to stop. I spent the following morning trying to catch up on my sleep, attempting to ignore Bernard whispering, 'Vaughan? Vaughan? With all your memory problems, you've probably forgotten it's quite rude to keep your curtains closed all morning.' It turned out that those were to be my last few hours in the hospital.

Suddenly the curtain around my bed was pulled back and there stood Gary with a smartly dressed blonde woman who looked younger than us.

'Ta da!' exclaimed Gary. 'Vaughan – meet the missus!'

The woman beside him gave me a nervous smile and attempted a rather girlie wave. 'Hello, Vaughan. Remember me?'

'Erm . . . no, I don't, sorry. Are you Maddy? Madeleine?' My voice was shaking having had her sprung on me like this. But if I had felt any anger towards her before 22 October, that emotion wasn't suddenly rediscovered by seeing her again. My wife was just a complete stranger – a woman towards whom I felt no particular hostility, nor, indeed, any attraction.

'Not *your* missus, you senile bastard, *my* missus! This is Linda!'

I felt the back of my head hit the pillow. Gary turned to her. 'See, I told you, didn't I? Like I said, he's forgotten bloody everything. So he won't remember that embarrassing affair the two of you had in Lanzarote.'

She giggled and gave him a playful slap on the arm. 'Honestly, Gary! What are you like! Don't worry, Vaughan – we didn't! I . . . am . . . Linda. Gary's . . . wife,' she explained extra slowly, as if speaking to a foreigner in a coma. She came forward to kiss me, but then diverted to a handshake when she saw the surprise on my face. 'Gary's explained what happened, and we're going to take you back home and look after you, aren't we, Gaz?'

Linda had already rung the ward to make her offer earlier that morning and apparently the hospital staff had embraced the notion of returning me to normal life. Of course it had been a big decision. The various medics who had been monitoring me had all given their professional opinions on my fragile psychological and physical state and whether a change of location might impede my progress. Then they balanced that against how much the hospital needed my bed and said, 'How quickly can he leave?'

With Gary and his wife having convinced the hospital of their credentials as close friends and suitable carers, Dr Lewington formally presented me with a leaving present. 'I'm afraid there is no guarantee that your memory will not wipe itself all over again, leaving you stranded and lost as before. So I want you to wear this identity tag around your neck at all times; it has emergency contact details for this hospital.'

'And it's metal,' added Gary. 'So even if your body was, like, horribly burned, we'd still know it was you.'

I had a series of future appointments scheduled, which I was rather tactlessly told not to forget, and then I was allowed a little time to gather up the rest of my possessions. Apart from the clothes I had arrived in, these totalled half a packet of tissues, some mints and Bernard's *Improve Your Memory* book.

'Do pop over and say hello when you're back for your check-ups,' said Bernard, a little forlornly.

'Of course I will, Bernard. If you're not out of here by then!'

'Have you got the same thing as Mr Memory Man here?' Gary asked him.

'No. I've got a brain tumour!' he said brightly.

'Oh,' said Linda. 'I'm very sorry to hear that.'

'Oh, I don't let a silly old tumour get me down. I say anything that rhymes with "humour" can't be all that bad.'

'Right,' reflected Gary. 'Well, that seems like a very sound medical diagnosis. Makes me feel a lot better about that dose I had that rhymes with "Snap"!' And Linda giggled and slapped him on the arm again.

Linda was not the spouse I would have cast for Gary. If he had taken the trouble the day before to mention that he was married, I think I would have expected some spiky-haired punk chick with piercings in uncomfortable-looking places, or perhaps an old hippy with hennaed hair and a big purple velvet skirt. Linda was not only conventional, but surprisingly young and posh, and glowed with the vigorous good health and self-confidence that came from generations of healthy diets and skiing holidays.

'Actually, we do have some rather big news since we last saw you,' said Linda, standing by the lift and smiling knowingly at her husband, who frowned slightly that she was going down this path. 'You know we've been trying for a baby . . .'

'No?'

'Oh. No, of course not. Well, the wonderful thing is – it's happened! We're going to be a proper family!'

She said this as if it was the cue for me to scream in excitement, and when I merely gave my polite congratulations she looked a little put out. As we travelled down in the lift she began to provide anecdotes and accounts of past episodes as if to prove that I really did know them very well. Apparently I had been Gary's best man at their recent wedding; I had played football with Gary every Tuesday night for years; I had even been on holiday with them, and Gary chipped in with the detail of how I had memorably fallen off the side of a fishing boat as he had pulled a huge tuna on board.

'Well, Gary didn't actually pull it on board. The man we'd chartered the trip from took over for the last bit, but it was very funny,' added Linda.

'No, *I* caught the fish,' interjected Gary with an edge of irritation in his voice.

'Yes, you hooked it, but the man hauled it on to the deck at the end and this huge fish flapping about made you jump backwards into the sea, Vaughan – it was very funny!'

'No, you're getting mixed up,' insisted Gary. 'He helped that American lady, but I pulled my own fish out of the sea – back me up here, Vaughan – oh no, you can't, can you?'

'Well, it doesn't matter whether the man helped Gary a little bit—' said Linda.

'Though he didn't—'

'The point is that you fell in the sea and the man had to pull you on to the boat.'

'Unlike the fish, which I did myself.'

'I'm sorry, I don't remember any of it,' I mumbled. 'I just feel like I'm being incredibly rude, you know? It's like I was the best man at your wedding but now I don't even know what Gary and I have in common. I mean, what did we used to talk about? I don't know.'

They thought about this for a moment.

'I don't think you ever had an actual conversation,' said Linda. 'You just compared apps on your iPhones.'

Beside me in the back of Gary and Linda's family car was an immaculate new baby seat strapped into position, but with the label still attached. 'So when exactly is it due?'

'In about nine months' time,' sighed Gary.

'No, it's less than that,' corrected Linda. 'But we want to make sure everything is perfect for Baby.'

'*The* baby,' corrected Gary.

'It's just this seat was on a discount, and it's one of the safest ones for Baby.'

'*The* baby . . .'

It was a sunny, windy day as we drove out of the hospital car park. The leaves were still on the trees, but looked as though they wouldn't hold out for much longer. I had presumed that we would be going straight back to Gary and Linda's flat, but they clearly had other plans.

'Okay, groovy people, we are welcoming you to aboard on Gary and Linda's famous Magicking Mystery Tour!' announced my driver, doing his best impression of a German tour guide, or maybe it was a Dutch MTV presenter: the accent tended to wander slightly. 'On this evening's super-hip sightsee trip, we will be point out some of most famous landmarks of Vaughan's life, which is pretty cool, yah?' Linda was laughing at his mid-Atlantic, Swiss/Scandinavian/American accent. 'And we will be give a bit of history surround some of fascinating locations we passing will be.' Now he just sounded like Yoda.

We were still some distance from any significant personal landmarks, but Gary did point out a pub we'd popped into about ten years ago, and then a sports shop where he'd bought some trainers, though he was pretty sure I hadn't been with him. He had given up on the comedy foreign accent, though the concept of the tour guide was still just clinging on. 'If you look out of the left-hand window you can see a branch of the celebrated restaurant chain McDonald's, which is where your parents and tutors always hoped you might work if you realized your full potential. Tragically, it was never to be, and you became a history teacher instead. And coming up on our right here is the first school you ever taught at! There – spark any distant memories?'

I looked at the large Victorian building, recently refurbished with fountains, electric gates and CCTV.

'It says "Luxury Flats".'

'Yeah, well, they closed the school down once you joined, didn't they?'

'Oh, Gary – you are rude sometimes! It wasn't your fault they closed it down, Vaughan. It was something to do with education cuts, which I'm actually *against* because I think children are the future.'

From there we crossed the river and Gary pointed out a couple more pubs we had frequented. Churches, gyms and health-food shops were passed without comment. Gary and Linda were surprised that I recognized some roads and not others; it seemed that a generic knowledge of London's main streets and bridges had survived, but nothing that was particular to my own personal experience. After a picturesque dual carriageway and graffiti-covered underpass, we pulled up outside a huge modern comprehensive.

'This is where I teach?'

'Wow – it's worked! You remember it, you clever bastard!'

'No – you just said my school was in Wandsworth and so I found Wandle Academy on the internet.'

'Oh. Well, anyway, guess what? This is where you teach! Not exactly fucking Hogwarts, is it?'

The concrete edifice did look a bit shabby and foreboding. The entrance was strewn with litter and, as if to symbolize the growth of young minds, a couple of young silver birch saplings had been planted near the entrance, and then snapped off before they'd barely started.

I already understood that Gary's rudeness about my job and the school must signify some sort of grudging respect – that this was the way we must have talked to one another, and that I would have to learn to give as good as I got.

'So am I just a classroom teacher or a head of year or anything, yer bastard?'

'What?' said Gary, suddenly looking slightly offended.

'Do I have a job title?'

'But why did you call me a bastard?'

'Er – sorry. I just thought that might be how we talked to one another.'

'You can't go round calling people "bastards", you stupid bastard! You joined the establishment, you're *one of them*, man.'

Linda was marginally more illuminating, explaining that during my time at the school I had been promoted to 'Head of Humans, or something'.

'Humanities?'

'Yeah, that sounds right – I thought it would be a bit weird to have one person in charge of all the humans . . .'

'So how long have I been teaching here?'

'Oh, ages now. Over ten years anyway,' said Linda.

I felt a twinge of worry that I was supposed to be on the other side of the gates, that there were classes of children wondering what had happened to Mr Vaughan.

'But my own kids don't come here?'

'Don't be ridiculous! Maddy knows what the teachers are like!'

'They go to a school closer to where you live,' explained Linda. 'Actually Dillie's only just left that primary. That's where we want Baby to go, isn't it, Gary?'

'*The* baby.'

Although I could remember nothing about these friends, their characters or personal histories, I had not forgotten the code of etiquette that made this feel rude.

'So – er – anyway, what do you two do for a living?'

'What?'

'You know, what line are you two in?'

'What is this? A Rotarians' Christmas cheese-and-wine soirée or something?'

'I don't know – it just felt a bit impolite to keep talking about me all the time. I didn't want to appear self-obsessed or whatever. First impressions and all that . . .'

'Second,' said Linda.

'Oh yes, second impressions. For you anyway.'

'One thousand and second,' said Gary.

'Okay. Well, I'm – this is weird – I am in recruitment,' said Linda, 'and Gary is in computers – internet and all that.'

'Right.' I nodded neutrally. 'Not data-recovery by any chance, is it?'

'Ha! No, though I know a few people who do specialize in that. They'll just say you should have backed your brain up on a memory stick. No, I work for myself, designing websites, developing new ideas for the net, you know.'

'Wow! What sort of ideas?'

'Okay, well, I might as well tell you about our big project, then.'

'*Our* big project?'

'Yeah, you and me have been developing this together. We're developing a site that will completely revolutionize how we consume news.'

'How's that?'

'This is going to be the future of current affairs.' I noticed a sudden degree of zealous self-belief in Gary. 'See, currently all news is top down. Some fascist corporation decides what's the most important story, sends some lackey to report it, who then serves up all the Murdoch lies to the trusting public.'

Linda was nodding supportively.

'The internet allows you to turn that model on its head. Imagine millions of readers writing up whatever they might have just witnessed around the globe, uploading their own photos and video footage and text. Millions more readers are searching and clicking on stories that interest them, and hey presto! The story with the most hits becomes the main item of news on the world's most democratic and unbiased news outlet!'

'It's ever so funny,' added Linda. 'Front page yesterday was a transsexual doing it with a couple of midgets, ha ha ha . . .'

'Yeah, obviously, we're still working on the filters and all that. But YouNews is the future, you said so yourself. You can search by region, subject, protest movement, whatever.'

'You must check it out,' said Linda. 'I've learned how to upload stories. I put up a lovely bit of video yesterday: this cute kitten being surprised by a cuckoo clock!'

'No, Linda, that's not news! That's not what the site is for!'

'So, no reporters or editors?' I observed.

'Exactly! No hacks filing their expenses from around the world, no expensive studios or equipment, and no press barons protecting their political allies or paymasters.'

I thought about this for a moment, and then pinpointed what made me uneasy about the whole idea.

'But how do you know it's true?'

'True?'

'Yes, a story that some member of the public has uploaded. How do you know they haven't just made it up?'

'Well, if they've made it up,' explained Gary, 'then you always said that other members of the public will say so in the comment thread and it will lose credibility. Or they can re-edit it themselves – it's like Wikipedia, but for current affairs. You're really into it, believe me! You and me – we're going to take on the world!'

My feelings about Gary's website echoed a deeper worry I had had ever since my brain had first pressed Control+Alt+Delete. How could I know whether anything was true? I was still fighting a tiny voice in my head that questioned whether my name was really 'Vaughan', that I was in fact a teacher and that my marriage was really over.

Eventually we reached the address where I had been living right up until my fugue. I learned that between moving out of my family home and taking up a residency on the fourth floor of King Edward's Hospital, I had sofa-surfed between a number of temporary addresses, most recently housesitting near my old neighbourhood for a rich family who were in New York for three months.

'Wow, what an amazing house. And I had it all to myself?'

'Yeah – but you didn't like it. It made you, like, really tense being responsible for all the fancy furniture and that. You were always like "Gary, don't smoke dope indoors! Gary, stop borrowing his clothes! Gary, don't piss on the herb garden!" Yeah, it seemed to make you a bit uptight, if you don't mind me saying . . .'

When I had disappeared, I had left my clothes and my belongings there, which were now in boxes round at Gary and Linda's.

'Yeah, there was some pretty hard-core porn in amongst all your stuff.'

'Really?' said a shocked Linda.

'No,' I said with a smile, already better at recognizing Gary's wind-ups than his wife was.

The family were apparently now back home, probably still picking the fag ends out of their tropical fish tank, so this private mansion was no longer an option for me.

'And you don't recognize that either? That is really amazing! So is there anything you can remember?'

'Actually, there is this scene that keeps coming back to me. I have this vague memory of really laughing with a girl when I was younger. And we're sheltering under a canopy or something but still getting wet, and we don't mind. But I can't remember who she was or what she looked like or where we were. I just remember being really, really happy.'

Gary and Linda looked at one another but said nothing. We turned into a residential street just off Clapham Common. Rows of mid-size Victorian houses were interspersed with a few ugly 1950s blocks, where post-war builders had done a poor job of disguising which house numbers had been removed by the Luftwaffe. On the corner was number 27, which looked like the best house in the street, with dormer windows at the top and a little turret which gazed out over the London skyline.

'Recognize this?'

'Don't tell me – it's where I was born? Ah, but there's no blue plaque.'

'No – have another go.'

'Did I stay here as well?'

'Er, well, yeah, in a manner of speaking . . .'

At that moment the front door opened and a striking redhead stepped out into the autumn sunshine and dropped a bag into the wheelie bin.

'Wow! Who is that?' I whispered. 'She is gorgeous!'

The woman stopped to remove a couple of dead geranium heads from the window box, tucked a strand of hair behind her ear, and paused as if to check the weather.

'Was she living there when I was? Should we go and say hello?'

'Blimey, Vaughan, you've gone bright red!' said Linda. 'Gary, we probably shouldn't hang about. We don't want her to see us here.'

He was already putting the car in gear and pulling away.

'Hang on, you haven't explained anything . . . Where are we? Who is that beautiful woman?'

'That, Vaughan, was the house you lived in for twenty years,' said my tour guide. 'And that was Madeleine. That was the woman you're about to divorce.'

Chapter 5

As you came in the front door, the first thing you saw was a baby-gate across the foot of the stairs and a brand-new stroller folded up by the coat hooks. There were plastic safety covers over the electrical sockets and in the lounge was a big Thomas the Tank Engine rug with primary-coloured bricks stacked up against the wall.

'Sorry, are you expecting *another* baby, or will this one be your first?'

'No, it's just the two of us at the moment,' confirmed Gary. 'It's just that Linda likes buying all the stuff, you know.'

'I always loved your home, Vaughan,' enthused Linda, 'brimming with children's toys and everything. I said to Gary that I wanted our place to be just like that.'

'Right. Well, it's good to be prepared, I suppose . . .'

'You see, this isn't a *house*,' she said meaningfully. 'It's a *home*.'

'And it isn't a *house*,' added Gary, 'because it's a *flat*.'

Linda proudly showed me into the room where I would be staying. In the corner was a brand-new cot, surrounded by musical mobiles with rotating light patterns. Cartoon teddy-bear wallpaper was softly lit by the low-wattage light from a Disney lampshade. Linda lovingly adjusted one of the soft toys, which looked settled in for a long wait. The extended sofa bed that had been made up for me rather spoiled the nursery atmosphere; it jutted out towards the primary-colour baby gym and the padded changing mat.

This was where my new life would begin – in a room with a nightlight and a baby monitor so that Linda could hear if I started crying. On the ceiling I noticed a poster with letters of the alphabet constructed out of contorted farmyard animals. The curtains featured rabbits parachuting off the edge of the moon. There seemed to be an unspoken presumption that this baby would be heavily into hallucinogenic drugs.

'Isn't this a lovely room?' she said proudly. 'Obviously you'll have to move out when Baby comes . . .' she said.

'*The* baby,' came Gary's voice from down the hall.

Inside a low wardrobe hung a range of men's second-hand clothes. These had either been collected for Baby when he grew up and reached middle-age, or were all the jackets and jeans that had belonged to me before my fugue. I had gone for the default casual-smart look of jeans, shirts and sweaters, as lazily favoured by millions of middle-class men from Seattle to Sydney. There were a few frayed-looking suits which had presumably been my teaching uniform, and some uninspiring ties that seemed doomed to be worn at half mast.

Linda had kindly prepared everything for my stay and there was even a new toothbrush still in its packet.

'This is the bathroom, Vaughan – I thought you might fancy a bath. You have to pull that lever there if you want to use the shower—'

'Do you think she looked sad?'

'Who?'

'Maddy? I thought she looked a little sad . . .'

'Er, no, she looked pretty much how she usually looks to me . . .

Dirty laundry goes in there, and I'll show you how to use the washing machine.'

'Maybe she was suddenly just a bit cold – the wind was quite cold, wasn't it?'

'Er, yeah, that could be it.'

The thought of a relaxing bath was appealing after a week or so in hospital and so a few minutes later I was taking off my clothes in the private space of virtual strangers. I felt like the intruder in a family bathroom. There was all her make-up and there were his razors; around me were other people's lotions and towels. I still wanted to ask them so much more; I felt like I'd just had the barest glimpse of who I was before the mirror was steaming over. When did things go wrong with Maddy? Did I move out? Did she kick me out? Did one of us have an affair?

The bath was foamy and scented and I lay there for so long that the hot water needed topping up again. I submerged my aching head under the suds, letting my senses deaden to the outside world. Now I could hear only my own heartbeat. That's all there is really: your own heartbeat, and your own eyes looking out at everything.

I slowly came up for air and looked at the ceiling. This was the most relaxed I could remember feeling. My head felt completely empty. A tiny spider was hiding in a crevice by the window. And then it happened. From nowhere and with no mental association or logical thought process, I recovered my first memory. It was just as if I were actually there, living it in real time, feeling the emotions, the sounds, even the weather – the whole episode fell into my head all at once.

Maddy and I are walking up a grassy hill hand in hand, nimbly hopping over cowpats and rabbit holes, until we stand at the summit and feel the wind and sun on our faces before indulging in another quick kiss.

'So where do we go from here?' I say, looking down towards the sea.

'I dunno. Move in together, maybe ten years of domestic bliss until I discover you've been having an affair with your assistant.'

'My assistant? Why not my secretary?'

'That's the big surprise. Your assistant is a man.'

'Yes, I am a repressed homosexual. That's why I find you so attractive . . .'

'Ten years! God, we'll be nearly thirty. How ancient is that?'

'I'm planning to look quite distinguished as I grow older. Like that man on the Grecian 2000 advert, with "just a touch of grey hair" at the side.'

'And your voice badly re-dubbed by a British actor.'

'Definitely.'

Without really thinking about where we are going, we continue on to the next hill, the backpacks and camping gear doing little to slow us down as we march optimistically across the Irish countryside. This is our first holiday together – it is sunny, we have a brand-new tent – what can possibly go wrong?

'Oh, no! I don't believe it!' exclaims Maddy, sounding genuinely alarmed.

'What? What is it?'

'I forgot to send off that postcard to Great-auntie Brenda. Again!'

'What, the racist one?'

'It's not racist. It's just an affectionate Irish stereotype.'

The postcard to Great-auntie Brenda features a smiling cartoon leprechaun drinking a pint of Guinness and bears the caption 'Top o' the mornin' to yers!!' I suggest that it might be of questionable taste, but Maddy stands firmly by her selection of a suitable postcard for her very elderly widowed great-aunt.

'I thought she'd like it. She has gnomes.'

'She has gnomes?'

'You know, in her garden.'

'Well, obviously in her garden. I didn't think they were infesting her hair.'

The leprechaun is not looking any less cheerful for having been stuffed into the side pocket of Madeleine's rucksack for three days. She has already written a short upbeat message on the back, lovingly completed the address and affixed a specially purchased Irish stamp. Just that last detail of actually putting the card in a postbox keeps eluding her. And when Maddy gets back to England and unpacks her bag, there is the leprechaun, still wishing her the top o' the mornin'. She resolves to stick an English stamp over the Irish one in the hope that Great-auntie Brenda won't notice, or has not yet found out about Ireland gaining independence in 1921. She gives it to me to post when I am going out that evening, and I place it carefully in my inside jacket pocket. It is several months later that I find it there, and wonder how I might possibly tell my girlfriend that I have forgotten to send off the vaguely racist postcard to the legendary Great-auntie Brenda.

Maddy and I have hitched and walked through west Cork and now gaze down on a huge stretch of sand known as Barleycove. Hills on either side lead down to a perfect beach with steep, grassy dunes behind. A shallow stream sweeps around to a tidal saltwater lake; occasional white bungalows speckle the hills and the hazy horizon is punctured by the tiny outline of the Fastnet lighthouse.

'Why don't we camp here for the night?' I suggest enthusiastically. 'We could have a swim and make a fire out of driftwood and have a back-to-nature barbecue with those economy sausages and the Pot Noodle?'

'But the lady in the pub said there was going to be a storm, remember? We could go back to Crookhaven. That pub had a few rooms upstairs.'

'Come on – it's blazing sunshine. This is the perfect spot. This is what it's all about!' and I am already taking off my backpack.

Six hours later, we are awoken by the tent's top sheet coming loose in the gale and flapping aggressively above us. Now the rain drums even more noisily against the canvas sound box in which we're supposed to be sleeping as water trickles down the tentpole, forming a puddle at our feet. Despite the foolhardy decision to ignore the local prophet, the night-time storm has actually made us even cosier inside; it is exciting and romantic to be thrown together in this contrived crisis.

'I told you to take no notice of that woman in the pub.'

'You were right. Everyone knows it never rains in Ireland. Famous for its desert-like conditions. That's how Bob Geldof developed his interest in droughts.'

Another violent gust of wind makes the tent shudder and then the guy ropes break free on one side, the poles fall inwards and the roof collapses on top of us. I swear loudly, sounding momentarily scared, which prompts shrieks of laughter from Maddy, who is still enjoying the effects of a bottle of white wine shared as the sun went down.

Now I attempt to right the tentpoles from inside, but the gale pulls the tent flat again, as a stream of water flows on to our things. Maddy laughs all over again, then sticks her head out of the tent to see what she can see.

'Maybe you should go out and try to fix it from the outside?' she suggests.

'Why me?'

'Well, because I don't want to get my T-shirt wet – whereas you can go out there like that.'

'But I'm completely naked!'

'Yeah, well, there's not going to be anyone out there on a night like this, is there?' she points out. 'Go on, I'll have a towel ready for when you come back in!'

And so my pale, naked frame steps out into the night to do battle against the wind and rain as Maddy zips the door closed behind me. It is then, from inside the tent, that Maddy hears an elderly-sounding Irish man nonchalantly ask me if I am 'all right there'.

'Oh, hello, er, yes, thank you very much. Our tent blew over in the storm . . .'

'Ah, well, I saw that you'd camped down here,' the old man muses from the shelter of a golfing umbrella, 'so I thought I'd better check you hadn't blown away, like.'

I can just hear Maddy giggling inside the tent – she had obviously seen him coming and deliberately set me up.

'Not yet!' I quip, and my fake laughter goes on far too long.

'There's a barn up the lane. I'd say you could always move up there if you want.'

'Thank you, that's very kind.'

'But you don't want to be prancing about in this weather stark-bollock-naked. You'll catch your death of cold.'

I hear another snort of laughter as I stand there in the driving rain, trying to make casual chit-chat with a local farmer while cupping my hands over my genitals.

'Oh, this? Well, I didn't want to get my clothes wet, you see. But good advice – I'll get back inside right now. Thanks for checking on us!'

The guy ropes are never re-set, and the tent stays collapsed on us all night, but it doesn't matter that we barely sleep and have to dry out our things tomorrow, because right now all we want to do is laugh and laugh. I suppose we are showing each other how upbeat we can be in the face of adversity. Maddy doesn't mind that I ignored her advice and was proved wrong; nothing is going to be allowed to spoil our happiness. We are young and can doze with canvas on our faces, and arms half wrapped around one another; we are immunized against discomfort by the euphoria of just being together.

'I've had a memory!' I exclaimed, running out of the bathroom. 'I've just recovered a whole episode of my life!' Gary and Linda were delighted for me, though their joy was slightly tempered by the vision of an almost naked man laughing manically and dripping foamy bathwater all over their kitchen floor. In fact, I wondered if being stripped and soaking wet was the association that triggered the memory, but somehow I knew that it was having seen Maddy. Linda fetched me her pink towelling dressing gown, and put the hand towel I had used to protect my modesty straight into the washing machine.

We sat around their kitchen table and they assured me that this was only the beginning, that other memories would surely start to flow back.

'That lady's bathrobe rather suits you, Vaughan,' said Gary, ''cos you always had a bit of a thing about dressing up in women's clothes.'

Linda laughed, then reassured me that I had not actually been a transvestite, adding, 'Well, as far as I know, anyway . . .'

I wanted more stories, more memories of Maddy. But while I wanted to find out more about my marriage, Gary felt I needed to focus on the ending of it. They had obviously had a conversation while I was in the bath and now I was reminded that I was due in court on Friday, for the final stage of what they earnestly assured me had been a very long, painful and expensive business.

'To put it off now would be the last thing you would have wanted,' Gary told me.

'You have to jump through this last hoop, Vaughan, for Maddy and the kids' sakes as much as your own,' added Linda.

The proposition that Gary was putting to me was that I was going to have to go to a court of law and pretend to a judge that nothing had happened to me in order to terminate a marriage I knew nothing about.

'But what if they ask a question I don't know the answer to?'

'Your lawyer will be in there with you – he'll just tell you what to say,' Gary assured me.

'And he'll know about my condition?'

'Er, well, probably not,' said Gary. 'I mean we could risk telling them, but what will they do? Insist on postponing the case and charge you another ten grand you haven't got.'

'Maddy and the kids are geared up to it happening on Friday. They need closure,' said Linda.

'I'm pretty sure this last hearing is already scripted. You just repeat your position to your judge, he makes his ruling, you swap

CDs with Maddy and then it's straight to the pub to flirt with the Polish barmaid.'

Gary was insistent that I would deeply regret not having gone through with the divorce if my memory suddenly returned and I awoke to discover that I had lost the chance to break free from an unhappy marriage.

'Yes, you *say* it was an unhappy marriage . . .' I ventured.

'Well, you *are* getting divorced,' pointed out Gary. 'That is sometimes a sign . . .'

I had sensed that our split had been an acrimonious one, but on digging a little deeper I learned that it was not until the actual divorce process was under way that things had turned really nasty. Apparently when Maddy and I had first separated we had still been behaving towards one another like reasonably civilized people. It was only after we were swept along in an adversarial legal system, and learned of the provocative claims and demands being made by the other side's lawyers, that personal hostilities spiralled out of control. 'I remember the history teacher in you compared the divorce process to war,' recalled Gary. 'You told me that in 1939 the RAF thought it was immoral to bomb the Black Forest to deprive the Germans of timber. But by 1945 they were deliberately creating firestorms to kill as many civilians as possible.'

'Maddy and I hadn't quite reached the Dresden stage, I hope?'

'No, you two were at, sort of, June 1944. She'd invaded Normandy, but you still had the Doodlebug up your sleeve.'

'Right. So I'm the Nazis in this metaphor?'

However persuasive they were that we'd be better off apart, I felt I couldn't agree there and then to take this momentous step in the dark. My authority was not helped by the fact that I was still wearing a pink lady's bathrobe. When I was dressed, I announced that I'd like to go out for a walk on my own, to have a bit of a think, and somewhere between Linda's nervous concern and Gary's total indifference, we reached a compromise that it would be fine as long as I took an *A–Z* with their address and phone number written in the back and twenty pounds in cash, which I promised to return.

'Are you sure you'll be okay?' repeated Linda at the door. 'You don't want one of us to come with you?'

'No, really – I just fancy getting out. After a week in the hospital and everything that's happened, I just need to clear my head a bit.'

'I think your head is cleared enough already, mate,' heckled Gary, from the kitchen.

And then as soon as their front door was closed behind me, I began retracing my steps the mile or so to where we had seen Maddy coming out of her front door. I was going to talk to her. I was going to meet my wife. I had resolved that she had to know about my condition; the event had major consequences for her own life, our children, the court case. I owed it to her to tell her face to face what had happened. It should be done before the children were home from school and with time to postpone the court hearing; and that meant I had to do it right now.

'In any case,' I told myself, 'before I divorce my wife I'd like to get to know her a bit first.'

Chapter 6

Gary had related the remarkable course of events that had led to Maddy and me becoming the owners of a large Victorian house in Clapham. The dilapidated building had been boarded up in the 1980s, with visible holes in the roof and shrubs growing from the upstairs balconies. After university, Maddy and I had been friends with a group of housing activists who'd identified the long-abandoned property as a potential squat. But when it actually came to it, Maddy had been the bravest of all of us. While I hovered behind, worrying whether we needed someone's permission to do this, Maddy took a jemmy to the heavily fortified front windows. Over the following weeks, we raided skips for fire-wood and propped heavy furniture against the doors to make ourselves secure at night, and it transpired that the council was too chaotic ever to evict us. Friends came and went, including a couple of anarchist performance artists whose idea of turning the whole building into a 'Permanent Free Festival and Events Laboratory' rather petered out due to their inability to get out of bed in the mornings.

A few years later we formed ourselves into a registered housing association; it was easier then for the authorities to permit us to stay there. But it was apparently *me* who did all the paperwork and took legal responsibility for it all, and Maddy and I were the only ones still living there when the law was changed giving housing association tenants the right to buy. In two decades Maddy and I had made the journey from radical squatters to respectable owner-occupiers without ever leaving our front door. The bay window where Maddy had taken a crowbar to the corrugated iron now had a little poster advertising our kids' School Autumn Fayre. There was a sticker on the letterbox saying 'NO JUNK MAIL'. I'm guessing we wouldn't have been so bothered about junk mail when there was a small bush growing out of the kitchen floor.

And now I stood before the family home once again, a place with so many memories, but none of them currently mine. My intention had been to march right up and ring the doorbell, but instead I found myself just taking a moment to summon up my courage. I was thrown by the fact that the bell was actually an intercom system, which meant that my first words to my wife might have to be through the alienating electronic filter of a voice-distorting microphone. When I had left Gary and Linda's flat, it had seemed so clear to me that this was what I had to do. But now my finger was shaking as I reached for the button. I left it hovering there uncertainly. What if one of my children was off school and rushed down to say hello? I imagined the terrifying scenario of my daughter emerging with a friend and me not knowing which girl I was father of. It was not just my own mental health that was at issue here.

But it had to be done. I flattened my hair down, pulled my shirt straight and pressed the buzzer. To my surprise this prompted the sound of loud barking from the other side of the door. There was a dog! No one had said anything about a dog. But this was the furious bark of a guard dog in the house on his own – an angry defensive warning that was not mollified by any owner coming down the hallway, calling him away from the door. Maddy was out. I had just presumed she would be at home because she had been there earlier in the day. I realized that I didn't even know if she worked or not – perhaps I had subconsciously presumed that she didn't. I rang the doorbell again, on the unlikely off-chance that she had not heard the commotion the dog had caused downstairs, and this set the barking off all over again. I peered through the letterbox, calling an optimistic 'Hello?' and instantly the dog's demeanour changed. Suddenly he was howling with joyful excitement as he recognized me; his tail was wagging so much the whole back half of his body wiggled from side to side to side. He was a big golden retriever, licking the hand that held open the letterbox, then breaking off to howl his emotional hellos, before manically kissing my hand all over again. I had never even thought about whether I liked dogs or not, but I instinctively felt affection for this one.

'Hello, boy! What's your name then? Yeah, it's me! Remember me? Did I used to take you walkies?'

That word made the dog even more manic, and I felt momen-tarily guilty for getting him so excited when I was going to have to walk away again.

Back on the pavement I studied the house for any more clues about the people who lived there. I crossed the road to get a better view of the place. I noticed it was less well maintained than the houses around it: the paint was peeling on the balustrade, and the panels in the front door didn't match; one was vintage patterned glass, the other was plain. Looking at this house and what it represented, I was struck by what a beautiful home we'd created. It was brimming with character, with brightly painted shutters and blooming window boxes. The quirky glazed turret that crowned the roof had space for perhaps just one person to sit and read or gaze out over the London skyline. Dormer windows peeked out from the slate-tiled roof, suggesting cosy teenage bed-rooms with sloping ceilings. The middle floor had a balcony, and from the side I spotted a faded sun canopy, overlooking the back garden where a chaotic Virginia creeper was in its final blush of copper.

I tried to imagine myself sitting out on the balcony with Maddy, sharing a chilled bottle of white wine on a summer's night, as the kids played in the garden. Was I recovering a vague memory, or was this some idealistic fantasy that our domestic problems had made impossible? Looking at it all with fresh eyes, I couldn't help thinking it was the old Vaughan that had needed the psychiatric help for letting all this go.

So lost was I in speculation and fantasy that I almost didn't notice a car drawing up a few spaces away. I felt terror-stricken and thrilled all at once when I realized who it was and dived behind a parked van. I crouched down out of sight and watched in the van's wing mirror. Leaning out of her open window, Maddy reversed the slightly grubby car into the tightest of spaces, rather expertly, I thought, which strangely gave me a momentary flush of pride. She stepped out, wearing a funky orange coat that flared out below the waist. She looked classy and more professional than she had seemed before. Her hair was up and she wore small earrings.

And seeing her again, I couldn't help but feel as if some enormous administrative mistake must have occurred – that the authorities were proceeding recklessly with the wrong divorce. Surely neither of us had ever requested such a thing. Why would I want to stop being married to such a beautiful woman? Well, now was my chance to meet her properly; this was my moment to introduce myself to my wife.

But just as I stepped out from behind the van, the passenger door of Maddy's car opened, and now I slipped out of view again as I spied a man getting out. The two of them immediately set about taking large frames out of the back of the car and began carrying them up to the front door. Who was this? A business partner? A brother? A lover? The man was younger than me, and too snappily dressed to be a delivery man. He was very matter-of-fact about the job in hand, stacking the frames up by the front door and then going back for more. Was Maddy a painter? An art dealer? Why hadn't Gary and Linda mentioned any of this? Or, rather, why hadn't I asked? Crouched down on the pavement out of view, I felt increasingly uncomfortable and slightly dizzy, but I was transfixed as I eagerly scanned the situation for any further clues. He definitely knew her, but there was nothing to suggest that these two were in any sort of relationship. He was comfortable handling heavy-looking frames; my guess was that she had bought them off him and now he was helping to deliver them. But that was a more personal service than you'd expect from a high-street picture framer. I wanted to see if this man followed her into the house or whether he made his own way back.

Maddy unlocked the front door and patted the excited dog, who circled her, wagging his backside and emitting the extended howl with which he had greeted me. I was relieved to see that the family dog showed no affection for the man who was moving the larger frames into the hall. The dog manically sniffed the air as she went inside, but instead of following her, he started down the steps. Maddy called his name, but the dog had got the scent of something, and then I saw the panic in her face as he headed towards the road, ignoring her calls. She put down a smaller picture and started to chase after him; I could tell this behaviour was out of character, but the dog had clearly got something in his nostrils and looked unstoppable.

And that was the moment I realized that the scent the dog had picked up was mine. He could still smell the missing member of the family who'd been here a minute earlier, and he was running across the road towards where I was hiding. Maddy was following and would find me lurking there, and my first encounter with her since my breakdown would be as some creepy stalker with a bizarre mental illness. Behind me was a shady passageway that led down the side of the house opposite ours. I ran down there and dived around the back of a wooden shed. Almost immediately the dog caught up with me, excitedly wagging his tail and jumping up to try to lick my face.

'Woody! Woody!' Maddy was desperately calling, getting closer.

'Go home, Woody,' I whispered, but the dog took no notice.

'Woody – come here!' she shouted, getting closer.

'WOODY, YOU BAD DOG!' I scolded in hushed desperation. 'GO HOME NOW, YOU BAD DOG, GO HOME!' and, amazingly, a rather disappointed Woody turned around and scampered back in the direction he had come. I heard her say, 'There you are, you naughty dog!' and it was weird hearing her voice. She had a slight northern accent, Liverpool maybe – it was hard to tell.

But I was safe. She wouldn't come down here, so I could wait a while until she was inside and then perhaps I should just slip away. I realized that more than anything I had just wanted to see her again, and now the idea of giving her bad news filled me with dread. I closed my eyes and leaned my head on the creosote-scented shed as I let out a huge sigh of relief.

'Excuse me, what are you doing in my garden?' said an indignant upper-class voice. I turned round to see a rotund, ruddy figure in his early sixties armed with what looked like a gin and tonic. 'Oh, Vaughan, it's you! Sorry, I thought it might be some sort of intruder. How the bloody hell are you? Haven't seen you for ages.'

'Oh, er – hello!'

'I think I know . . .' said this rather self-consciously raffish figure with a cravat under his open-neck shirt '. . . I know why you're here.' My mind was racing. How much did he know? Had he seen me spying on my own wife?

'Do you?' I stammered.

'Neither a borrower nor a lender be!' And with an expectant grin he gave me a knowing nod.

'Er – Shakespeare?'

'The bard himself! You want your thingamajig back, don't you?'

'My thingamajig?'

'Yes, you know – God, what do they call those things?'

'Um . . .'

'God, I've gone completely blank. Umm . . .'

'Yes, what are they called?'

'I meant to bring it back ages ago – very remiss of me. Anyway, help yourself – it's in the shed.'

I obediently opened the shed door and stared at the chaotic arrangement of garden furniture, abandoned lawnmowers, rusting barbecues and plant pots piled up before me. I wondered about making a guess; maybe I should just grab the old bicycle wheel and say, 'Ah, there it is! Well, if you ever need to borrow it again, you know where we are . . .'

'How's Madeleine?' he enquired, as I pretended to scan the space in front of me.

'She's, er, fine. Oh, actually, she's just been out in the car!' I blurted, perhaps slightly too proud that I did have one genuine snippet of information to share.

'Oh. Anywhere special?'

'Er, not sure. Collecting some big pictures?'

'She never stops working, does she?'

'Doesn't she? No, I mean, she doesn't, does she?'

'Well, you two must come round for dinner soon.'

'Thank you. That's very nice of you.'

'Really?'

I seemed to have given a reply that surprised him. In that moment I understood that previous offers must always have been rebuffed.

'Great, well, what about this weekend? Arabella was just saying we hadn't seen much of you and we're not doing anything on Saturday.'

'Ah no, Saturday . . . Saturday evening's not good . . .'

'Lunch then?'

Without even knowing him or his wife, I could already sense

that the bitterness of my marital break-up would not be ameliorated by committing Maddy and myself to a dinner party with these neighbours.

'Er, it's a bit difficult at the moment, actually. Maddy and I are getting . . . erm, well, I think we're going to be a bit preoccupied for a while . . .' His silence demanded more details. 'Well – we're having a trial separation.'

'A trial separation?'

'Yeah, you know . . . and a trial divorce. Just to see how that goes for a while . . .'

At least this embarrassing news cut the conversation short. The neighbour put down his drink and came into the shed himself, where it turned out the thing I had come round to collect was right under my nose all the time. 'Silly me!' I tutted.

Ten minutes later I was standing on a busy underground train, noticing that people were giving me more space than might usually be expected. Perhaps it was the three-foot-long serrated blade of the electric hedge trimmer I was clutching. It was too heavy to carry back to Gary and Linda's, so I had made the brave decision to take public transport. I attempted a faint smile at a nervous-looking mother, who then moved her children further down the carriage. I affected to carry the unwieldy weapon as if I was barely even aware that I was holding it, as if I often travelled on the tube during rush hour with a yard of sharpened steel teeth in my right hand. A couple of hoodies were eyeing me warily. 'Respect!' muttered one, as he got off at the next stop.

Chapter 7

I felt as if I had stared at my bedroom clock for an entire night. Lying there, in the half-light of the nursery, everything was quiet and completely still except for the manic pendulum on the wall opposite. It featured a happy clown clinging on to a rainbow, swinging back and forth, for ever. His situation still seemed to make more sense than my own. By about half past three it became clear that the clown was not going to take a rest, so I got up and tiptoed into the kitchen for a glass of water.

When dawn came it would be the day of my court case. I sat at the pine table for a while, listening to the rhythmical dripping of the tap. I looked at the cooker. Did people still kill themselves by putting their heads in ovens, I wondered, or would that not work with an electric fan oven? There were little informative images beside the various settings – a fish, a chicken, but no picture of a depressed person's head. Pinned on the noticeboard by the fridge was a telephone bill. 'Have you updated your Friends and Family?' it asked. I spotted Gary and Linda's address book and I started to flick through the pages. 'Vaughan and Maddy' was filed under 'V', neatly typed, with the address set out underneath.

Then a green biro had crossed my name out and scrawled a new address sideways down the margin. That had subsequently been crossed out and then another address scribbled in blue underneath that, which was so squeezed in, it was virtually illegible. No one had planned for any separate space for 'Vaughan' on this page; it just ruined everything. There was my family's telephone number glaring at me from the yellowing paper, a series of digits that I must have effortlessly recited a thousand times. I could just dial that number right now and talk to Maddy. Although ringing up my ex-wife at half past three in the morning might not be the best way to reassure her of my sanity.

My personal effects had been rediscovered in a jacket pocket at the bottom of a bag of clothes and now, seated at the kitchen table, I carefully dealt out the cards from my wallet like some sort of sociological Tarot reader. 'That's the Blockbuster video card. It represents stability and culture – a sign that you might be the sort of person who would own a DVD player and enjoy renting movies. Combined as it is with a Lambeth Library Services card and a Clapham Picturehouse membership, this sequence suggests that you are quite a cultured person, although of course there is no card from the British Film Institute or Friends of the National Theatre. The Virgin Active Gym card would at first suggest that you are a health enthusiast, except you have to look at how the card is lying. It was actually stuck inside the wallet with the embossed numbers having imprinted their shape into the leather pocket, suggesting it has never actually been used. In terms of wealth, there is only one basic credit card, not a series of high-status gold or platinum cards. But on the plus side, your Caffè Nero loyalty card shows that you are only two stamps away from a free cappuccino . . .'

I took a pen and a notepad and attempted to copy the signature on my bank cards. I could produce nothing even vaguely similar. My phone was completely out of battery, which had been something of a relief to me. I had been frightened by the idea that people could just ring me up; that names would flash urgently on the screen, expecting to pick up where they had left off with me and I would know nothing at all about them. But now, under cover of darkness, I plugged it in and watched the screen come back to life. I had forty-seven missed calls and seventeen messages. I scrolled through my contacts, reading the cast list of the play in which I was about to make my entrance. I tore off a clean sheet of paper and prepared to write down all their names and what they wanted.

I didn't recognize the first caller. 'Vaughan, hi, it's me, there's a curriculum problem I need you to sort out. I've spoken to Jules and Mike, and if you could check the rota for Day 6—' And then I stopped it and just pressed 'Delete All'.

I rested my forehead on the kitchen table for a while and thought about the ordeal of the day ahead. The court case had not been postponed because I had never been assertive enough to insist that Maddy or my lawyer was informed about my condition. Gary had maintained that we were definitely doing the right thing, and that my life could begin again once this 'last little formality' was out of the way. I was to learn the hard way about the wisdom of taking legal advice from a man with an earring.

I was woken by the sound of some crockery being placed on the kitchen table beside my head.

'Sorry to wake you there, Vaughan, mate. I'm just doing breakfast. Do you want any prawn balls?'

'What?'

'With sweet and sour sauce. And some special fried rice, though it's a bit less special than it was a couple of days ago, to be honest.'

The microwave gave out a beep and Gary bit into a reheated spring roll.

'Er – no, thanks. What time is it?'

'It's getting on a bit, actually. You're supposed to be in court in an hour – although you might want to iron the creases out of your face first.'

*

Gary observed that I wasn't as laid back as I used to be. He felt there was no need to run from the underground station to the court. 'Relax, they're not going to start without you, are they?' I still had no idea just how bad a husband I had been. Thankfully, as I approached the courtroom steps there was no angry mob surging forward against police barricades, spitting and shouting, 'Bastard!' as a grey blanket was put over my head.

'Vaughan! There you are!' said a posh young man with a voice even louder than his tie. 'I thought you wanted to meet a bit earlier?'

'Are you Vaughan's lawyer?' said Gary. 'We spoke on the phone yesterday.'

'Yes, hello. So, Vaughan, according to your friend here you wanted to go through all the questions likely to come up in court, so that you know what you should say?' He made this sound like a bizarre request.

'Er, that's right. Yes.'

'*Again*,' he said pointedly.

'Again?' I asked, without checking myself.

'Well, that's exactly what we did last time I saw you. And we're not supposed to do that in any case.'

'Er, Vaughan said that was incredibly useful,' interjected Gary, 'but when I was just doing a final, final rehearsal with him, it turned out that he was a little confused about one or two minor aspects of it, weren't you, mate?'

'I see,' said the lawyer, opening his leather file. 'We haven't got long. Which particular areas would you like me to go over again?'

I looked forlornly at Gary, hoping that he might have the words to answer this. He didn't. 'Well, the whole, general sort of area of the whole thing, really . . . you know. Getting divorced? That bit.'

I found it difficult to concentrate when I was looking over his shoulder to see if I could spot Maddy coming in.

'As I say, I'm afraid Mrs Vaughan is being incredibly unreasonable,' commented the lawyer on one of the minor points of contention relating to our financial settlement.

'Well, there are two sides to everything,' I interjected. 'I mean, her lawyer probably thinks I'm being incredibly unreasonable too.'

He seemed to be pulled up short by this comment. 'Well, Mr Vaughan, I must say you seem to have mellowed in your feelings somewhat.'

Gary was anxious that my attitude did not arouse suspicions. 'I think with the actual divorce so close, you're already preparing for the next psychological stage, aren't you, mate? Forgiveness, reconciliation, cooperation. It's all in *Divorce for Dummies*.'

'I haven't read that one,' said the lawyer. 'I don't think it was in the Bodleian.'

The lawyer had never actually told us his name, so I found myself saying things like 'what *our colleague* here is saying'; 'going back to the earlier point made by *our esteemed lawyer friend* here'. Plus I was still looking out for the beautiful woman I was divorcing, and so the patter of unfamiliar legalese became just incidental background noise as I drifted in and out of concentration.

'So you're completely clear about the CETV?' he said.

'What? Oh, er, almost completely . . .' I stuttered. 'Will the judge ask me what that stands for?'

'No! The Cash Equivalent Transfer Value is the valuation technique both parties have agreed to pursue with regard to the pension.'

'I knew that . . .'

'The difficulty being that Maddy is demanding half.'

'Sounds reasonable,' I commented cheerfully. His stunned silence went on for so long I was worried the extra time would be added on to my bill. 'I'm sorry, Mr Vaughan, but we have been absolutely adamant on this point up till now.'

'See, mate, you paid nearly all of the contributions into the pension,' interjected Gary, 'so you didn't see why she should receive half of it.'

'But if she was looking after the kids or whatever, how could she pay any money in? She was making, like, a non-cash contribution, wasn't she?'

'That is the point that *her* lawyer will be making. But one of the reasons you are having to go to court is because you don't agree with what you just said.'

'I don't?'

'*No, you don't.* We have consistently agreed that she could have worked when the children were young if she had wanted to, but that she *chose* not to.'

'Ah, well, that's a difficult one, isn't it?' I mused philosophically, pressing my index fingers together. 'I mean, was there a genuine choice? Deep down, you know? If I was working so hard at my job – teachers' bureaucracy, staff meetings, marking, cleaning the blackboard . . . do teachers still do that? – perhaps all that closed off the possibility of her resuming any meaningful career after we had children.'

My lawyer pressed his fingers to his temples as if he had suddenly developed a powerful headache, and his exasperation seemed to increase as I went on to question the pre-arranged position on the division of the house and the custody of the children. 'I just think we are pursuing a rather hard-line and unreasonable stance.'

'This is the Divorce Court, Mr Vaughan, not Disneyland. You either fight your corner or you get utterly destroyed.'

The lawyer insisted that there was no alternative but to proceed on the basis already agreed, and Gary pointed out that if I won, I'd look all the more generous to Maddy if I didn't insist on all the court's terms. But I was alarmed at some of the stands adopted by my former self. To solve the practical problems of my demand that I have custody of the children, my lawyer had suggested that the kids move schools to the comprehensive where I was a teacher. Gary drew breath at that one.

John O'Farrell

'I'm not sure you want to do that to them, mate . . .' Now it seemed wrong to want to cause further disruption to the children's lives; I couldn't understand the thinking of the Vaughan who had previously gone along with this. Finding out more and more about myself was like peeling an onion. And the more I peeled away the layers, the more I felt like crying.

'Right, shall we go in?' suggested the lawyer before I complicated things any further. I discovered that Gary would not be allowed in the courtroom, and so I alone was solemnly escorted to the innermost chamber where marriages went to die.

The courtroom itself was smaller and more modern than I had anticipated; nothing like the great oak-panelled room that had been planted in my subconscious by climactic trial scenes in forgotten TV dramas. It smelt of furniture polish and new carpet tiles, and on the wall hung an old portrait of the Queen to remind divorcing couples that there were always families more dysfunctional than their own. We were joined by a pupil barrister and then a solicitor and trainee, and eventually Maddy and her team bustled in and placed themselves at the parallel bench. I felt my insides fizzing as I saw her again and I leaned over and attempted a smile, but she had clearly decided that our final divorce hearing was not the occasion for friendly little waves across the room. Her lawyer mumbled at her for several minutes and she listened in intense concentration, only glancing up once, accidentally making eye contact with me and then quickly looking away. She was wearing a smart dark jacket and skirt, with a plain white blouse underneath. 'That's exactly what you should wear for a divorce hearing,' I thought. Well, if you were a woman, anyway. Though if you wore that when you were a man, at least the judge might have an idea why the marriage had failed. I was troubled by how little Maddy seemed able to smile. Of course I understood that this was not a happy occasion, but I still found myself wanting to make her feel better. As it turned out, my performance in court was to have exactly the opposite effect.

As the judge entered the room, I was struck by the fact that he was not wearing the traditional headpiece. 'Oh, no wig!' I heard myself blurt out. The judge heard and looked at me. Now I was suddenly worried that he was in fact wearing a toupee, and that saying 'no wig' might not have been the best way to get on his good side.

'Divorce judges don't wear wigs, Vaughan – it's not Open Court,' my lawyer whispered. And we both attempted a polite smile at the judge, but my willpower was not quite strong enough to hold eye contact with him and I glanced momentarily at the top of his lushly carpeted head.

There then followed some procedural overtures that I hoped might help the judge forget about our poor start before the hearing began in earnest. It was as if he and the two lawyers were performing some sort of secret coded mumbling game, in which the judge would say something incomprehensible and the lawyers would have to go through the charade of muttering back the unfathomable but presumably correct answer. They might as well have been discussing the transformations of Pokémon characters.

'Counsel for the petitioner? Jigglypuff evolves into?'

'Jigglypuff turns into Wigglytuff, m'lud.'

'Let the record show that Jigglypuff's evolve is Wigglytuff. Counsel for the respondent, Pikachu becomes?'

'Pikachu transforms into Raichu, m'lud. Via the use of the Thunder Stone.'

I gradually understood that they were establishing the stages of the divorce process so far, the areas of agreement and divergence, during which I found my eye wandering back to the other half I hadn't known I'd had. She was looking straight ahead, vacant and unemotional, listening to the protracted history of our separation and just enduring the ordeal; coping alone, waiting to move on from there. I so wanted to make this easier for her, to make that blank expression crack into a smile.

The previous night I had worked hard to think of every possible question that might be thrown at me if I had to take the stand. My trainer Gary had said I should go into court feeling confident and completely in control. 'This is only for insurance, mate. I'm pretty certain you won't have to say anything at all. There's just a load of special phrases and that, and then at the end you just have to agree by saying "amen" or something.'

'That's church.'

'Oh yeah. Not "amen". It's "not guilty" or something. "The ayes have it!" I'm sure you'll pick it up once you're in there.'

I was wishing that he could be in there just to see how very wrong he had been. Right at the beginning they caught me out with a trick question that it was completely unreasonable to expect me to know.

'Could you state your full name, please?'

'Oh! My *full* name?' I stammered. 'Do you mean with, like, middle names and everything?'

'Yes.'

'Ooh, erm . . . let me see . . . Well, I'm Jack Vaughan, though everyone calls me Vaughan, but my full name . . . my full, complete, legal name with the middle name . . . or names, well, that would be . . . Mister . . . Jack – sorry, I've gone blank, help me out here, er, lawyer person, sorry, I've forgotten *your* name as well, actually . . .'

The whole room was now staring at me as if I had decided to come to court completely naked, which I knew I hadn't because the tie around my neck felt as if it was slowly tightening. 'Bit nervous, sorry.'

My lawyer gazed at me uncertainly, perplexed by this mystery new tactic. 'Well, your full name, is er, well, it will be on the original submission. I didn't think to check you knew that – it's in these papers I think – hang on, not this pile, the other one . . .'

'It's Jack Joseph Neil Vaughan,' recited Maddy, in a tone suggesting years of exasperation with the uselessness of the man she was divorcing.

I leaned across and mouthed, 'Thank you,' and her look back seemed to say 'What the hell are you doing?'

'My name is Jack Joseph Neal Vaughan,' I declared, with exaggerated confidence.

'Is that Neil with an "*i*" or with an "*a*"?' interjected the over-weight clerk.

'It's with an "*a*"!' I declared confidently.

'It's with an "*i*",' came the voice from the other side of the court.

'With an "*i*", sorry. Of course, Neil with an "*i*".'

The officially un-wigged judge stared at me silently for a moment; he seemed to be lamenting the long-lost power of the judiciary to impose the death penalty at will. I pictured him with a black cap on his head. At least it might have covered up the toupee.

The next section was manageable if a little uncomfortable. Before I swore an oath I was asked my religion. I took a calculated guess that I was probably not a Hindu or a Zoroastrian and so swore an oath on the Holy Bible that everything I would say would be the truth. I learned that I was the petitioner (amazingly to my mind, *I* was the one who had initiated divorce proceedings) and I confirmed my date of birth as the one I had seen printed on the forms. 'So what does that make me?' I thought as I considered this seemingly randomly allocated birthdate. 'What star sign is May – that's Taurus, isn't it? Mind you, it's a load of rubbish anyway . . .'

'And your occupation?'

'Teacher!' I snapped back, like a smug contestant in a TV quiz show. At last – I had got a couple of questions right. That must have stood me in good stead, I thought.

Above us a large, angry fly was trapped inside the light casing. To my heightened senses, its manic buzzing and spinning was as loud as the monotone voices of the two lawyers talking a language I barely understood. Maddy poured herself some water and then

I did likewise. My lawyer nodded to me as if to suggest that something had just gone according to plan, though I had no idea what
that might possibly be. Eventually the judge instructed the
counsel for the respondent to begin their case, and after his opening statement we came to the moment I had hoped would never
happen: the part of the proceedings when I was to be cross-
examined by my wife's lawyer.

'Mr Vaughan, I want you to cast your mind back to 1998.'

'Erm, okay . . . I'll do my best . . .'

'You and your wife first employed the service of a financial
adviser in that year, did you not?'

The lawyer looked at me, almost miming my expected
agreement.

'Quite possibly.'

'I'm afraid we need to be clearer than that, Mr Vaughan. Did
you and your wife employ the services of a financial adviser in
February 1998?'

I looked across at my estranged wife, who was staring directly
ahead.

'I have no reason to disbelieve Madeleine if she says that we did.'

'And did you not make a decision at that meeting on the seven-
teenth of February 1998 that, in addition to your teacher's pension,
to which we will come later, you would also make freestanding
additional voluntary contributions in your name only, because you,
Mr Vaughan, as the only taxpayer at that point, could then benefit
from more tax relief than if they had been in Madeleine's name?'

I would have struggled to follow these financial details even
with my brain in normal working order.

'Erm, I don't know.'

The judge leaned forward. 'Think hard, Mr Vaughan. It's
important that you try to recall the key points.'

'Er, well, it sounds quite possible. If there is a record of the
payments being made after that date, then obviously I did take out
an additional pension in my name.'

'The existence of this pension plan is not the issue, Mr Vaughan. The point is that you verbally assured your wife that this personal pension was intended for your joint benefit, but that it was only taken out in your name to save tax. Is this not the case? Is this not what you told your wife in 1998?'

I was perspiring in places that I hadn't known had sweat glands. I thought of lying and just obligingly going along with the plausible picture being presented to me, but I felt a higher duty to be as honest as it was possible to be in this uncomfortably dishonest situation.

'I have to say, in all truth, that I really can't remember,' I declared with a sigh. Maddy's lawyer looked completely stumped. As if I had craftily outmanoeuvred him.

'Brilliant!' whispered my own counsel.

'You can't remember?' scorned the opposing barrister. 'How convenient for you . . .'

'No, I really can't. I mean, I might have said that to her. But I might not have. It was a long time ago, and I just can't recall.'

The judge intervened: 'Would it not have been possible to get a statement from this, er, "financial adviser", if he was present at this meeting?'

'We did attempt to, your honour. But he left the country after he was declared bankrupt.'

'Oh, this is getting us nowhere . . . Can we move on?'

'You don't remember any subsequent assurances to your wife, do you, Mr Vaughan?' improvised her lawyer, now sounding a little desperate.

'Er, no. No, I don't.'

Maddy shook her head in contempt and disappointment. 'It's not enough that you have all the money,' she spat. 'You have to come and take the hedge trimmer away as well! You don't even have a garden any more!'

'Quiet, please,' said the judge.

'I don't want the hedge trimmer. You can have it back . . .'

'Quiet, PLEASE!' insisted the judge, and as her lawyer moved on to the next matter, I tried to catch Maddy's eye, to mouth to her that the trimmer was hers – I'd buy her a new one if she wanted. She couldn't even bear to look at me.

The memory test now moved on to the next stage: the years of our marriage and how they reflected the respective investment made by both parties.

'Mr Vaughan, while you were at work, would you attempt to claim you were also doing fifty per cent of the childcare?'

'Er, I doubt it. It sounds like I was always still at work when they came home from school for a start.'

'Quite,' he commented meaningfully. 'Would you even attempt to put a figure on the proportion of the childcare you did?' He theatrically pretended to imagine the sort of tasks this might involve. 'Picking them up from school? Helping with homework? Cooking their tea? Running them to clubs and swimming lessons? Did you do forty per cent of this, thirty per cent, or indeed virtually none of this type of work?'

'Well, it's very hard to say *exactly*,' I said truthfully. 'Much less than Madeleine, I'm sure.' I glanced nervously to my lawyer, whose indignant frown suggested that he'd personally witnessed his client doing years of baths and bedtime stories.

'Would it be fair to say that if Madeleine had not done so much of the domestic work involved in raising a family, then you would not have been able to work the very long hours that both parties accept you put into your career?'

'I guess you're right . . .'

I noticed Maddy look up.

'So would you not agree that seventy:thirty represents an unfair reflection of the paid *and unpaid* work done by the two of you during this period?'

'Yes, it is unfair. I think a fifty:fifty split would be fairer.' And I stared directly at my wife. She looked completely astonished.

There was a moment of slightly confused silence, punctuated only by the mad spinning of the fly trapped in the light. I was rather disappointed this was not some huge courtroom with press and witnesses and a packed public gallery; for it was at this point that it would have burst into an excited hubbub, forcing the judge to bang his gavel and shout, 'Silence in court!' Instead, Maddy's lawyer seemed utterly bewildered. It was as if he was only pro-grammed to disagree and contradict; he tried to reach for words but none would come. Now my own representative felt compelled to respond to what had just happened. He stood up.

'Your honour, the respondent's counsel is putting words into my client's mouth. Surely it is for the court to make a ruling after we have put our own case for a seventy:thirty split.' And he urgently gestured for me to shut up.

'It appears, Mr Cottington, that you and your client have come to court without agreeing in advance on the apportionment you are seeking.'

'Mr *Cottington*,' I thought. 'So that's my lawyer's name.'

I had feared that the judge might be irritated, but in fact he seemed to be suppressing a certain degree of excitement that something slightly out of the ordinary had finally happened. He made a self-consciously formal pronouncement reminding both counsel of the importance of preparation, and resolved to put this issue to one side for the moment as there were a number of other matters to be settled. He entered into a whispered exchange with the alarmingly overweight clerk while I was left standing there. Although I felt certain I had done the right thing, I could feel my legs shaking underneath me.

Then, in the middle of the most stressful situation I could recall, I suddenly got my first negative memory. Maddy was angrily berating me and I was shouting back. I even felt a twinge of resentment rise up in me as I recalled how over the top she had been about a little thing like a battery in a smoke alarm. This memory was hazier, but the argument had arisen because I had apparently 'endangered the family' by taking the battery out of the smoke alarm to put in my bike light.

'Why the hell didn't you replace the battery?' she is shouting.
'I forgot, okay? Don't you ever forget things?'
'Not where the safety of our children is concerned.'
'Well, this was for the safety of your husband – so that he was visible on the dark, busy roads! Isn't that important too?'
'No, actually – it's not as important. Though you could have bought a replacement battery anyway – you just forgot all about it. You just forgot about us but remembered you.'

Looking at Madeleine standing there in the court, I couldn't believe that there was such an irrational and aggressive side to her; that she was capable of so much anger about something as trivial as one AA battery.

The court had come to consider the key point in the settlement, the decision on the Property Adjustment Order. With no agreement on the house, it would have to be sold, but negotiations had completely broken down over a fair split of the money, the furnishings and who was going to have to talk to the estate agent. I had been allowed to stand down, but the more I listened to the arguments from both sides, the clearer it became that neither Maddy nor I would be able to afford a house in the same area that would accommodate two children and an excitable golden retriever. It would mean moving the kids far away from their school, maybe either parent having to sleep on a sofa bed in the living room when the kids were with them; it would mean no garden and the children having tiny bedrooms and no space for friends to come and stay. Maybe they should keep the house, I thought, and we could take turns to borrow that collapsing tent we'd had in Ireland.

One blindingly obvious solution to all this was not being suggested by anyone in the courtroom and I felt a duty to point it out.

'Excuse me, your honour – is it possible to . . . change my mind?'

'I beg your pardon?'

'Can I change my mind? Or is too late?'

'You want to go for a different arrangement regarding the property assets as well?'

'No, no – about the whole divorce thing,' I heard myself say. 'I mean, looking at it afresh, as it were, I wonder if we really ought to try and give the marriage another go?'

'Vaughan, stop it!' said Maddy. 'This is not a game.'

'Vaughan, what are you doing?' pleaded my lawyer.

'If I'm the petitioner – can't I, like, withdraw the petition?'

It seemed like a reasonable question. I hadn't actually seen any petition, let alone asked any members of the public to sign it. But the judge's patience had now been exhausted and he seemed at a complete loss over what to say. Even the fly in the light fitting went silent. Deep down I had been hoping for the judge to declare 'This is most irregular, but, given the circumstances, this court instructs Vaughan and Madeleine to jet off to the Caribbean for a second honeymoon, to share a beach hammock in the moonlight and for Mrs Vaughan to fall in love with her husband all over again.'

Instead, he reprimanded my lawyer for not having checked whether his client actually wanted a divorce and declared that this case was 'a disaster'. Looking at the time, he said he was faced with no alternative but an adjournment. We would return at a later date when, he said pointedly, he hoped we would be a little clearer on what it was we actually wanted the court to decide. Inside I felt a rush of elation, which lasted for just a split second as I watched Maddy burst into tears and then dash outside. She didn't even look at me, but was followed by her lawyer who was trying to tell her how well it had actually gone.

Mr Cottington, on the other hand, looked utterly shell-shocked. He chose to say nothing at all to me; instead he gathered up his papers into his briefcase and just left, followed by his trainees and accomplices. The judge had already departed so I sat there in silence for a moment, trying to take in what it was I'd just done.

'Well, I've been in this job over twenty years and I've never seen anything like that before,' said the clerk.

I attempted a brave smile. 'I just think we should be really sure,' I ventured. 'You know, before we finally cut the knot.'

'Right.' The clerk was straightening the chairs. 'As I say, people are usually pretty sure by the time they get here.'

I felt embarrassed and a little bit foolish. Part of me had wanted to rush after Maddy, but I didn't want to experience the angry side of her that I had just remembered. I sat staring straight ahead, wondering where I could possibly go from here.

The clerk had finished gathering her things. 'That was the last case before lunch, but I'm afraid I can't leave you in here on your own.'

'No, of course,' I said. 'Only – would you mind if I unclipped this light fitting? There's a big fly trapped inside, and he's been going mad.'

'Oh. Well, there is a maintenance officer . . . but, yes, all right. I think it just unclips on the side there.'

'Yes, I can see it.'

And so I climbed up on a chair and released the light cover, and stood back to watch the grateful insect fly free. Instead it fell straight to the floor and spun around buzzing on its back.

'Urgh, he's enormous, isn't he?' said the clerk. And she stepped over towards where it was struggling, and the spinning and buzzing gave way to a final crunch as her big fat foot came squelching down on it.

'There!' she said, with a smile. 'Good luck sorting out your marriage – or we'll see you back here in a couple of months . . .'

Chapter 8

Maddy and I are on a train. It is before people have mobile phones, because no one is shouting, 'I'm on a train!' We have not been out of university that long and approach the prospect of a long rail journey with a different mindset from the sensible reading opportunity that we'd settle for later. Basically, we don't view this space as a train so much as a moving pub. I find the perfect double seat facing one another in the smoking compartment, which only adds to the bar-room atmosphere.

As soon as we are settled, I go and buy enough drinks for the whole journey; an hour or so later Maddy goes off to the buffet car to buy the food I neglected to get. But she is taking much longer than I had, and I find myself glancing down the aisle looking to see what has happened to her. There is still no sign of her when a message comes over the tannoy.

'This is a passenger announcement . . .' (Back then we are only 'passengers'; it is before we are re-graded as 'customers' so that we can be that much more indignant when we don't get what we have paid for.) For a split second I think, 'A female train guard – you don't hear that very often.'

'British Rail would like to apologize for the fact that the man serving in the buffet car is such a sexist wanker. British Rail now accept that none of the female passengers on this train wish to be asked if they have a boyfriend, nor be asked for their phone number by a middle-aged man wearing a wedding ring and a name badge saying Jeff.' Maddy has the dull monotone delivery to perfection. Other people in the seats around me are suddenly looking at each other with widening grins, while my heartbeat has just got faster than the train. 'They would also appreciate it if Jeff could attempt to maintain eye contact while serving the All Day Breakfast Bap instead of staring so obviously at the breasts of the female on the other side of the counter. Our next station-stop is Didcot Parkway, where Jeff really ought to consider alighting from the train and lying on the track in front of it. Thank you.'

There is a spontaneous round of applause from all the women customers in our carriage. A couple of them even cheer. Only the old lady sitting nearby carefully listens to the whole thing with concerned concentration, as if it were just another official announcement.

I can't wait for Maddy to come back. I am so fantastically proud of her; she is funny and brave and has made total strangers on a train start laughing and talking to one another. The hubbub is still going as she saunters through the door with a completely straight face as if nothing has happened. 'There's our rogue announcer!' I boast loudly, demonstratively clearing the table so that the star of the moment can put down my beer cans and the now famous All Day Breakfast Bap. It is probably a mistake to tell the whole carriage like that. But we don't particularly mind being turfed off the train at Didcot Parkway. I mean, it's not as if there is absolutely nothing to do in Didcot on a Tuesday evening.

The defining characteristic of this memory was the powerful sensations of love and pride it conjured up. Her entrance into our carriage felt like one of the funniest moments in the history of the world. Just the insouciance with which she calmly sat herself down and began eating the bap; it was a deadpan comedy triumph.

And yet it was deeply frustrating to have so little else of our past lives in which to place it. It was as if I was living in one tiny cell, my head bumping against the ceiling as I paced back and forth re-examining every familiar brick and floor tile. My life-map was incredibly detailed on everything that had happened since 22 October and then there were just a few aerial snapshots of the uncharted continent beyond.

The train-tannoy memory had come to me as I had woken up, with no logical associations or identifiable trigger. Except that I had been thinking about Maddy when I went to sleep and I was still thinking about her when I woke up. It was a few days after the court case and for once I had slept in late. I desperately wanted to have the story officially verified by Gary and Linda, but the two of them had already left for their appointment at the hospital. I think Linda may have booked an extra scan to prove to Gary that there really was a baby in there.

I made myself a cup of tea and thought I would try it without sugar, the way the old Vaughan took it. If I was going to return to normal, I reasoned, I should try to do everything as I used to. I took one sip, winced, and reached for the sugar bowl. I wandered around the flat in my pyjamas. I looked at the spines of the books on the shelves, rows of celebrity life stories ghost-written by someone else. I turned on the television and flicked through dozens of channels, old repeats of soap operas featuring families screaming at one another, punctuated with adverts of families laughing and getting along. I turned it off and stared at the blank screen for a while. Beyond the television stand were various entangled wires, cables and redundant VHS plugs. It could be as chaotic and knotted as you liked behind the scenes as long as the right plugs stayed in the right sockets. 'Come on, come on!' I said out loud, and smacked my forehead in frustration, as if the picture might revert to normal if I hit the top of the set.

I resolved that I was going to go and talk to Maddy alone. She was probably still furious with me after my *volte-face* in the courtroom, but I felt I owed it to her to tell her, one to one, what had happened to me. If she was not at home, I had the address of 'the studio' where she worked. I had learned that Madeleine was not a painter, but an artist none the less, selling huge framed photos she had taken of London landmarks, which funded her more experimental photographic works displayed in galleries and exhibitions. It made me that little bit more proud of her. Maddy was a photographer, and a classy one by the sound of it. It was a relief that the woman I was divorcing did not spend every Saturday taking pictures of brides and grooms.

An hour later I was finally ready to leave the flat to face her. I took a last look at myself in the hallway mirror. And then I went and changed my entire outfit again.

'What the bloody hell are you doing here?' said Maddy, opening her front door.

'Hello.'

'Well?'

'I wanted to meet – I mean, *talk* to you. Properly.'

'You've got a bloody nerve.'

Our first moments alone together. In my fantasy reunion I had imagined her being more pleased to see me.

'I thought I owed you an explanation. Are you alone?'

The dog was barking from the back garden.

'What business is it of yours?'

'It's just – well, it's complicated, and if the kids are in, then . . .'

'No, they're at school, obviously.' I hovered there for a decade or so. 'All right, well, you'd better come in,' and she turned and headed inside. I stood in the doorway, looking at a huge black-and-white photo of Barleycove for far too long, until she came back out from the kitchen and said, 'Well? Are you coming in or not?'

'Sorry, yeah. Do I need to take my shoes off?'

'What? When have we ever done that?'

'I dunno – I forgot . . .'

'Makes a change . . .' she mumbled to herself.

The dog came bounding down the hallway and nearly knocked me over with his enthusiasm. I tried to give him some attention as I gazed around in wonder. It was not one of those pristine and perfectly furnished homes you see in glossy property magazines. It would have been an unconventional interior décor consultant who suggested that the fruit bowl might also be the ideal place to keep that old phone charger and a ping-pong ball.

I could feel myself shaking as we entered the kitchen. I didn't know quite where to start with my news. I didn't want it to spoil my first moments with her. A battered iPod was plugged into some speakers and I recognized the song.

'Hey, you like Coldplay! I love Coldplay!' I said.

'No, you don't. You hate Coldplay. You always made me turn it off when you were in the house.'

'Oh. Well, I like it now . . .'

'So, what's going on, Vaughan? You ignore all my emails and texts and then you turn up to the court and pull a stunt like that.' Her brow went all creased when she looked concerned.

'Erm, well, the thing is, that a couple of weeks ago – the twenty-second of October to be precise, at some point in the late afternoon I think—'

'Yes?'

'I was sort of . . . reborn.'

She looked at me with suspicion.

'You've become a Christian?'

'No! No, although you saying that now tells me that I wasn't a Christian before, which I didn't know.'

'What are you talking about?'

'I was in hospital for a week or so, following a psychogenic fugue.'

'A what?'

'It means that my mind completely wiped itself of all personal memories. I lost all knowledge of my own name, identity, family, friends. I still haven't got my memories back. I've been told that we've been married for fifteen years and that I've known you for twenty. But standing here right now, it's like I'm talking to you for the very first time.'

There was a pause while she just regarded me suspiciously.

'Fuck off!'

'It's true. You can ring the hospital—'

'Bollocks. I don't know what your scam is, but you're not getting this house!' Her accent was more pronounced when she swore; it was a soft Scouse, presumably diluted by a couple of decades spent down south.

'Yeah, Gary told me that we were getting a divorce, although I don't remember why. The doctor said the stress I experienced from the marriage break-up might be what triggered the fugue.'

'The stress *you* experienced! You weren't ever here to experience any stress; you were staying late at work, or going round to Gary's to fart around on computers while I was being stressed all on my own, and I haven't forgotten that, I can tell you.'

'It's a lovely kitchen. Really homey.'

'Why are you being so weird, Vaughan? And why are you patting the dog like that, you know he doesn't like it—'

'No, *I don't know*! I don't know anything. For most of last week I had a hospital label on my wrist saying "UNKNOWN WHITE MALE". Look, I've still got it. And see this metal tag around my neck? It has my name and contact numbers on it in case my brain wipes all over again and I'm left wandering the streets not knowing where to go or who to call.'

She had made me a mug of tea and plonked it down unceremoniously in front of me.

'Do you have any sugar?' I asked.

'You don't take sugar.'

'That's what Gary said. He reckoned I used to smoke as well.'

She leaned closer and smelt me. 'That's what's different about you. You don't stink of stale nicotine. I can't believe you finally gave up.'

'I didn't give up. It's like the addiction was wiped along with everything else.'

She was leaning against the sink with her arms folded and seemed perplexed as to why I should make up such an extra-ordinary story. Then she pulled out her mobile phone and I heard one end of a conversation with Linda. She was looking at me as she talked, her eyes widening and her face draining of colour. When she had finished she just slumped down on a kitchen chair and stared at me.

'That is so typical of you!'

'What?'

'All that crap I'm still dealing with and then you just wipe the slate clean and forget all about it . . .'

'Oh. Sorry.'

'My God, how are the kids going to take this? It's bad enough that we've split up, but this means – well, now their own father doesn't even know them!'

She seemed close to tears, and part of me wanted to comfort her, but her body language did not suggest I should move in for a hug.

'The doctors reckon there's a chance I could return to normal – though I don't think any of them really understand what's hap-pened.'

'They'll be home from school in a few hours. What do I tell them? You can't be here – they'll be scarred for life.'

'Whatever you say. You know what's best for them – I don't.'

'Yeah, well, no change there.' And she glanced up and saw me looking a little lost in the middle of her kitchen, then softened slightly. 'Sorry. It's just . . .'

'It's okay. Where's the bin for the tea bag?'

'Same as always. Oh, I mean you pull out that cupboard there. This is too weird . . .'

'Oh, that's clever – the lid lifts up as you open the cupboard. It really is a lovely kitchen.'

'I thought you were being a bit odd in court from the outset. All that trying to catch my eye and give me little waves.'

'Sorry, it's just that normally you get to meet your wife *before* you divorce her.'

'God, you were under oath in that courtroom – you'd promised to tell the truth.'

'I *did* tell the truth – I said I couldn't remember.'

'So . . . I still don't understand – you literally cannot remember us? Or any of this?'

'Not really.'

'Not really?'

'All right – not at all. Although a couple of moments have come back. I remember the tent collapsing in Ireland and you using the guard's tannoy on some long rail journey?'

'Oh yeah, we got kicked off the train for that.'

'Didcot Parkway.'

'No, it was Ealing Broadway.'

I didn't contradict her, but it was definitely Didcot Parkway.

'But that's all, so far. Except the other night I had a powerful dream about someone nicknamed Bambi.'

Maddy blushed slightly but said nothing.

'What? You know, don't you? Who's Bambi?'

'Bambi is what you used to call me. Years ago, when we were at university.'

'Bambi?'

'You said I had the same eyes. Can't believe I fell for that.' She mimed putting her fingers down her throat.

'But Bambi was a boy, wasn't he?'

'Yeah, and a deer as well. Apart from that, I looked just like him.'

'Yeah, well – if it's not too forward of me – you have got very nice eyes.'

Maddy seemed momentarily lost for words and sipped her tea. 'You really have forgotten everything, haven't you? I have "nice eyes"? Where the hell does that come from? You said I was a selfish cow, you said I was ruining your life.'

'Did I? I'm sorry if I said that. But I just don't remember.'

'Yeah, well, how nice for you.'

'It's not very nice really,' I said slowly, staring at the floor. 'It was incredibly distressing to start with.'

'Sorry. It's just a bit hard to get my head around it. So – like, you didn't know your own name or anything?'

'Not for the whole week I was in hospital. All I could think about was who I might have been before my amnesia. I began to worry whether my life had been a good one, whether I had been a good person, you know what I mean?'

'I suppose you would . . .'

'But now I discover my marriage failed and I've been sleeping on people's sofas and have spent all my money on divorce lawyers.'

She didn't quite know what to say to that. Instead her eyes welled up and then she began quietly crying. I so wanted to kiss her at that point; just to put my arms around my wife and press my lips against her – that would have been the most wonderful thing in the whole world. I hovered there for a moment and finally leaned across and gently rubbed her arm.

'What are you doing?'

'Er – comforting you?'

'Well, don't!'

Instead the dog went across and licked her hand, which was acceptable from Woody, but probably not from me.

'I'm sorry to be the bearer of bad news,' I mumbled eventually. 'I just had to tell you face to face.'

In the difficult silence I became aware of the low steady gurgle of the dishwasher. It sounded like my insides felt. It was then that

I spotted a photo on the fridge. 'Are these our children? Is this what they look like?' The girl had a big, open-hearted smile for the camera, while the boy was doing his best to look cool. What was so striking was how the two children seemed like miniature versions of their parents. Dillie looked just like her mother and Jamie looked just like me.

'Wow! They're beautiful,' I said. And she nodded and stood to share the moment with me.

'That was in France. Dillie's a bit taller than that now. Jamie hates having his photo taken.'

It was a surreal moment. The mother couldn't help but be proud of her children as she showed their father what they looked like. Maddy put her tongue out slightly as she lovingly straightened the photo on the fridge, and in that moment I wanted to float up to the ceiling. All the emptiness I had felt since 22 October was filled with an overwhelming certainty. Just that tiny gesture, that sweet movement of her mouth, made me feel whole, yet light-headed; vigorous and fully charged and, at last, completely alive.

'Beautiful,' I said again. 'Really beautiful.'

On the walk home the whole world seemed different. Those first few fireworks exploding in the sky were all for my benefit. I wanted to tell passing strangers that I had just met this wonderful girl; I held a newsagent's door open for a young mother with a buggy. Then my walk broke into a jog, and in the end I ran all the way back to the flat and I was panting but still elated when I found Gary in his kitchen with the insides of a laptop spread across the table.

'Gary! Something incredible has happened! I think I've fallen in love!'

'Wow! That's great news, man! What's her name?'

'Maddy. Madeleine. I've just met my wife and she is something else, isn't she?'

Gary groaned and tossed down his tiny screwdriver.

'Yeah, she is *something else*, Vaughan – she is your ex-wife. You split up, remember?'

'No.'

'You can't have fallen in love with Maddy, you stupid nutter – you're in the middle of divorcing her!'

'I know – we already have that in common. She's got this gorgeous little nose that turns up at the end and her eyes, they're this beautiful hazel brown—'

'Vaughan, listen, mate, this must be related to your condition.' He indicated the computer circuit boards scattered on the pine table. 'Your hard drive has wiped and this is like an emotional memory coming back or some shit, I don't know. Just don't do anything stupid – it'll soon fade.'

'No, it's not going to fade, Gary. This is for ever, I'm absolutely certain of it! It feels as if all my life I've been waiting for that special someone and I've finally met Miss Right.'

'Okay. Except that all your adult life you've been married to her and finally decided she was Miss Wrong.'

'All right, I know we're getting divorced and that. But every relationship has to overcome a few obstacles – look at Romeo and Juliet.'

'Yeah, they both die . . . You don't love her, you're just going through a phase.'

'No way. I know for an absolute certainty that this is for ever. I feel like I should get a tattoo. Like a big heart on my forearm, with "MADDY" on it.'

'Yeah, right, great idea! Or you could tattoo "IDIOT!" across your forehead. You're delirious. Come on, let's get some food inside you. I'll make you a sandwich.'

Gary sat me down at the kitchen table while I told him about the train memory. He confirmed the story. 'Oh yeah, she was always doing shit like that.' He laughed. 'Like when that posh bloke blocked in her car at the pub and was really rude and refused to come out and move it for her.'

'What did she do?'

'Well, when she finally did squeeze her car through, she stopped and got out and then scratched a huge message on his bonnet with her key.'

'What did it say?'

'*Please be nicer.*'

I laughed out loud.

'I think it's important to say "please" in these situations,' added Gary.

'Absolutely. Maddy's great, isn't she?'

Gary put down his plate. 'Look, Vaughan, there are millions of girls out there. If you're looking for someone who might be interested in making a future with you, I'd say the very last woman in the whole country you should go after is the woman who has tried being married to you for fifteen years and decided she can't stand the sight of you.'

'It's not like that. You don't know Maddy like I do—'

'No – I know her *better*. It's not going to happen, Vaughan. You've got to move on.'

I sulkily pushed away my untouched sandwich. 'So what exactly are you doing to this laptop?' I asked after a while. I think he was grateful to me for finally changing the subject.

'Oh, I'm just putting in more RAM.'

'What's that?'

'RAM? Well, that stands for, er . . . Random Access . . . well, it's a technical term, I shouldn't worry about it. Listen, I've had a brilliant idea for how you can find out more about your past . . .'

Chapter 9

Dear All,

As you may be aware, I recently experienced an extreme form of amnesia that has completely wiped all my personal memories. This means that I cannot recall anything that happened to me before 22 October this year. However, with your help I am hoping I can reconstruct my own personal history from the fragments that you yourselves can remember.

It would be greatly appreciated if you could take a moment to look at this Wikipedia page that I have begun, and then add in any extra details you remember, or edit anything that you feel may be incorrect. For example, I have already put in the basic fact that I attended the University of Bangor. But if you were there with me, you might add in the names of tutors I had, or clubs I joined or particular anecdotes that you feel are worth recalling. My hope is that this online document will grow to become a complete account of my life before my amnesia; and this in turn might help me regain the actual memories of these events.

Many thanks,

Vaughan

With his zealous belief in the power of user-generated content, Gary had come up with an initiative to establish a detailed account of my life to date. My appeal went out via email, Facebook and, for what it was worth, the features pages of YouNews. I had been desperate for a way to restore ownership of my personal story; I wanted to learn the history of my own Dark Ages, to swot up on the dates and key events and understand how it all fitted together.

'Half-knowledge is a dangerous thing,' Gary had sagely quoted at me.

'Who said that?'

'I dunno. Alexander somebody . . . Aha ha ha!'

So here was the Facebook/LinkedIn/Friends Reunited profile taken to a new level. I was going to have my own memoir collaboratively written online. Uniquely, I would not be the editor of my own life story; I didn't even get a couple of sessions with the ghost-writer. The old manuscript had been lost, so now it would be completely rewritten, this time from the witnesses' point of view. I barely existed in the first person yet: my life story was all 'you' or 'he'. I wondered how this perspective might affect the reader's sympathies. It would be like the United States having its history rewritten from scratch by Britain, Mexico, Japan, the Native Americans and Iraq.

'It's an interesting idea,' said Dr Lewington, as I proudly told her how my personal memories were going to be compiled by others. It was now three weeks since I had had the fugue and this was my first appointment back at the hospital. 'Though you should continue to keep a separate record of your own memories. Are you writing them down?'

'Yes, I have a little notepad by my bed. With lots of blank pages.'

'And how are you feeling in yourself? Because I can still refer you to a psychiatrist or a counsellor if you feel that would be at all helpful.'

'No, I'm fed up talking about it, to be honest. People think I'm mad enough as it is, without me seeing a psychiatrist.'

'There's no stigma attached. What you have experienced is very traumatic – it is a form of mental illness.'

'I'm fine, really. Things are looking up. I think I've fallen in love . . .'

'Well, that's wonderful news. Because I seem to remember you were getting divorced.'

'Yup, that's her. She still wants to get divorced, but I was hoping she might marry me again after that.'

'Right. As I say, the offer of a psychiatrist is always there if you need it . . .'

At the end of our session Dr Lewington asked to see my online biography, and I found myself feeling a little nervous as she clicked on the link. It had not been live for even twenty-four hours, and I worried that one or two people might take advantage of this situation to settle old scores or exercise some ancient grudge. But I had not anticipated the viciousness of the treatment I had received in those first twenty-four hours. No one had written a single word about me.

Over the next day or so I kept returning to the document and clicking on 'Refresh', but my life story just read '*This neurology-related article is a stub. Please help Wikipedia by expanding it.*' I could tell from checking the article history that quite a few people had opened the page, but no one had taken the trouble to write anything. Gary had been on Facebook and mentioned that everyone I knew had found time to update their own status and upload new photos of themselves.

Not even Maddy had responded to my round-robin email and I worried about how she was dealing with the bombshell that her own husband had forgotten their entire marriage. But then Linda took a phone call from Maddy; apparently she wanted to meet up with me for a coffee 'and have a serious talk'.

'Ha, that's almost like a date, isn't it?' I suggested optimistically.

'Um, I don't think so, Vaughan. I think she wants to talk about where the two of you go from here.'

'No, I hear what you're saying. It's just two adults meeting up to discuss a very difficult situation.'

A few minutes later I came out of my room to ask Linda's advice.

'What do you think – is this shirt too bright? Would this one be better?'

'It doesn't matter, Vaughan – they're both fine.'

'What about these shoes? Too formal?'

I had been through all my old clothes, but I reckoned that Maddy must have seen me in those. And Gary's shirts somehow combined looking as if the washing instructions had been consistently ignored with looking like they had never been washed at all.

'Have I got time to go out and buy a new outfit?'

'It doesn't matter what you wear, Vaughan. Just be yourself.'

'Fine. Just be myself. So, er, what is "myself", exactly?'

I was ridiculously early to the café and chose a seat outside so I'd be able to see her coming. I sat down with a book, and re-read the same line about twenty times. She had chosen a café in Covent Garden and the piazza was so busy I kept momentarily mistaking other people for Madeleine. Finally she approached and I stood up, but there was no big smile or exaggerated wave from her when she spotted me. I went to give her a peck on the cheek, but she didn't move towards me at all and so I was forced to pretend I was leaning over to pull out her chair.

'Hi! Great to see you! You look nice . . .'

'Shall we get on with it?' she said, playing it rather cool, I thought.

Today she was wearing her hair down, and I decided that she wasn't so much a redhead as a strawberry blonde. I asked her what sort of coffee she wanted; she requested a double espresso and insisted on handing over the exact amount in loose change.

'Hey, double espresso! Same as me!' I said, with enthusiasm, wondering what that might taste like.

'No, you always have a cappuccino.'

With her already knowing me so well, there was less of the exploratory trivia that I would have liked to warm up with.

'Anyway, listen, I talked to my lawyer and I think it's actually good that the final hearing got postponed.'

'Oh, great!' I said, trying not to wince at the strength of my black coffee.

'Yes – he said that if the hearing had gone ahead and it was then discovered that you were not in a fit state to be in court, then the whole divorce might have been invalidated. Far better to get divorced when we know it would be a cast-iron *decree nisi.*'

'Oh.' I sighed. 'I see.'

In the distance a street performer was juggling or balancing on a unicycle, or possibly both, and his bombastic self-commentary was punctuated with occasional ripples of applause.

'See, I told him about your amnesia and he says you have to get medical attestation that you have the mental capacity to give instruction. Do you need to write that down?'

'No, I can remember that.'

'So you need to see a psychiatrist or neurologist or whatever as soon as possible so that we can finalize the divorce.'

She had already crushed the tiny part of me that had hoped she might be just a little bit flirty. We were only able to sit outside because of the large metallic mushrooms that appeared to have sprouted between the tables, but even these huge heaters struggled to revive the summer in the face of the plummeting temperature.

'So have you seen a psychiatrist yet?'

'I'm not mad. Why does everyone think I need a psychiatrist?'

'What, you and me give the marriage another go? That was pretty mad, you must admit.'

A round of applause echoed across the piazza. If she could only get to know me, she would surely see how sincere and attentive I was. She'd forget all that negative stuff she'd heard about me from her divorce lawyer and would be convinced that here, finally, was the man for her.

'How are the kids?' I was keen to hear about them, and I wanted to remind her of the things we had in common.

'They're fine. I've tried to give them an inkling of what's happened to you, but Dillie was quite upset by it all. So we're going to have to handle it very carefully . . .'

Privately I was frightened of being introduced to my own children. I was desperate to make the right first impression on two people who had known me all their lives. Surely they would see it in my eyes – my distance, my coldness.

'Okay, I'll follow your lead. But tell them I can't wait to meet them.'

'No, I won't say that.'

'I mean see them. *Again*.'

I ripped open the top of a sugar sachet and shared the contents between my coffee cup and the surface of the table.

'Still taking sugar then?'

'For as long as I can remember . . .'

'But you're not smoking? I can't believe all those years I begged you to give up and you said it was impossible. And then you give up just like that!'

'Yup, that's all it takes, a bit of willpower. And a psychogenic fugue. Are you sure I can't get you a blueberry muffin or anything?'

'When have I ever eaten blueberry muffins?'

'I don't know, do I? I do not have the *mental capacity* to choose you a muffin.'

'Sorry, I forgot.'

'Hey, that's my catchphrase.'

'So just how much can you remember now? If you can remember the camping holiday when you ignored that gale warning and the time you got us kicked off the train . . . is it all starting to come back?'

I thought about her shouting at me about the smoke alarm. 'No, there's not much else yet.'

'Well, maybe that's a blessing.'

'I don't remember why we split up – it feels like it doesn't make sense. I was serious about what I said in the courtroom. About us giving it another go . . .'

'Come off it, Vaughan – we had long enough to make our marriage work. It was over a long time ago.' And then she put down her coffee cup and her demeanour changed as if she had made a decision to stop being so restrained and adult about this. 'God, when I think of the shit I had to put up with!'

'Hey, it wasn't all me, you know!' I had no evidence to back this up, but I felt no responsibility for things of which I had no memory. 'It takes two people to make a marriage fail.'

'Yeah, that's what Dr Crippen said . . .'

'Anyway, there is something else I remember,' I said triumphantly. 'I remember you being too cross about trivial things. Going ballistic because I forgot to replace the battery in the smoke alarm—'

'Trivial?'

'In the broad scheme of things, yes. I mean I don't see why it was such a big deal.'

She looked at me as if I was completely stupid. 'Because there was a fire.'

At first I thought this must be a joke. I had spent too much time with Gary.

'What?'

'Because there was a fire. That's why I was cross. There was a fire in our kitchen while we were all asleep, and the smoke alarm failed to go off because you had taken the battery out.'

This is why it is best to be in full command of the facts when you get into an argument.

'Shit! That sounds scary. I – I don't remember that bit . . .' I mumbled.

'But you remember me being cross about it?'

'Vaguely . . . Were we outside?'

'Er, yes, because our house was on fire. The whole family was standing in the back garden in pyjamas while the fire brigade chucked all the charred, smouldering kitchen units out on to the patio.'

I tried to picture the scene but it was still lost to me. 'Blimey. So who raised the alarm?'

'Er, well, I got the kids up when you nudged me and asked if I could smell smoke.'

'Oh, well, so at least I raised the alarm.'

'You woke me up and said "Can you smell smoke?" And then I leapt up and ran to the children.'

'But I was the one who smelt the smoke? So that sort of cancels out removing the battery?'

'No, it does not – we could all have been killed! We had to completely refit the kitchen! That could all have been avoided—'

'I might have smelt smoke quicker than the alarm would have detected it . . .'

'Okay – you were the hero of the hour! Wow, that's quite a rewriting of history there. Silly me – I must have remembered it all wrong.'

I couldn't help thinking that this was our first tiff, but thought it best not to mention it.

'A rose for the lady?' said a flower-seller, in a powerful Eastern European accent. The scent of roses was slightly lost in the fug of tobacco smoke from the wet cigarette hanging from his lip.

'Er, no. No, thank you.'

'Hey, lady – doesn't he love you? You want him buy you romantic flower?'

'No, thank you very much.'

The vendor wandered off, but his appearance had punctured the increasingly dangerous atmosphere.

'You can't just wipe the slate clean and start again, Vaughan.'

'But that's exactly what's happened! Okay, I've forgotten everything, but then so have you. You've forgotten how you used to feel. I meant what I said in the courtroom.'

'Look, you're attracted to this romantic idea of Vaughan and his happy wife, because you are understandably desperate to get your past back. But your past isn't what you imagine it is. You can't just go back to the happy bits. It wasn't all drunken giggling in a tent, I can tell you.'

'I'm not thinking about the past, I'm thinking about the future. When I first saw you and the home we made together . . . If you could have seen all that through fresh eyes like I did, you wouldn't want to just let it all go.'

'Yes, but your eyes can't see *you* spoiling the view. It's like seeing a pretty house from the motorway and thinking, "I'd like to live there."' A ripple of applause came from the crowd, as if to compliment Maddy on a point well made.

'Look, people change,' I pleaded. 'Clearly I have changed. And I'm really sorry about all the things that hurt you when our marriage went wrong. I can't imagine why I would have done them, but if it's any consolation I clearly found it all so traumatic that my brain completely wiped any memory of it along with everything else. And now the only thing I can remember about you is how passionately I felt when we first met.'

'Yeah, well, you wait till you get the rest of your memory back. You don't love me, Vaughan. Your mind is still playing tricks on you.'

The chain-smoking flower seller had had no success and by now had started on the next café along from us.

'Excuse me!' I called across to him.

'Vaughan, no!'

'How much are the roses?'

'Four pounds a stem,' he said, rushing over. 'Beautiful rose for beautiful lady.'

'Vaughan – do *not* buy me a rose.'

But the nicotine-stained fingers were already pulling out one cellophane-wrapped instant love token.

'No, no,' I said. 'I'll give you fifty pounds for the whole lot.'

'All of them?'

'Vaughan – you're wasting your money.'

'Sixty pounds!'

'Fifty quid and you can finish work now.' The man gave an impassive nod and quickly exchanged the notes in my hand for a huge bunch of skinny red roses.

'He love you very much.'

'Actually, we were just finalizing our divorce,' she explained.

'Your wife – funny lady!' laughed the flower seller. But neither of us joined in. My dramatic gesture had only irritated Maddy further and now she just brusquely worked her way through her checklist of all the practical things she needed to sort out. Though our lives would continue to require contact and cooperation, she did not want to be my friend.

Desperately, I made one last pitch to her.

'My memory loss might be the best thing that ever happened to us!'

'For God's sake, Vaughan, one of the things that used to drive me mad about you was that you forgot everything I told you. If it was anything about *your* life then you remembered it all right, sure, but if it was something I was doing, then it wasn't important enough for you to register. And suddenly you don't remember a thing about me and you think that's going to make you more attractive to me? I'd say this was just the logical conclusion to the way the whole relationship had been going for twenty years. First you forget the milk I ask you to pick up on the way home; then you forget I've got an exhibition coming up, or that I asked you to come home early so I could get to the processors; then you forget our anniversary or that you gave me the same Christmas present last year; until finally you completely forget every single thing about me – my name, what I looked like . . . you completely forgot I even existed. I don't see what the big deal is with the doctors and neurologists, because you forgot I existed years ago. This isn't a mental illness. This is just who you are. It's over, Vaughan! We are getting a divorce. End of story. End of us.'

And she got up and walked away, leaving fifty red roses on the table in front of me. I sat there, wincing at my overpowering cold espresso until the heater beside me flickered and then went out. Daylight was fading and I realized I was shivering. What had I been thinking – it was ridiculous to believe you could keep the summer going for ever.

Across the square I observed an elderly lady with a walking stick. She had stopped walking altogether and just stood still in the middle of the pavement, staring at the ground. She looked worn out; defeated even. Determined that some good might come out of all of this, I picked up the over-large bunch of roses and strode towards her.

'Excuse me, would you permit me to give you fifty red roses?' I said, with all the charm I could muster.

She looked at me suspiciously for a moment. 'Pervert!' she said.

Chapter 10

'Vaughan. I've got some bad news, mate.' It was exactly a month since my fugue and I had come in to find Gary seated in the kitchen, using a bread knife to try to skewer the last pickled onions in the jar.

'What? What is it?'

'Maybe you should sit down?'

'Is it Maddy – is it one of the kids? Just tell me.'

'No – it's your father. He's had another heart attack.'

A stunned pause followed.

'*My father?!* I didn't know I had a bloody father. My father is alive? Why didn't you say that my father was alive?'

'Er, well, I just assumed you knew. I mean, you never specifically asked . . .' Gary raised his hands defensively as if to say it was nothing to do with him.

'But you talked about my parents in the *past tense*. You said they *were* a great couple.'

'Well – the past is like, when I knew them. So, anyway, that's good news, then, if you thought he was dead. He's not – he's alive. Just. Although you might not want to leave it too long, mate . . .

Heart attack – that's quite serious, isn't it?' And then, as if he thought it might be some sort of comfort, 'Do you want a pickled onion?'

Questions I wished I had asked long before were fired at Gary faster than he could fail to answer them.

'How old is he?' 'Is he conscious?' 'When was his last attack before this one?' And even harder to answer than the others: 'What do I call him?'

'What do you mean?'

'Do I say "Dad" or "Daddy" or "Pop", or call him by his first name or what?'

'I dunno. "Dad", I think. Yeah, I'd say anything else would have been unusual enough for me to remember it.'

All Gary knew was that Madeleine had called to say that she was going to the hospital with the kids to see their grandfather. He was out of intensive care, and could be visited for a short period.

'Madeleine called?'

'She called Linda's mobile. She said she thought you should know.'

'Oh. Did Maddy say anything else? Did she want me to ring her?'

'No.'

'No, she didn't say?'

'No – she said don't ring her. She left the number of the hospital. But here's a funny thing . . .'

'What?'

'The number of the hospital ends in all ones. It's like one, one, one, one. That's weird, innit?'

I slumped into a chair and now that Gary could see the bad news had finally hit me, he did his best to empathize, in his blokey, awkward way.

'It must be, like, really difficult for you, mate.'

'Yeah, well . . .'

'Not remembering anything about him, and then finding out the old ticker's gone kaboom.'

'Yeah – it's not good.'

'Not good. Exactly. That's exactly what it is. It's *not* good. These taste a bit off. Can pickled onions go off?'

'Do you know exactly when Madeleine's going to be visiting him?'

'Er, no. But you could ring them. It's because they're in fancy vinegar, like balsamic or whatever.'

'Maybe I should call her anyway. You know – to find out what time she's going to be there and how it works and everything.'

'You could do. Except she said don't call her. Hmm – I feel a bit sick now.'

I had not felt ready to meet my own children yet, anxious that I should feel fully prepared. But with my father, events now forced me to arrange an immediate introduction. I had to get to know him so that I could be properly upset if he died.

There was a moment as I entered the hospital when I wondered if I ought to buy my dad something from the gift shop. A card perhaps, or some flowers? Or something to demonstrate confidence in the idea that he would soon be much better: a magazine maybe, or even a book? Nothing too long, though; *War and Peace* or the fourth Harry Potter would clearly be over-egging it. But of course I had no knowledge of my father's tastes or interests. 'Dad' was currently an amalgam of all the paternal role models that had survived my amnesia. Baron von Trapp and King Lear were mixed up with Homer Simpson, Darth Vader and the jokey father from that 1970s gravy advert.

On the fourth floor I was directed towards my father's room, and as I entered I was pleasantly surprised by the apparent health of the stout, dark-haired old man lying in the bed in front of me. So this was my father. This was Dad. I sat down and dutifully took his podgy little hand.

'Hi, Dad, it's me. I got here as soon as I could.'

The old man regarded me for a second. 'Who fuck hell are you, fuck-bastard?' he said, in a strong foreign accent. I saw the Arabic name on the patient's plastic wristband and leapt up and out of the room.

I sat in the corridor for a moment to calm myself down. I had pumped myself up into a state of some emotional tension which it was hard to maintain once I'd realized I was holding the hand of the wrong old man. Or maybe that had been the right old man, and Gary had forgotten to tell me that my father was also a Syrian spy who'd risen up through the ranks of the Royal Air Force, despite his incomprehensible accent and penchant for grammatically incorrect swear words.

Now I was standing outside a room where the occupant shared the same surname as myself. I steeled myself and went in. Lying in the hospital bed, surrounded by purring machines, tubes and wires, was a skeletal old man – discoloured skin pulled tight around his skull, the lips almost non-existent. The contrast could not have been greater; the digital monitors and expensive technology seemed self-consciously space age, while the body at the centre of it all looked like a Bronze Age corpse preserved in a peat bog.

'Hello?'

'Is that you, son?' he said through his oxygen mask.

'Yes. Yes, it's me.'

'You are very good. To come and see me.' His voice was very weak and he didn't turn his head to speak.

'Oh, that's okay. It's the least I could do. Is there anything I can get you?'

'No, sit down. I'm fine,' he said, though he clearly wasn't.

I had ascertained from the hospital that my father was conscious and compos mentis, but I had somehow expected the patient to be sleeping or unable to talk through an oxygen mask and that, as the dutiful son, I would just have to sit there for a bit and then go home again.

'How are you feeling?'

'Ooh, you know. Just pleased to be here.'

'Are you in any pain at all?'

'A little. Not too bad really.'

'And there's nothing I can get you?'

'Large whisky. No ice.'

I smiled at the old man's light-heartedness and realized I already liked my dad. He managed to be humorous even though he was at death's door. In fact, he looked like he'd gone straight past death's door, into death's hallway and was heading towards death's lounge to make himself comfortable. The room smelt of disinfectant failing to mask bodily decay.

'Maddy and the kids. Were here . . .'

'That's right.'

'Wonderful children. So charming.'

'They are.' And then I struggled to think of anything else to say. 'And they've coped so well with it all.'

The old man seemed not to respond at first, but finally processed what I'd just said.

'Coped with what?'

'Well, you know . . .'

'Is something wrong?'

Instantly it hit me that the old man knew nothing about our marriage break-up. Of course – my father had a heart condition, he was old and vulnerable: why would we have added the stress of telling him that his only child's marriage had failed? And by the same token, he clearly hadn't been told that I'd gone missing or was suffering from chronic amnesia.

'I mean, they've coped very well, both of them, you know . . . with their grandfather having a heart attack.' And in a perverse way I was grateful to this medical emergency for coming to my rescue.

Suddenly an alarm sounded on one of the monitors. I leapt up, uncertain what I should do. A red light was flashing on a machine just above the bed. Was this it? Was this the moment that my father died, a couple of minutes after I'd first met him? I was about to run and get help when a nurse strode in, casually flicked a switch to silence it and headed back towards the door without saying anything.

'Is everything all right?'

'Yes, it's just that machine. It does that sometimes.'

'Thank you!' said the old man, but the nurse had gone. 'They're marvellous here.'

'So you're keeping your spirits up?'

'Oh yes. Mustn't grumble.'

'Well, you've just had your second heart attack. You're entitled to grumble a little bit if you want.'

'No, I'm very lucky. The staff are very kind. Absolutely marvellous.'

It was indeed 'absolutely marvellous' my father could find nothing negative at all to say about his present condition. I had not known whether to expect him to be tired or scary or grumpy or martyred, but the heart-attack victim just seemed incredibly big-hearted.

On the side was a home-made card, and I could see it had been signed 'Dillie'.

'I like Dillie's card.'

'Bless her. So thoughtful.'

I listened to his laboured breathing. I tried to imagine this man holding my infant hand and leading me across the road; I pictured myself as a little boy being allowed to change the gears in an old-fashioned car; I visualized us kicking a leather football together in some imaginary back garden. But none of it came into focus.

'Do you remember us playing football when I was little?' I asked.

'How could I forget? You were always . . .' and he paused for a moment as his ageing mind searched for the right words '. . . so *useless*!'

I chuckled at his joke.

'Yeah, but I was only a kid.'

'No, no. Even when you were older. Completely rubbish!' His tired face muscles still managed a smile. Obviously my father's memory was not going to be as sharp as it had been, and I attempted to move on.

'No, well, football was never really my thing. Gary was reminding me how I used to sing in a band.'

'Oh, yes. What a voice!'

'Oh . . . thanks.'

'Like a strangled cat.'

'What?'

'Bloody terrible.'

'Ha! I suppose rock music's always going to sound like that to the older generation.'

'The audience clapped –'

'Well, that's good.'

'– slowly. While you were singing . . .'

It seemed that this was another relationship based on mickey-taking, but I just didn't expect strangers to be this rude.

Once I'd made the adjustment, I realized it was wonderful that my father was still able to tease me like this from his hospital bed. It showed what a bond we must have had; this was clearly my dad's way of showing his affection.

'But none of that matters,' declared the aged mystic, who could see a time that was invisible to his pupil. 'Because the big thing in life . . . you got right.' His voice was sounding increasingly strained now.

'What – my job?'

'No. *Your wife.*' With all his effort, he turned to face me. 'You married the right girl.' His breathing was becoming more laboured and I struggled to hear the whispered sentences under his mask. 'You two. Are perfect together.' And he closed his eyes, perhaps to picture me returning to Madeleine this evening and how happy that thought made him.

I suppose my father's physical condition added a little extra value to these words. Any sentence can seem apt and profound if it's uttered on your deathbed. You could use your last breath to say, 'You know, you should take your coat off when you're indoors or else you won't feel the benefit', and the onlookers would nod reverentially at the wisdom of such an insight. But for my own father to spare the breath to tell me that Madeleine and I were perfect together – it was the first time anyone had had anything positive to say about my marriage.

'Yes, she's one in a million,' I agreed.

'Just like . . .' and now he needed another gasp '. . . your mother.'

Then suddenly my time was up. It had only been about ten minutes, but already the fuel tank was empty. 'Bit tired now, son. Can't talk any more.'

'Okay.' And then I forced myself to say it. 'Okay, *Dad*.'

Dad fell quiet and the noise of his breathing changed gear as he sank almost instantly into a deep sleep. I sat there just staring at him for a while, trying to spot myself in those weathered features. A trolley rattled past the door, but no one came in. I had worried that seeing an unrecognizable parent would make me want to cry, but actually I found myself feeling uplifted. His instinct about Madeleine was the same as mine. 'Perfect together' is what he had said. If it had been my heart connected to the ECG machine, the alarm would be going off by this time.

A few minutes later a nurse came in and said that he would sleep for hours now.

'He's surprisingly upbeat, isn't he?'

'He's just one of those people,' smiled the nurse, 'who makes you feel good to be alive.'

'He's my dad.'

'Yeah.' She smiled. 'I know.'

*

I was disappointed to find Gary and Linda's flat empty when I got back. I had so wanted to tell them all about my father, what he had said about Maddy, to share what the nurse had said about him. Maybe I could call Maddy now and talk to her about him. What could be more natural, the two of us catching up about our respective visits to the hospital? I had already learned the number off by heart and I pressed all but the last of the buttons and left my finger hovering over the final digit. Then I hung up and walked into the hall. I lay on the carpet for a while staring up at the smoke alarm giving a tiny blink every few minutes to show that no one had taken the battery out. And then almost without thinking I got up and just dialled the number and was shocked that it was answered almost immediately.

'Hello?' said a girl's voice, friendly and almost surprised that anyone might call. 'Hello, who is it please?' she said after a pause. 'Mum, they're not saying anything but I think there's someone there . . .'

'Hell-ooo?' said Maddy, taking the handset. 'Hello? Oh – can you call back, please, we can't hear anything at this end . . . Thank you, goodbye.'

And I could just hear Dillie saying a shocked 'Mum!' before the line was cut off. That was the first time I had heard my daughter's voice.

I had used my own mobile phone, but had withheld the caller's ID. I wondered if right now they would be trying to find out who had intruded. Looking at the phone in my hand I suddenly noticed the camera icon on the menu. I excitedly scrolled across to find another icon labelled 'Photos' that I had never been told about. Just one click and I uncovered a whole gallery of pictures of Jamie with the dog or Maddy with the dog or myself with the dog. Then there were about another hundred pictures of just the dog. I was hatching a suspicion that Dillie may have used the camera feature slightly more than I had ever done. But there were a few images of her as well, always stopping to pose and give a big smile to the photographer. I scrolled through them all slowly again, looking at these actual human beings that Maddy and I had produced. And then I nearly ran down the battery staring at pictures of Maddy, trying to discern her feelings in every photo, imagining the actual moment that had been captured, the words that might have accompanied these silent stills. And no rational thought could counter the overwhelming gravitational pull I felt towards her. The wife that Gary had said I could never win back. The woman my father had said was perfect for me.

An hour later I stood in front of the bathroom mirror and raised the blade to my throat. I took one last look and then went for it. Soon, big grey-streaked tufts of beard were falling into the sink; wiry clumps of old Vaughan were scooped off the porcelain and dumped into the pedal bin. The uneven stubble was harvested as close to the skin as it was possible to go, before it was smothered in masculine-scented foam and then scraped off with a brand-new razor that boasted far more blades than can have been practical or necessary. Bit by bit, I saw the shape of my face emerge from where it had been hiding ever since the late 1980s, when apparently I had read somewhere that Mrs Thatcher disapproved of beards.

The birth of my face was not without a little blood and pain. I was a novice shaver, and pressed too hard around the chin and missed annoying tufts under my lower lip, but eventually I washed and moisturized my pale shiny face to see a new person looking back at me. I tried to persuade myself I looked rather square-jawed and handsome, like James Bond or Action Man – an effect only slightly spoiled by the specks of blood and deadheaded spots that needed immediate patching. The clean-shaven figure was still wearing the crumpled, shabby old clothes I'd found in Gary and Linda's bedroom cupboard, but now I set about part two of my action plan.

*

Gary had said to me that my fugue was just some sort of mid–life crisis, an accusation I had vigorously denied since I felt as if I were right at the beginning of my life. 'Honestly, what a bloody fuss about approaching forty,' he had said. 'Why can't you just get an earring and a red sports car and have done with it?' His words came back to me as I strode into the menswear section of a large department store, announcing that I was looking for a new suit or two.

'Of course, sir.'

'Something classy, you know, sort of smart and sophisticated . . .' and then I noticed in the shop mirror that a blood-stained fragment of toilet paper was still stuck on my face.

The makers of the suits I liked best had even spent money where no one else would see it: there were fancy flowered linings and neat little extra pockets on the inside. I felt myself standing an inch or so taller in front of the mirror; I looked sharp and in control, and the assistant deigned to share his expertise that this was a 'very nice suit'. The outfitter had regarded me rather disdainfully when I had first trespassed into his department – an attitude that was not ameliorated by my inability to remember the PIN number on my credit card. A frantic text to Maddy then informed me of my PIN, my mother's maiden name and my secret password. Re-armed with the knowledge required to survive modern life, I bought three designer suits, three shirts and two pairs of shoes. I kept one of the suits on; my old clothes were placed inside the shopping bags, even though I could never imagine wearing them again.

One month after my fugue I was self-consciously launching Vaughan 2.0. Yes, there had been teething problems with the operating system, and sure the memory was limited, but this model would look cleaner and sleeker; it would have a more user-friendly interface; it would not emit smoke or cause battery problems. My hope was that it would be exactly the sort of hardware that someone like Maddy, for example, might find desirable and, before long, indispensable.

'There you are, sir!' said the shop assistant, passing over the suits in big, expensive-looking bags. 'Special occasion, is it?'

'Sort of. I've just met my wife.'

'Congratulations! When are you getting married?'

'Well, let's not get too hasty,' I said, popping the receipt into the bag. 'I've got to divorce her first . . .'

Chapter 11

Today is the first day of the rest of your life, said the greetings card with the cute seal looking up at the camera. It made me feel optimistic about my own situation. I opened the card to see a Canadian seal clubber waiting a few yards away, with the caption: *Oh, and it's the last day of the rest of your life too.*

I browsed along the shelves of over-priced cards, bewildered at the endless but empty choice. Did Dillie like cute animals? Did she like photos of cool older girls? Surely she was too old for Disney princesses? I so wanted to get it right. Here was one specifically for me. *Sorry I forgot your birthday* . . . I opened it up to read the punch line: *I was having a bad hair day*. I examined the front of the card again. It featured a dog with scruffy fur. I read the punch line again: *I was having a bad hair day*. My amnesia must have wiped the part of my brain that would have got this joke. There were quite a few cards that said, *Sorry I forgot your birthday*, but none of them went on to say, *because I suffered an incredibly rare neurological disorder known as a psychogenic fugue.*

I wrote in Dillie's card that I would like to take her out and buy her a birthday present, but this was only after I had spent hours walking up and down the aisles of a toy shop seeking inspiration. Inside her late card, I placed a small passport photo so that the kids would not be too taken aback by the image of their beardless, suited father. And also just to make sure that they really did know what their dad looked like. Part of me couldn't quite believe that they had ever met me before.

When I came back from the post office, Linda had returned from work and was in the kitchen stirring a saucepan. She looked round, let out a startled scream, then fought off this approaching stranger by striking me with a wooden spoon covered in leek and potato soup.

'Linda! It's me!'

'Bloody hell, Vaughan – you look completely different.'

'You've got gunge all over my new suit!'

'Sorry, I didn't recognize you. Where's the beard? And you look so smart! Well, you *did* anyway . . .' She took my jacket and was wiping it clean as Gary wandered in.

'All right?'

'Well?' she said to her husband expectantly.

'Er – new frock?'

'Not me – what about Vaughan?'

'What?'

'He's shaved his beard off!!'

'Oh yeah, that's what's different. I thought he'd just washed or something.'

'And the suit?'

'Oh yeah! Of course, it's the big day on Monday, isn't it? First day back at work . . .'

I had indeed resolved to return to my former workplace; some instinct had told me that sitting around Gary and Linda's flat all day was not doing anything for my fragile sanity.

'You didn't tell me that, Gary,' snapped Linda, sounding increasingly dangerous. 'Why didn't you tell me that? You never tell me anything.'

'Well, that's not actually possible, is it? If I *never* told you anything, you wouldn't know my name or anything about me . . .'

The sirens sounded and the crowds rushed towards the shelters. A massive marital row was coming. The man who had just given me the theory on marital arguments was now going to demonstrate the practical. It was bound to happen. If I was going to be the house guest of a married couple, sooner or later they would attempt to jog the memory of my break-up by thoughtfully having a massive bust-up right in front of me.

There are few things quite as embarrassing as being stuck with a husband and wife having a bitter, personal argument. The only possible course of action is to stare at the floor pretending you can't actually hear it, saying nothing, even though at every turn you are thinking, 'Ooh, I wouldn't have said that,' and then, 'Ooh no, but I wouldn't have said that back in return either – that's only going to make it worse!'

Every marriage has its own San Andreas Fault running right underneath, and even the slightest rumbling or tremor can be attributed to that basic fracture deep below the surface. The fault line might be 'You only married me because I was pregnant' or 'You're never there for me when I really need you', but most of the time these powerful forces remain suppressed. But then, from nowhere, the crockery starts to vibrate and a family picture will smash on the floor, and before you know it the subterranean tectonic plates have collided and the screaming measures 8.2 on the Richter Scale.

It wouldn't have taken a professor of advanced psychology to work out that the central tension underlying Gary and Linda's marriage was their differing levels of enthusiasm for Baby/*the* baby. There were men in history who had looked forward to a baby less than Gary. King Herod springs to mind. But although every argument was really about this, they almost never argued about it directly– as if the seismic forces were too powerful ever to disturb.

'You're so bloody wrapped up in yourself, you don't ever tell me anything. You don't even notice Vaughan's shaved his beard off. And stop fiddling with your bloody iPhone!'

'I'm not fiddling. I'm activating the Voice Record app.'

'YOU ARE RECORDING OUR ARGUMENT?!!'

'Yes, because you always misquote me afterwards, or twist my words around, or just make up stuff I never said.'

'Oh, not this again! You always bloody say that—'

'No, I don't – and I think if you listen back through the files, you'll find I said it once, tops.'

'You mean you recorded other fights too??'

'Yes – I told you that ages ago—'

'No, you didn't.'

'Yes, I did – hang on, I've got the recording on here – you can listen back to it yourself.'

It transpired that Gary had a definitive record of all their marital disputes, dated and filed in chronological order. At some point he was planning to cross-reference them by subject index as well. Sometimes a fight might look like it was building, and he'd activate the Voice Record application only to feel a slight sense of disappointment when Linda said something conciliatory and then he'd have to delete the file.

This was the only relationship I had witnessed first hand since my memory loss, and it perplexed me that this must be a stronger marriage than my own failed one. What had been the ancient fault line that eventually ripped Maddy and me apart, I wondered; what was it that had ultimately brought our house crashing down?

That night I could hear the noisy love-making coming from the next room and wondered if Gary recorded that on his iPhone as well. They were as emphatic in their love-making as they were in their fighting; one minute they were screaming in anger, the next in ecstasy. Gary and Linda seemed to have a bipolar marriage.

I resolved that as part of my mission to seize control of my life, I would eventually have to move out of Gary and Linda's house and find somewhere more peaceful. Basra, perhaps. Plus, I worried that I was outstaying my welcome. Earlier in the day Linda had been hoovering in my room when she suddenly came into the living room looking very agitated. 'Why is there a huge electric hedge trimmer hidden under Baby's cot?'

'Oh, that? Oh, yeah, there's a perfectly simple explanation—'

'It's a yard of razor-sharp steel! What if Baby had crawled on to it?'

'*The* baby,' said Gary without looking up.

I felt Linda's scenario was a little unlikely. 'Well, to be fair, the baby isn't actually going to be born for quite a long time—'

'What if Baby had plugged it in and played with it?'

'*The* baby.'

With their new arrival now only six months away, I felt it was time to give the parents a little bit of space to shout at each other in peace. It had been a few weeks since the debutant Vaughan had first been presented to society and already I was gaining in confidence. To begin with I had felt like a gatecrasher at my old life. And not just some uninvited student at a chaotic corridor party, but worse than that – like a stoned Hell's Angel with mirror shades gatecrashing a genteel dinner party in the Home Counties.

I had, however, found that I had quickly developed a new skill: I could measure the degree of shared personal history on a new face. All these people were strangers to me, yet their eyes revealed different levels of expectation. Those who had known me for years seemed to plead for some sort of recognition or acknowledgement, whereas the indifferent glance of casual acquaintances demanded nothing in return.

'Hello, Vaughan, you look well. Great to have you back,' said the receptionist at my old school as I walked into the building, and I could judge exactly how well she had known me. Rather helpfully, Jane Marshall wore a card around her neck that told you her name, her job and that the school needed to invest in a better digital camera.

I had made sure I knew the principal's name before I came back to the school, but now I didn't know whether to call him 'Peter' or 'Mr Scott'. He had personally undertaken the job of welcoming me back and talking to me about my 'reintegration into the school community'. The two of us were walking around the corridors, giving me a chance to meet staff and 'refamiliarize' myself with the building. Everyone was behaving so normally, they'd obviously had a serious talk about behaving normally. In the school office, one administrator hurriedly removed the sign above her computer saying, *You don't have to be mad to work here, but it helps.* Each of them smiled and proffered a warm hello as I passed, and then got back to pretending to work. And in the background was the sound of furious keyboard tapping – the office communication system must have nearly crashed with the weight of gossipy messages flying back and forth about whether I was faking the whole thing.

I had been paid in full for all the time I had been off on leave, and today there would be a meeting at which we'd discuss what work I might realistically be able to undertake.

'I've been re-reading the syllabus – I'm keen to start teaching as soon as possible,' I declared.

'No hurry,' said Peter, or Mr Scott, regarding me with some surprise. 'You take as long as you need.'

'No, really. If my classes are being covered by supply teachers, I feel I owe it to the students to get back to work a.s.a.p.'

'Goodness. You really have forgotten everything, haven't you?'

And two pupils disappearing round a corner shouted 'Oi, Boggy Vaughan! Where's your bog-brush?!' and then ran away laughing.

'Boggy Vaughan?'

'I'm sure it's just a very small minority of students who call you that. You're known for many other things here. Apart from the one time you cleaned all the toilets.'

'All right, Boggy? Good to see you,' said a dinner lady, walking past us.

'Why did I clean all the toilets?'

'To set an example to all the students about "declining lavatory standards". You got a bit of a bee in your bonnet and made a big announcement. I wouldn't have held up a toilet brush in assembly myself, but you got their attention, I suppose.'

'Hey, Boggy Vaughan's back!' came a voice from the atrium as we passed.

'Oh, well, I'm sure it'll blow over . . .'

'Maybe. It's been a couple of years now. To be frank, Vaughan, you seemed to lose your confidence around then. I know you were having problems at home, but you stopped loving your job as well. And kids can always tell.'

Perhaps I wasn't quite ready to face the students just yet. I explained to Peter, or Mr Scott, that I had further appointments with the neurologist, so they agreed that I might perhaps start with a little administration in the school office. This would be made official by the Occupational Health Officer as soon as he was back from sick leave. But I was starting work again! This was my place of work. I popped to the toilets on my way out. 'These are disgusting!' I thought. 'Why can't somebody just clean them?'

Although there was part of me saying, 'Well, I wouldn't be starting from here', I was still excited to be accumulating the attributes that made up a whole person. I had a job, a family; slowly I was groping my way towards some sort of purpose. Today really was the first day of the rest of my life. I still didn't have a past, but like everything else in the modern world, you simply had to look it up on the internet. I had forced myself not to look at my online memoir for forty-eight hours, but that evening I logged on to see that the picture had changed completely. A second email to everyone requesting that they write something had obviously had some effect, as now my life story was filling out. Although not everyone had entered into the exercise with the strict neutrality or serious academic rigour that I had hoped for.

Jack Joseph Neil Vaughan, commonly known as 'Vaughan', was born on 6 May 1971. His father Keith Vaughan became a senior officer in the Royal Air Force while his mother had worked as a bi-lingual secretary. With his father being posted overseas, Vaughan spent his childhood in many different parts of the world. He attended Bangor University where he got a 2.2 in History, unlike his friend Gary Barnett who got a 2.1 (and a distinction in his dissertation). The two friends played football together, although Vaughan soon became a substitute while Gary became the top scorer for two seasons in a row and was runner-up as the player of the season.

In his first year at Bangor, he met his future wife, Madeleine. (MORE HERE PLEASE) Maddy is hot, she is a MILF. Hands off! She's my secret fantasy, not yours, you perv, even if she's like 35 or something.

Vaughan and Maddy have two children: Jamie who is 13 and Dillie who is 11. In 2001 Mr Vaughan began teaching history at William Blake Secondary School in Wandsworth, which became Wandle Academy. Last year he got to go on the history field trip despite a superior application from another teacher who had actually achieved better results than him. His nickname is 'Boggy Vaughan' because he loves cleaning the bog. He is the Bogmeister General, Bogimus Maximus, the Boginator. Boggy! Boggy! Boggy! Oi! Oi! Oi!

Vaughan was a speaker at the 'Lessons Worth Behaving For' Conference at Kettering and was very boring. Like, dull, dull, dull. Not content to just drone on about a load of deadly dull data, he did a PowerPoint presentation where he had written up all the deadly dull data, and then at the end handed out a printout of all the same deadly dull data.

Boggy Vaughan's all right coz he didn't tell the police when we nicked that llama from the City Farm.

Mr Vaughan's home is four doors down from Mr Kenneth Oakes, one of Britain's leading exponents of Close Magic, member of the Magic Circle and popular choice for corporate events and family parties; 'a great traditional magic act' says *The Stage*. Vaughan plays 5 a side football every Tuesday night and has all the grace and skill of a pissed ostrich. Vaughan lives in South London. His birthday is May 6th. Hello, Vaughan, long time no see, mate! Sorry to leave this message here, but Gary said something about you wanting everyone to write stuff about your life and shit – he was trying to make out you were off your nut or something which I knew must be one of his wind-ups! Anyway, tell us where you want people to write stuff and I'll give it a shot! Cheers, mate! Karl ☺

I went to bed that night telling myself that the past was past and there was nothing I could do to change it. Apart from deleting the bit about how boring I was at Kettering – I could change that bit. And quite so many references to how bad at football I was – it didn't need all of those. Or even one reference really; it was not worth mentioning. Did the high level of sarcasm and mockery demonstrate affection and confidence in a shared sense of humour? And why did they call Maddy a 'MILF', whatever that was?

I later Googled the word on Linda's computer. That left me with some explaining to do.

Chapter 12

It is the early 1990s, and Madeleine and I have been a couple for less than a year. Maddy has gone to Brussels with a friend. When she checks in at the hotel, the concierge says there is an urgent letter already waiting for her. She opens the envelope to find the battered postcard of the leprechaun still raising a pint of Guinness to her. I imagine her laughing, and maybe explaining the context to her bemused friend. But she never ever mentions it to me.

Many months after that, I receive a huge mystery parcel in the post. I set about cutting through the excessive tape, only to find that inside is another, slightly smaller, cardboard box. Inside that is some packing material protecting a posh presentation case. I open this to find a gift-wrapped present. After a dozen layers, I finally get through to a small embossed envelope, and although by now I realize that someone is playing an elaborate joke on me, it still has not occurred to me that I am about to get back the ludicrous postcard that I was supposed to have sent to Great-auntie Brenda.

And so the iconic symbol was passed back and forth down the years, with neither of us ever mentioning the game to the other. That had quickly become one of the unwritten rules. The recipient would never ring up and say, 'Oh, you got me there!' I would simply smile to myself at the ingenuity of my partner, hide the card away and then bide my time as I plotted an even more elaborate and surprising way of placing it back into Maddy's custody. Receipt of the card meant that it was now that person's responsibility to remember to post this bloody thing to Great-auntie Brenda, even though Great-auntie Brenda had long since died and the address on the card was now occupied by a family from Bangladesh – the task was still effectively the custodian's responsibility unless it could be planted on the other person when they least expected it.

One day when Maddy turned on her new computer, the screen was filled with a digital photo of the leprechaun, with instructions to check inside the printer tray. When Maddy suggested I ordered myself a pizza from my usual home-delivery service, I opened the big flat box to find that Madeleine had arranged with the local pizza company to deliver me Great-auntie Brenda's card instead. When Maddy had put tasteful framed black-and-white photographs of the children up the stairs, she came home one day to notice that every single frame contained a colour photocopy of a grinning Guinness-drinking leprechaun saying 'Top o' the mornin' to yers!!' with the original in a huge clipframe of its own surrounded by flashing fairy lights.

The memory of all this came back to me in one split second, sitting in front of a computer terminal during my first day back at work. It was as if the search facility in my brain had finally located a certain file extension. I wanted to tell everyone seated around me, but the school admin team seemed uncomfortable enough with having one of the teachers suddenly parked in their office like this, without me drawing attention to my strange mental illness.

I wanted to contact Maddy right now to share all the memories of our running private joke, but I sensed that to do so would also kill it. Nor could I add the episodes to my online memoir. Instead, despite having been desperate to remember details just like this, I had to tell myself to try to forget about it for the time being, in order that I could actually get on with my life right now.

My first day in my new job felt empowering. I was making a contribution; I had a reason to get up in the morning. Being the temporary administrative assistant in an inner-city comprehensive came with more status and variety than all the other life experiences I could remember, such as lying in a hospital bed or watching repeats of *All-Star Mr & Mrs*. Now I was returning to school to undertake my own education, revising the complex syllabus of where I fitted in and what sort of school I worked at.

I had in front of me access to detailed information on a thousand pupils. I could click on any name and know their Key Stage 2 Sats, their GCSE or B.Tech targets, whether they were on free school meals or had English as an additional language. Yet access to data on Jamie and Dillie was still restricted; none of my records of my children's lives could be summoned. My task for the day was supposed to be entering data on 540 Key Stage 3 pupils. But I couldn't prevent my mind from returning to two children in particular whom I was going to be meeting that very evening.

I had agreed to go to the house at six o'clock to take my son and daughter out to the Christmas funfair on the Common, which seemed like an appropriate divorced-dad sort of thing to do. Then we would meet Maddy for a pizza, and by the end of the evening I would, I hoped, feel like a father again. They had been told about my neurological condition, though I was not confident they would understand the extent of my amnesia. But Maddy had been kind enough to tell me that they were looking forward to seeing me and her suggested arrangement was that I was to come to the house for a cup of tea and a chat and then take my children across to the Common on my own. 'Make sure you get a good look at them before you go to the fair,' warned Gary. ''Cos you'd feel a bit stupid at the Lost Children's Tent, saying you had no idea what your kids looked like.'

I arrived at the house twenty minutes early. I walked up and down on the frosty pavement for a while until Madeleine opened the front door and shouted over to me.

'So are you going to ring on the buzzer or what?'

'Sorry – I was a bit early and didn't want to . . . you know, like, inconvenience anyone.'

'That's okay – I think they've seen this particular episode of *Friends* a hundred and twelve times before.'

Without pausing, I put my hand over to pull back the catch on the gate the moment I pushed it open.

'Hey – I just opened the gate!'

'Well, yes . . .'

'But without thinking about how to do it! It's a subconscious memory!' It made the place feel part of me. Madeleine was wearing a red spotty dress that had an almost humorous edge to it, but, standing at the open door, she folded her arms against the cold as I approached.

'Kids!' she called out. 'Your dad's here!'

An avalanche of enthusiasm came thundering down the stairs. The force of it hit me all at once, knocking me off balance as both children threw their arms around me and hugged me tightly.

'Daddy!' exclaimed little Dillie, and I stood there uncertain as to what I should do, ending up patting them a little self-consciously on the back. They smelt of washing powder and hair conditioner – my children were all fresh and new. The dog, circling this melee, barked in enthusiasm. My heart definitely remembered what my head had forgotten: I felt like I had regained a couple of limbs that I had not realized had been amputated. I would have to learn how they operated, I would need months of practice to be able to love them really properly, but it was still a miracle – Maddy and I had made these beautiful human beings together, these two separate individuals; it was the wonder of new life that struck me most powerfully.

I resolved to follow their lead and just be as natural as possible. I asked them what they'd been up to, and listened to funny stories from school, and I could sense Maddy watching me interact with them and noticed her smile a couple of times as I found the confidence to joke with them both. For all my worry in advance of this meeting, they just made it incredibly easy. They were confident and chatty – when Dillie was excited she talked faster than I had imagined was humanly possible, segueing wildly from one subject to the next in mid-sentence, and I had not yet learned that it was not even worth trying to keep up. 'Oh-my-God-it-was-so-funny-Miss-Kerrins-told-Nadim-in-science-not-to-bring-in-his-rat-yeah-cos-like-it-always-gets-out-and-freaks-out-Jordan's-slow-worm-oh-I-like-your-suit-is-that-new-anyway-he-put-it-in-her-handbag-on-her-desk-we-had-curry-for-lunch-today-yum-and-you-could-see-it-moving-around-in-the-bag-oh-I-got-an-A-in-Maths-by-the-way-so-he-got-sent-to-the-referral-but-he-left-his-rat-behind-with-Jordan-who-put-it-on-his-head-and-she-is-like-totally-phobic-about-rats-so-she-screamed-and-ran-out-of-the-classroom-and-it-was-so-funny-can-we-record-*Friends*-on-Comedy-Central-before-we-go?'

Perhaps this was why her brother spoke so little; there just weren't enough gaps. Although it seemed he had developed the skill to extricate the important points.

'Yeah, why are you wearing a suit, Dad?'

'Yeah, why did you shave your beard off? Are you having a mid-life crisis?'

'Oh, I thought I should make a bit of an effort. Fresh start and all that. Is it too much?'

'No,' said Maddy. 'It looks very nice.'

I wanted to thank her, but couldn't quite find the words.

'Dad, you're blushing. Why are you blushing?'

The four of us sat around the kitchen table as I drank sugary tea. The dog completed the perfect family scene, gazing longingly at us all casually eating biscuits, his head hanging in shame at the guilty thoughts going through his mind. 'Oh, God, I feel so weak and worthless, but I cannot fight these dark desires inside me for those sweet-scented HobNobs. Oh no, now my mouth is salivating, I am disgusting, I'm sorry, I despise my own base obsession . . .'

'No, Woody, stop scrounging,' said Jamie.

'Ah, poor Woody. Don't tell him off in a cross voice,' said Dillie.

I used up one of my prepared questions and asked them what they were hoping to get for Christmas. Dillie's wish-list seem to go on for about twenty-five minutes and might have carried on indefinitely through all the different brands of make-up and trinkets from Accessorize if I hadn't eventually cut her off and said, 'What about you, Jamie?'

'Dunno.' He shrugged. 'Money?'

'Last year we gave a goat to an African villager,' recalled Maddy. 'We thought this year they might just prefer a Nintendo Wii instead.'

'Good idea,' I concurred. 'Or an iPad maybe?'

'Oh, can I have an iPad?' suggested Dillie. 'And a goat?'

'No, you can't have a goat,' I decided unilaterally. 'Because you might take it into school and scare Miss Kerrins—'

'What?' said Jamie and Maddy in unison.

'Was I the only one listening to Dillie just then?'

'Yes,' they both said nonchalantly.

The kids were impatient to go to the Winter Wonderland funfair but, standing in the hallway by the scorching radiator, they insisted that it wasn't cold enough to require woolly hats and gloves. I deftly headed off an argument by suggesting I carried all their sensible insulation until they'd been outside for a few minutes, by which time they'd be begging for extra layers.

'Are you sure you don't want to come?'

The Man Who Forgot His Wife

'No,' said Maddy, with a half-smile. 'You've got too much catching up to do to have me in the way.'

'Well, I have a lot of catching up to do with you as well.'

Maddy raised her eyebrows as if to suggest that I was dangerously close to crossing the line. 'See you at the pizza place at half seven.' And the door was closed.

Inside the Hall of Mirrors I saw my distorted face smiling at the kids laughing and waving at our bizarre reflections. Jamie was stepping back and forward to change the length of his neck, and Dillie was putting her hands out and laughing as they stretched to the length of her body.

'Of course, this might be what we actually look like,' I ventured. 'Maybe the mirrors we have at home are the crazy ones.'

'No, because then our eyes would have to be wrong as well,' pointed out Jamie, whose intelligent point was rather undermined by his forehead being longer than his legs.

'Depends what our brain does with the info it receives. Maybe we just see everything the way we want to see it.'

In the mirror, I saw Dillie think about this for a second as she made eye contact with her distorted father.

'Dad?' she asked after a moment. 'Did you really completely forget me and Jamie?'

'Erm – well – it's all still in there,' I said, banging my forehead in an exaggerated comedy manner that brought a smile to her face. 'But I just can't find where I left everything. So at the moment I don't remember lots of facts about you, but I haven't forgotten how I feel about you.' I felt excited enough to say it and it seemed important. 'I haven't forgotten . . . how much I love you.'

'Aaaah,' she said, touched by the sweetness of these words, while in the mirror I could see Jamie miming putting his fingers down his throat.

The only other visitors in there were an enormously fat couple who had presumably come in here to see themselves looking normal. They moved slowly from mirror to mirror without laughter or comment, remaining stony faced and utterly neutral in response to everything they saw. In contrast, Jamie and Dillie dashed about, jumping forwards and backwards, and even people walking past outside the tent must have been infected by their laughter. I stopped looking at my own distorted image and just watched my new son and daughter instead. They were so full of enthusiasm and energy, living in the moment, delighting in whatever the world offered next. They made me feel as if my lost past wasn't important; it was right here, right now that really mattered.

'Dad, your head has got another blob of head hovering above it.'

'Oh yeah, I hate it when that happens. It's so embarrassing.'

'Urgh – look what's happened to my body!' shrieked Jamie.

'That's what I say to the mirror every morning.'

'Aah no, Dad,' said Dillie. 'You're in quite good shape. You know, for someone who's, like, really old.'

I actually felt ten years younger today. The children's energy and optimism was infectious, and although I still had no memory of them before my fugue, I felt a cocktail of pleasure, anxiety, responsibility and delight that I realized was how it must feel to be a parent. There was a tinge of sadness that there was no one I could excitedly call to announce the arrival of these children into my life. 'Mum! Dad! It's a boy! A hundred and forty pounds and three ounces! We've called him Jamie and he's got blue eyes, quite a lot of hair and he's already feeding really well. Candyfloss, mainly. Oh, and guess what? Maddy had a little girl as well! Yeah, Dillie – slightly smaller than her brother, but she's already walking and talking. Talking quite a lot, actually.'

'Dad can we go on the waltzer now?'

'Sure, we'll all go.'

The children looked unsure, and explained that I couldn't go on rides like that because they used to make me throw up.

'Really? Nah, that was the old Dad. You see, that's what I was trying to say back there about our brains and preconceived ideas and everything. Maybe I used to be sick on the waltzer because that's what my mind told my body I always did. But that expectation has been erased, and now I'll probably really enjoy it.'

Five minutes later I staggered off the waltzer and puked up behind a generator.

'Are you all right, Dad?'

'Do you need a tissue?'

I was sick once more, and sat on the tow bar with my head in my hands, the sirens and the lights flashing in the dark adding to my nausea.

'Do you want me to get you a bottle of water?'

'No, it's okay. Sorry,' I groaned. 'I'll be all right in a minute.'

Maddy was already seated in Pizza Express when we arrived. She laughed when she saw her two kids; they had evidently prepared for dinner by seeing how much candy floss they could get stuck to their hair and faces. This response was surely a signal of approval, I thought. She could have been angry with me; a woman who was 100 per cent set on divorce would have interpreted this as evidence of my incompetence or irresponsibility. Over dinner she asked about my father, she took an interest in my return to work, she even laughed when I told her that Gary was now recording all his rows with Linda on his iPhone. 'Honestly, what are some married couples like?' suggested our shared laughter. 'Why can't they just sort it all out and get on with one another . . .'

The comfortable atmosphere prompted Dillie to ask if I was going to come and stay for Christmas, but Maddy took this opportunity to go to the Ladies. Her unwillingness to have this conversation in front of the children was not a good sign. Or maybe she was composing herself in the toilet right now, rehearsing the right words to suggest I move back home so that we could give the marriage another chance.

'So, kids, let's go out again soon. Or if your mum is busy one day, I could come round to the house and look after you.'

'Hey yeah!' said Dillie. 'Or when Mum goes away after Christmas, you could come and stay instead of Granny. Please, Dad, please!!'

'Oh, that would be wonderful. I'd love that.'

It was almost too perfect. I had somehow got myself invited to come and stay in the house, to live with them while Maddy was away.

'So, where's Mum going?'

'She's going to Venice with Ralph,' said Dillie, as her brother shot her a look.

'Ralph? Who's Ralph?'

'Durr! Ralph is Mum's boyfriend.'

And Maddy returned to the table and took a sip of her wine.

'Everything all right?'

Chapter 13

'Oh, Vaughan *is* marvellous!' said Maddy's mother, Jean, as I carried a couple of dirty plates from the table and placed them vaguely near the dishwasher. 'Look at that, Ron – now he's clearing the plates. Isn't he marvellous, Madeleine?'

'It's only a couple of plates, Mum. It was *me* who went out and bought all the food, made the stuffing and all the trimmings, set the table, made the gravy, and carved the turkey.'

'Well, I think it's wonderful when a man helps around the kitchen. Look at that! He's scraping the plates into the bin. He *is* good.'

I said nothing, but couldn't resist stirring things a little more by offering to make everyone coffee.

'Oh, you are a dear. No, you sit down; you've done enough already. I'll make the coffee. Madeleine, can you give me a hand, dear?'

Christmas dinner had been easier than I had expected. Everyone had admired the huge steaming turkey surrounded by bacon rolls and mini-sausages; especially the dog, who hung his head in disgrace at the sinful thoughts going through his head. 'Oh, I am so ashamed, but oh, the moist tender meat so physically close to me yet so utterly out of reach; oh, God, I'm drooling again, I can't stop myself, the indignity of it all . . .'

Maddy's mother had shown no hostility to her estranged son-in-law; on the contrary, I found my apparently abundant qualities constantly highlighted, usually when Jean's own husband was in earshot. 'Vaughan has brought some Christmas crackers! How thoughtful. Did you see that, Ron? Vaughan brought crackers. That's nice, to think of contributing something.'

It might have been more honest for Jean to hold up large cards explaining the sledgehammer subtext every time she spoke. 'What a good dad he is! Did you hear that, Ron? Vaughan took the children to the funfair the other day. They are lucky children to have him . . .' That would have come with the subtitle: *You never did anything with the children, Ron. Why couldn't you have been more like Vaughan?* Or, 'Your father never helped around the house, Madeleine. You must be finding it harder now, without Vaughan here to help?' telegraphed the message: *My husband was much worse than yours, but I stuck with it.* And finally: 'Why don't you and Vaughan bring the children to stay this summer? It'll be lovely to have all four of you together, and I can help Ron with some of the jobs on the house that he still hasn't started . . .' This angle of attack was too unsubtle for a mere sign; it should have come with a klaxon and flashing lights, as a police negotiator shouted through a megaphone: 'DO NOT GET DIVORCED, MADELEINE! YOUR MOTHER WASN'T ALLOWED TO GET DIVORCED, SO WHY SHOULD YOU BE?!'

Maddy's father, Ron, might have felt offended by the stream of unsubtle reminders of his apparent failings as a father and husband had he been listening to any of it. But long ago he had developed the skill of tuning out the background noise of his wife, reacting only to occasional trigger words that might be of interest to him.

'Vaughan offered to make the coffee. That was nice of him, wasn't it, Ron?'

'Coffee? Oh, yes please.'

The whole day had gone reasonably well considering that most civil wars can trace their origins back to a difficult family Christmas. I gave the children their presents, having previously spent a happy afternoon at the shops so that Jamie could actually come with me to the cashpoint and choose his money himself. Dillie had wanted a little electronic diary into which you could type your secrets and no one could read them because only you knew how to access it. A bit like my brain, I thought, except that she hadn't forgotten the password yet.

I had been unsure whether or not I should get Maddy anything. I was guessing that divorcing husbands don't usually give their ex-wives Christmas presents; the house is usually enough. But I happened to stumble upon a beautiful but understated gold necklace after browsing through a number of jewellery shops. And I have to confess there was a satisfactory moment of tension after lunch when Madeleine unwrapped it, gasped, and murmured, 'You shouldn't have.' I knew she really meant it. I had clearly spent a great deal of time and money choosing the perfect gift, which made it even worse. Right now Maddy would have preferred a useless present from her ex-partner, something that confirmed how wrong for her I really was. She shook her head when the children urged her to try it on, and put it back in the box, although later when she visited the bathroom, I noticed that the box went with her.

Jean was very effusive about what a lovely present the gold necklace was, as if somehow to suggest that she was not quite as thrilled with the shoe rack she had received from her husband.

'What have you got Vaughan, Madeleine? Are you going to give Vaughan his present now?'

'I didn't get him a present, Mum. We're getting divorced, remember?'

'Well, he's still your husband till then, dear. You could have made a bit of an effort . . .'

But my gift had clearly been more than a casual act of generosity and Maddy knew it. It was making a point; this was me showing my magnanimity, resolutely defending the moral high ground that I felt I had seized after discovering that she was seeing another man. ('She's not seeing *another* man,' Gary had insisted when I had told him. 'She's just seeing a man.')

So throughout Christmas Day I pointedly played the role of perfect son-in-law and attentive husband with my unexpected ally Jean, making the trip to Venice seem selfish and unnecessary. Jean was particularly worried about her daughter going on a boat after some of the stories she had seen on the news.

'For God's sake, Jean, Venice is in Europe,' repeated her exasperated husband. 'She is not going to be kidnapped by Somali pirates.'

'She might be. Several Westerners have been taken hostage.'

'Yes, off the Horn of Africa. Somali pirates are not going to sail all the way up the Red Sea, through the Suez Canal, across the Med and up the Adriatic just to kidnap a bloody gondola.'

'Well, it's all in the same direction, isn't it? Venice, Somalia. They're ruthless these people. In my day pirates were jolly, swashbuckling types, with parrots and wooden legs. I don't know why they have to change everything.'

Undaunted by this obvious danger, Maddy would head off to the airport the following morning at six, and I would be left alone with my children. I had initially worried that my mother-in-law might be indignant that she was no longer required to look after her grandchildren, but it transpired that Jean thought the idea of me returning to the family home was an excellent one. 'Isn't it wonderful that Vaughan's moving back in? We should have champagne!'

'He's not moving back in, Mum; he's staying here while I'm away.'

'And I'll be sleeping in the spare room,' I confirmed, with a glance to Maddy. 'The double bed is strictly reserved for the dog.'

'Still,' said Jean, 'it'll be lovely for the children to have their father at home. So many children don't have a father these days and I think it's a terrible shame.'

The seasonal tradition of too much food was followed by the tradition of too much television, with the grandparents setting the volume to 'Too Loud' and turning the central heating to 'Too Hot'. Ron initiated only two conversations: one asking after my father, to which I reported that he had been sleeping when I had seen him that morning in the hospital; and the other enquiring about my own condition, during which he surprised me by sharing a couple of books he had got from the library on amnesia and neuropsychology.

'He doesn't want to look at those, Ron,' said Jean. 'Christmas is supposed to be a happy time, not for reminding people they've gone mental.'

In the evening we watched a film together, despite the director carelessly neglecting to include a running commentary from Maddy's mother. Dillie had got the DVD of *Love Actually* for Christmas and I was entranced by Emma Thompson as the betrayed wife holding the family together despite everything. And I was utterly unconvinced by the little boy jumping the barriers at airport security and not being gunned down by armed police. 'I remember this bit!' I declared. 'Where he talks about how much love there is in the world by looking at the arrivals lounge in the airport.'

'Yes, but of course they love each other then!' said Maddy scornfully. 'That's because they've spent months in separate continents. Film the same couples a week later and they'd be back to shouting and screaming at one another.'

Jean had never really entered the spirit of *Love Actually* either. 'Kiera Knightley's a lovely-looking girl,' she said. 'Why's she marrying a black?'

*

The grandparents went to bed, as Jean needed a couple of hours before lights out to take things out of her overnight bag and then put them back in again. Then it was just the four of us, sat around the fire in the family home: mother, father and the two children.

'Let's play a game,' enthused Dillie.

'Yeah, we always play games at Christmas,' agreed her brother. 'What about charades?'

'Depends on your dad. Films and TV shows and everything? Personal or extra-personal memory?'

'Bit of both actually. Even if I know about the films, I don't remember seeing them. It's like *Jaws* is part of the general cultural furniture. But even though Dillie says I took her to see *27 Dresses*, I can't remember a thing about it.'

'Yeah, I think that's true for everyone who saw *27 Dresses*.'

'What about the water game?' suggested Jamie, to excited agreement from his sister.

'The water game? I don't like the sound of that.'

'You think of a category – like "Premiership football teams" or something – and one person has the name of a club, like say "Fulham", in his head. Then he goes around behind everyone, holding an eggcup full of water above their head, and the first person to say "Fulham" gets a drenching!'

'Okay, why don't you go first, Jamie?'

Jamie chose the category of '*Simpsons* characters' and although I could only recall Bart and Homer, the latter was sufficient to get the water tipped over my head, which the kids thought was hilarious. I had actually been surprised by how much fun was involved in this Russian roulette lite: the moment of tension as you said your selection out loud and the relief when the pourer moved to the next player. Now it was my turn to wield the eggcup. I chose 'Fruits' and selected 'orange' as the detonator.

'Banana,' said Dillie nervously.

'Starfruit,' declared Jamie, tactically. I moved on to Maddy.

'Orange,' she said.

There was a split-second pause. 'No . . .' and I moved on. I quickly revised my chosen fruit to 'apple', but Maddy said that next time round as well, so I changed it again. I was struggling to remember which fruit they had and hadn't said, and then there was an argument as to whether a tangerine was the same thing as a satsuma, and because Dillie was so desperate to have a go I just decided to pour the water over her whatever she said, which looked a bit suspicious when she said 'Potato'. But just as she was laughing and wiping her head with the tea towel, I suddenly had a strong memory of the four of us together, doing exactly this.

'We played this before. On holiday, by a swimming pool?'

'That's right, we did,' said Maddy. 'In France. You've had another memory!'

'And instead of tipping the cup on my head,' remembered Jamie, 'you picked me up and threw me in the pool!'

'That's right. And then I pretended not to notice Dillie creeping up behind me . . .'

'And I pushed you into the water too!'

The room fell quiet for a moment and then Dillie said, 'Can we go back there?' The silence answered the question for her.

'Maybe I'll take you back there again one day,' said her mother, unconvincingly.

'No, like, all of us. And play the water game by the pool?'

I had to stop myself looking at Maddy for an answer and I struggled to find anything to say to fill the heavy silence. Eventually Jamie rescued the situation with a tactful clarification: 'No, stupid. They're getting divorced.'

And finally came the moment when the children had gone to bed and there was only Maddy and me left downstairs. I made an effort to pick up stray bits of wrapping paper, rescuing Dillie's cryptic note to herself containing the coded top-secret prompt for her diary's password. It would take a team of genius de-coders many months to decipher the enigmatic clue: 'Our dog's name'.

'Well, that all went as well as can be expected,' I suggested.

'Better than last year, that's for sure.'

'Sorry, you'll have to remind me . . .'

'Last Christmas we had a huge row after you sat in that chair all day drinking yourself into a stupor. Which you claimed was "the only way to make this marriage bearable".'

I picked the last few bits of ribbon off the floor, brushed against a dangling bauble and another thousand needles fell off the non-drop Christmas tree.

'Forgive me for asking, but did we ever try and get any counselling?'

'Yeah, but we couldn't even agree on that. I wanted to share the problems with a woman counsellor, and you said not having a bloke would tip the scales against you from the outset.'

This did strike me as a difficult stand-off in which to find a compromise. Maybe we could have found a counsellor who was also a pre-op transsexual? But then I thought our marriage had been screwed up enough already, without me staring at the new breasts of our marriage guidance counsellor while trying to ignore his Adam's apple. I flopped on to the sofa and she sat down too, filling up her wine glass and offering the last of the bottle to me.

'I thought my drinking was one of the reasons you didn't want to be with me?'

'It doesn't matter any more, does it?'

I poured my wine into the potted plant she had just been given by her mother. 'Okay, so I'll stop drinking. What else was it?'

'I don't want to have this discussion now.'

'No, I have to know, because it doesn't make any sense. Why are we getting divorced? What was it that was so impossible for us to work out?'

'Oh it was just . . . everything.'

'You see, that's no good. You have to give me concrete examples, actual points of contention or issues.'

'I don't know.' Her head was tilted up towards the ceiling. 'When you were young you were so passionate about things; so incisive about what was wrong with the world and how we had to change it. But somehow over the years that just turned into general moaning.'

'Okay, that's one thing,' I noted. 'Allegedly—'

'I mean, it was so bloody boring! All these stupid unimportant things making you too cross.' She was in full flow now. 'I mean, I didn't mind that your hair thinned and turned grey, or the lines on your face, or your expanding waistline. It was the ageing of your soul that made you so much harder to love; all the goodness in you that got all flabby and unexercised.'

'All right! You don't have to be so bloody personal!'

I got up and disposed of the empty wine bottle rather too forcefully, so that it nearly smashed as it hit the others in the recycling bin. 'Anyway, that's hardly grounds for divorce, is it? You still haven't given me a good reason.'

'We weren't happy.' She sighed. 'We were fighting all the time, and it made the kids miserable. What better reason do you need?'

'But what did we fight about?'

'Lots of things. You'd always encouraged me to do more photography, to try and exhibit my pictures. But once it finally started to take off, you resented having to accommodate me not being there all the time. You talked the talk of a supportive husband, but when it actually came to it, on a day-to-day basis, taking up the slack, getting home from school in time or giving up stuff like fiddling around on Gary's stupid internet site, you were just never there.'

'Well, I must admit I don't quite understand why I wanted to get involved with YouNews . . .'

'It was just a reason not to be here, wasn't it? And then you couldn't believe that a certain gallery owner could be interested in exhibiting my photography. You said it was just because he fancied me.'

'Okay – well, that does sound annoying. Clearly, I was jealous of other men. You are very attractive, and perhaps this gallery owner thought so too.'

'But it shows you couldn't see me as anything other than a bit of skirt. I was feeling insecure about my work and putting it out there, and you made it a hundred times worse by demeaning my achievement of getting a gallery interested.'

'All right, fair point. I can see that must have been insulting and unsupportive.'

'I mean, why couldn't he exhibit my stuff because I was an interesting photographer? Why did you presume it was only because Ralph fancied me?'

I nearly dropped the empty glass in my hand. I don't think she had intended to let slip the name.

'What?! So this "certain gallery owner" was Ralph? You're saying I shouldn't have seen him as a threat or suggested he fancied you, and tomorrow he's taking you to Venice?'

'Yes, but things are different now. Back then he was just a professional acquaintance.'

'Who fancied you! I was right.'

'You don't know that!'

'Well of course I do! God, you act as if everything was my fault – at least I never ran off with anyone else! At least I was never unfaithful!'

'What are you talking about? Neither was I.'

'No? Isn't that your suitcase waiting by the front door? With two tickets to Venice in the front pocket?'

'That's what this is about, isn't it? You can't accept I might have met someone else.'

'No – I can't accept that you won't give our marriage another go when I still don't see why it failed.'

Early the following morning Maddy crept downstairs with her suitcase to find me already dressed and occupied in the kitchen.

'Wow – you're up early!'

'Oh, I wanted to unload the dishwasher and get the kids' breakfast things ready before your mother witnessed it and nominated me for a knighthood. Here – I've made you a cup of tea.'

'Thanks. "*Did you see that, Ron? He made his wife a cup of tea.*"' And the two of us were able to smile in a way that put the previous night's argument behind us.

The darkness outside seemed to add to the illicitness of this encounter – she was about to fly off with her boyfriend, but here she was sharing a half-joke with her last partner.

'What was it like sleeping on the sofa bed?'

'Yeah – it was fine. Except Woody hogged most of the duvet . . .'

Maddy got a text message. 'Oh, that's . . . er, the car's outside.'

She wheeled her bag to the doorway and the two of us hovered there for a moment. 'Okay – 'bye.' And she gave an exaggerated wave, the sort of gesture you would make to someone who was a long, long way away, and it was clear that I was not to lean in and kiss her. 'Send my love to your wonderful dad when you see him.'

'I'm taking the kids to see him on Wednesday. Hope that's okay?'

'Yeah – that's good.'

'So, have a great time.'

'Thanks.' She unlocked the front door and forced an awkward smile.

'Just out of interest,' I mused, 'did we ever go to Venice?'

'No. I always wanted to go and you always said you'd take me . . .' she broke off eye contact '. . . but it never happened.'

'Oh. Sorry.'

'It's okay. I'm going now, aren't I? 'Bye.'

And the door closed and I heard a muffled man's voice and Maddy's upbeat response and the sound of a car taking her away.

Chapter 14

If the name of the place was supposed to fill you with excitement and wonder, it didn't work on me. In fact, I was highly suspicious that Splash City might not be a proper city at all; almost certainly lacking the basic local government and municipal infrastructure that would have justified it applying for official city status. So when the kids launched their plan to go to this massive indoor water park, I was not quite able to share their enthusiasm.

'Splash City?'

'It's like a giant swimming complex with flumes and wave machines and everything.'

'And they have, like, a realistic beach with sand and stuff.'

'And a dead gannet covered in oil?'

'You do that joke every time, Dad.'

'Do I? Oh, it felt like I just thought of it. It's a lovely idea, kids, but I don't think it'll be open on Boxing Day.'

'Yeah, it is. We checked online.'

'Ah no, but you see, I don't think I actually have any swimming trunks.'

'Yes, you have – they're still in that bag in the airing cupboard.'

'Ah, but, the thing is,' I stammered, 'the reason I don't think I can take you swimming, my darling children, is . . . because I don't think I can remember how to swim.'

For a moment I seemed to have them stumped.

'We'll teach you!' squealed Dillie excitedly.

'What?'

'Yeah, we'll teach you to swim! Just like you taught us!'

An hour later I found myself standing in a pair of baggy swimming shorts, plucking up courage to skip through the freezing footbath between the changing rooms and the pools. A large sign said that children under fourteen must be accompanied by an adult. It didn't say anything about those kids teaching their parents how to do doggy-paddle.

Once inside I was struck by the scale of the place. It was an enormous post-modern cathedral built to the twin gods of water fun and athlete's foot. Huge human-swallowing tubes spiralled through the air; children and adults alike were digested one by one, screaming as they disappeared down the fibreglass gullet. On zigzagging stairways, queues of almost-naked, shivering refugees patiently waited in the hope of escape, only to find that the tunnel that led outside cunningly re-entered the building further down and then spat them out into a deep pool beside the base of the same staircase.

The humid, echoey atmosphere overwhelmed me and I just stood there trying to take it all in. When a jarring siren went off, I optimistically wondered if this might be a fire alarm, but instead children excitedly grabbed body-boards and lined up to surf towards an unconvincing beach featuring plastic palm trees and an assortment of soggy sticking plasters lapping at the shore. Dillie and Jamie had arranged to meet me 'at the beach' once they had been down their favourite flume, and they found me looking suspiciously dry, leaning against a killer-whale litter bin. We agreed to start my lesson in the Little Tadpoles pool in the far corner, where a sprinkling of under-fours splashed around with over-keen parents and an inflatable great white shark, which, on closer inspection, told you that it was not a life-saving device.

The warm water of the learner pool came halfway up my thighs, so I decided it might be a little less embarrassing to squat down as the children debated the best way to proceed with Dad's first lesson.

'We could both sort of hold him underneath while he practised kicking his feet?' said Jamie.

'Yeah, I remember he did that for me. Or there are some inflatable water wings in that basket. He could put those on?'

'Shhh – I can't wear those!' I protested. 'They're for the under-fives!'

'No answering back in the learner pool!' declared Dillie.

'Yes, be a good boy and if you're very brave we'll buy you an ice cream!'

The kids seemed to find this reversal of power hilarious. Another parent looked our way and I tried to adopt the air of a responsible dad supervising my own over-large kids who really ought to be swimming by now.

'And if you want a wee, DO NOT do it into the pool!' said Dillie too loudly.

'Especially off the top diving board!'

They were in hysterics now. I was sure that when I had taught them to swim it wouldn't have involved me utterly humiliating them first.

'So how are we going to do this, then?' I demanded as a four-year-old swam confidently past me.

'Well, er . . . why don't you just push off the side and see if it all comes back?' suggested Jamie.

'What?'

'You know – just start kicking your legs and moving your arms and stuff, and just see if you can do it?'

'Is that it? Is that how you teach something?' My children had turned into a 1930s information film for no-nonsense parenting. *Today: How to teach swimming. (1) Put the non-swimmer in the water. (2) Tell him to swim.*

But I recognized that there was actually a simple logic to it: just push off from the end and see if it comes back.

'All right! I will. Here goes . . .'

'Go on then!'

'I'm going to just try to swim . . .'

'Yeah. Get on with it!'

And then I just fell forwards into the water. It felt unnatural and foolhardy, but I just closed my eyes and braved the depths of the Little Tadpoles splash pool. I put my hands out to break my fall and discovered that actually my arms could reach the solid bottom of the pool, so I pushed my body upwards again. But now I found my arms were sculling and my legs flexing and pushing me onwards, and as long as you kept moving forwards you didn't sink. I was swimming! I knew how to swim – it seemed the most natural, instinctive thing in the world.

I could hear my two kids cheering and applauding, but I didn't want to stop, so I swam to the end of the pool, turned and pushed off again, punching the water now in a forceful front crawl, twisting my head to the side every third stroke to breathe, and I was at the other end already. I did a flawless tumble-turn, pushed off and powered my way through the water, breaststroke, backstroke, even butterfly – it was all still there in my repertoire. I was an alpha-male macho-swimmer, clocking up the lengths as I pushed my body to the limits. And then I became aware of a lifeguard blowing a whistle, and I stopped and stood up to see that the parents of the toddlers in inflatable armbands were clutching their frightened children and staring at me.

'Oi, mate, this is the children's pool!' said the young Australian.

'I can swim!' I told him delightedly.

'Yes, we can see that. If you want to swim like that, use the Olympic pool, you idiot.'

*

I had a memorable lunch with my children. The gourmet food guides had yet to decide the number of stars they would award this restaurant, but surely it could be only a matter of time before they were struck with the debonair ambience of the burger franchise that sat within the Splash City fun park. Because families came to this complex for the whole day, the eatery boasted a convenient waterside location at which it was traditional to dine in the ultra-casual dress of soggy swimming trunks and nothing else. At no other restaurant in the world was it possible to see so clearly both the food and its dietary consequences. And how utterly charming to be entertained by the parade of the bare body shapes of those who were regular patrons. Sure, no Michelin stars yet, but no shortage of real-life Michelin men squeezed on to the bar stools, eating Whoppers and Fries, their bellies hanging over their skimpy Speedos. After lunch some of them lay stretched out in the shallow area of 'the beach', where teams of Greenpeace activists would pour buckets of water over them and try to help them wriggle back out to sea.

'May I have a hamburger, please, and, er, some chips and, er, a lemonade as well?

'You want a Meal?'

'Yes. Of course I want a meal. That's why I'm ordering all this food . . .'

The kids quickly took over the ordering while simultaneously pretending not to know me.

'So are you going to move back out when Mum comes home?' asked my daughter sadly, finally taking a break from a huge vanilla chocolate shake.

'Dillie! Shut up!'

'No, it's okay, Jamie.'

I blushed with suppressed satisfaction at this question. Clearly the implication was that my daughter would prefer me to stay at home for ever.

''Cos I was thinking you could move into the summerhouse.'

'Dillie, shut up!'

'That's a very sweet thought, but I think when couples get divorced they're generally supposed to live apart. I've been looking for a little flat as near to home as possible – they're just very expensive. But wherever I live, we'll still see lots of each other.'

'I want you to move back home,' said my daughter straight out.

'Well, that's very nice of you . . .' My smile faded as I noticed the thunderous expression on Jamie's face.

'No! No, you can't do that!' he snapped. 'Because then you and Mum will just end up shouting at each other all the time again . . .' and tears were streaming down his red face. His white plastic chair fell over as he stood up and stomped off.

'Jamie! Jamie, come back!'

I didn't know whether to jump up and run after him or just give him some time to cool off. Plus there was an additional complication in that Dillie had taken advantage of the opportunity to help herself to his chips.

'Dillie, don't do that. He's upset!'

'If you get down from the table it means you've finished eating. That's what you always said . . .'

I watched my son march around the perimeter of the big pool, his pace gradually slowing before he sat down, looking as indignant as it is possible to appear while seated on a plastic octopus. I watched him for a while, aware that he was casting the occasional sideways glance in our direction. And then I thought that the chips would be cold soon anyway, and it was a shame to waste them. I made a half-hearted attempt to suggest to Dillie that she shouldn't go straight back in the water after lunch, but I wasn't sure if I even believed this old cliché myself. 'If you jump in the water straight after eating, you could get stomach cramps. And then a swan might break your arm, or something.' So while she was queuing for a giant slide I walked all the way around and finally flopped down next to Jamie.

'You can push me in the pool if you want.'

'No. It's all right.'

'But we ate your chips.'

'They're not chips, they're fries.'

'You know, the whole point of me moving out of the house was so that you and Dillie didn't have to put up with all that shit any more.'

'Yeah, but then it's just different shit, isn't it?'

'What sort of different shit?'

'Mum crying in her room at night. Us having to move house.'

'But eventually things move on and you realize that the new shit isn't as shitty as the old shit. You know, I don't think this casual use of swear words is making me seem like a cool dad . . .'

And then Jamie's face broke into a smile.

'Do you want me to replace those fries we ate?'

'Don't say "fries", Dad; it sounds stupid coming from you.'

When we got back home, I asked Jamie to help me see if I could still ride a bike and, to my amazement, that came back to me instinctively, too. Jamie clapped and cheered and proudly claimed to have taught his father to ride a bicycle, and I allowed that little bit of distorted history to stand. But there had not even been a single wobble; it turned out that you really did never forget how to do it. It was the same as swimming: as long as you made an effort to keep going forwards, you were okay.

'Yeah, it's like marriage,' said Gary on the phone that evening. 'You can't just freewheel or simply hope to float along; you always have to be working at a relationship . . . LINDA, SHUT UP! I'M ON THE FUCKING PHONE!'

Though swimming and cycling had returned easily, it seemed that other basic skills would have to be relearned. I did my best around the home, but it was very difficult for me following my amnesia, because I had clearly forgotten how to use an iron or a hoover.

'Wow, Dad's using the Hoover!' said Jamie. 'I've never seen that before!'

'I know, and he was actually doing some ironing this morning!'

I stripped the beds where Maddy's parents had slept, and when Jean rang to say they had got home safely, this detail somehow slipped into the conversation. 'Oh, Jean, I found a hairgrip when I was stripping your bed. I've put it on the bedside table for next time you're here.'

'Did you hear that, Ron? He stripped the beds. Oh, you are marvellous!'

'Oh no, it's nothing. I'm just glad I found it before I put the sheets in the washing machine.'

'And you washed them too? Did you hear that, Ron – he does washing!'

I felt empowered by discovering that physical memories had been unaffected by my amnesia. 'So if I can still do all the things I learned before,' I reasoned, 'that means I can still drive. It's like the swimming and the cycling – you just have to go for it!' I waited until the children were out at friends' and then picked up the car keys. 'I must have sat in that driver's seat a thousand times before,' I told myself. 'I'm just going to get in and drive!'

Forty minutes later the garage truck arrived to hoist the car off the ornamental wall at the front of number 23. Previously the Parkers' front garden had been separate from the pavement, but now it was all much more modern and open-plan. And instead of having to park on the street, I had created an entirely new parking space for them on top of this pile of bricks and the remains of the hedge, as long as you didn't mind securing your front wheels in their goldfish pond.

'I'm terribly sorry. Obviously I'll pay for all the damage,' I said to Mrs Parker, a very nervous American woman who only seemed to leave the house for Neighbourhood Watch meetings.

'I thought it was a terrorist attack!' she stammered. 'I thought this was my nine/eleven.' She had stayed inside for some minutes after the accident. I think she may have been waiting for a second car to crash into the other wall.

A couple of police officers arrived fairly promptly, though not the elite anti-terrorist unit that had been suggested by the person making the emergency call. One officer fiddled uncertainly with a new laptop on which he was supposed to log the accident details, while the other was perplexed that I tested negative for alcohol and that no calls seemed to have been made on my mobile phone.

'So there was no other vehicle involved,' continued the older policeman, 'and it was broad daylight on a straight road . . . I'm struggling to understand how you managed to crash into a garden wall.'

'Well, I sort of forgot how to drive.'

'You forgot how to drive?'

He looked at the scattered remains of the ornamental wall, with a badly dented Honda Jazz brought to a halt halfway through it.

'Er, Dave, there's no box for that . . .'

'What?'

'On the new form – there's no box for "Forgot how to drive".'

'Let's have a look? Hmm . . . Are you sure you didn't "Swerve to avoid pedestrian or animal", sir?'

'Sure.'

'"Skidded on treacherous road surface", perhaps?'

'No, no – it was completely my fault. I'm sure I used to be able to drive, but I forgot.'

'And when did you forget, exactly?'

'The twenty-second of October.'

The older policeman looked at me uncertainly. 'And are you planning to attempt to drive again?'

'Not until I remember.'

The policeman on the computer chuckled at this unintended jest, but immediately dropped his smile when the senior officer shot him a glare. It was time to bring this to a close. 'Put that he swerved to avoid a cat.'

'Got it!'

'Tortoiseshell, wasn't it, sir?'

'No.'

'Swerved to avoid animal,' mouthed the second policeman as he ticked the appropriate box, and another little bit of history was made official.

'What were you thinking?' said Maddy, on the phone from Italy, when I had decided that it would be best to be completely honest and open about the tiny little scrape on the car. 'Why did you imagine you'd suddenly be able to drive?'

'You mean I *couldn't* drive?'

'No! You never learned on principle. It was one of the things that used to really piss me off. You thinking you were all ecologically sound and pro-public transport, and then asking me for a lift everywhere when I wasn't running the kids from one place to another.'

'That's a shame, and it was such a nice car . . .'

'What do you mean, *was*?'

When the Honda was finally delivered back from the garage, I gave it a good clean in the street outside, prompting the raffish neighbour who had borrowed our hedge trimmer to wander across for an extended chat.

'Hullo there, Vaughan. Giving the old motor a wash and set?'

'Ha ha!' I chuckled politely. 'Yes . . . it wouldn't fit in the dishwasher.'

The neighbour thought this was hilarious, and I was unsure about the etiquette of resuming washing the car before the laughter had died down. I did my best to navigate the treacherous line between normal good manners and actually encouraging this man's friendship, but a moment's lost concentration saw me offer too chatty a response with just a bit too much eye contact, and suddenly the neighbour pounced.

'Anyway, Arabella was saying the other day that with Maddy away at the moment, you must bring the kids over for their tea one evening. She could cook them some fish fingers or something?'

Approaching behind him I spotted Jamie and Dillie, returning from the Common with the dog. The mime was unambiguous: the word 'No!' was mouthed over and over again, while the kids acted out shooting themselves in the head, hanging themselves and slashing their wrists.

'Ah, well, that's very kind,' I said, appearing to suppress a cough or hiccup or something, 'but I've already planned and bought their meals for the whole week, so another time perhaps?'

I had actually promised the kids home-delivered pizzas that evening, and was now forced to make an elaborate arrangement with the driver to meet me a hundred yards up the road so that the moped wasn't spotted bringing our dinner to the door. But I grew more confident in the kitchen, cooking from recipe books and serving up the kids' favourite dishes by special request. They were incredibly supportive, telling me exactly how it all used to work before. Apparently I always stacked the dishwasher immediately after dinner and they weren't expected to do any clearing up at all, because Mum and I were always really insistent that they went and watched *Family Guy* 'while their food went down'.

And I knew that they were winding me up, but I let them watch television anyway on the grounds that they'd made me laugh. That was the rule: if their pleas or excuses were witty enough, they generally got their way. 'Dad, I haven't had my pocket money – have you got six pounds fifty?'

'Six pounds fifty? Mum said you got a fiver.'

'Yeah, but there's a one pound fifty handling charge.'

I had originally said no to Dillie's suggestion that the twins from her class came for a sleepover. But then she indignantly insisted that the twins couldn't stay at home because the builders had just discovered their house was possessed by the Antichrist.

'Oh really?'

'It's true,' added Jamie. 'The council are sending round an exorcist, but you have to wait six weeks unless you get a private one.'

And a few minutes later I was dragging the double mattress into Dillie's room.

Dillie's own bed was a masterpiece of creative carpentry. Angled steps at the rear, like on an old-fashioned London bus, led up to a cosy upper bunk, while underneath was a den that hid a pull-down desk featuring hand-built drawers and cubby holes and special places for books or soft toys. Car stereo speakers were built into either side of the headboard, which led to an iPod dock, radio and CD player. The audio books for which this had been conceived remained in their cellophane wrappers, while a selection of music CDs were scattered across a shelf with a special hole for a water beaker, which currently held a can of Dr Pepper.

'Wow – fantastic bed!' I said. 'Where did you get that from?'

'You built it!' she said with pride.

I looked it over more carefully, beaming with pride at the crafts-manship, checking the strength of the joints, learning that I must have an instinctive flair for design and carpentry I had not realized I possessed.

'And what about the clouds on the ceiling? Did I paint those?'

'No, that was Mum. She said she got the idea from the boy's bedroom in *Kramer vs. Kramer*.'

'Right. That was a Dustin Hoffman film, wasn't it? I think I remember it. They get back together at the end?'

'No – they get divorced.'

This home was just another Victorian terrace like so many others in the surrounding streets, but on the inside our family's character had been stamped on every room. I found myself staring at Maddy's photographs for hours. Her signature creations featured elaborate digital collages made up of hundreds of tiny thumbnail photographs of interesting locations or people, which combined to make one huge image of an individual face. There was so much in them, and I was fascinated by the choices Maddy had made in these giant portraits. When I looked in the mirror I could see my own image, but still couldn't make out all the hundreds of people and places that had made me. Yet having gone from sleeping in a hospital ward to camping in a baby's nursery, I felt I'd finally found the place where I belonged.

I learned that I had put a lot of effort into the renovations. It had been me who had done the refit of the kitchen, it was me who'd made the built-in wardrobes. I had even constructed the wooden summerhouse at the bottom of the garden, and the decking outside the kitchen doors. It was strange that I was able to feel a little abstract pride at these achievements. Unlike all those negative stories, which were nothing to do with the new Vaughan at all.

When this property came to be sold, the clouds would be painted over and my hand-built bed ripped out for something to the new owners' taste. And what about the invisible handiwork that Maddy and I had done in raising our children? Soon they would be adolescents: how would they react to losing the security of their family home and shuttling between their estranged parents? Would all their sparkle and charm end up on the skip with everything else?

I was still consumed with the mystery of how this had become a 'broken home', as Jean insisted on calling it. That night, when the children were asleep, I closed the lounge door and furtively connected an old VHS player I had found under the stairs in order to watch some old home movies with promising titles like 'Christmas 2007'. I felt guilty, but was sure that all men secretly watched films of themselves and their wives enjoying a healthy, happy marriage. Maybe there was even stronger stuff on the internet; maybe it was possible to download illicit images of Vaughan and Madeleine holding hands on the beach or running through fields of poppies together.

Baby Jamie had clearly been something of a superstar, playing the title role in countless thrilling-sounding movies such as 'Jamie's First Mashed Banana' or 'Jamie Sees the Sea!' (an interesting interpretation by the lead, who chose to play the whole of this scene fast asleep). The second baby must have failed a screen test or something, because she barely made an appearance. Seeing them as toddlers was thrilling and heart-wrenching at the same time. It was like I was seeing our babies for the first time, but with the added bonus of knowing the people these infants would turn into.

There was more footage of them as they got a bit older; once they could be put down, the camcorder could be picked back up again. An angelic little Dillie sang a song in her Brownie uniform, though I can't believe it was Brown Owl who had taught her 'Heaven Knows I'm Miserable Now'. And Jamie was filmed running towards the finishing line at his infant school sports day. I was actually quite excited watching this, because Jamie was in the lead – my son was going to win the race! And then, a yard before the tape, he saw me filming and stopped and waved at the camera as all his classmates swept past him.

I took a break and got myself another couple of beers from the fridge before resuming the home-movie marathon. There was footage of my wife and kids at the seaside, our voices almost inaudible over the rumbling wind on the microphone. Woody was a puppy, scared but entranced by the water, barking at the waves and then running at manic full speed up the beach, falling over his own legs and running back down towards the water again. The children were younger and fantastically cute, yet I could see that they were essentially the same people as now. Their memories of this holiday would probably have been reconstructed by this film; their brains would have tricked them into thinking they remembered the day on the beach rather than the recording they had seen many times since.

That was what this whole experience was teaching me: that memories are continually revised, that people re-script past conversations and change the order of events. The view from the divorce courts would have pushed Maddy's negative memories to the fore; she needed her version of our years together to be a distorted, Fox News version of events. I sifted through the films, looking for more positive evidence for the Counsel for the Defence. And there I was – perhaps just a couple of years ago, judging by the age of the children – in the back garden of this house, tending a barbecue while Jamie filmed and gave his account of what was going on from behind the lens.

'I could always cook the meat in the oven first? And then you could put it on the barbecue to finish it off?' suggested Maddy, as the raw chicken legs failed to look even vaguely warm and the wisps of white smoke from the briquettes gradually petered out.

'No, it's getting there,' insisted the chef, despite all evidence to the contrary. Jamie's cheeky commentary on my failed barbecue became less sardonic and increasingly hungry every time filming resumed, and by the end there was an edge of desperate starvation in the boy's voice. With the light of the midsummer evening fading, Dillie did a spoof appeal into the camera lens on behalf of the starving children of South London and then Maddy came into shot with a grill pan to transfer the meat to her own domain, where it would be ready in twenty minutes' time.

Then the atmosphere suddenly turned. 'Just let me fucking do it for once, will you?' I snapped, as I took the chicken back. 'I said I'd do a barbecue and I'm doing it.'

Jamie then lowered the camera, and to the blurred footage of my son's shuffling feet, I heard Maddy and me shouting at one another.

'Why do you have to be such a bloody control freak?'

'I'm not a control freak. I'm just making sure the kids get something to eat.'

'So dinner is a bit later than usual – so what? You moan that I don't cook enough and then when I do, you march in and take over.'

'What cooking? There's no heat! The chicken is completely raw two hours after you started. I suggested you got the barbecue going hours earlier and you told me to keep my nose out of it.'

The footage of the floor gradually moved indoors as Jamie crept away from the scene and the bad radio play of domestic rancour faded into the background until the camcorder was finally turned off. But the argument had got increasingly personal and bitter, moving from the specific to general character flaws in the other partner, lines that were not designed to prove a point, merely to wound the other person.

I watched the tape a couple more times, noticing that I'd had a beer bottle in my hand, and that there were a few empties on the table nearby. As the camera swung down at the exact moment that the atmosphere turned sour, it caught Dillie's depressed expression. Her nine-year-old face had a resigned sadness to it, as if she had witnessed scenes like this before. I had no memory of ruining a summer barbecue and, despite the incontrovertible evidence before me, found it hard to believe that that really was me.

Then I lined the tape up to the end of Dillie's comic appeal and pressed 'Record' on the VHS player. The last five minutes of this story would now be wiped clear; the downbeat ending had got a negative response in the test screenings, so the studio ordered the ending be re-cut.

'Do you remember that lovely summer's evening when we had a barbecue and the coals wouldn't light and Jamie did a sarcastic commentary on the cooking?' I imagined Maddy fondly reminiscing.

'Oh yeah – and Dillie did that mock charity appeal to camera?'

'That was a funny evening, wasn't it?'

'Yeah . . .'

When I returned to the kitchen, I noticed the recycling bin

brimming with empty lager bottles. I stared at the six pack of beer on the sideboard. I took the first can, tugged on the ring pull and then poured the contents down the sink. I opened the next one, and smelt the hoppy aroma as it fizzed around the plug hole. I pulled open the third. It was thirsty work this, and it did seem rather profligate. Buying beer and pouring it down the sink – that's not very green, is it? So by the end of the evening, I did dispose of all the beer, but in the less wasteful manner of drinking it all.

And then I noticed Ralph's business card in the kitchen and, even though it was the middle of the night, I dialled 141 followed by his mobile number.

'Hi, this is Ralph,' said the recording. 'I'm in Venice at the moment. Please leave a message and I'll get back to you in the New Year.' He didn't have to boast about it.

I watched the re-edited videos again with the children on New Year's Eve, and they were thrilled and delighted to see the way we used to be. Then Dillie ran and fetched a box of photos and the two of them narrated me through the blurred cast of relations and family friends that had not been obscured by my fat thumb half-covering the camera lens.

'That's Great-uncle Simon, Granny's brother who moved to Australia—'

'Understandable.'

'Dad!'

'Look at Mum in that one – she looks so cool!'

Oval stickers had been placed on some of the poorer-quality photos. *Subject out of focus. Cause: lens may not have been correctly adjusted. Subject too dark. Cause: flash may have failed. Subject cannot be recognized. Picture-taker may have suffered dissociative fugue and wiped all personal memories.*

'Who's that lady?' I asked, looking at a very old picture of a woman standing alone in some tropical location.

'That's Granny Vaughan. That's . . . your mum . . .'

I held the faded colour photo in my hand for a moment. She was smiling directly at me – a modest introductory hello from another universe. She had on a wide-brimmed hat and was wearing a smart two-piece and clutching a leather handbag over her arm; a formal pose in front of some important former colonial building. I dearly wished I could have reported experiencing some sort of instant love or bond, but instead I was only aware of a powerful vacuum where sentiment and longing were supposed to be.

'Are you okay, Dad?' said Dillie.

'It must be a bit weird,' added Jamie.

'Yeah – I'm fine. It's just . . . she looks nice.'

'Yeah, she was,' said Jamie. 'She always gave us chocolate and pound coins and said, "Don't tell your dad!"'

'What else did she say?'

And my children allowed me to stay up late as they told me all about the times I couldn't remember, and we found more photos of my mum and dad and of me as a child, and they made me laugh with family stories and tales from the olden days.

'Happy New Year, Dad!'

'Happy New Year.'

The next day I took Jamie and Dillie to see their grandfather and I felt an enormous pride in them being so valiant and mature, so affectionate towards him, unembarrassed at showing that they cared. His face looked slightly yellow, and there was long white stubble in the wrong places, but Dillie didn't hesitate to lean in and kiss him. She had brought a hand-made card as always and Jamie even lent his grandfather his iPod; he had cleared his own music collection to fill it up with audiobooks he had downloaded himself.

'That button is "Play",' Jamie explained. 'That's if you want to skip to the next chapter,' he continued, and even though I doubted whether his grandfather would have the energy to listen to an audiobook, the vision of my teenage son taking this much trouble brought me close to tears.

'You are so kind,' said my father. The children told him all about their Christmas, and reported what presents they had got and all the places we had been. And when it was time to go, they instinctively knew to hug him long and hard.

'Goodbye, Granddad,' said Dillie.

'Goodbye, dear.'

'See you, Granddad,' said Jamie, leaning in.

'What lovely grandchildren! Thank you for coming. You must have more important things to do.'

'No,' said his grandson, firmly, suddenly seeming twenty-five years old. 'Not more important than you.'

The week passed far too quickly. On the final day I cleaned the house from top to bottom, prepared a dinner and packed my bags ready to move back out. Maddy arrived alone at the front door and embraced the excited children as I hovered in the hallway. She had presents for them and pictures to show of cute dogs in Italian ladies' handbags, and an inscrutable smile and a hello for me.

'Wow, it all looks very clean everywhere. We should send photos to my mum!'

I had invited myself to stay for dinner by cooking a big casserole, and afterwards Maddy and I had the chance to talk on our own.

'So how was your holiday?'

'Oh, you know . . . One minute I was travelling in great comfort in a gondola, the next moment I was travelling in extreme discomfort with a budget airline. They sort of cancel each other out.'

'Well, it was great being here with the kids. They're so funny and clever and interesting and everything . . .'

'Yeah, they get that from their mother.'

'Though I don't understand how they can prefer *The Simpsons* to *All-Star Mr & Mrs*.'

'Listen – I've been thinking,' she announced. 'What you said in the courtroom . . . We don't actually have to get legally divorced, if you really don't want to.'

I stood up and gently pushed the kitchen door closed.

'You're so much easier to talk to since your amnesia that I wondered if we could just work something out like adults? If we didn't spend so much on lawyers, we might just be able to hang on to the house.'

'For you and the kids to live in without me?' I had started stroking the dog, but now I could feel my fingertips digging quite hard into his fur.

'Well – this is my proposal. The kids live here all the time, keep their rooms, keep Woody, keep walking to school with their friends. But you and I split the cost of a little flat somewhere cheap, and take turns to live in that when it's not our turn to be here with the kids.'

The dog grunted in pleasure at the rigour of fingers digging into his mane.

'What about the summerhouse? I could live in there. Or the spare room?'

'I'm just trying to find a way to protect the children, so that their lives are not disrupted. Once they have grown up and left home we can sell the house and work out how to split the proceeds. But just for the next seven or eight years, we could both have the same second home . . .'

Privately I had to concede that this seemed like a constructive and mature suggestion. I'd get to have every weekend in this house with the children. Dillie would still have her lovely bedroom and Jamie could still do his schoolwork in that summerhouse with Woody lying at his feet.

'So part of the time you'd be here,' she said with a smile, 'and the rest of the time it would be me and Ralph.'

'What?'

The dog turned round, indignant that he was no longer being stroked.

'So this is Ralph's idea, is it?' I said, feeling my face heating up. The neglected dog let out a bark. 'No, Woody, shut up!'

'No, not exactly . . . I only meant eventually, if Ralph and I decide we want to live together. The kids would have to be cool with it, of course – they'll always come first.'

'So your great plan is, we don't have to legally get divorced to save money so that Vaughan lives in a shoebox in the slums, while Ralph moves into my half of the double bed here?'

'No – that's not it at all . . .'

The dog barked again.

'No, shut up! Bad dog, do you hear me?' and I pushed him away. 'You're very bad and I don't want to hear it any more.'

'You're distorting it all – Ralph said we shouldn't rush into anything—'

'Oh, well, if that's what Ralph suggests, then that's definitely what we should do! I can't believe you try and dress it up as what's best for the kids, when really it's just your fancy man trying to save on his rent bill!'

The kitchen chair fell over as I brushed past it on the way to the front room to give my children a farewell kiss. Madeleine was still trying to talk to me in the hallway as I marched to the door and put on my old coat, which was hanging by the door.

'Um . . . that's Ralph's coat,' mumbled Maddy.

'What? No, this is mine – I've been wearing it all week.'

'No – it's Ralph's. He left it here, it's his. But I'm sure he wouldn't mind you borrowing it . . .'

Chapter 15

'Right, Year Elevens, it's good to be teaching you again. Today we are going to be talking about the causes of the Second World War,' I predicted a little optimistically. 'Now, Ms Coney, who I understand was taking you while I was away, has told you all about the Treaty of Versailles, which was of course greatly resented in twenties Germany, but today we are going to ask how extreme politics came out of an extreme economic situation—'

'Sir! Mr Vaughan, sir?'

'Yes, Tanika?' I was pleased to demonstrate my apparently effortless grasp of all their names. It had involved much time staring at school photos of spotty faces and committing the matching names to memory. 'Is this a question about hyper-inflation in the Weimar Republic?'

'Not exactly. Are you a mentalist, sir?'

'I beg your pardon?'

'Dean said you'd gone mental in the nut and shit and didn't know summit or nothin'.'

'Well, first of all, can you not use that word in my class—'

'What – "mentalist"?'

'Well, yes, that one as well actually, but I was thinking of the swear word. And in answer to your question, it is no secret that my absence last term was due to me suffering a very rare neurological condition from which I am rapidly recovering and which in no way affects my abilities to teach you about the fall of the Weimar Republic.'

I pressed a link on the interactive whiteboard and was proud to see it display an image of a one-million-mark banknote.

'Yeah, but are you off your nut, sir?'

'No, Tanika, I am not *off my nut*, as you so charmingly put it.'

'Are you a loony, though? Do you, like, bark at the moon and shit?'

'No, but I might be in a minute. Since Tanika insists on referring to my memory loss, it's worth asking whether it is possible for whole countries to lose their memory as well. That's why history is so important—'

'Are you a psycho, though? Are you a nut job, sir?'

'What exactly a nation chooses to remember or forget comes to define the identity of its people and affect their future choices. And I would suggest, for example, that we in Britain opt to remember too much about the parts of the Second World War that we are comfortable with, and we prefer to forget about all the colonial wars of conquest that weren't a million miles from what Hitler was attempting.'

This point seemed to have made them think, and a few different hands went up.

'Yes – Dean?'

'But are you a mentalist, sir?'

'Do you think you're the Messiah, sir? Are you going on a shooting spree in McDonald's?'

'Could we concentrate on the lesson plan, *please*. Now, the failure of democracy in Germany to deliver economic security increased the attraction of a traditional militaristic leader—'

'Did you find them, sir?'

'Did I find what?'

'Your marbles, sir. Oh no – have you still not found them?'

'Do you want some fruitcake, sir? It's really nutty . . .'

'Do you foam at the mouth, sir? Are you afraid of water?'

'LOOK!' I finally snapped. 'THIS IS THE BLOODY EASY STUFF! THE RISE OF HITLER AND THE BLOODY NAZIS – THIS IS THE EASIEST HISTORY I CAN BLOODY TEACH! IT'S ALL THEY EVER SHOW ON THE HISTORY CHANNEL, SO BLOODY LISTEN OR WE'LL DO MODULE FOUR INSTEAD AND WE'LL TALK ABOUT THE REPEAL OF THE CORN LAWS, ALL RIGHT?'

'Ooooh!' said Tanika, seemingly vindicated. 'Boggy Vaughan's gone mental.'

After my first lesson with Year 11, I slumped into my chair in exhaustion and reflected on the distressing revelation that I seemed to lack the natural authority required to teach a challenging class of inner-city teenagers. Younger students were just as disrespectful; in fact, it seemed worse hearing the same swear words in higher-pitched voices. Deep down I already knew something, but now this depressing truth was fighting its way to the front of my consciousness: I was not the inspiring, life-changing teacher I had imagined when I had first learned of my occupation.

I stayed at my desk all through lunchtime, marking homework, doing lesson plans and ringing the parents of one particular student to try to understand how their child might have developed an attitude problem.

'Hello, it's Mr Vaughan here, Jodie's history teacher.'

'Oh yeah, Boggy Vaughan . . . You're the mentalist?'

Perhaps there might be something a little more positive on my online memoir. Perhaps by now former pupils had recalled how I had transformed their lives and future prospects with one interesting lesson on the causes of the Agricultural Revolution?

John O'Farrell

When I logged on I found that a number of students had indeed discovered my Wikipedia page, although their accounts of my past did not smack of the rigorous accuracy for which the open-source encyclopaedia has become so famous.

For example, I was sceptical about whether I had indeed genuinely been the so-called 'Fifth member of Abba', playing the oboe and tambourine on 'Gimme, Gimme, Gimme (A Man After Midnight)' and supplying backing vocals and handclaps on 'I Do, I Do, I Do, I Do, I Do'. I read with interest that I had spent three years fighting alongside Islamic militants during the Second Chechen War, eventually deputizing for Akhmed Zakayev during the 1999 Siege of Grozny and then switching sides to the Russian Federation 'because they had nicer trousers'.

Once the sixth-formers had become aware of this open document, it seemed that a competition had ensued for the most outlandish back story to the mystery of Mr Vaughan's life before he taught history at Wandle Academy. I learned that I had been assistant editor of *What Caravan?* magazine but had been sacked following a fist-fight with the editor over the merits of the new Alpine Sprite and the easy-to-reach butane regulator mounted on the front bulkhead. I was pleased to learn that I had single-handedly identified the genome of the Giant African Badger, though less proud that I had threatened to kill myself on the steps of Nestlé's headquarters unless they promised that in future Quality Street would have more of the yummy green triangle ones.

Looking at the document's history, I could see that new facts about me had been replacing old facts every day. 'Jack Joseph Neil Vaughan was previously "Ingrid Fjola Johansdottir", a popular and notorious West End nightclub hostess who, despite her well-documented sexual exploits with Eastern Bloc diplomats during the Cold War, increasingly came to feel that she had been born into the wrong body. With the fall of the Berlin Wall, the "Icelandic Mata Hari", as she was known to MI5, was no longer able to procure Communist military secrets for sexual favours and so decided to have a sex change and adopt a new persona as a male history teacher in a South London comprehensive.'

I considered taking down the Wikipedia page, but the worthy teacher in me decided that it was providing a valuable outlet for student creativity and literary experimentation on the blurred borders of fiction and non-fiction. Some of the original true facts that I had put in about myself had been left up there beside the students' bizarre inventions, but this just had the effect of making everything I had written seem invented as well.

Dr Lewington had asked me to come up with some memories that I had recovered, and to think of some significant life events that were still out of reach in my memory banks. I duly arrived for another brain scan with a wide selection of episodes from my past life – happy memories like scoring my first goal in a junior school football match, and unhappy memories like being informed that the teams had changed ends at half time. I was to concentrate on these moments and my brain activity would be compared to the chemical and temperature changes that occurred when I tried to recall chapters that were still blank.

The new brain scanner itself looked as if it had accounted for most of the NHS budget for the previous financial year. It was a huge, hi-tech, gleaming-white module, roughly the size of Apollo 13. There was a gentle whirr as the conveyor transported me inside the pod, and it seemed to know when to stop once my skull was in place for the internal mapping to commence. The idea of a female doctor being able to see inside my brain made me feel slightly uncomfortable. 'Don't think about sex,' I told myself, thus immediately doing so. How would that show up on the screen? Could she search through past thoughts and go back over my imagination's last browsing session? Over the hum of the machine I could hear Dr Lewington giving me instructions into her micro-phone and so I duly summoned up a significant recollection.

*

It is the memorable summer of 1997, and the newspapers are consumed with the new young Prime Minister who can do no wrong and the irredeemable Princess Diana and her scandalous new boyfriend. I am feeling a little stiff and nervous in my new suit, as I stand outside the mildly controversial non-religious venue for our marriage service. Madeleine did not want a traditional church wedding with a big white dress and bridesmaids and the church organist playing Bach's 'Cantata for Looking Around And Waving At Relatives'.

'She's not pregnant – she's just very political,' explains Maddy's mother to various elderly relatives. 'Hello, Joyce. Doesn't Madeleine look lovely in red? She didn't want a traditional white dress. It's not because she's pregnant or anything—'

'Mum, will you stop telling people I'm not pregnant.'

'Why – are you?'

'No, but it's perfectly normal to want a non-religious service.'

'I just don't want people thinking the church wouldn't have you. Or they might take the red dress as a sign . . . you know, that you were a fallen woman.' The last two words are whispered, as if it's shameful even to think of such a notion.

'A fallen woman! What is this – Hardy's Wessex? It's the nineties, Mum. It doesn't matter if a woman is pregnant when she gets married!'

'Oh, are you pregnant?' says Great-auntie Brenda. 'Oh, well, it's good that you're getting married, dear. It's better that the baby isn't a little bastard.'

'No, she's not pregnant, Brenda,' says Maddy's mum, slightly too desperately. 'She's just very political.'

'Political?'

'You know – doesn't believe in things.'

'Mum, I do believe in things. That's exactly why . . . oh, it doesn't matter.'

'Don't let it spoil your day, Madeleine,' says kindly Auntie Brenda. 'You're still the bride, dear, even if, you know . . .' and she

gives a supportive glance in the direction of Maddy's womb. And after Great-auntie Brenda has done the rounds at the reception, Maddy can be overheard politely thanking other elderly relatives for the compliment that she looks 'blooming', or denying that she 'must be tired' and insisting that one portion of food is quite enough.

The ridiculous notion that Maddy must be 'in the family way' was memorable because the two of us had laughed about it in the following years; it wasn't just a neutral series of isolated conversations – I recalled it as a funny anecdote. Maddy and I had imposed a narrative on to it and that became how it happened. As a rule, all my strongest memories had a sort of story to them, either real or subsequently fashioned in the retelling.

I guessed that the same must also be true of the other moments from the wedding that I recalled, as the various images of the day melted into each other like an edited-highlights package. I thought of Maddy waltzing with my father, as he gracefully led her round the scuffed wooden floor like a gentleman ballroom dancer. I could picture a rather drunk Gary remembering every single move to 'The Birdie Song', even though the DJ was actually playing Oasis. And I remember Maddy giving me a long and meaningful hug at the end of the evening, the moment before we got into the car. We could have skipped the service and the big party; that embrace was what made me realize that she loved me and wanted to be with me always.

One tradition had been upheld during the wedding ceremony itself, when Maddy and her dad had been the very last people to enter the civic chamber. Her entrance had been delayed outside the building, when a young lawyer had stopped her and handed her an important-looking wax-sealed envelope that he insisted she must open and read before she could proceed with her marriage. With the selected music for the bride's entrance already filtering through from inside, a flustered Maddy tore open the envelope. Was it a legal bar to their marriage? Did her intended already have a wife? Was her intended an illegal alien, a fraudster, an escaped convict? Finally she had the thing open and she pulled out the contents. It was a postcard of a leprechaun saying 'Top o' the mornin' to yers!!'

The brain scanner hummed and whirred and from outside this huge sarcophagus Dr Lewington instructed me to try to think about something significant of which I currently had no remembrance. I tried to picture my mother, searching for the moment when I had learned of her death, or the funeral that I must have attended with Maddy and probably our children. Now I could see myself standing in a country churchyard, throwing a handful of earth down on to a wooden coffin. It was a detailed image, featuring distraught mourners dressed in black as a lone church bell tolled nearby. I could easily have convinced myself that this was exactly as it had happened, except that I had already learned that my mother had been incinerated in a large municipal crematorium. Even though I knew it was pure fiction, I found it vaguely comforting to have this classic funeral scene to cling to.

Now I was instructed to concentrate on any episodes I had that were only partially reconstructed. I had deliberately saved the most negative moment I could recall to contrast with the bittersweet memories of my wedding day, and had intimated to Dr Lewington that this was what I would be thinking about.

It was the day that Madeleine said she didn't want to be married to me any more. Without quite understanding why, the memory felt infused with a numbing mixture of injustice, frustration, powerlessness, desperation and anger.

Maddy and I are getting ready for bed late one night, somehow both irritated, but failing to ignore one another in our tiny bathroom. I attempt to suggest that I have had a very tough day at school, but she is not interested. What I have forgotten is that Maddy has just had the results of a test for a health scare that has consumed her for the previous couple of weeks. She had found a lump under her arm and had become convinced it is cancer, and my attempts at reassurance have been interpreted as dismissive.

'What the hell is non-Hodgkin's lymphoma?' I had said when she first mentioned it. 'You can't diagnose something like that just from looking it up on the internet.'

'I have several of the symptoms. And a couple of people said it sounds really serious . . .'

'What people?'

'I don't know their real names. It was on a blog about women's health issues.'

From the outset she has interpreted my scorn for online medical chat as lack of interest in her wellbeing. Now she gets into the other side of the bed, but noticeably as far away from me as it is physically possible to be. And then she starts sobbing.

'What? What is it?'

'I got the results of my cancer test today.'

Two blows strike me almost simultaneously. First, there is the sudden shame I feel at not having remembered that today was the day she's been so worried about. I had said I would ring her immediately after lessons, but that worthy intention had been overtaken by the demands of the school.

But now such petty details count for nothing in the wider scheme of things as I absorb the far greater blow: the follow-up, knock-out punch that comes from nowhere. Maddy's sobbing tells me that the cancer test must have been positive. Despite my scepticism about self-diagnosis on the internet, despite the little bit of inconclusive research I have done myself, she really does have non-Hodgkin's lymphoma. Suddenly I see a future in which the kids might lose their mother, and a weakening Maddy will have to endure chemotherapy and operations and we will all be consumed with fear and uncertainty and the pain of seeing her endure an illness that none of us had even heard of until a couple of weeks earlier.

She shakes off my tentative offer of a comforting arm as she

*weeps, and I try to ascertain what exactly the doctor has said to her
and what the treatment options are. She wipes her eyes on her nightie.
Finally she is able to say a few words through the tears.*

'It was negative. I don't have cancer.'

'What?'

'The lump is benign.' She weeps. 'And he said all the other symptoms were probably just a bug or something—'

'Oh, thank God for that!' and I go to hug her but she pushes me
away and now her sobbing seems worse than ever.

'Maddy – it's fantastic news! I thought from the way you were crying that you must have non-Hodgkinson's disease or whatever—'

'Non-Hodgkin's lymphoma. You can't even get the name of the
illness right.'

'Well, it doesn't matter, does it, because you haven't got it! God,
you had me going there, the way you were crying and everything!
God, what a relief.'

She wipes her face on her nightie again, and it occurs to me that she
never wears anything like that in bed; she always wears one of my
baggy T-shirts. Perhaps there hadn't been any in the drawer.

'You forgot to ask me about the results.'

'Yeah, I know – I'm really sorry, but can I just tell you what
happened at school today and you might understand—'

'You didn't even remember to ask! You don't care enough to ask if
I'm going to live or die, to find out whether I have cancer or not.'

'Well, obviously I do care whether you live or die, that's just
ridiculous. As it happens, I never thought that you did have cancer,
although I could see you were worried about it.'

'But you didn't come to the hospital, did you?'

'Because you never asked me to.'

'You still should have offered.'

'Where's the logic in that? If you had said, "Please come", I would
have come; but you never asked, so I judged from that that there was
no need. For God's sake, you don't have cancer – why are we arguing
again? We should be celebrating.'

'Our marriage has cancer. Aggressive non-operable terminal cancer. If you can't be there for me when I go through something like this, then I don't think I want to be married to you any more . . .'

'Look, it's understandable that you're not thinking straight. The worry of this whole lymphoma thing means that you're getting this out of proportion. I'll take a couple of days off work, and maybe we should take the kids down to your parents—'

'It's too late, Vaughan. You've never been there for me. You never made the jump, you never actually got married – it's always been about you, never about us . . .'

And I realize that she wouldn't have sobbed like this about the uncertainty of cancer; she would have been silent and thoughtful. She is crying because she feels that something has died.

Lying in the scanner, I could almost feel my head throbbing as I trawled over that terrible night again; homing in on the tiny details that made it feel so real and recent. The moment when we finished talking and she got up from the bed and went to sleep in the spare room, never to return for all the time that we stayed under the same roof. The broken light bulb that I had meant to replace in the bedside lamp. The throbbing ache on the back of my skull and the crippling headache that kept me company until dawn.

Then, lying there inside that machine, I realized I had just had an actual new memory. Live on camera, the scan would have seen what happened when a new file was opened up and my brain accessed previously lost information. I had had a blow on the head! I was sure of it; the whole time this marriage-ending argument was going on, I had had an overpowering headache and could feel a large, tender swelling on the back of my head. Yes, I had been concussed. That was what I had been trying to tell her: I had been confronted outside the school by an angry father, who had accused me of picking on his child. He had shoved me over and I had hit the back of my head on the kerb and I had been concussed. I had refused to go to hospital, but despite my attempt at heroics, I knew it had been a pretty bad blow.

Now I realized that my amnesia might be a delayed reaction to that injury. That was why I had forgotten Maddy's medical results! I wasn't being indifferent or selfish – I was concussed. It was the first symptom of an amnesia that was later to swallow me completely.

Back in her office, Dr Lewington listened to the whole episode. She was interested in the detail about the blow to my head but, to her excitement and wonder, it seemed that nothing would unlock the mystery of what had happened to me. She showed me the results of the different scans. One image showed lots of blues and reds in the middle part of my brain. And in all the others there were lots of blues and reds in the same part of my brain. 'Isn't it wonderful? Absolutely no difference whatsoever!' she enthused. 'The brain really is such a fascinating enigma.' Even the moment when I recovered the brand-new memory revealed no brain activity that was discernibly different.

On her desk was a life-size ceramic human head, with lines and writing all over the cranium denoting the confident Victorian nonsense that had been phrenology. Things had moved forward enormously in a hundred and fifty years. Now they knew that they knew nothing.

'Of course, we have to be aware that the memories you are recovering may not be all that accurate . . .' she commented cautiously.

'What do you mean?'

'Well, there's plenty of research proving how memories change over time. You might be regaining memories that were already distorted, and they might have been twisted further in the recovery – they might even be completely false.'

'False?' I exclaimed, feeling vaguely offended. Each returning episode had made me feel a little bit more normal. Now Dr Lewington was suggesting that I might be growing madder with every one.

'Certainly. I've had patients with vivid recollections of things that happened when they weren't there. They can become quite angry when their versions of their own past are directly challenged. Such is the wonderful power of memory to affect our emotions!' she enthused, clicking her computer to close down my file. She made another appointment to see me in a couple of months and I realized that that would be after I was officially divorced. The ceramic head showed all the different parts of the human brain that were supposed to correspond to the major functions of the mind: 'veneration', 'caution', 'love'.

'Just as a matter of interest,' I said, as I stood up, 'is there any scientific basis for what they say, you know, that "there's a fine line between love and hate"?'

'Yes, actually. Both emotions occur in the same neural circuits, located in the putamen and the insula. Neurologists at UCL recently logged levels of emotion from the amount of activity in that part of the sub-cortex.'

'What, so you can actually scientifically measure how much you love someone?'

'Well, it might be love. It might be hate. Their scans only measured the strength of feeling.'

The memory of my concussion increased the sense of injustice I was already feeling inside. Now I was the determined defence lawyer who had just unearthed a crucial piece of evidence proving the innocence of the wrongly accused. I had to confront Maddy with this new development; she had played the neglected martyr about her worrying health test, but at the end of that fateful day she did not have a serious medical condition and I did. I went directly to the house to share my revelation with her. I don't know how I was expecting her to react; perhaps I was just seeking some sort of vindication. But I knew the children would be at school, and I think I was actually looking forward to a really good argument with her. That's the problem with being single: there's just no one there when you feel that physical need for a really good row. Sure, you can pick up a woman in a bar and have a one-night spat, but deep down you know it is an empty, meaningless experience. Companionship, mutual attraction and regular fights – that's what makes a marriage work. In the fantasy scenario spinning around in my head, she was actually conceding that she had been over-hasty and pleading with me to take her back. 'No, it's too late now,' I told her. 'You had your chance but you threw it away.'

Forty minutes later I had worked myself up into a state of indignation as I skipped up the front steps and pressed the entryphone buzzer hard enough to break it. There was a pause and then a buzz.

'It's Vaughan! I need to talk to you.'

There was another long pause and then the door lock buzzed and clicked and I pushed my way in. The dog greeted me enthusiastically, but Maddy did not appear as quickly as my state of excitement demanded. Through the ceiling I could hear her walking about in the bathroom above, and I fantasized that she might be putting on a little make-up before she came down to see me. Eventually a toilet flushed and I heard her footsteps. I stiffened in anticipation of the coming difficult conversation. But it would be more awkward than I expected. Coming down the stairs was not Maddy, but her boyfriend, Ralph.

Chapter 16

I recognized him before he introduced himself. I had already guessed that the man I had seen helping Maddy with the picture frames must have been Ralph. In any case, the confident way he jumped down two steps at a time wearing a towelling dressing gown suggested that he was probably not a telephone engineer or a burglar. He was tall, and maybe a decade younger than me, and indeed Maddy. His hair was wet and he looked fresh and clean compared to the flushed and sweaty mental case who had just rushed here on his bicycle.

'Hi, Vaughan – I'm Ralph! Great to meet you.'

I felt I had no alternative to accepting the outstretched hand.

'Maddy's out at the moment. Sorry about my state of undress – just showered after my run!'

'Ah, right. Hence the dressing gown. "Hilton Hotels"!' I hadn't intended this to come across like an accusation of theft, but that was how it sounded.

'Yes, it's Egyptian cotton – they were selling them in the Venice Hilton so I thought, why not?'

I was disorientated by the detail that he had taken Maddy to a luxury hotel, and found myself forced into polite conversation.

'Yes, Venice, of course. How was that?'

'Amazing! What a city! You ever been?'

'Er, no. Maddy always wanted to go – but, you know . . .'

We stood there for a moment. I was sure the clock in the hall didn't usually tick that loudly.

'Yes, so – Venice,' I mused. 'Is it still sinking?'

'What?'

'Venice. Wasn't there some problem with it sinking or something?'

'I dunno if they sorted that out or not.' Ralph concentrated hard, and went to put one foot on the first stair so that he could place his elbow thoughtfully on his knee, but then became aware that this was opening the front of the dressing gown and so he deftly reversed the movement. This meeting was embarrassing enough without him contriving to show me his penis. 'But then, er, I suppose even if they did stop it sinking, now sea levels are rising it's going to be back to square one!'

'Honestly, if it's not one thing it's another.' I tutted.

'You just do what you can . . .'

'Yes,' I agreed carelessly, although it was a pretty safe bet that neither of us had ever done very much. 'I mean, I used to order the Veneziana in Pizza Express because they added twenty-five pence on to your bill for the Venice in Peril fund.'

'Well, that's great! And do you still have the Veneziana now?'

'No – I got fed up with the sultanas.'

'Urgh, sultanas on pizza? No!'

The dog yawned and I knew that it was time at least to acknowledge this tense situation and say something about his relationship with Maddy.

'So . . .' I said ominously, and I saw him prepare himself. 'I wonder . . . if they've thought about building, like, a huge tidal barrier across the strait of Gibraltar?'

'What?'

'You know – like the Thames Barrier, only really massive so it could stop the rising Atlantic flowing into the Med and flooding all the low-lying coastal areas?'

Ralph was also aware of the need to clear the air; he must have been feeling defensive about where he stood with regard to the children and the difficult emotional journey of Maddy and everyone else wrapped up in this.

'Nah – it's about twenty miles between Spain and Morocco!' he said. 'I mean, the engineering logistics alone would be insurmountable, before you'd even considered all the political and funding obstacles . . .'

The arrogance with which he dismissed my idea rubbed me up the wrong way.

'Well, something's got to be done!' I said, hearing my voice rising. 'We can't just do nothing and leave things as they are.'

'There's no point – it's all too late anyway. Just accept it.'

'Oh, right, so we can put a man on the moon or organize the D-Day landings, but don't bother trying to safeguard the homes and livelihoods of a billion people?'

'All the other coasts are going to disappear anyway – just deal with it!'

'No – I'm not going to "just deal with it"! I'm going to try and do something about it. I'm going to start having the Veneziana again. Even if I have to pick off all the sultanas!'

Admittedly my idea had been a bold one, and this had probably not been the forum to hammer out all the minutiae. Ralph might have tried to clinch the argument by pointing out the geo-political strategic power that control of this barrier would bestow upon Spain or Morocco, but instead he opted for a personal blow way below the belt.

'So, I understand you've been having some mental-health issues?'

It was at this point that I felt that my argument for this massive engineering project would become unanswerable if I punched

Ralph in the face. It seemed to me that this deft tactic would crystallize all the arguments and make the point more emphatically than anything I might say. I felt my fist clench and my face redden as an alarmed Ralph suddenly took a step back. Only in the last nanoseconds of this thought process did something inside me put the brakes on. I had no memory of ever hitting anyone, and I had just remembered how stupid and upsetting the incident with the psycho-dad at school had been. That's why I had come here – to tell Maddy about my concussion.

'Where's Maddy?' I demanded.

When he told me, I instantly knew I wanted to be there too. Failing to bother with the niceties of saying goodbye, I turned and slammed the door on my way out, feeling my hands shaking as I unlocked my bike. It was not a short cycle ride, but it was made considerably quicker by just how fired up I was. Frightened cabbies swerved out of my way, pedestrians didn't dare step on to zebra crossings.

'Hello, Maddy,' I said quietly, as I pushed the door open.

'Oh, hi. I didn't know you were coming.'

'No, well – spontaneous decision. Hi, Dad, how you feeling?'

My father's gaunt face peeked out of the top of the NHS blanket, which failed to conceal how thin and frail the body was underneath.

'Is that you, son?'

'Hello, Dad. You're looking a little better.'

'That's for seeing. Your lovely wife!' he suggested breathlessly. 'You don't. Normally. Come together.'

Maddy and I glanced at one another.

'Well, we thought you'd prefer more frequent visits, so we take it in turns,' improvised Maddy, rising from her chair to remove the paper from her flowers and put them in a vase.

'Yes, that!' I blurted. 'But – it's nice to be here together, isn't it, Maddy?'

I was still angry with her and Ralph and realized that there would be nothing she could do if I put my arm around her waist. I felt her stiffen as I placed my hand just above her hip, but I held it there as we stood before the old man's approving gaze. Maddy did not pull away; instead she explained to my father that she had put the flowers in a vase now, and that they certainly brightened up the room. Her waist felt softer than my own bony body; there was a tender, perfect hand-shaped ledge above her hip that felt like the most natural place in the world for a man to place his hand. But I wasn't sure that this was an affectionate act; part of me worried that I had wrapped my arm around her in the search for some sort of sarcastic revenge. I could feel the warmth of her leg against mine, and her perfume could be detected over the odour of the hospital and its patients.

'Look at you two!' wheezed my dad. 'You still make such a lovely couple.'

I gave her an extra squeeze towards me, and I was contemplating planting a kiss on her cheek. But this was Madeleine's cue to pull away from me and adjust the blanket where a discoloured foot had become exposed. She quickly sat down and told him what the children had been up to, and I sat in the chair beside hers, chipping in with inferior contributions inexpertly copied from her.

'Maddy's been. Very good.' His breath seemed weaker now; the effort of this visit could not be sustained much longer.

'Of course she's been very good!'

'She's the daughter. I never had.'

'You have a sleep now, Keith,' she said, in a cracking voice. I looked across at her and was startled to see that her eyes had welled up and that she was close to losing control.

'I'm just popping to the loo!' she blurted, as she dashed out to the corridor to cry in private.

Soon the old man was asleep and I went out and found our family car and waited to catch her there.

'Hi. You okay?'

'Your father is such a wonderful man,' she mused, her eyes still red.

'Yeah, I wish I could remember more, you know, of what he was like before.'

Madeleine seemed a little irritated by this, and said nothing.

'Look, I need to talk to you. Any chance of a lift if you're going back over the river?' Madeleine was too grown-up to refuse me.

'You didn't have to do the whole lovey-dovey thing in front of him.'

'I didn't want him to be suspicious.'

'Sure! Do that again and I'll stamp on your foot.'

'Yeah, well, I'll take whatever attention I can get.'

Maddy had put her seatbelt on and was just checking her texts when she suddenly looked up, astonished and a little nervous. 'So you . . . you met Ralph?'

'Oh – yes. We had a brief conversation,' I said, trying to affect an attitude somewhere between indifference and mild antipathy.

'Oh. Did you, like, work anything out?'

'Not really.'

'Not really? Well, come on, what did you say to him? What did he say back?'

'You wouldn't be interested.'

'What – my ex-husband and father of my children meets my boyfriend and you think I wouldn't be interested?'

She had put the ticket into the machine, and the barrier juddered upwards to let us out.

'Okay, well, he said you could never build a tidal barrier across the strait of Gibraltar, and I said it would be worth trying to stop all of southern Europe, North Africa and the Middle East losing their coastlines.'

She took her eyes off the road to look at me in confusion.

'Sorry? I don't understand.'

'Rising sea levels? Hello? Venice in Peril? He was actually quite dismissive of my idea of a massive Thames Barrier-type sea-wall.'

'Right. So you didn't talk about anything important?'

'Rising sea levels are important. But no, we never really talked about the elephant in the room.'

'What was the elephant in the room?'

'Well, *you*, obviously . . .'

'So you're saying I'm an elephant?' she said dangerously.

'No – the subject of you was like an elephant in the room.'

'So I'm a big fat elephant – that you can't ignore because I'm so enormous and fat?'

I couldn't quite understand how I found myself on the defensive. Her phone beeped again, and she read the next message at the traffic lights.

'He says he thought you were going to hit him!'

'What? Over a discussion on sea levels? Talk about paranoid! And as if I'd hit a man in a dressing gown!' That detail embarrassed her, which had been my intention. 'From which I am deducing that he's already moved in.'

'No! The kids were on sleepovers, so he stayed the night. They don't know he ever stays either, so don't say anything.'

'Anyway, I went round there because I wanted to talk to you about something. I had another brain scan today—'

'Okay – back to *you*, then.'

'It's important. I remembered something. The day you had the results of your test for non-Hodgkin's lymphoma. The thing is I had concussion that day – I had been shoved to the ground by an aggressive parent and I banged my head on the kerb. I think it might be related to my amnesia since October.'

'Did you tell the doctor?' She was being deliberately obtuse.

'That's not the point. We never slept in the same bed after that argument – but there was a *medical* reason for why I forgot to ask you about it, not to mention all the stress of the assault and the police and everything that I never got the chance to tell you at the time. Remember it was the final straw for you that I forgot to ask you about it?'

'The point of that phrase is that it takes a lot of other straws as well.'

'But the more I remember, the more I see that we didn't need to break up. I knew that from the moment I fell in love with you back in the autumn.'

'You didn't fall in love with me, Vaughan. You just loved the idea of being married.' She was cross now. 'And now I have to put up with everyone saying, "Oh poor Vaughan – he can't even remember his own wife!" But you always forgot your own wife – you just took your world view to its logical conclusion!'

The light had changed to green and a car behind was tooting impatiently. Maddy leaned out of the window. 'And you can fuck off as well!'

I was knocked back by the depth of her resentment, but had one more line I had prepared and polished and was ready to detonate.

'Have you any idea what it's like to lose your identity? And then to find out who you were, only to have that taken away from you too?' Frankly I was just grateful that we were no longer discussing whether or not I had called her an elephant.

'Do I know what it's like to lose my identity?!' she spat in disbelief. 'Are you serious?! Before I married you I was "Madeleine". Not "Vaughan's wife" or "Jamie's mum" or "Dillie's mum". I existed in my own right as *me*. I was Maddy the photographer who earned her own money doing something she loved. But then suddenly there was no time for that and nobody wanted to talk to *me* about me any more. It was all, "What does your husband do?" And, "How old are your children?" or, the double-whammy, "So will your kids go to the school where your husband teaches?" So do I know what it's like to lose my identity? Yes, I do. Every bloody wife and mother has known that since the dawn of fucking time—'

'Maddy, you're doing nearly seventy miles an hour in a thirty-mile zone—'

'And now I'm doing what I want for the first time I can remember! I'm going to Venice and I'm working towards an exhibition and I drive too bloody fast when I feel like it, and I don't have to compromise my entire existence any more.'

'I think that speed camera just flashed twice—'

'Yeah, well, I'll appeal, explaining that my ex-husband was being really fucking annoying. You think because you got a bang on the head I'm going to go, "Oh, that changes everything! It was all *my* fault . . ." It's not that simple. Didn't all the wiped files in your brain leave enough room for you to understand that? It's over – we are finished!'

I felt humiliated by her onslaught and clumsily tried to hurt her back.

'Don't try and chuck me, because I already chucked you.'

'What? Are we thirteen years old or something?'

'You suggested cancelling the divorce and sharing the house, but it was me who said no, so I finished with you.'

She pulled the car over to the kerb.

'Why don't you just get out here, before you make me run someone over? Or even better, get out here and then maybe I can run *you* over.' She gestured to the passenger door.

'Oh. But – couldn't you at least drop me where my bike is locked up?'

'Where's that?'

'At the hospital.'

It seemed that everything I said was somehow really annoying. I watched her speed off without glancing in her mirror. I stood there for a while in the winter drizzle and eventually crossed the road to catch the bus back in the opposite direction. When nothing came for ten minutes, I began to walk and soon the drizzle turned into rain. I picked a slightly broken umbrella from a litter bin. As soon as there was a small problem these days, you just threw it away and got a new one; umbrellas, computers, spouses: they were all casually disposable. But there must have been a time when a couple really valued their umbrella; when a snag or a tear was patched up and made good. Except I quickly realized that this broken umbrella was completely bloody useless and I dropped it in the next bin. Eventually I reached Chelsea Bridge with the hollow shell of Battersea Power Station towering behind me. The rain had eased slightly now, but I was so soaked that it had long ago ceased to matter. A huge rusty barge passed under the bridge and the dead drone of its engine boomed across the water.

Around my neck I could feel the dog tag that I wore in case my amnesia recurred. But so what if I lost my memory all over again? I might handle it all better second time around. This ID tag weighed a few grams but felt like a couple of kilos; it sparkled in the mirror and rubbed against my neck, a constant reminder of my broken brain. In a knowingly dramatic gesture, I pulled violently on the tag, but the chain didn't break, it just really hurt where it dug into my skin. Having looked around to check that no one had heard my squeal of pain, I now carefully undid the little clasp, looked for a moment at the emergency contact details and then cast it down into the swirling, murky Thames. I heard no sound and saw no splash. And then I just walked on to face the rest of my life without Madeleine.

Chapter 17

'I am never, ever, getting a mobile phone!'

'Yeah, you say that now . . .' laughs my fiancée.

'No – I know it for a fact,' I confirm. 'Cell phones are for twats. Come back to me in the year 2000 and even if I'm the last man in Britain without one, I guarantee you will never catch me shouting into a handset like those wankers on trains, who probably have a flat battery anyway, but are just trying to impress everyone else in the carriage.'

'It's different for a woman,' asserts Maddy. 'I might be stuck some-where at night and be worried about being mugged or something.'

'Oh, right, so you make sure you have something really worth nicking ringing away in your handbag like an advertisement! Sorry, but I can wait until I find a telephone box . . . as Gary said when he needed the toilet.'

This conversation came back to me twenty years later as I sat in the pub with Gary taking turns to show off the stupid apps on our iPhones. 'This one finds your location and tells you how many crack houses have been closed down in the area . . .'

'Hey – that's useful.'

'Or there's this one, where you can take a picture of yourself and then add moustache and sideburns to turn yourself into a seventies porn star.'

'I really don't know how we managed before these things came along . . .'

I had now officially moved out of Gary and Linda's flat, having felt increasingly less comfortable there as the weeks passed. Linda was now visibly pregnant, which at least reassured me that she was not just a nutter with a fetish for baby products.

'Gary, did you tell Vaughan about the new clothes I bought Baby?'

'*The* baby. No.'

'And I've bought a big sweatshirt that says on the bump, "Yes I am!"'

'And on the back it says "Mental".'

When I had popped back to leave a gift and return their keys, I found myself hovering on the step, unsure whether I should intrude on a screaming match that could be heard from the other side of the front door. Hoping it might blow over, I waited outside for a while, but eventually got so cold that I let myself in and tip-toed into the kitchen to find that there was no argument. Gary was alone, listening to an old fight on the iPod speakers while he was peeling some potatoes.

'Hi, Gary. Listening to your Greatest Hits tape?'

'Yeah. Fifteenth of August last year – it's an interesting one.'

From the expensive trendy speakers, a tearful Linda shouted, 'You never talk to me about anything! You always just go all quiet if I want to discuss things . . .'

'Because *this* is the alternative to quiet!' Gary's voice shouted back. 'You don't mean "talk", you mean "agree". You don't really want me to "talk", as in "put alternative point of view", you just want me to be like your friends who think it's somehow supportive to go along with every nutty thing you say.'

'Good come-back line, eh?' commented Gary. 'See, I was ready for her set-up. It's like the presidential debates – you've got to have your counter-arguments rehearsed.'

'Isn't the point to try to avoid the arguments?'

'No, you've got to have fights in a marriage. Otherwise what's the point of being together? What is it you see tattooed on people's fingers? "L.O.V.E." on one hand, "H.A.T.E." on the other. They're two sides of the same coin.'

'I don't hate Maddy.'

'You did before your brain wiped it all. You hated her because you loved her – that's how it works.'

'But why does it have to be "love" and "hate"? Why can't it be "compromise" and "mutual empathy"?'

'Tattooist would run out of fingers.'

It was a short walk to the pub – or it would have been, if we hadn't taken the route suggested by Gary's new 'Barfinder App'. In my defence, when I said I would never get a mobile phone, it was before you could do so many useful things with them. Gary and I generally used our phones to text one another, email, Facebook, though for some reason we never just rang one another up.

Many weeks had passed since Maddy and I had fought in the car and I had decided to make the most of my freedom and live in one of the world's great tourist locations at the perfect time of year. Which one was it to be: Paris in the spring, New England in the fall, or Streatham in March?

'So what's the High Class Hotel in Streatham like?' said Gary, returning from the bar with a couple of pints.

'Well, it's very high class, obviously. Except for the fact that it spells "class" with a "K". Oh, and "high" doesn't bother with the last two letters either.'

'Eye-catching . . .'

'But it's very cheap for me, because I'm the only guest who wants a room for more than half an hour. They have a sort of chambermaid pit-stop team changing the sheets after every punter all through the night.'

'Maybe you should make the most of the convenience. It must be a while . . .'

'What?'

'Since you had sex. When was the last time?'

'I don't know.'

'You don't know?!'

'Yes, I can't remember ever having sex. The experience has been completely wiped from my brain.'

Gary almost fell off his bar stool with laughter. 'Wow, you must have been really rubbish!' And then he laughed some more to the point where I stopped pretending to smile in the sporting manner expected of me and just sat there waiting for him to stop.

'Oh, my God, you know what that means, don't you? For all intents and purposes, that makes you a virgin!'

The pub jukebox had gone quiet at exactly that moment and now various regulars looked round to see who the virgin was.

'Don't be ridiculous. I've got two kids.'

'Makes no odds. You're a *born-again virgin*. You do not know what it is like to make love to a woman. Ergo, you're a virgo!' Gary was clearly really enjoying this and was now tapping his phone in search of suitable singles bars and pick-up joints.

'What are you doing?'

'We, my friend, are going to make a night of this. We are going to make a man out of you.'

Before we left, Gary popped to the toilets and came out with a small foil square which he thrust into my hand.

'What's that?'

'It's a condom. *Be prepared*. Wasn't that the Boy Scouts' motto?'

'I dunno, I never got my Casual Sex Badge . . .'

'Go on, take it. You'll thank me later. This is a once-in-a-life-time opportunity! Most men your age would love to be in your position.'

Had I not been so worn down, I might have put up more of a fight, but Gary's certainty about the rightness of his mission made him difficult to resist. I had no intention of sleeping with some stranger on the first date, but I agreed to humour Gary and see if meeting a few other interesting and sensitive ladies might prove to be the antidote for the disastrous crush I had briefly had on Madeleine.

'You all right, mate? You seem a bit down for a bloke who's about to lose his virginity.'

'Yeah – I dunno. I'm just finally coming to terms with it all. It seems like everything in my life was held up by the two tentpoles of Maddy and Vaughan.'

'Tentpoles?'

'Yeah – you know, I remember we had this old two-man tent which just needed two poles to hold it up. The ropes might have been pulling in all sorts of directions, but as long as both poles were there, the tent stayed up.'

'Er, well, our tent has this big bendy rod across the top, so I don't know what you're talking about. Are you thinking of going camping, then?'

'It doesn't matter . . . Without Maddy's pole, the whole tent of my life collapsed, didn't it – family, finances, home, my ability to do my job . . .'

Gary thought about this for a while and finally said, 'Well, you can probably get a replacement tentpole on eBay. But you don't have to sleep in a tent, mate – you can always come back and stay at our place, you know.'

I thanked him for his sensitive support and understanding and told myself that, though it would take time and patience and many false starts, there must be another woman out there somewhere. I was just slightly doubtful that I would find my own Miss Right here, inside Secret Whispers, the Gentlemen's Entertainment club to which Gary had led me. I stood on the threshold looking at the electric-blue outline of a naked lady jiggling her neon breasts.

'I can't go in here. What would Maddy think?'

'Vaughan, it's over. You said so yourself. This is just to get you in the mood. Look, they've got "Live Girls"!'

'What – as opposed to dead ones? Anyway, what about Linda?'

'She's not going to want to come to a bloody strip joint, now is she?'

'Just the two of you, is it?' grunted one of the bald-headed bouncers from behind a velvet rope.

'No, I can't go in there. It's . . . well, it's sexist.'

'Sexist? Where've you been, Vaughan? It's not sexist any more. Didn't you see that lap-dancer talking about it on the telly? It's empowering for the woman . . . to be in control of . . . something, something. I stopped listening to be honest because they cut away to her tits . . .'

'Are you coming in or what?' said the bouncer, dangerously.

'Don't you think it's sexist?' I asked him.

'Of course it's sexist, that's the whole bloody point. Sexy girls you want to have sex with.'

I was about to explain the nuanced difference in the etymology but Gary gave me a little shake of the head.

'But are the girls interested in the likes of me? I bought Olga flowers, I left chocolates in her dressing room, but she still goes home in the Porsche of the bastard club owner . . .' The bouncer didn't seem quite so intimidating any more, and rather than stand on the pavement consoling him, I followed Gary inside.

Fifteen minutes later we were back out on the pavement.

'Vaughan, you bloody idiot – what were you playing at?'

'I didn't do anything, honest. I was just trying to be polite.'

'First off, everyone knows you're not supposed to touch the girls.'

'But it seemed rude not to offer to shake hands . . .'

'It's a strip joint, not a bloody church fete. And you don't have to ask what she does for a living – she was doing it! Jiggling her breasts in the face of out-of-town businessmen is what she does for a living!'

'I'm sorry, I'm just not used to meeting women and I wasn't sure of the etiquette.'

'I can't believe I paid all that money for you to have a private dance in a booth and you get us both thrown out!'

I had indeed gone behind a crimson curtain for an 'intimate one-to-one encounter' with a sweet-looking Lithuanian lady called 'Katya'. Despite her wearing nothing but a leopard-skin thong, I had done my very best to maintain 100 per cent eye contact throughout and had found out some very interesting facts about her brothers and sisters back in the Baltic port where she had grown up.

'So why was she crying when she came out of the booth?'

'Well, I was just telling her about Maddy and the kids and everything. And then I mentioned my dad in hospital, and she said it was so sad, and that I was a sweet, kind man . . .'

'Bloody hell, Vaughan – you're just supposed to look at her tits.'

'Oh, not you as well! Honestly, Katya says that men in England are only interested in her for her body.'

'She's a bloody table-dancer, for God's sake! Not the Gender Equality Officer for Lambeth fucking Council!'

Gary was determined that the evening's mission should not be aborted, despite having to listen to my musings about equal opportunities tribunals as applied to lap-dancing clubs.

'You know, women are allowed to breastfeed their babies at work.'

'No . . .'

'Well, they are – it was a hard-fought battle. I just wondered if that included topless dancers?'

'What are you talking about?'

'Well, if Katya decided she wanted children, could the lap-dancing club legally sack her for getting pregnant? Or for bringing her baby into the workplace and then breastfeeding it while on stage?'

'Urgh! Is that what turns you on, then? 'Cos I'm sure there are websites—'

'No! It's just that seeing those women dancing naked up there – well, it made me think about employment legislation issues.'

'Yeah,' laughed Gary, 'well, that's men for you!'

Unsurprisingly, my condom stayed in its packet that night, despite Gary doing his best to re-create the cliché he'd seen in a hundred films where two men spot two unattached women in a bar and offer to buy them a drink. In six different pubs and wine bars, we found just one pair of women who were not with boyfriends or husbands and it turned out they were waiting for the rest of their book group to turn up.

'How old are you two anyway?' one of them had said to Gary, who came straight back with the unwitty retort 'Old enough!' This failed to make them want to abandon discussing their magic-realist novel and sleep with two middle-aged strangers instead.

But away from the over-eager, vicarious prowling of Gary, I did soon find myself in a situation where some women were interested in me. It was the night after school had broken up for Easter, and for once I accepted the invitation of the younger teachers to go to the pub after work. My work colleagues had always been cautious not to appear nosey about my medical condition, and generally tried to act as if nothing had ever happened. But after a few bottles of white wine, a group of female teachers finally broached the subject of just how much I could and couldn't remember.

'Well, I can't remember why my marriage broke up, so I'm feeling pretty sore about that, to be honest.'

'You poor thing . . . Can you remember your childhood and stuff like that?'

'Bits of it are coming back. I don't really remember my parents, or growing up or going to university or anything.'

'Maybe your mind has shut it out because you were abused?' suggested one particularly intense science teacher, who could usually be seen sitting in the staffroom reading misery memoirs with titles like *Cry Silent Tears Child 7*.

'Er – well, I don't think so.'

'Yeah, I've read about it. It's a self-defence mechanism so you don't recall being used as a sex slave by Catholic priests and then locked in the cellar as punishment by your abusive step-parents who fed you scraps from a dog bowl—'

'Jane, shut up, will you?' said Sally, the English teacher. 'But it must be weird to have no past. It sort of means you don't quite know who you are in the present.'

'Yeah, exactly. Though it's made me think none of us really knows who we actually are – we just invent a persona, put it out there and hope everyone else goes along with it.'

The others reflected on this profound thought for a moment.

'Or maybe you were a child prostitute?'

'Shut up, Jane!'

'Actually, my friend Gary says I'm a virgin because I don't remember having sex!' I joked, but this information sent an electric ripple through the crowd.

'What – you haven't had sex since your amnesia?'

'Well, no – my wife and I are separated.'

'And you don't remember having sex beforehand?'

'No – it's a complete blank!'

This bewitching detail instantly seemed to elevate me to the status of the most desirable man in all Europe. Suddenly my half-jokes were hilarious, my anecdotes were deeply fascinating, and any bit of fluff on my shoulder was urgently in need of brushing away as I was subjected to an hour of intensive flirting from a collection of beautiful and vivacious women.

They took it in turns to top up my wine glass and listen to my story about how I had spent a week in hospital not even knowing my own name. I told them about having no memory of my friends and family and then discovering my marriage had failed and that my father was dying.

'Ah, come here – you need a big hug,' said Jennifer, who helped late developers with special needs, which clearly included Mr Vaughan, as she held me close and rubbed my back for longer than might be considered just kind and supportive.

'Yes, you're badly in need of a cuddle,' agreed Caroline, who taught media studies and drama but seemed keen to expand to adult education, perhaps as soon as that very evening.

And I realized I was thoroughly enjoying the star treatment and the undivided attention of all these women, even though it felt alien and slightly scary to be this physically close to members of the opposite sex.

'And I have no memory of my own mother at all . . .'

Hug.

'And I'm trying to rebuild a relationship with my father from scratch, as he lies dying in his hospital bed . . .'

Hug.

'And, er . . . I had to re-learn all the history modules before I could teach Year Eleven their GCSE coursework.'

That one didn't seem quite so tragic, but they gave me a hug anyway.

The topography of the pub, coupled with the perseverance of one particular woman, meant that eventually I was no longer talking to a group of ladies but just to one, and a few drinks later it dawned on me that it was quite possible that I might spend the rest of the night with her. Suzanne was a tall, thin Australian brunette in her early thirties who worked in the PE and drama departments at the school. She had previously been a dancer, and it showed in her impeccable posture and penchant for woolly leggings. Where other women might have a cleavage, Suzanne's low top revealed a bony sternum that made you want to knock on it to see if it was as hard as it looked.

She had seemed fairly attractive at the beginning of the evening, but following several pints of beer and a bottle of red wine, I was even better able to appreciate her stunning good looks and seductive allure. The more she talked to me, the more convinced I became that I should sleep with her that very night. She taunted me with her provocative story of how she had introduced a B.Tech in dance for those not able to do the GCSE; her account of how she was unfairly passed over for the vacancy of Assistant Principal (Curriculum) seemed positively erotic.

'So you know you said you were going to Greenwich Market on Sunday?' I said. 'I have an *A–Z* back in my desk that you could borrow if you wanted.'

'I do own an *A–Z*!' she blurted out too quickly, immediately cursing herself as she realized that this had been offered up as her excuse to follow me out of the pub.

'Oh,' I said, seemingly defeated by the first hurdle. 'Oh, but my *A–Z* is, like, a ring-binder one,' I persevered, 'so you could actually keep the map open on the Greenwich page . . .'

'Oh, a *ring-binder A–Z*? No, my one isn't like that, no, that would be really useful, actually, yeah . . .'

''Cos then you wouldn't have to keep remembering the right page number . . .' I said, as if this was the most laborious, time-consuming business imaginable

'. . . and then opening the book to that page, blah blah blah – yeah, that can be a real drag . . .'

There was a moment's silence while we both wondered how to get round the second problem.

'The only thing is, my desk is really messy, so it might take me a while to find it.' I was concentrating hard now. 'So, if you like, you could finish your drink, with the rest of your department over there, and then I could meet you in school in about ten minutes?'

Kofi and John, the security guards, were well used to teachers coming in at all hours to work late on emails or collect piles of homework and thought there was nothing unusual in seeing me walk past the reception desk around midnight. They were friendly and respectful but they weren't going to let a senior member of staff distract them from the important business of sitting behind the counter all night reading the free local tabloid.

'Evening, Kofi. Evening, John!'

'Hello, Mr Vaughan, sir!'

'You working too hard, sir, isn't it?'

'Aha, ha, yes, work, work, work! Just picking something up, actually . . . Won't be long.'

I swiped my smart card to pass through the main doors and then headed up the stairs. It felt illicit to be in school so late. I had never heard the place so quiet; the cleaners had all gone home and the lights were dim and emitted a low buzz I hadn't noticed during the daytime. In the staff toilets I dragged a wet paper towel under my armpits and wetted down my hair. Looking at myself in the cracked mirror, I was excited and nervous that this could really be the night when it was finally going to happen.

In my form room I grabbed the requisite *A–Z* from my drawer. And now it could lead me to my first sexual experience: you just followed the route from talking to touching, kept going till you reached kissing and eventually that led you straight down to . . . And then I realized that I had no idea how you actually went from one to the next. Would I be any good at it? Would she think me ridiculous? Perhaps I should make an excuse and forget the whole idea? At that moment the beep of my phone made me realize how jumpy I felt. The text message read: 'Hve bought wine. Am in gym store. S.x'

Now I felt myself physically shaking. 'S.x' she had signed the text. It just seemed to put me in mind of something. This information changed everything. Suddenly I had been robbed of the journey home with her, the time to work myself up to the big moment. Suzanne had unlocked the gym store and was waiting for me in a room smelling of sweat and rubber. I was going to lose my virginity in the gym, like some jock in an American teen movie.

The door was slightly ajar, and Suzanne was sitting on a pile of exercise mats with a bottle of red wine and two plastic cups in front of her. The room was a chaotic jumble of five-a-side goals, folded-up ping-pong tables, netball poles and running hurdles, with coloured bibs and balls of every shape and size scattered around the place. Suzanne made sitting cross-legged look so natural – she was like a Buddhist statue, a yoga teacher, while my gangly legs refused to fold underneath me and my limbs grew stiff as they worked hard to make me look relaxed. In the end I perched myself on the edge of a low bench and drank my wine far too quickly, while we pretended to have a conversation.

'Are you okay, Vaughan?'

'Yeah, great, fine. Why?'

'Your leg is tapping, like, really fast.'

'Oh, sorry. There, it's still now. Do you want some more wine?'

'No, I've still got my first one.'

'I'm sure there are rules about members of staff drinking alcohol in the gymnasium after midnight,' I joked.

'Who's going to know? Kofi and John never leave the reception desk, and anyway, I can always lock the door!' She got up and did so with a suggestively raised eyebrow and I worried that I might have given out a slight whimper.

But still the Rubicon had to be crossed. We were still only chatting; we were just two work colleagues who had met in the pub earlier and officially were now just having one perfectly innocent drink in the locked store room of the gymnasium after midnight.

'It's incredible to think that you have no memory of having sex!' She chuckled as she sat beside me, looking directly into my eyes.

'Yeah, but you know, I got in the swimming pool and immediately remembered how to swim. And I got on a bike and I remembered that . . .'

'Oh, right, so you can still cycle and drive and everything?'

'Er, well, actually, no. I tried driving. And I demolished my neighbour's wall—'

Her insane laughter made me realize that she was even drunker than I was.

'Maybe I should give you a few driving lessons?' She laughed.

'Well, no, I think it's important to have a proper instructor, with dual controls and everything. Oh, I see—' The rest of my sentence was cut off at source as she kissed me full on the lips.

Her skin smelt quite distinctive: it was how the perfume counter in a department store might smell if it was moved into a pub. Her lips contorted around mine. I could smell hair lacquer. She was either wearing too much of it or had started drinking it when the bar had run out of vodka. 'Okay, we're doing this now,' I thought. 'I understand that this is one of the required stages along the way.' I wondered how many women I had kissed like this in my previous life. Gary had given me the impression that I had always been the shy one, that I had dismally failed to match his tally of conquests at university, and that I had not even looked at another woman after I had met Maddy.

Finally I broke off the kiss, ostensibly to have another glug of wine. I had tried my hardest, but had failed to keep Maddy out of my mind. This woman's body was so completely different from that of the mother of my children. And I knew which I preferred. Madeleine's body was softer than a man's; she had curving hips and breasts and tumbling red hair that wasn't cropped short for sport. And then I did something I did not feel proud of. As Suzanne launched her face at mine once more, I imagined it was Madeleine. I closed my eyes and kissed harder now, and eagerly pulled her close to me. Suzanne let out an approving grunt that I finally seemed to be getting into it, and I wrapped my arms around her and kissed her with passion and meaning, pretending she was the woman I had told myself that I was over.

She put her hand under my shirt and I felt Maddy's hand tenderly stroking my back. Maddy's other hand ran through my hair. Her lips were softer now, her skin smelt sweeter. I tried to put Maddy out of my head again. My mission this evening was to lose my virginity; it was a target I had set myself, like running a marathon or climbing a peak. I had to remain focused on my goal,

however uncomfortable I felt along the way. Despite the accumulating evidence, I still didn't dare believe it was actually going to
happen, and so a thrilling tingle of excitement shuddered through
me as each station was reached along the way. When I ran my
hand up inside the back of her top and my hand brushed against
the mystery mechanics of her bra, she invitingly suggested that I
made her 'more comfortable'.

Undoing a lady's bra – this was definitely the furthest I had
ever been! I was virtually being granted access to her breasts!
She wasn't screaming or turning round and slapping me in the
face – she actually wanted me to do it. Her bra-strap had three
separate hooks, but one of them seemed to have become caught in
a loop of cotton thread from which it refused to be disentangled.
I tried to keep kissing her as if there wasn't an awkward problem
going on at the end of my left hand, but there was no denying it
once the final sharp jerk at her back actually dislodged her face
from mine.

'Ow! What are you doing?'

'Sorry! Sorry – one of the little hooks seems to be caught in a
bit of material there . . .'

'Oh, just give it a tug – doesn't matter if you rip it.'

I yanked it firmly, but still the thread of cotton was stronger
than I was. 'Hang on a minute, I might be able to see the problem
properly if I put my reading glasses on . . .'

The sexual tension dipped more than a little as I reached for my
jacket and took out my glasses case, opened it up and eventually
had a good look at this little problem, like an old clockmaker
studying the inside of a pocket watch.

'There! Got the little monkey!' I finally announced. But I
feared that just advancing straight to her breasts now might seem
a bit perfunctory, so I just left the strap hanging loose across her
back and resumed kissing her again in the hope of building up
another head of steam.

I was surprised by how forward she was, effortlessly undoing my buttons to rub her hands over my chest. At each stage she was ahead of me. She wriggled out of her top and her bra in one deft movement and then moved to pull my shirt and vest over my head. I could see Suzanne's breasts now. Even though we hardly knew each other, she seemed to have no qualms about baring the upper half of her body to me. I tentatively went to touch them, like a wartime child who had never seen this particular exotic fruit before and wasn't sure how you approached it. She wriggled out of her tights and I thought I ought to follow suit by taking off my trousers. 'But would it look too forward if I took off my under-pants as well?' I thought. 'I mean, this might be as far as she wants to go – I don't want to come across as some creepy flasher exposing himself in the school gym store.'

'Have you brought something?' she suddenly enquired.

'Well, I've got some wine in my bag, but you already had a bottle, so—'

'No – a condom. Have you got a condom?'

That was definitely it, then. That surely was confirmation that sexual intercourse really was going to happen.

'Oh, sorry, yes, I've got one in my wallet.' And I reached across to my discarded trousers to find the little sachet that Gary had bought me a few days earlier. 'But that doesn't mean I was auto-matically expecting, you know . . .'

'What?'

'I wouldn't want you to think that I presumed you would have sex with me so I put a condom in my wallet—'

'Who gives a fuck? Quickly, just put it on . . .'

'Right, will do.'

I tugged at the foil, and for a few seconds was unable to open the packet. In my urgent desperation I attacked it with my teeth, and I bit the serrated edge of the foil, recoiling as the seal broke and I got a tiny taste of the sterile lubricant inside. Once the thing was in my hands I couldn't help but think how pathetic it was. 'All that fuss over this?' I thought. 'A wet bit of crumpled polythene?' But my disdain masked a certain amount of fear. I had no idea how to put the thing on. The Year 9 pupils had recently been shown how to put on a condom as part of their health and social care curriculum, but I had thought at the time that it might seem a little strange if I turned up to the lesson to find out myself.

Finally the deed was clumsily done and Suzanne and I were ready for proper intercourse to commence. Suzanne lay back below me and I was ready to make love to her. Actually 'love' was far too strong a word. I barely knew her, I quite liked her; I would be 'making quite like' to her. The pile of exercise mats had a musty rubber smell, and there was a piece of blackened chewing gum on the top one. And so, with a shift of my body and a clumsy grope to find my way, I became a man again. 'That Rudyard Kipling poem really should have included something about this bit,' I thought, as I focused on the achievement, the milestone that *this was it*!

'Whoa! Whoa! Slow down a bit, Vaughan – it's not a race to the finish!'

'Sorry . . . Is that better?'

'Nice and gentle – that's right.'

I felt a huge gratitude to this older woman for showing me the ropes, even if she was about a decade younger than me. But I couldn't help thinking that this whole business really was remarkably intimate; I barely knew Suzanne, and yet our two naked bodies were now interlocked in a secret room.

I did my best to go slowly, to be considerate and attentive, with occasional tender stimulation of various parts of her body, even if Suzanne had never particularly thought of her elbow as an erogenous zone. I had got into a rhythm now, and felt pretty much in control. Unfortunately my foot seemed to have got tangled in the netting of a folded-up five-a-side goal that was propped against the wall, but I wouldn't let that stop me. I was actually having sex; this was what it felt like! That foot was not shaking free, however much I tried to wiggle it about. I looked around to see that it was completely wrapped up in the netting and I wondered whether I might be able to just leave it there until this was over. While still ostensibly focusing on Suzanne, I gave one final tug and suddenly the whole metal goal frame was pulled from where it was leaning and came crashing to the floor with a deafening clatter.

'Jesus Christ, what was that?!' She had leapt up in fear of being crushed by falling metal bars, and I was horrified that she had pulled herself away from me.

'Sorry! Sorry! The goal net was tangled in my foot. Sorry, did I make you jump?'

'Do you think the guys will have heard that from the reception desk?'

'I doubt it. Don't they normally have the radio on? Shall we just carry on?'

'Did they have a radio on? I don't remember them having a radio on.'

'It didn't make that much noise,' I claimed, despite the ringing in my head and the fear that my eardrums might now be bleeding. 'Shall we just go back to where we left off?'

But the moment had gone. Whereas before her drunkenness had made her adventurous and provocative, now she was excessively paranoid and I was appalled to see her getting dressed.

'We could get in big trouble,' she suddenly decided. 'I have a professional duty to look after this equipment,' she continued, which seemed a bit rich from someone who had minutes earlier demonstrated her professional duty to the exercise mats by having sex on them.

It was over before it was finished. I had seen an 18 certificate but had left before the end; I had smoked pot but hadn't inhaled; I had learned to put on a condom, but it hadn't really been required. Probably best not to save it for another time, I thought, as I shoved it in a tissue inside my jacket pocket. 'Did this count?' I wondered. I had had sex with a woman, but there had been no climax. Was that enough to admit me into adulthood? Yes, that still definitely counted, I concluded. I had broken my duck, I had lost my second virginity. Now I could look Mick Jagger in the eye.

The two of us got dressed and there was no pretence that we ought to spend the rest of the night together or anything soppy like that. She suggested I should leave first and she would tidy up in her store room and leave ten minutes later, so that the blokes on the door didn't suspect anything. I gave her a peck on the cheek and thanked her probably too much, and then headed out into the main part of the gym, still feeling like a super-hero. There in the middle of the wooden floor was an abandoned football. I saw the goal at the far end of the room, and I took a short run-up and kicked the ball with all my might, watching it curl with perfection into the corner of the goal. And I raised both arms in the air in triumph. 'He shoots! Goooooaaaallll!'

I was feeling extremely pleased with myself. I was the cock of the walk, I was the king of the world, I was the Six Million Dollar Man. I was still feeling mightily proud when I said goodnight to Kofi and John, who seemed a little strange towards me, and red around the eyes as if they had been crying or something. Or laughing, perhaps. And I looked up to the small security monitor above the desk, to see a black-and-white image of Suzanne just putting her coat on in the gym store, and then I heard them burst out laughing again as I slunk out of the main door.

Chapter 18

When Maddy was particularly fed up with the inner city, she would occasionally buy a property-porn magazine called *Coastal Living*. It featured sun-bleached seaside cottages where the only item on the kitchen table was some freshly gathered samphire or an artistically positioned shell. Freckly children in stripy T-shirts with sand on their knees ate crusty brown bread grabbed from pale-blue kitchen sideboards.

I wondered if there should be a special lifestyle magazine for where I found myself now? *Vaughan divides his time between his cosy bedroom in Streatham's Hi Klass Hotel and the en-suite bathroom, where he is cultivating a range of black and green moulds on the non-slip bathmat. 'I love living in a cheap South London hostel used mainly by prostitutes,' says Vaughan, 39. 'From my grubby fourth-floor window I have a perfect view of the huge extractor ducts of the kebab shop opposite.' Vaughan says that having no cooking or washing facilities helps keep life simple, and he likes to remember the various takeaway meals he has enjoyed by keeping the congealing cartons piled up all around the room.*

In my imagination, the Easter holidays had loomed in the

distance as a vast tract of unlimited free time during which I would get completely on top of all my marking, lesson plans and personal admin, while also grabbing some quality time with my children and visiting my still hospitalized father. It was not until I emerged from under the cheap hotel bedsheets to glance at my bedside clock on Wednesday afternoon that I accepted I might be letting the opportunity slip by. All my good intentions had presumed a degree of energy and enthusiasm for life that seemed to have been mysteriously drained from me. Both my laptop and mobile phone had run out of battery power long ago. It would have been no effort to plug in their chargers, had my own batteries not been so low as well.

I was no more unshaven on Wednesday than I had been on Tuesday – it seemed as if even my stubble couldn't be bothered any more. I looked so unhealthy that I decided I ought to eat some vegetables, so I rooted around among the old curry cartons and found the three-day-old polythene bag of shredded lettuce that had come with the chicken tikka masala.

I turned on the television again. I flicked to the 24-hour News Channel, but extra news was still stubbornly refusing to occur to fill the additional allotted time. I watched part of an American daytime show that featured a couple who were divorcing because they'd found out they were brother and sister. At least that was one problem Maddy and I had never had. Well, as far as I knew anyway, though if Jean turned out to be my mother that might just be enough to finish me off.

I occupied just one side of the double bed, as I always did. I'd only just realized that I instinctively preferred to take the left half of the mattress, subconsciously leaving the other side free. But now I was staring at a piece of paper that would do away with the need for such considerations.

I had verbally agreed to all the terms in this legal document some time ago; now all I had to do was sign the embossed papers where indicated, in front of a witness, and return it in the expensive-looking stamped addressed envelope and my marriage would be history. It was just a five-second task of signing my name, yet during four whole days of doing nothing I had still not found the time to do it. I had placed the document on the rickety bedside table, but now clambered off the crumpled blankets and hid it out of sight amid the clutter on the other side of the room. It wasn't just the final act of formally ending the marriage that crippled me, but that extra little humiliation of having to ask a witness to watch me sign the form.

I had wondered if could ask the fat man from the former Soviet republic of Something-astan who ran the Hi Klass Hotel. Except that I sensed he rather resented the way that I paid the nightly tariff for my room and then proceeded to sleep in it for the entire night. Every time I saw him, I felt guilty that I wasn't sheepishly vacating my room fifteen minutes after arrival. I could always ask one of the ladies who regularly entertained clients here, I thought. *Witness Occupation: Prostitute*. That would look impressive.

Overhearing people having sex did not particularly lighten my depressed state. Occasionally I thought about that moment in the gym store, but it had clearly left me feeling empty. More significant than the physical experience of the night with Suzanne was the recovery of my memories of sex with Madeleine. These weren't summoned up to be titillating or erotic, but prior to recovering them it was almost as if I'd been ending a marriage that had never been consummated.

I remembered that Maddy talked during sex. Not in the way that women are scripted in male fantasies – she didn't groan an ecstatic 'Oh, that is amazing! Oh yes, yes!' That wasn't really Madeleine's style. No, on the particular night of passion that came to mind we were in the final throes of sexual intercourse and, as I grunted and grimaced with Maddy lying beneath me, she suddenly said, 'Oh, I must remember to give in the form for Dillie's school trip . . .'

I recalled that she had often done this. When I'd imagined that she was totally consumed in the ardour and intimacy of the moment, she would volunteer the information that she had booked the car in for a service, or would wonder out loud whether she could move that chiropodist's appointment from Monday to Wednesday. I doubt that these were lines you'd ever hear in a pornographic movie: a beefy, oiled-up gym instructor having athletic sex with a silicon-breasted peroxide blonde, who in the moment of climax mumbles, 'Oh no – I forgot to post Mum's birthday card!'

But I suppose what Maddy had really been saying was that she was very comfortable with me; that she knew me really, really well. That's how used to one another we had been – completely familiar with our partner's quirks and idiosyncrasies. Like the two trees in our garden that had grown side by side, their trunks intertwining over the decades to accommodate and support one another.

And then I recovered another memory. It was an argument that had begun with Maddy wanting to throw out a plastic shower curtain and me insisting that it just needed cleaning.

'Just needs cleaning by me, is what you mean,' she says. 'Because it would never occur to you to clean a shower curtain.'

'But a shower curtain doesn't need cleaning; it has a shower every day.'

'Yeah, you take a shower every day and I have a bath, and you said you would clean the shower, so why didn't you clean the curtain as well?'

'Because I forgot, okay? I forgot to clean the curtain when I cleaned the shower. I forgot, just like everything else that you endlessly point out that Vaughan forgets . . .'

But the argument wasn't about that at all: it was actually about sex as well. The previous evening I had suggested that we had intercourse and she had said no, and we had not so much as touched one another for weeks, and I felt angry and frustrated.

'You notice a bit of grime on the curtain, but you don't even notice your own husband,' I say, escalating the conflict.

'What?'

'You care more about a bit of black mould in the shower than you care about me.'

'Why are you being so horrible?'

'Oh, look, the lid is off the toothpaste because Vaughan forgot to put it back on!' and I run to the toothpaste and make a big show of replacing the lid. 'Ooh, look, the toilet seat is up because Vaughan forgot to put it down.' And I slam down the toilet lid. 'Well, it's better than forgetting you're supposed to be married to someone!'

I was able to place this incident to about a year before we had separated. The drama churned over in my head and I felt ashamed that my sexual frustration had translated into anger in such an extreme manner. But, with hindsight, I now understood that sex is so important in keeping a marriage together that it really shouldn't be left to husband and wife alone. There are people who come round to check your burglar alarm and window locks; we have health checks and visits to the dentist, and an engineer who makes sure the gas boiler is safe. There really ought to be someone from the council who pops round regularly to make sure that married couples are having sex every weekend. 'Hmm . . . I see there's a two-week gap at the beginning of the month. I'm going to have to log that in the system, and it means you will receive an official letter warning you of the dangers of neglecting physical intimacy.'

The document from my ex-wife's solicitors had to be signed. I owed it to Maddy. I pulled on my shoes and threw on a jacket and quickly checked myself in the mirror before I presented myself to the outside world. Then I took my jacket off again, removed my shoes and went to shower and shave. I gave the bottom of the shower curtain a wipe down before I was finished.

My reintegration into civilization seemed to go unnoticed by the rest of society: evening shoppers passed me by, busy commuters were more focused on their own journeys home than noticing the lonely man forcing himself to keep walking down the high street despite having no particular place to go. It reminded me of my time before I found my true identity, the sense of separateness from the rest of the world, as if everyone else knew the part they were playing but I'd never been given a script. Inside my jacket pocket, however, was the death certificate for my marriage that I had set myself the task of posting. In my head I was scrolling through all the people who could witness my signature, but somehow I didn't want to admit my final failure to any of my friends.

I walked two miles and found myself at the front door of the only person I felt I could ask. I had never been here before, but I had memorized the address from when I had worked in the school office. Suzanne, the dance teacher, seemed very surprised and a little alarmed to see me.

'Vaughan! What the bloody hell are you doing here?'

'Sorry not to call – my mobile's flat. I came to ask a favour.'

'Er – it's not very convenient . . .' She glanced back down the hallway.

'Who is it?' said a gruff man from inside the flat.

'Just someone from school.'

Despite Suzanne's acute embarrassment, I persuaded her that this wouldn't take more than a minute, and I was whisked into the kitchen where I produced the divorce agreement for her to witness and sign. The nature of the favour threw her yet further.

'Vaughan,' she whispered, 'I don't want you to divorce your wife just because of what happened the other night . . .'

'No, I was going to divorce her anyway.'

'I mean, Brian and I are very happy. I can't leave him for you, Vaughan, just like that – just because of one naughty little fling.'

'No, really. I just needed someone to witness my signature, and I was just passing, so . . .'

'You won't tell anyone what happened, will you?' She glanced nervously in the direction of the lounge where Brian was watching a home improvement programme. 'I mean, I was drunk and you were drunk and it didn't mean anything, did it?'

Her name was hastily scribbled and signed. It was barely legible, but the deed was done.

I stood before the pillar box, nervously double-checking that the envelope was properly sealed and that the stamps would not fall off. Then, in a short private ceremony, The Future formally surrendered to The Past and I put the letter in the box. Rather than return to my dismal hotel room, I picked up a free newspaper and went into a high-street 'tavern'. The pub had got a signwriter to advertise its many attractions in old-fashioned Shakespearean script. This worked quite well for 'Ye Real Ales' and 'Ye Fine Foods' but looked less convincing for 'Sky Sports in High Definition'. Even with the sound turned down, the large TV screen was impossible to ignore, as the silent presenters on Sky News searched for the least appropriate footage to match the song playing on the pub jukebox. Images of floods in Bangladesh served as an edgy rock video for Lady Gaga. The remains of a roadside bomb in Afghanistan added an extra poignancy to a new power ballad from the latest winner of *The X Factor*. The info-bar scrolled the changes in the stock markets or Europa League football scores as I finished a third packet of pork scratchings and tied the foil packets into tiny knots. A couple came into the pub hand in hand, and I was disgusted by such an ostentatious public display of sexual passion.

In the toilets I paused for a while to stare at the craggy face of the man whose life I had inherited. 'You stupid idiot!' I shouted at my reflection. 'You only get one life, and you completely screwed your one up, didn't you, eh?'

Perhaps the drink had made me slightly aggressive, but right now the only person I wanted to fight was myself. 'You don't know your own kids! Your wife hates you. You can't even remember people's names, you senile bastard—'

Then a slurred voice spoke up from behind a locked cubicle door. 'Who is this? How do you know so much about me?'

I set off to walk the length of Streatham High Road, the night lit briefly by the blue strobe of a passing police car. Alcohol used to make me excited and up for a laugh, but these days it just made me really drowsy. Throw a party for people in their forties and too much alcohol just makes everyone want to go home and go to bed. 'Oh wow, look at all this vodka! I'm going to drink a whole bottle and get completely . . . tired.' 'Yeah, and then let's have a load of tequila slammers so we get like, really, really *sleepy*.'

Walking down the wide, uneven pavement, I found myself over-compensating for the sudden appearance of a litter bin and, in trying to give it a wide berth, I nearly staggered into some bike racks where bicycle frames could be locked up if you didn't want their wheels any more. Finally I skipped up the steps to the hotel front door, displaying a certain casual aplomb, I felt. But aiming the front-door key accurately at the uncooperative lock was a more demanding challenge and I missed the keyhole several times, unaware that I was using the wrong key anyway.

I leaned against the unlocked door and discovered it just needed pushing open, then I was surprised to see someone sitting in the chair in the corridor. Occasionally this seat was occupied by punters waiting for a lady, or a lady waiting for a room, and in my drunken confusion I could not work out why my ex-wife Madeleine was now working as a prostitute at the Hi Klass Hotel in Streatham.

'Maddy? What the bloody hell are you doing here?'

'Hello, Vaughan,' she said calmly.

She looked deadly serious, and now that I had worked out that she was here to see me, her unexpected appearance at this time of night, looking as ragged and red-eyed as this, alarmed me.

'Look, I'm sorry,' I blustered. 'I posted it today. I had to get a witness signature and so I asked, well, I asked a teacher at school, but I didn't get round to it till today, but I have sent it off, I promise—'

'It's not that. We've been trying to ring you, to find out where you were . . .'

'What? What is it?'

'Your father. It happened in his sleep. I don't think he suffered. I'm so sorry.'

I could almost feel my body sobering up as I stood there trying to comprehend the shocking but not at all shocking news that my father had died.

'But – that's not fair,' I heard myself blurting out. 'That's just not fair.'

'I'm really sorry, Vaughan,' repeated Maddy, but I felt too numb to respond. My grief was for something I hadn't had. He'd died before I had got to know him properly or before memories of him had returned. Was that selfish of me, I worried – shouldn't I have automatically loved my father on first meeting, and now grieve him as any child would mourn a lost parent?

'Oh. God. That's so sad . . .' Maddy and I just stood there for a moment looking at one another. And then she put her arms out to embrace me and I accepted the invitation. Now my emotions were really confused. Just as I had been getting to know my dad, my only living parent had been taken from me. I was angry that my stupid broken brain had denied me the chance to know him better. But mixed in with all of this was the realization that the woman I had given up on was hugging me, and it felt right. And tentatively, I put my arms around her and hugged her back. Was it wrong to *like* this?

'It's what he would have wanted,' I told myself.

Chapter 19

It was a touching and selfless gesture. That Maddy could put all her pain aside to comfort her former adversary in his moment of loss would have been enough to restore anyone's faith in human nature. The only slight blemish upon the tenderness of the scene was the hotel manager munching on a kebab and saying, 'You no fuck hoe in lobby. You pay for room. Condom three pounds extra.'

Madeleine did not take the proprietor up on his charming offer. Instead she suggested that I should come and stay in the spare room at home, so that I didn't wake up on my own and could be with the children in the morning.

In the front room that I now remembered us decorating and furnishing down the years, we stayed up for an hour or two, sharing a bottle of wine and talking about my dad. She told me of holidays when he had joined us down in Cornwall, and the enormous patience he had always shown with the children. There was no friction in the air; in fact, looking at her sitting opposite me on the sofa, her legs tucked up underneath her, I couldn't understand how I had ever not been in love with her. Eventually I took a moment to visit the toilet and, looking at the family pictures on the wall in there, I recovered another memory. I was regaining them every day now, and this one was of a trip to central London with the kids when they were roughly the age they appeared in these photos.

We are in Madame Tussaud's. There must have been an era when a visit here was a great family treat, but as far as our own kids are concerned, shuffling along in crowded rooms looking at waxy replicas of has-been celebrities has not been their idea of a thrilling day out. The display of the British Royal Family has singularly failed to compare with the excitement of the Nemesis ride at Alton Towers; in fact, I think it is actually a bonus for our kids that a couple of the figures have been removed for refurbishment. After a disappointing and increasingly fractious hour or so, we are close to abandoning the whole trip, when a little light goes on in my wife's eye. I recognize that mischievous glint – I'd last seen it when the make-up lady in the department store asked her if she would like to try the coconut cream and a slightly demented-looking Maddy said okay and started eating it. Just as a group of tourists is about to join us in the room, Maddy steps over the velvet rope and strikes up a pose on the empty pedestal, where she maintains a suitably blank yet regal expression as she stares into the middle distance.

Little Dillie and Jamie are already thrilled at her mischievousness, when some foreign tourists join me as I stare hard at the apparent wax model on the pedestal.

'Dad – who is this model of?' says Dillie, pointedly, hoping we can make Mum start laughing.

'Oh, you recognize her, darling. That's Princess Rita. Of Lakeside Thurrock . . .'

Maddy's expression does not alter one iota, though I know she must be bursting inside.

'Excuse me, what relation would she be to the Queen?' asks an American lady, who is now studying the impressively life-like figure in front of us.

'Princess Rita? Oh, well, she's not actually related to the Queen.

Rita is the bastard offspring of the Duke of Edinburgh and, um, Eleanor Rigby,' I explain, as Jamie emits a strangulated coughing sound.

'Eleanor Rigby? Like the Beatles song?'

'Yeah, that's why she was so lonely – the Duke wouldn't leave the Queen for her. He couldn't afford the alimony.'

'Oh, I never knew – that's really interesting! Thank you.'

And then as they walk away their teenage daughter lets out a scream.

'Dad! Dad! Princess Rita just winked at me!'

'No, honey – you're imagining things.'

'I swear it did! It just winked when I looked at it. It's coming to life, Dad! The waxworks are coming to life!'

When I rejoined her in the kitchen, Maddy was putting the wine glasses in the dishwasher and turning off the downstairs lights.

'When did you stop doing stupid stuff?' I asked her.

'Stupid stuff?'

'You know – pretending to be a statue at Madame Tussaud's. Making your own announcements on the train tannoy. You were always making us laugh with daft stunts like that, but somehow they just sort of petered out.'

'Yeah, well . . .' She shrugged. 'People change, don't they? I think life probably knocks the fun out of us all in the end.'

Ten minutes later I was lying in the dark in the poky spare room, reflecting on what she had said and thinking of the last time I had seen my father, still clinging on to life, but a shadow of the man I had seen in the photos. 'Is that how people die?' I wondered. 'Incrementally?' My father's life may have ended that day, but he had gradually died over the course of the previous months. Madeleine's spirit had diminished since our marriage had crashed; a part of us both must have died with every injury and disappointment.

This little room where I now lay had once been Dillie and Jamie's nursery and the smell took me right back to when my children were tiny. Little luminous stars still glowed on the ceiling from where they had long ago been stuck by a younger, optimistic father. I stared at the random constellations, thinking how many years it had taken for the light from those stars to reach me here and now; the centuries that seemed to have passed in between me putting up the stickers for my newborn baby and this lonely moment in the visitor's bed in my own house, watching their glow slowly fade.

I recalled how delighted Maddy was when she saw what I'd done for our new baby, how I'd proudly pointed out the little crescent moons and tiny spaceships. And how we both laughed as I confessed to having started trying to re-create famous constellations, and then had given up and just stuck them up at random. 'Those stars there are in the shape of the Plough. Not the constellation, but the pub on Wandsworth Road.'

I remembered, a few years later, how thrilled and entranced Dillie was when I'd shown her the luminous stars one winter's night, and we both just lay on our backs in the dark, whispering and pointing at the magic of the tiny lights on the ceiling.

Now I was surprised to feel an emotional geyser building up inside me. I felt the tightening of my throat, the surprisingly autonomous flush of moisture across my eyeballs. So much had been lost, so many moments gone for ever. I pictured the old man I had got to know on the hospital bed, misty-eyed, with his saggy lizard neck. And I thought of Dillie and Jamie visiting him, and that final hug they gave him, understanding that he would soon be dead.

Now I wept out loud at the simple sadness of it all – at the hollow sense of loss: disappearing childhoods, irrecoverable decades; a family I had taken for granted but one that I now understood could not be there for ever. I checked myself, wiping my face on the pillow case. Then another wave came over me and I cried again, turning my face to the wall as if ashamed of myself.

And when at last I was quiet, I could hear Maddy crying on the other side of the bedroom wall.

In the morning I hugged my daughter long and hard as she wept for the loss of her grandfather. Dillie wore her emotions on her sleeve, quite literally, judging by the amount of snivel she had wiped on to her cardigan. Her brother, on the other hand, attempted to play the stoic young male, but he too crumbled when I asked him for a hug. Maddy herself could not help but break down as she watched them standing there in the middle of the big kitchen where they had learned to crawl and walk and talk and read and, now, mourn. Then the group hug was joined by the excited dog, who jumped up and wrapped his front paws around my jeans and started to hump my leg.

'Ah, that's so thoughtful of you, Woody,' I said, as the children pulled away. 'You could sense that what Dad really needed now was to have his leg humped by a golden retriever.' Their crying turned into laughter. 'Perhaps you could come to the funeral and do that to some of Granddad's old RAF colleagues?'

The kids switched from grieving for their grandfather to eating their cornflakes in front of the television, and Maddy and I tidied up in the kitchen. It was strange how all the ordinary things still had to be done. Maddy's mobile phone got a text with a slightly too comical ringtone, considering the message was about a bereavement.

'Ah – okay.'

'What is?'

'Oh, it doesn't matter . . .'

'Ralph?'

'Yes. But – he was just saying he was sorry to hear about your father.'

'Okay.'

'He said he lost his own dad a few years back so he knows what you're going through.'

'I doubt that very much.'

'Sorry, I shouldn't have mentioned it.'

I wiped down the surfaces, perhaps a little too vigorously.

'You know, it's okay. I don't expect you to like him.'

'No, he was fine.' I pouted.

'I really don't mind if you have an issue with him.'

'Okay. I just thought he wasn't very "can do", that's all.'

'He wasn't very "can do"? What are you talking about?'

'He just came across as one of those people who sees the problems first.'

A moment's puzzled bemusement was followed by the penny dropping and then Maddy laughed out loud. 'Because he foresaw difficulties in building some massive dam? He's not very "can do" because he thought it might be difficult to get Italy and Israel and France and Russia and everyone else to agree to Vaughan's pet project?'

'Russia wouldn't be involved,' I said. 'It doesn't have a Mediterranean coastline.'

'Well, maybe it will after global warming . . .'

'You see, you're on my side! You're already thinking big. Ralph's the one with the negative attitude.'

Without realizing it, we were unloading the dishwasher in tandem, Maddy doing the glasses, me doing the cutlery as I had always done. I cleared away the breakfast things, instinctively knowing that the leftover cereal went in the dog's bowl and the tea bags went in the compost bin. Madeleine could have been angered by my criticism of Ralph, but to my annoyance she actually found it quite amusing. Still, the subject of her new partner hung in the air and I felt the need to show a little humility.

'I posted the settlement, by the way.'

'Yeah, you said. Blimey! Since when did you pick the little bits of food out of the plughole?'

'What? Oh, I got a memory back that you hated it that I never did that, so now I try and do it even if I'm on my own.' I was pleased that she had noticed. 'So, is Ralph going to move in here?' I said, while I could get away with asking. 'I mean, have you got a timetable in your head for it or anything?'

Maddy let out a long sigh. 'Oh, I don't know. Sometimes I think it would have been so much easier to be a lesbian . . .'

'What does that mean? Ralph's not a lady-boy as well, is he?'

'No, it's just that . . . It doesn't matter . . .'

I hoped that I was coming across as a good listener, when in fact I was just being nosey. 'It's okay, you can tell me. I was married to you for fifteen years.'

'All right, I'll say it. We had a big fight. He's filled his gallery with these awful abstract things by this new painter. And, well, I think it's just because he fancies her.'

'Oh dear,' I lied.

'Maybe I was never meant to be with anyone. I'll be one of those old ladies with seventeen cats and an injunction from the council about the smell coming out of my kitchen.'

Inside I was surprised to feel as if I wanted to punch the air in triumph, but I remained determined just to carry on as normal, finishing the routine cleaning up around the sink like any modern, house-trained man.

'Vaughan, it's okay – you don't have to sort the bits from the sink into compost and recycling . . .'

She told the kids to get dressed once *Friends* had finished, unaware that on this channel that meant some time later in the week, and I announced that I should be on my way. I thanked her for letting me stay the night so I could tell the kids the sad news myself, and added that it had been good to have someone to talk to. Maddy avoided eye contact, busying herself with wiping some glasses. She was slightly embarrassed that she had revealed more than she had intended, and wanted to leave me with a clear signal that we both had to move on.

'You know what you need, Vaughan? You need a girlfriend.'

Even though I had my coat on, I began stacking the dirty plates into the dishwasher.

'Hmm . . . I don't think I could handle the emotional involvement. Maybe I could house-train some of those cats you're going to get and work up from there.'

'It doesn't have to be Miss Right straight away. Just someone to have a fling with, someone to make you realize that there are plenty of other women out there.'

'What – you'd actually like me to have a fling?'

'Well, it's nothing to do with me, is it? But I think it might help you move on.'

I think I must have been enjoying the attention, because now I could not resist sharing my secret with her.

'Actually, there was this woman from school . . .'

'What woman?'

'Suzanne. She's a dance teacher, Australian.'

'What? And you fancy her?'

'Actually, in the cold light of day, I can't say I do, really . . .'

She had stopped the housework and just stood there looking at me.

'But I had a one-night stand with her. Like you said – just to try to help myself move on.'

'Oh.'

Suddenly it seemed her eyes didn't know where to look.

'It was last week. It was just a one-off.'

'A dance teacher? Skinny, is she?'

'Yeah, not really my type.'

'What's that supposed to mean?'

'It doesn't mean anything – I just don't much care for that particular look, that's all.'

'Oh, well, that's . . . there's some news, then. That I didn't know.'

The dirty mugs were being placed in the dishwasher with more force than was strictly necessary.

'I mean, I wasn't seeking it or anything. Suzy just happened to come along.'

'Oh, she's called "Suzy"? It's all right – *I*'m stacking the dishwasher. It doesn't take two of us.' And we both pretended not to notice that she had just chipped Kate Middleton's face on the Royal Wedding mug.

Walking towards the bus stop my breath steamed and the wind felt cold on my cheeks, but it was a crisp, clear day and the rest of the busy world seemed not to have noticed that my father had died or that Maddy's demeanour towards me had changed. Above everything else, I was still consumed by a sense of resigned sadness for the death of the old man I had got to know in the hospital. It was almost as if, during our talks together, this old man had become something of a father figure to me.

Other cultures have developed traditions for coping with death, which involve a week of communal mourning – singing, dancing and religious observance. Western society, on the other hand, has decided that what the bereaved family really need is a huge in-tray of complicated admin. Suddenly I was responsible for all sorts of legal duties and organizational tasks that took me the entire week. I learned that I was the executor of the will, that it fell to me to register the death, book the cremation, choose the hymns and decide on the appropriate number of *vol au vents* and sliced carrots for the hummus dip.

Who was I supposed to invite to the funeral anyway? I settled on a tactic of writing to all the names that had not been ominously crossed out of my father's address book. There was a very charming letter back from John Lewis explaining that there was no actual 'John Lewis' as such, and that no one from the department store would be able to come to the funeral. They sent me their condolences all the same.

And so a couple of weeks after his death I stood at the top of the sweeping drive of the 1960s suburban crematorium, ready to fulfil my duty as the chief mourner and only son of Air Commodore Keith Vaughan CB. The fact that my father had some special letters after his name had been news to me, although it was not an award I had ever heard of. It turned out a CB was like a CBE, but shorter. It meant that, for services to the Royal Air Force, my father had been declared a 'Companion of the Bath', which was an ancient honour bestowed by the king in the Middle Ages when it didn't sound quite so gay. There was even a little medal, which I had found in the pitifully small shoebox of personal items that had been forwarded from the old people's home. This box now lived under my bed in case I ever needed an Air Force service book, a wind-up watch or some regimental cufflinks.

I had paid the extra to be driven in a black car to the crematorium, just so that I had someone to talk to. Now the previous service had finished and the family was filing out of the chapel. They had obviously had a fantastic time inside, because they emerged laughing and joking and slapping each other on the back; a death in the family had obviously cheered them up no end.

The first of my guests to turn up were a couple of elderly ladies from the rest home where my dad had spent his last years. They looked the building up and down as if they were researching a venue for their own cremation. They shook my hand in a theatrically respectful manner and went inside to check out the action on the coffin-rollers. They were followed by a reasonably young man in an RAF uniform, who didn't stop to talk and marched straight past without making eye contact. Then my heart lifted as I saw Maddy and the children approaching. The kids looked so smart, and seemed a little nervous as to what expression might be appropriate.

'Are you okay, Dad?' asked Dillie, giving me a hug.

'Yeah – I'm fine.'

Maddy told me that I didn't have to stand outside waiting for everyone and, once her parents had arrived, we all went inside to take our seats.

'What did you tell the children, dear?' whispered Maddy's mother, conspiratorially, as they led the way inside.

'I told them their grandfather had died, Mum.'

'So that's the story, is it? Shall we all stick to that?'

Our host for the afternoon seemed to be somewhere between the sympathetic parish priest and the bored bloke in the hi-vis jacket who directs the traffic on to the car ferry. He led the traditional mumbling of the hymns and did an impressive piece of reading from the Bible, in which he managed not to change the emphasis or note of his voice by one iota for the entire duration of the passage. I hadn't found time to meet and discuss exactly how I wanted this funeral to proceed, so had requested in an email that we would require 'the standard traditional service; I'll just go along with whatever is the most popular format that you normally do.' In retrospect, I should have checked exactly what this involved. Even if I had stopped to think about it for a moment, I would perhaps have guessed that this would include a speech from a close relative.

We sat down following the second hymn and my mind drifted off as he muttered another incomprehensible prayer, but then I could have sworn I heard the vicar say, 'And now Keith's only child will say a few words about his father.' No – surely I imagined he just said that? But there was the vicar, stepping aside from the pulpit, gesturing to me to come up and share a lifetime of recollections of my dad, unaware that I had none. I glanced around and saw the elderly mourners looking at me in antici-pation, nodding to me that the highlight of the service was indeed about to begin. I made eye contact with Maddy, who looked slightly panic-stricken on my behalf, but who was just as power-less to get me out of this impossible predicament.

'So,' he repeated, with a firm smile, 'Vaughan, if you would—'

'Oh no, I er . . . I can't. I mean . . .' I mumbled from my seat in the front row.

But I could almost feel the waves of expectation coming from the congregation. For the elderly faces staring at me, I sensed that this oration was to be a highlight of their social calendar. They clearly didn't get out very much any more; a speech at a friend's funeral was the best entertainment they generally got.

'Obviously it can be very difficult,' said the vicar.

'You have no idea . . .' I thought, and with everyone waiting and the vicar not taking the hint to skip to the next section, I felt myself slowly standing up and walking to the pulpit.

The congregation looked at me with the default smile of empathy. I took a deep breath. My legs felt unreliable behind the lectern as I gripped on tight.

'What can I say about my dad?'

I gave a long, significant pause, which I reckoned bought me another second or two. One retired RAF colleague nodded meaningfully at this rhetorical question.

'Dad! My old dad . . .'

There was a wheezy cough from the back row.

'Well, there's so much to say it almost seems wrong to attempt to sum it all up in a few minutes . . .' an old lady sitting in the third row frowned slightly at this notion '. . . but obviously I'm going to have to,' and the woman looked reassured. 'He had a distinguished career in the Royal Air Force, rising to the very senior rank of Air Commodore and serving his country with such distinction that he was awarded a CBE. No, not a CBE, a CB. There was no "E". Er, he was posted all over the world, but always wanted his family there with him.' Time just to start making stuff up and presume it was true. 'Because he was always a great father and a wonderful husband to my late mother . . .' This prompted a few nods; there was a sense of reassurance that the tribute was now properly under way. Even if it had turned out that this last detail was wrong, I had felt it unlikely that anyone would dare to contradict me. I couldn't remember going to any funerals, but I was pretty sure that heckling was generally frowned upon. I saw Dillie looking at up at me admiringly.

'But he was a wonderful grandfather too. I remember on family holidays in Cornwall –' I chuckled to myself at the memory of it – 'he was always so patient with his grandchildren.' This detail seemed to go down well; they were anxious to know exactly how this quality had manifested itself. 'Like, he would always . . . be really patient with them . . .'

There was another cough.

'He and my mother made very powerful home-made wine . . .' A few smiles at that. 'And he had a long and distinguished career in the Royal Air Force . . .' I realized I'd already said that, and now was pretty sure I was completely out of things I could say about him. 'He had some interesting sort of regimental cufflinks, and an old-fashioned watch.' Then there was a long pause and I let out an extended sigh, shrugging and shaking my head slightly as if to say, 'To be honest, there isn't much else.' I could feel a bead of sweat run down my back and I noticed my hands were shaking. In my internal panic, I could think of no other course but the lowest one available to me. I clutched my thumb and forefinger to the bridge of my nose and just said, 'And I'm going to really miss him . . .'

It was all the more convincing for the fact that I had gone completely red in the face out of pure embarrassment, and now I bit my lip and shook my head. But in fact, having resorted to this posture, I realized that I did really miss him. He had always been so delighted to see me, and made the world seem such a positive place, lifting my spirits when I was supposed to be lifting his. Perhaps my emotions were more overt than I realized, because as I glanced up from behind where my hand rubbed my furrowed brow, I saw the ladies who had been the first to arrive clutching their tissues to their noses. An old couple who had apparently known me since I was a baby now wiped away a tear. And, directly in my eye-line, right in front of me in the front row, sat Maddy with tears streaming down her cheeks. Only my children were holding it together; in fact, they seemed rather appalled to see a room full of supposedly superior grown-ups totally losing control like this.

Witnessing Maddy being so upset like this suddenly flicked a switch inside me. 'And one of the other things about my dad was that he really thought the world of Maddy,' I said, looking directly at her. There was more I wanted to say and I started to speak with a fluency and feeling that had been absent up till now. 'When he was in the hospital at the end, her regular visits were the highlight of his day. He pointed out her kindness and intelligence to me, as if to warn me against the risk of ever losing his beloved daughter-in-law. He was not to know that he was already too late. With him being so ill, we took the decision that he should be protected from the bleak truth that his own son was unable to hold a marriage together in the way that he had done in far more difficult circumstances.'

There was tension in the room, tinged with sadness at the news that Keith's son's marriage had not worked out. Only the municipal priest was not enthralled and noticeably checked his watch, clearly anxious to keep a regular supply of coffins feeding the furnaces.

'Maddy brought his grandchildren to see him one last time, and I think we all knew then that he would never see them again. The kids were so grown-up about it, so affectionate yet gentle with him, and he refused to let a little thing like his own imminent death get him down. "How wonderful to see you all!"' I said, impersonating him. "What a lucky man I am, to have such a wonderful family!"'

The crowd recognized Keith's optimism and smiled at the memory. '"What a lucky man I am!" he said to us, with tubes sticking out of his body. "What a lucky man I am!" he said, through the pain and discomfort. "What a lucky man I am! Just to be alive for a few more days."'

I was speaking with some passion now. I had stumbled on my thesis and was conveying it with a missionary zeal. 'And maybe the best way we could all remember my father is for each of us to take that world-view away from this crematorium, and try to remember Keith whenever we are feeling a little bit irritable or sorry for ourselves. "My flight has been delayed; what a lucky man I am to have spotted a bookshop and a coffee bar where I can read!" "My wife and children don't live with me any more. But what I lucky man I am to know them all, to be able to recall so many wonderful times together, and have so much to look forward to as they grow up . . .." '

The vicar's body language was suggesting my speech was almost at an end. A few more minutes and it felt as if he'd press the switch to send the coffin through the curtains whether I'd finished or not.

'I know every bereaved son must think this, but believe me when I say, I wish I'd had a bit more time with him. I feel I should have got to know him better. It's made me determined to spend every possible moment with my own family, to grab every memory that I can – even though I can't be there as much as I would like, and Maddy now has someone else.'

'No,' interjected Dillie. 'She dumped him.'

The heckle had not been a loud one: the children were in the second row. It was more a mumbled point of order than a public declaration. But I had heard her clearly enough, and then caught her whisper, 'But they have!' when Jamie chastised her for speaking out like that during the service. So Maddy and Ralph had broken up. Maddy avoided eye contact, but I looked at her mother and the undisguised satisfaction on her face confirmed that this was indeed the case.

'What a lucky man I am!' I said, but I didn't qualify this with any further information. 'That's what I think. What a lucky man I am!' And I sat down, trying to hold back a beatific smile.

Now I understood the therapeutic value of a funeral, because a curious sense of peace and serenity washed over me. The world seemed like a better place. 'I'm glad to have been here today,' I thought, as the coffin set off on its short journey to the sound of the Carpenters. They had been Dad's favourite band, although in retrospect I realized that 'We've Only Just Begun' was probably not the best choice of song to mark an old man's demise.

'Don't sing along, Vaughan,' whispered Maddy behind me.

'Oh. Sorry.'

Chapter 20

'Sir, Mr Vaughan, sir, why weren't you in on Friday? Were you in the loony bin, sir?'

'Are you having a lobotomy, sir? Were you being fitted for your straightjacket?'

'That's enough, Tanika.'

'Have you been sectioned, though? Do you have a padded cell and shit?'

'Tanika, Dean, you are both on a first warning. Any more disrespect and failure to focus on today's lesson outcomes and you will be one step away from removal from this classroom, detention and a telephone call home.'

I had relearned the official script and was hoping that my most difficult pupils would recognize the magic words and instantly change their behaviour.

'We never said nothing. You must be hearing voices, sir.'

'Are you a serial killer, sir? Do you eat your victims?'

'Second warning, Tanika!'

'I'm not Tanika, though. Your memory's gone all loopy again. I'm Monique, sir.'

'That's your last chance, Tanika.'

'No, it's not, sir – they changed the Behaviour Policy. It's five consequences now, and then you go to the referral. You must have forgotten it when you went all mental.'

'Sir, do you bury your victims under the patio? Is that where you was on Friday? Burying a victim?'

'If you must know, I was burying someone.'

The moment I said it, I felt it was probably a mistake, but the room fell into a stunned silence that demanded some further explanation.

'Er, well, it was a cremation, actually. I wasn't in because I was at my father's funeral, okay? He had been ill for some time and he died during the holidays, so that's why you had a supply teacher on Friday, for which I apologize.'

The teacher-baiting stopped after that. They must have thought that it was hard enough for Boggy Vaughan to have lost his dad without being reminded that he was a mentalist as well. They cooperated with the lesson, answered the questions and wrote down their homework assignments at the end. In fact, I was wondering if I could get away with announcing a family bereavement at the start of every class, but guessed the sympathy might diminish a bit after a couple of weeks of dead great-aunts and elderly in-laws.

After the students had all filed out, I noticed Tanika hanging back to speak to me alone.

'Er, I'm sorry about your dad, sir. I didn't mean to disrespect him and shit.'

'That's okay, Tanika. Only, just ... let's drop it with the "mentalist" thing, eh? I didn't have all my memories of my father back before he died, so I do have some sort of mental condition that is still affecting me and can be quite difficult at times.'

She didn't say anything, but didn't go to leave either.

'Was there anything else?'

'Sir? My dad died ...'

I had never seen Tanika drop her cocksure guard before, but could sense that this was anything but a wind-up.

'I'm very sorry to hear that, Tanika. Was that recently?'

'No, it was when I was three. He was shot.'

'Shot!' I exclaimed, unprofessionally revealing my alarm.

'It was on the London news and that. They said it was a drugs-related murder, but it wasn't. Would you like to see a picture of him?'

She had already got a photograph from the little plastic wallet that held her travel pass and her dinner card. It looked scuffed and crumpled, but there through the misty plastic was a tiny toddler version of Tanika standing next to a tall man smiling for the camera.

'He looks like a very nice man.'

'It wasn't drugs-related though.'

'I believe you.'

'They just said that to make everyone feel better.'

The queue of Year 7s waiting to come in for the next lesson was peering in the door, and I pushed it closed.

'What do you mean?'

'If people see a picture of a murdered black man and then the free newspaper says it was like 'drugs-related', all the posh white people think, "Oh, that's all right, then, it won't happen to me."'

This was a level of analysis that I had not witnessed in Tanika before, but clearly her father's death was always going to engage her more than the collapse of the Deutschmark.

'Well, losing your father at three is much, much harder than losing your dad at my age. I can't imagine what you must have gone through . . .'

She was no longer staring at the floor but making direct eye contact with me. There wasn't any sadness or emotion there; instead I understood the hard shell that had grown over her to make her top dog in the classroom.

'Tanika? You know you have to do an independent history module for your final bit of coursework?'

'I'm gonna start it – shut up, man!'

'Why don't you set the history straight on your dad?'

'What?'

'Your project doesn't have to be about something that happened centuries ago. Why don't you gather all the records of your dad's murder – in the newspapers, online or whatever – and then set about correcting them with the true story of what really happened?'

'Are we allowed to do that?'

'What you said about how things get distorted to make people feel more comfortable, that has to be part of it. You're right – that's exactly how history gets rewritten.'

I was already worrying that I should have reflected upon this perilous idea before suggesting it, but Tanika's education was going to end soon unless I could find a way of getting her engaged. 'Anyway, have a think about it,' I said, and she nodded blankly, put the photo away and started to head out. An eleven-year-old boy had placed his open mouth against the glass in the door and was inhaling and exhaling like a giant human slug.

'Sir, what the other teachers do to stop them doing that is, like, spray the glass with a really disgusting cleaning fluid. Just thought you might have forgotten . . .'

'Ah, thanks, Tanika. I might just try that.'

After school I sat at the computer screen in my form room, battling a fresh onslaught of emails, grimly aware that for every one that I killed off, two would pop up to replace it. I resisted the siren voices of the internet for as long as I could bear it, but after a whole minute and a half of actual work, I finally succumbed to the significant distraction of a window to everything in the whole world. Gary's user-generated news site had an interesting main story on its front page explaining how the BP oil spill in the Gulf of Mexico had been deliberately staged as part of a white supremacist conspiracy between Buckingham Palace and the American Military-Industrial Complex to destabilize Barack Obama. Surprisingly, none of the major news outlets had yet picked up on the YouNews exclusive:

> British royal family (Jews) told BP poodles to be faking oil spill for to keep blood-money of oil-dollars, yes, and not to tell how they kill Lady Di, for Obama 'black' president, (Africa) like Dodi, will face same fate as M. L. King, Malcolm X and Marvin Gaye – all executed, yes, by zionist CIA (true).

It made me feel marginally less guilty for having told Gary I didn't want to resume my involvement in YouNews. He thought I had sold out; he couldn't believe that I didn't want to topple those evil, all-powerful, super-rich media moguls and become an all-powerful, super-rich media mogul.

I had not looked at my online Wiki-biography for a week, following a session when I had methodically reversed all the facetious edits, deleting the claims that I 'could talk to the animals', that I had 'discovered France' and had 'a spare pancreas'. One joke in particular had played on my mind afterwards:

> On 22 October, Vaughan experienced a psychogenic fugue on learning that he had won the National Lottery. The shock was so great that he suffered chronic amnesia and still doesn't remember that he is entitled to £4 million on production of the winning ticket that he put in a very special hiding place for safekeeping.

It was clearly an inspired wind-up; I was not going to let it bother me any more. Especially now that I had looked in every hiding place imaginable.

Previously when I had deleted such yarns they had soon been

replaced with new jokes, but in the time since I had last corrected the document no further changes had been made. The writers had clearly just got bored; reinventing Mr Vaughan's life had been fun for a bit, but apparently the creative young minds had now moved on to other things. I couldn't help but feel a little hurt.

But then I noticed a new paragraph under 'Career' that I had never read before. It said:

> Mr Vaughan was the best teacher I ever had. When I left the sixth form to work in JD Sports he kept coming into the shop to persuade me to come back. I would never have got my A levels or gone to university if it wasn't for Mr Vaughan.

This one comment from a former pupil utterly transformed my mood. I had been a good teacher after all, I reasoned. There *had* been a time when I had transformed lives. 'Now I am manager of JD Sports,' boasted my former pupil.

Despite the accumulating evidence and recovering memory, I still found myself regarding the negative side of Vaughan Mk 1 with a dispassionate objectivity. The marital break-up in particular was an event that had happened to another man. And the Maddy before the fugue had been a completely different person from the woman I knew now. The first was just a fictional character from some trashy half-remembered domestic drama; the other was a living, breathing woman who, despite all our problems, seemed to understand me better than I did myself. But what was so irrational about this Maddy was that she kept getting the two genres mixed up. She minded about things that had happened to her imaginary counterpart; she resented real-life Vaughan for things that fictional Vaughan had done. I was different now, she had acknowledged as much; but I was not going to be allowed to forget things I couldn't remember.

I had found myself pondering how much my brain-wipe had altered my actual character. I suggested to Gary that this question raised all sorts of issues about the philosophical relationship between memory and experience. We were sitting in a busy pub, beside a noisy quiz machine. It was probably not the best setting for an existential debate about the influence of the conscious and subconscious on the evolution of the ego and id.

'What I'm trying to say is, when I had completely forgotten all the events of my life, was I suddenly no longer shaped by them? Is it possible that my personality could have reverted back to my essential core nature, with the nurture starting all over again based on subsequent experiences?'

'Well, you were shit at football before, and you're shit at football now. So what's that tell us?'

'Well, I'm about average at football actually . . .'

'No, you're really shit. I mean you run like a girl, and the last goal you scored bounced in off your arse.'

I felt the philosophical discussion was drifting from the central thesis.

'What I'm saying is: is it possible that all the character-defining experiences of my life were wiped along with the memories of them? I had a teenage cycling accident which I don't remember. I still have the scar on my leg. But do I still have the mental scars of a failed marriage and all the other disappointments and unrealized ambitions, whatever they may have been?'

'Being shit at football—'

'Yes, you said.'

'Can't drive a car . . . never shagged enough girls at college . . . can't hold your drink . . . appalling dress sense . . .'

'Yeah, all right, you don't have to list them all. I'm just saying, don't you think this offers a unique case study in the whole "nature versus nurture" debate? Surely we don't have to remember something to be affected by it? None of us can recall every single thing that's happened to us, yet all of it helps shape our personalities.'

'Nah,' Gary said, taking a sip of his beer. ''Cos you were

always into all that philosophical bollocks. Can I eat your crisps?'

But even Gary's rhinoceros sensitivity was gradually being affected by the outside world. The photo on his iPhone was from the scan of his unborn child. And no moustache or sideburns from his favourite app could make the foetus look like a seventies porn star. He was actually coming to terms with the notion that we might not be an inseparable pair of radical students any more. He even had an idea about a possible girlfriend for me.

'Do you know who I thought you ought to ask out on a date?'

'Who?'

'Maddy!' he declared, as if this was the radical brainwave of a total genius. 'Think about it. You've got loads in common with her already – and I've got a hunch you've still got a bit of a soft spot for her.'

'Wow! Thanks, Gary. I'll bear that in mind.'

Deep down, I feared that as more memories of my marriage came back, I might reacquire some of the bitterness and cynicism of my pre-fugue incarnation. I could now recall various stages of our marriage. The power struggle in our home seemed to have escalated like a small regional war. I had been insistent that the shelves above the television were the historic homeland of my vinyl LP collection, and demanded an immediate end to the provocative settlement of scented candles and framed photos in the disputed territories.

Madeleine upped the tension in the region, with the infamous 10 July massacre of all the history programmes stored on the TV planner. Dozens of recorded documentaries about the Nazis that I definitely intended to watch at some point were systematically wiped out; her ethnic cleansing of the Sky Plus box had been Maddy's final solution to end Hitler's occupation of the recorder's hard drive.

The general resentment meant we ended up fighting about all sorts of stupid things. 'No, they are completely different types of songs!!' I remembered shouting. 'How can you possibly compare "Fernando" to "Chiquitita"?' And the tension following any fight would continue for days, with a coded war of attrition fought on a dozen different fronts. Maddy would insist that she filled up the car with petrol, and then deliberately let the price slip to £50.01 just because she knew how much that annoyed me. Her critical appraisal of detective thrillers on the television became unreasonably sympathetic towards the deranged wife who murdered her husband. Traditional little kindnesses between us disappeared: favourite treats were no longer placed in the supermarket trolley; just a single cup of tea was made at any one time. Years earlier the news of other couples splitting up would have been recounted in the same tones as a car crash or a serious illness. Now the reporting of such events sounded more like an innocent person being let out of prison.

None of this, of course, featured in this Wiki-memoir that I had pulled together, where I had taken care to be as neutral and objective as I could be. In any case, I was uneasy about trusting my own memories of the marriage; in the narrative I had reconstructed in my mind, the unhappy ending still didn't seem to work. I could remember the Maddy who had been my companion, my best friend, my soul mate. Was that the last stage in all those marital self-help books? Or was a bitter divorce always going to be the final chapter in this case?

Over the past months, I had spent many long hours thinking about this relationship and wanting to understand why it had fallen apart as it did. Like a detective continually mulling over the clues leading up to a crime, I had kept staring at the basic life events mapped out in front of me, wondering where the wrong turning had been taken. And then in a flash I saw what was wrong. *I was only thinking about me.* That was the only history I had investigated, the only perspective I had viewed. Could it be that the problem with my marriage had been the same as the shortcomings of this memoir? That I had approached it as an individual, not as one half of a pair, or one quarter of a family?

Feeling inspired by this flash of insight, I created a new document, a private one this time, and wrote the title at the top: 'The life story of Madeleine R. Vaughan'. And then I deleted that and put in her maiden name. In no particular order, I began to recall everything I knew about her story. Her family background, her interests and, with all the objectivity I could muster, details of boyfriends before me. I took care to write as much as I could about her work. The struggle of being a professional photographer, and how she had to reinvent her work completely when the digital revolution came along. I described some of the brilliant photo-montage creations that she developed once the childcare had become less exhausting. I recalled the excitement she had felt when buyers began to be interested, and the indignant fury she had sometimes expressed when she suspected me of regarding her job as less important than my own.

I attempted to chronicle our own entire relationship from her point of view. Memories I was unaware I had recovered poured out of me: of the day we had squatted our home, and how we had spent a frightened first night failing to sleep downstairs, expecting at any moment to be physically dragged out by security guards. I wrote about her pregnancy and the birth of Jamie – how she had confessed to feeling frightened before it all began and the tearful explosion of joy as she held the bruised and waxy newborn in her arms. I wrote about the time she was called up at home by a telephone salesman and she pretended to be really, really stupid. 'Yer wha?' she just kept grunting to every question, no matter how many times he repeated it. I pictured her being stopped by a chugger in the King's Road, pretending to be deaf as she used rather unconvincing sign language to ask if he signed too.

My fingers were still eagerly pecking away at the keyboard two hours later. Fellow teachers, cleaners and daylight had long since drifted off; now it was just me, lit by the glow of the computer screen in the darkening classroom. Even if I did not agree with what I understood to be her analysis of my own faults and mistakes, I recorded them in this document. I was determined to see our two lives from her point of view. Finally, I brought the story right up to date. My first draft of Maddy's pocket biography ended with her splitting up with Ralph and then grieving for her father-in-law. I had felt almost as moved writing about Madeleine's response to my dad's death as I had felt myself at the time.

In just a couple of hours of trying to see the world through her eyes, I felt as if I had discovered an extra hemisphere in my brain. I didn't pretend that now I completely understood Maddy's psyche, but at least I had found a way in.

We used to have these stupid arguments about nothing, which had driven me mad with their self-defeating illogicality. 'What's wrong with you?' I would finally ask, having failed to ignore Maddy's meaningful sighs.

'It doesn't matter,' she would lie.

'Well, it clearly *does* matter,' I would say, with the emotional sensitivity of Mr Spock. 'If there's something wrong, just tell me what it is.'

'I shouldn't have to tell you. You should just know.'

And I would feel exasperated and aggrieved that not only was she angry but she was also immensely disappointed in me for not being a circus psychic with magical telepathic powers. But now I think I understood what she had meant. 'I shouldn't have to tell you. You should just know.' It was Maddy-speak for, 'Did you ever once stop to look at the world from my point of view?'

She had seemed so quiet after the funeral, pensive and distracted. Obviously she was upset about my dad, and splitting up with Ralph must have been distressing, but there was something else going on in her mind: she had not heard the offers of egg-and-cress sandwiches, she had not heard the elderly relations informing her that her children had grown. At one point I had caught her on her own in the kitchen and had asked her if she was all right.

'I just don't know what I think any more,' had been her enigmatic reply.

'Don't know what you think about what?'

'About anything,' and I thought for a moment she might be about to put her head on my shoulder.

'I don't know what I think about bloody anchovies,' boomed Gary, striding into the kitchen carrying a can of lager. 'Sometimes I love them; sometimes I hate them.'

'Maybe you should have married an anchovy, Gary?' said Maddy, and I laughed, but she was already wandering back out to the reception. I didn't get another chance to talk to her after that; there were just a few words about practical arrangements as she left. I gave the kids some money for their school ski trip and told her that I could walk the dog at the weekend if that was helpful. I had wanted to be her counsellor and confidant, but instead I was watching her car drive away while I was forced to listen to an old man in a beret explain that he had been stationed with my dad at Northolt.

'Ah yes,' I said, 'my dad often spoke of you fondly.'

'Did he?' said the old man, seeming pleasantly surprised. 'Oh – that's nice to know.'

Sitting in the empty classroom on my own, I felt a deepening worry on Maddy's behalf. Maybe I possessed an intuition that was unique to me: instinctive empathy with her acquired through two decades of marriage; perhaps it had remained hardwired within me. I glanced at the time in the corner of my computer screen and realized it was now too late to go round there and just check that she was all right. I should have rung her over the weekend, I thought; I should have gone round to see her. I could go past in the street and just see if any lights were on? No, it was a ridiculous idea. I was making something out of nothing; I was just flattering myself that she needed me to talk to – she was probably completely fine. And then I shut down my computer, packed my things away and hurried out of the door.

'Working late again, eh, Mr Vaughan?' chuckled John and Kofi on security, before scrolling through the CCTV locations on their monitor, hoping to find a female teacher putting her clothes back on.

Even before I was close, I could see that lights were on all over our house, which struck me as quite unlike Maddy. Even the outside porch light was still glowing like a beacon. I watched the place from the street for a while, but couldn't see her moving about inside. I could have telephoned first, but didn't want to give her the chance not to pick up my call. Finally I climbed up the steps and hesitantly reached for the button, as if pressing it gently would make it buzz slightly less loudly. I didn't quite understand why, but I was relieved to see some movement from the other side of the glass. She checked the peep-hole and then opened the door. But to my disappointment, it hadn't been Maddy on the other side but her mother, looking fretful and anxious.

'No, it's not her!' Jean called back into the house. 'It's Vaughan!' She urgently beckoned me in. 'I was going to ring you, dear – I was going to ring you if we didn't hear from her this evening. It's been two days – we've been worried sick . . .'

'What? What is it? Where's my wife?'

'She's disappeared, Vaughan. She's completely vanished.'

Chapter 21

My first thought was that Madeleine had experienced exactly the same sort of neurological breakdown that had befallen me. That at this very moment she was wandering the streets, not knowing who she was or where she belonged. This was not such a fantastical notion: one of the early theories put to me by Dr Lewington was that I had contracted viral encephalitis – perhaps Maddy could have literally caught this amnesia virus off her ex-husband?

I remembered my own bewilderment and confusion as the strangeness of myself crept upon me and hoped that nothing so severe had befallen Maddy. She might be in a hospital somewhere labelled 'UNKNOWN WHITE FEMALE'; she could still be trying to talk to hurrying passers-by unwilling to unplug their headphones to listen to her pleas for help.

Then I wondered, if she had been struck with retrograde amnesia, would this manifest itself in exactly the same way? Would she now fall passionately in love with me all over again? Would she be just like when we were nineteen? Isn't that every middle-aged couple's fantasy – to feel that white-hot passion burning as fiercely as when they first fused together? In recent years it had seemed impossible to keep the last few embers of that bonfire alive. The only time you stare into each other's eyes when you've been married for twenty years is to check whether your partner's looking guilty.

Though it remained possible that Madeleine had experienced a psychogenic fugue, the more I heard about the manner of her disappearance, the less likely it felt. If Maddy's brain had suddenly wiped all memories, it was a very convenient moment at which to do so. On the Saturday morning both children had left for the school's skiing trip. It occurred to me that this would have been the first time in twenty years that she'd had her home entirely to herself. At least it would have been, had her mother not insisted that they stay for the week to keep her company. Maddy's mysterious disappearance had occurred at the end of a period of enormous stress: she'd had her ex-husband disappear and then resurface wanting to turn back the clock; she'd got involved with another man and then broken it off; she'd taken her children to their grandfather's funeral.

Enduring all that and then having her mother in her house completely focusing on her twenty-four hours a day might be more than any sane person could be expected to endure. 'But I can't comprehend why Madeleine would just disappear like that. I can't comprehend it. Can you comprehend it, Ron? You see, Ron can't comprehend it either – it's completely incomprehendible—'

'Incomprehensible . . .'

'It is! Completely incomprehendible! Isn't it, Ron?'

'It's "incompre*hensible*".'

'Completely. Shall I phone the police? I think I should phone the police. Ron, will you phone the police? It's nine, nine, nine, dear. Three nines.'

'Hold on – let's not phone the police just yet,' I counselled.

'It's all right, I'd forgotten the number anyway,' said Ron, with a twinkling smile towards me.

'It's nine, nine, nine, Ron. It used to say it in the middle of the dial, but it's all buttons now. I don't know why they have to keep changing things . . .'

Ron had clearly come to the same conclusion as me: that his daughter's sudden disappearance might not be so mysterious after all.

'The thing is, Jean,' I said, pausing to find exactly the right words, 'perhaps Maddy just needed a bit of space?'

'Space? She's got lots of space. You had the loft converted, didn't you? And had the cellar dry-lined. Did you know that, Ron? Why couldn't you ever do anything like that to our house?'

'Well, we never had a cellar.'

'No, I mean headspace – from all the pressures she's been under recently. You know, some time on her own.'

Maddy had only been away for thirty-six hours, and although it was understandable that Jean might have expected an explanation before her daughter simply took off, the required conversation with her mother might well have used up most of that time. I assured her that Madeleine would call soon, but was forced to concede that it was 'Not Normal'. For Jean, 'Not Normal' was a catch-all condemnation that included women's football, nose piercings and Asian presenters reading 'our news'.

Privately I remained worried. To leave her parents alone in the house without so much as an explanation was unlike the Maddy I thought I remembered. She was always so ultra-considerate, always thinking of the feelings of others. Whenever an air hostess did the safety talk before take-off, Maddy always felt really sorry for her being ignored by everyone. So there would be forty rows of seasoned travellers blithely reading their magazines, and one supportive-looking mum on the aisle seat, visibly concentrating and nodding and pointedly looking round when she indicated the emergency exits. Her sweetness contrasted sharply with her husband's grumpiness: he was convinced it was really rude when the passenger in front reclined their seat.

These memories prompted a thought. I knew where she kept the family passports. If she had really wanted to get away, to flee abroad for a few days, that would be an obvious clue. I slipped upstairs to the bedroom, where a large Victorian bureau stood beneath the window. I slid open the little drawer for essential documents. There was our marriage certificate (I was surprised we hadn't had to give that back). There were her childhood swimming medals and the dog's vaccination record. There was the stub of an old parking ticket, which had obviously had enormous sentimental value. But my hunch had been correct. Maddy had stolen herself away; the person who had always put herself second had emerged from her cocoon of commitments and responsibilities and just flown.

I stood looking around our old bedroom, imagining her hastily packing a bag while her parents were out walking the dog. I wished I could have seen it as an exciting, spontaneous declaration of independence. But she had left no note, there had been no text message; it smacked of a moment of crisis, a woman at the end of her tether. And then I sat on the edge of the bed and tried to imagine where she might possibly be.

Putting myself back into Maddy's mindset, this is the sequence of events that I finally projected on to her.

It was unseasonably hot for April and I pictured her skipping nimbly over some rocks to where the water was deep enough to dive in. She would have stopped for a moment and just inhaled the sense of space, the arc of emptiness that was her favourite beach in the world. In the distance a few sheep populated the grey-green hills that surrounded the bay, but no cars came along the coast road. It was so tranquil here: there was only what Maddy called 'good noise' – waves and wind and seagulls.

I saw Maddy positioning her bag and towel by a crevice in the rocks, and then she prepared to dive in. The water would be cold, but Maddy always said that she never regretted a swim. Then an unhesitant leap and a splash. The grace and beauty of her dive would probably have been slightly undermined by her coming to the surface and swearing loudly about the iciness of the Atlantic Ocean in springtime. But Maddy was a strong swimmer and I saw her doing a powerful front crawl across the bay. This beach had lifeguards in summer, but she would have checked the tides and stayed close to the shore, and maybe she had spotted a local, collecting wood at the far end of the beach, who might be keeping one eye on the mad swimmer.

When the cold had finally penetrated the fillings in her teeth, I could see her hauling herself back on to the rocks. She knew she could climb out here – she had never forgotten that swim on this beach all those years ago, the shared bottle of wine and the snugness of the little tent before the storm pulled it from its moorings. Now the light spring breeze felt like an icy wind and her little towel seemed wholly inadequate as it barely wrapped around her freezing shoulders. The figure at the far end of the beach had lit a fire which sent a plume of white smoke up over the dunes. She wanted to go and warm herself by its flames but she could hardly wander up to a strange man in her wet swimming costume just to recover from an insane swim far too early in the year. But then again, this was Ireland: people were friendly, strangers talked to one another; to wander over and chat would be a perfectly normal thing to do here.

Carrying her sandals, she walked barefoot along the length of the dunes, smelling the tantalizing wood-smoke as she got closer. It was hard to see in all the smoke whether the man was still there or not, and she was quite close before she attempted a friendly good afternoon.

'Good afternoon,' replied an English accent she recognized. And then the smoke changed direction and right before her stood her ex-husband, smiling warmly, holding out a canvas bag.

'I brought your cashmere hoodie,' I said with a smile. 'I thought you might be a bit cold.'

*

Once I became certain that this would be where Maddy had gone, it had been easy enough to follow her here. I had already done the more difficult journey: getting to the point where I finally under-stood her. Now Maddy looked at me as if too many thoughts were racing through her head for her to articulate any one of them.

'And I just made a fire to warm you up. But I know you prob-ably came here to get a bit of space from everything, so I'll be on my way. If you fancy meeting up for a drink later, I'm not flying back till tomorrow, but it's completely up to you,' and with that I turned to head back up the beach.

She took quite a few bewildered seconds to call after me and I started to worry that she was actually going to let me just walk away.

'Wait! Don't be stupid. How did you . . .? How come . . .? Are my mum and dad all right?'

Now I stopped and turned. 'They're fine.' I laughed. 'See, you can't help it! You can't help thinking about other people!'

'Mum wasn't too upset, was she? How did you guess I'd come here? How did you find me?'

'Well, I remembered that whenever you couldn't hear yourself think, when there were sirens in the street and jumbos roaring overhead and problems overwhelming you, you'd always say, "I wish I was at Barleycove."'

'You remembered that?'

'And finally you just did it! I saw your passport had gone and I just, you know, worked it out . . . But then I saw that you hadn't taken your cashmere, and I thought, Oh, she's going to want that.'

She had already pulled it on and her sea-scrubbed cheeks were glowing in the warmth of the fire.

'Oh, and I've got some sausages and bread by the way, if you fancy a sandwich?'

'Are they vegetarian sausages? You didn't forget I'm vegetarian?'

For a split second I believed her.

I was careful to cook the sausages slowly and thoroughly. This was a special day, and having Maddy on her knees vomiting into the sand as a result of my cooking might have slightly taken the edge off the atmosphere. But to Madeleine's post-swim appetite, these bonfire-roasted Irish sausages were the best meal she'd ever eaten, and when I brought out a small bottle of wine and a plastic cup, I think she had to stop herself hugging me. We sat on the dunes looking out at the blurred horizon, chatting and laughing as the tide went out and our shadows lengthened. I felt so at peace with the world. I didn't even mind when Maddy interfered with my fire. Well, not much anyway.

Madeleine explained that she had spontaneously decided to disappear abroad without saying anything to her mother, as the only other option would have been to bludgeon her to death with a Le Creuset saucepan. 'I think Mum sensed that I was a bit depressed, so she thought she might cheer me up by listing all the things that her lucky daughter had that *she* hadn't had when she was bringing up children.'

'And did you feel grateful that you hadn't had to endure a marriage to your father?'

'Yesterday I learned that my dad had always been very selfish. *Sexually speaking.*'

'Oh, that's the sort of detail a daughter wants to know!'

'Yes, and all the other people in the supermarket queue found it very interesting as well. So I thought I would slip away before she got on to the details of which actual sexual positions she had found so unsatisfying.'

Maddy had spotted a cheap flight to Cork (she just happened to be glancing at a budget airline website) and realized that if she left straight away she could make that flight and ring her parents later. 'But then my phone was out of battery and the telephone box was broken, and actually, it felt quite thrilling for a moment, just to be that selfish.'

'Don't worry – we'll just say that you rang me and asked me to tell them. But then my dodgy memory wiped any trace of it.'

'Hey, that's a good idea. On second thoughts, that's exactly what *did* happen!'

We talked for a while about my amnesia and just how much had come back to me. Neither of us wanted to refer to the worst memories, but she knew what I meant when I said I was gradually processing it all, good and bad. We watched a distant tanker disappear around the headland and threw our crusts to a slightly scary seagull. When she offered to fill my glass she noticed I wasn't drinking.

'Why? Are you driving?' she joked, then looked as if she regretted being so unkind.

'Well, um, actually I am. I've got a little rented car up the hill . . .'

'You learned to drive?'

'Yes. I did this intensive course and haven't demolished a single garden wall yet. I can chauffeur you back to Crookhaven later if you like, in my luxury Nissan Micra. It's got a broken wing-mirror, but that wasn't my fault; a tree came too close outside Skibbereen.'

She didn't say anything; she just looked at me long and hard as if she was processing this new person she had known all her life.

When the fire had faded and the temperature had dropped, we headed back to the village and Maddy tried not to grip on to the passenger seat too obviously as we wove around the coast road. We had a drink at the pub where Madeleine had booked a room and we both got an excited skiing update text from the children that we spent a good twenty minutes deciphering. Maddy rang her parents and apologized, then we took turns to quote Jean, remembering how the children had been unable to suppress their laughter at Christmas dinner. 'Vaughan puts the toilet seat down when he's finished weeing, you know, Ron,' said Maddy, in her mother's voice. 'Ron splashes urine all over the seat;

you're much more careful with your penis, aren't you, Vaughan?'

'Oh, that's one of the many qualities my mother-in-law reports back to her friends about me. My excellent penis-aiming skills.'

'Vaughan, why don't you show Ron how you hold your penis when you wee?'

I asked Maddy about her work, then she asked me about mine and I went on for far too long about the breakthrough I had had with my most difficult pupil, finding myself getting carried away with the excitement of being able to tell her all about it at last: '. . . and then Tanika stood up in front of the whole class and talked about how her father's death had been misrepresented in the media and you should have seen it, Maddy – I was so proud of her. She did this really impassioned speech saying a lie is like a cancer; you can't just leave it because it will eat away at you, and it was all the stuff we'd talked about in history – how getting the past wrong will send you off into the wrong future. And she's written to the *South London Press* to ask them to print an article setting the record straight on her dad's death, and the whole class was cheering her, and she shouted that she was going to *kill the lie*: "Me and Mr Vaughan are going to kill the lie," she repeated above the cheers, "and I know my dad is looking down from heaven, saying thank you."'

'So you've remembered that too,' Maddy said with a smile.

'Remembered what?'

'Why you loved teaching. You used to talk with that sort of passion often in the old days. I always loved that about you . . .'

Eventually Maddy went up to her room and hung her damp towel out to dry, and since the pub had a couple of other rooms free, I took the cheapest of those.

She gave me a peck on the cheek as she said goodnight before the old wooden door closed behind her. An hour later I was still wide awake. I wasn't used to trying to sleep feeling this strange sense of peace.

Without either of us ever directly referring to it, something momentous had occurred. The two of us had forgiven one another. Eventually I felt the adventure of the long day catching up with me: the flight, the anxious drive, and most of all the very real worry I'd had that she would be utterly appalled that I had followed her here to spy on her like some crazy stalker. But she had been amazed and delighted to see me. It had gone far better than I had dared hope. And then, just as I felt myself losing consciousness, my door opened and Maddy whispered, 'Budge up,' and climbed into bed beside me.

I wanted to sit up and hug her, but something told me she'd prefer it if I just shifted across the bed and made sure there was enough quilt for my ex-wife. Or my wife, maybe? I couldn't be sure.

'Have you got enough room?'

'Yeah, I'm fine.' She was still whispering. 'Sorry if I woke you.'

'No, I was awake. How did you know which room I was in?'

'I didn't – I tiptoed into the room opposite first. I nearly got into bed with that fat German who was up at the bar earlier.'

'Could have been interesting . . .'

'Anyway, you found me in the West of Ireland. I don't think finding the right door is quite as impressive as the feat of mind-reading you pulled off today.'

She put her head on my shoulder. 'You knew I'd come here!' she said in amazement. 'You just knew!'

And we didn't talk any more, but just lay beside one another, my arm around her, her body pressed against me. I had remembered things I never would have remembered before my amnesia. I had remembered her favourite place in the whole world, I had remembered that she loved to swim but never took warm enough clothes, I had remembered that she'd said that sausage sandwich we'd shared on that perfect beach had been the best meal she'd ever had.

And I had also remembered her Gmail log-in so I could check where she had booked her flight and accommodation – but it didn't seem the moment to mention that right now.

Chapter 22

If a historian had to put a date on the absolute low-point in our marriage it would most likely be 11.15 p.m. on 13 February, eight months before the sudden onset of my amnesia. On that night I had come home late to discover that Maddy had actually carried out her threat to change the locks on our front door. She would not come to the door or answer the phone; indeed she pretended not to be at home and in my anger I struck my hand against the front panel, accidentally smashed the glass and ended up taking myself to casualty, where I had a few stitches, the precise number varying with the level of injustice I felt at the time of recounting this particular episode. In my mind, that blood all over my sleeve was Maddy's doing; that scar across my hand was from a wound she had inflicted upon me when she barred me from my own home.

The next morning was Valentine's Day and the shop windows were adorned with giant pink hearts and over-sized cards. I had a white-bandaged hand that showed dark specks of red if I used it too much; which I did, subconsciously proving some sort of point. I refused to speak to Maddy for weeks after that, until I had already got divorce proceedings under way.

The undignified exit from my marriage was not a new memory to me; its recovery had been prompted some weeks earlier when I'd asked Gary about the scar on my left hand. Linda had pointed out that it cut across the 'heart line' on my palm. 'That signifies a difficulty in a relationship . . .'

'Yes, I know it does, Linda – it's a scar from the night my marriage finally ended.'

'No, I mean you could have discerned a possible break-up, just from reading your palm.'

'Yes, except my palm was wrapped in a blood-soaked bandage from where I smashed the glass because Maddy had changed the locks to our house. That would have been another clue.'

But this morning the memory came back to me again, lying in bed with Madeleine in an old-fashioned guest room in West Cork. I had heard the sound of broken glass being swept up outside the pub and the sorry episode had rudely leapt into my consciousness when it was least welcome. I glanced down at where Maddy stirred, and was glad the noise hadn't jolted her awake.

After I woke that morning I had been unable to remember where I was for a few seconds – it reminded me of how entire days had felt when I'd first lost my memory. But then there had been a surge of elation as I remembered how Maddy had quietly tiptoed to my bed the night before and cuddled up next to me. And there she still was, stirring slightly, placing her dozing head on the Madeleine-shaped dip below my shoulder as she had so often done in a previous life.

We had not had sex the previous night. I had been tempted to make physical advances in that direction, but I was haunted by what Maddy had reported about her mother earlier in the day. In years to come I didn't want Madeleine telling the children that I had been 'sexually selfish'. I was stroking her hair as she dozed, but now I could not get the memory of 13 February out of my head. I recalled feeling utterly humiliated as I stood on my own front doorstep, alternately demanding, then pleading, then screaming through the letterbox to be let in. It had felt like she was stealing my whole life from me; literally robbing me of who I'd been for the previous couple of decades.

I stopped stroking Maddy's hair. Her head was actually quite heavy on my collarbone and I shifted my body so her head fell on to the pillow. She had actually changed the locks on the house where I lived with my children! I hadn't been violent or unfaithful; she just didn't want me living there any more, so she had changed the locks. How was that not a monstrous thing to have done?

Madeleine shifted slightly in her half-sleep and pulled the quilt off my body. I felt my indignation rising, the deferred anger resurfacing as I thought about the injustice that had been done to me. Now I climbed out of bed, thinking I might go and have breakfast alone, but she rolled over and opened her eyes and smiled dreamily at me.

'I seem to be in your bedroom . . .' she said playfully.

'Yes,' I mumbled coldly, avoiding eye contact, finding myself obliged to focus on the cheap kettle on the side table instead.

'Why don't you come back to bed?'

'No, I'm, er, just going to see if I can make some tea.'

And I took the kettle to the sink, but it banged quite hard against the tap as I did so.

'Are you okay?'

'Fine,' I said, as if denying a monstrous allegation. 'Oh, the bloody kettle doesn't fit in the sink – how's that supposed to work? That is so stupid!'

'Fill it up using the cup. Or use the cold tap in the bath.' Now she was sitting up in bed. I noticed that she was back to wearing my T-shirts in bed, which I understood was quite significant in the complex code of marital diplomacy.

I banged cups and saucers, and used more force than was strictly necessary to tear open individual sachets. I had felt obliged to offer Maddy a cup too and now, as she sipped it, she said how lovely it was to be brought a cup of tea in bed. I failed to return the smile and countered that I hated those little cartons of UHT milk, which I had only mentioned several thousand times before over the course of our marriage. The moment had come to vocalize my fury about what she had done. I knew it might ruin everything, but I couldn't hold down my anger about the way I'd been treated. I glanced up at her sitting against the pillows, her smooth pale skin still slightly creased from where she had slept. She looked back me with a coy smile and then she pulled the T-shirt over her head so that she was now completely naked in the middle of a soft white bed. 'So, why don't we have sex and then go downstairs for a big cooked breakfast?'

'Oh God, oh God . . .' I groaned a few minutes later. 'You are so beautiful . . .'

'All right, shut up!' She tutted. 'Blimey, I must look a right state – just woken up, with my hair all sticking up and big bags under my eyes.'

Now that sexual intercourse had occurred, the case of the lock-changing was re-examined and found to be a trivial, inconsequential matter that had really been blown out of all proportion. Actually, now I thought about it again, the fact that in my drunken state I had smashed a window rather vindicated Maddy's decision to keep me locked out. I recalled that 'make-up sex' had always had an extra passionate edge to it, so it was unsurprising that 'make-up after getting divorced' sex proved to be even more potent. I was still lying on top of her, but we knew each other well enough by now for her to admit this wasn't actually all that comfortable. So we lay side by side for a moment, and I stroked the stretch marks from way back when she had been pregnant with Jamie. I couldn't remember sex like that with Maddy. At no point during intercourse had she blithely mentioned that the car was making a funny rattling noise or wondered out loud if her mother still had her school reports in the attic.

After breakfast we walked by the port, hoping to buy

Madeleine's parents a present for looking after the house and dog. Only the Post Office and General Store was open at this time of year, and Maddy was torn between a linen tea towel featuring Irish winners of the Eurovision Song Contest or a tub of live lugworms. In the height of summer the quayside buzzed with blubbery local boys hurling themselves into the sea and tourists in chunky jumpers emerging from the pub with trays of Guinness and Tayto crisps. But now the village felt ghostly and suspended; boats were wrapped in damp tarpaulins; eye-mask shutters covered the windows of the hibernating holiday homes.

'Do you want to go back to Barleycove? You know, for one last swim?'

'No, thanks, I'm not risking pneumonia a second time. Anyway, it's nice here – we could walk up to the headland maybe?'

'You're right, it's a lovely spot. We should have stayed at that pub when we were students instead of bloody camping.'

'Yeah, well . . . Some things take you twenty years to learn.'

This hadn't meant to be significant, but now that the words were out it seemed to demand some sort of clarification about where the two of us stood. We stared out at the bobbing yachts and listened to the chorus of cables slapping against aluminium masts.

'I came out to West Cork to decide something,' Maddy said finally. 'And yesterday, staring into that fire at Barleycove, I think I came to a conclusion.'

I felt my heart accelerate and inadvertently whispered my next sentence.

'What did you decide?'

She took both my hands in hers as she looked me directly in the eye.

'That next time I'm going swimming in the Atlantic in April, I'm buying a fucking wetsuit.'

'That seems reasonable . . . I might not always be there with your cashmere.'

'Oh, that was the other thing.' She looked back out across the water. 'It would be quite nice if you were.'

A couple of seagulls seemed to laugh together in the distance. After about twenty seconds Maddy said, 'Can you stop hugging me now as I'm having trouble breathing?'

We walked out of the village and towards the cliffs, and I took her hand and she let me hold it, even though the narrow path soon became single file, which made walking like that ridiculous. The wind was stronger up on the hills beyond the village, and the path ahead looked challenging. Finally we were at the cliffs looking down on the bay, sitting on a weathered bench that a bereaved husband had erected in memory of his late wife.

'Look at those dates,' I said. 'Fifty-five years they were married. Do you think we could stay together fifty-five years?'

'Depends. You might go off and have an affair tomorrow, and then I would have to kill you . . .'

'Really? Is that the very worst thing?'

'No, actually. If you immediately confessed to a one-off infidelity, I might just forgive you. But if you didn't tell me and then I found out, well, I would kill you slowly and painfully and post the video of your execution on YouTube.'

'I find that hard to believe. You managing to post anything on YouTube.'

We reminisced fondly about the first time we had come on holiday here; how we had hired bicycles and put them on the ferry to Clear Island, and eaten pub lunches and swum on deserted beaches, and found a beautiful loch in the hills above Ballydehob and camped up there on the edge of the woods for a few nights with nobody seeming to mind. We delighted in parading these liberated memories; during the years of fighting, such stories had been officially suppressed as they had done nothing to help the war effort. Now these folk tales were being positively encouraged as part of the ongoing peace process; we were writing a new history of our marriage, one that suited the new ending of the happy, loving, divorced couple.

'So tell me, are we actually legally divorced yet?'

'No, that's in a few weeks' time – there's one last court thing, but we're not expected to go to it.'

'Well, maybe we should go?' I half joked.

'Hey, yeah! I could wear my wedding dress again – and you could wear your best suit, and we could have confetti outside and a big reception afterwards?'

'Oh, fantastic!

'Fantastic?'

'Yeah – you're up for doing stupid stuff again!'

Suddenly I decided I really ought to do this properly, and by the bench on the windswept headland in our favourite part of the world I took her hand and got down on one knee. 'Madeleine Vaughan, would you do me the immense privilege of becoming my ex-wife? I'm asking you – no, begging you: will you divorce me?'

A sheep stared at us as, as if it had found its intellectual match.

'I would be honoured!'

This was going to be a divorce like no other. We both accepted it would be far too complex and expensive to try to reverse the whole process now, so we resolved we would have a different kind of *decree nisi* with champagne and speeches and a big party to celebrate that we were going to live happily ever after now that we were finally divorced. We talked about how the children might adjust to having us both at home again, how we had to be careful not to argue in front of them when disagreements eventually came along. Which then happened immediately . . .

'I'm sorry I couldn't just take you back after your fugue. But I had to be really sure that you wouldn't walk out on us again.'

I was slightly shocked by just how distorted her version of our split was. For a second I wondered if I could just let this pass, but it seemed too fundamental to leave it in the official record.

'Erm . . . it seems a shame to drag this up now, but . . . I didn't actually walk out on you. It was you who changed the locks, if you remember?'

'Changed the locks? What are you talking about?'

'You changed the lock on the front door, like you threatened. That was the moment I realized the marriage was beyond saving and I had to start divorce proceedings.'

'I didn't change the locks, you stupid idiot! I know I used to say it, but I'd never actually do that!'

'Yes, you did. And you pretended to be out – even after I cut my hand on the glass in the door.'

'What? That was you? We thought someone had tried to break in! I'd taken the kids to stay at my parents to give them a break from all the fighting – I left you a note and everything. But when I came back the window was smashed and you weren't there and wouldn't return my calls for weeks afterwards . . .'

'Yeah, because you'd gone and changed the locks!'

Maddy turned to look directly at me. 'Had you been drinking?'

'What?'

'When the particular key you selected from your keyring didn't work in the front-door lock? Had you been drinking?'

There was a long pause while I opted to forego the incredible view from the cliffs and found myself staring down at the muddy path.

'Look, er, if you like, I can move my vinyl LPs out of the lounge . . .'

Chapter 23

It was spring, when a middle-aged man's fancy turns to divorce. Maddy and I entered the court arm in arm and walked ceremoniously down the central aisle. Fortunately, Madeleine's old wedding dress had not been a traditional white puffy meringue number, with five-foot train and cascading bridal veil, or else she might have been charged with contempt of court by wearing it to her final divorce hearing. But she was unmistakably a bride, in a classy crimson-silk three-quarter-length dress, clutching a bunch of roses that matched the single rose in her coquettish hat. This was only the second time she had worn this outfit, and I complimented her that after two children and fifteen years she could still get into it.

'Thank you. Oh, and if an expensive new dress purchase happens to show up on our credit card, then we must have been the victim of identity theft.'

Despite all my recent efforts jogging on my dog walks and giving up alcohol, I failed to fit into the suit I'd worn on my wedding day, which was just as well considering the size of the shoulder pads and the way the sleeves were meant to be pushed up on the jacket. Neither did I have sufficient hair to replicate the bouffant 1990s fringe that was already out of date first time round. But I hired a smart grey morning suit and wore a rose in my buttonhole, and we stood side by side in the Principal Registry of the Family Division, ready for the judge to pronounce us man and ex-wife.

The judge himself initially checked that we weren't in the wrong building when what appeared to be a bride and groom entered his court for the next *decree nisi* on that morning's roster. Both our long-suffering lawyers were present, now themselves finding some sort of common cause in the obstinate refusal of this impossible couple to follow the traditional script of bitter acrimony. The legal settlement still had to be decreed, but this part was now purely academic. It no longer mattered who got the house or how much I had to pay Madeleine each month, as we would all be part of the same unit.

Only a few minutes were normally allotted for such cases, all financial and custody disputes having generally been sorted long before a separation reached this final formality. Except this time, the stock answers to the usual questions did not quite apply, and it seemed that the judge's day had been brightened up by this unconventional couple. 'Sounds more like a marriage than a divorce!' he observed.

'You could say that, m'lud,' said an embarrassed lawyer, and Maddy proudly showed the courtroom a new bejewelled ring on her wedding finger.

'Counsel, may I just ask the petitioner directly – are you absolutely certain, Mr Vaughan, that you wish to divorce this woman?'

'Oh yes, your honour.' I looked lovingly at Maddy, who smiled back. 'I've never been so sure of anything in my whole life!'

The judge then declared that since there were no other legal impediments, the *decree nisi* was granted and the pair were now legally divorced. And then my lawyer mumbled sarcastically to himself, 'You may now kiss the divorcee.' So I did.

There was no notice outside the divorce court saying that the throwing of confetti was forbidden, so as Maddy and I emerged hand in hand, a small gathering of friends and family showered us with tiny coloured bits of tissue paper. I had to stop myself being concerned about creating litter. Our children were particularly generous with the confetti, tipping whole boxes of the stuff on to their parents' heads, before asking if they could ride in the white Rolls-Royce that had been booked to drive us to the reception. And so the whole family climbed inside and pulled away to the applause of the crowd, Dillie in the front passenger seat, desperate to be spotted by someone she knew.

'This is so cool. Can we go to the Ritz for lunch?'

'Too expensive. We could buy you some Ritz for lunch?'

But for Jamie and Dillie's benefit, the Rolls-Royce took a scenic route home, passing along the banks of the River Thames, over Chelsea Bridge, and taking in the drive-thru McDonald's, where the uniformed chauffeur leaned out of the window to order the kids a Happy Meal and chocolate shake. By the time we pulled up at our home, most of the guests had arrived for the reception and were already sipping champagne in the large marquee which took up most of the garden.

Our friends had happily dressed up in their best wedding out-fits to mark the occasion. Only Madeleine's mother struggled to process the irony of the thing and was circulating among relatives, explaining that they weren't really going to be divorced because they were actually back together now and would probably get remarried again like Richard Burton and Elizabeth Taylor. Except, she added as an afterthought, without the second divorce and battles with alcoholism.

Most of our social circle had been delighted to learn that one of their favourite couples were back together, although some of Maddy's women friends found themselves regretting having agreed quite so emphatically with her when she had said how terrible her husband was. 'When I said "I'd always thought you were too good for him", I, er, meant you were too good for how Vaughan was behaving when you were getting divorced, um, as it were. But apart from that I always thought he was just the right man for you, lovely bloke, the perfect husband. Or ex-husband, whatever you're going to call him . . .'

Now that they'd all had a couple of weeks to get used to the idea, there was a sense of real euphoria amongst the friends gathered here on this special day. Jokes were funnier, food was tastier, the sun was sunnier; this was the perfect party because everyone present was resolved that it should be so. 'Oh, this is so romantic!' said the heavily pregnant Linda. 'Why can't we get divorced?'

Today Gary was taking the role of best man, or 'worst man', as he enjoyed telling everyone, even claiming he'd had the idea that Maddy and I should get back together. In his waistcoat pocket he checked he still had the original wedding rings that we had not worn for months but would later place on one another's finger in front of everyone we knew and loved.

Dillie was officially the world's most charming and delightful twelve-year-old girl, seemingly genuinely interested and surprised as a succession of adults informed her that she had grown. Jamie would have blushed when he was asked if he had a girlfriend, had he not already been asked the same question eleven times already that day. 'No, I'm saving myself for Miss Right' got an appreciative chuckle from elderly relatives; the follow-up, less so: 'Or *Mr* Right, depending on how I turn out.' The family dog actually did come out of the closet, having been given the confidence by our cravat-wearing neighbour, who brazenly fed him endless chicken goujons and sausage rolls. Woody had never felt so liberated: 'At last – this is the real me! Yes, I adore food! Is that so bad? Must I always feel such shame for the love that dare not speak its name? Finally, I'm coming out! I am a gourmand! A foodie! A glutton! I am greedy and I am proud – get used to it!'

Ron danced an old-fashioned dance with his beautiful daughter and Jean looked on with brimming pride at the two of them. With the champagne flowing through her veins, she suddenly erupted into tears of joy to see the uncomplicated love between the two most important people in her life. 'He always was a splendid dancer,' she slurred. 'He's always been such a wonderful husband. I'm so lucky to have him, I really am . . .' I nearly choked on my chicken drumstick.

Eventually it was time for the mock ceremony; and Gary guided people towards the raised decking in preparation for the service. A decade and a half before, Maddy and I had given a set of vows before the council registrar and elderly relations in hats. We had promised 'to have and to hold from this day forward, for better, for worse, for richer, for poorer, in sickness and in health, to love and to cherish, till death us do part.' On reflection, we had to accept that we had fallen a little short of these demanding promises, and perhaps should have aimed a little lower first time round. 'With this ring, I thee wed for a bit. With my body, I thee worship, even if I thee repel with my habit of leaving toenail clippings in the bidet. With all my worldly goods I thee endow, except my big book on the history of nude photography, which I naively imagine you haven't spotted in that box in the loft.'

For this special 'second time around' ceremony we had resolved that we should still publicly commit to one another, but this time with a completely new set of revised, more realistic vows. These pledges were designed for the more mature couple under no illusions about the compromises and occasional disappointments of a lifelong partnership. 'I promise to sometimes pretend to listen to you going on about stuff, when really I'm thinking about something completely different'; 'I promise to love you in an everyday, familiar, best-friend sort of way, but not expect gushing declarations of devotion, with flowers, chocolates and love sonnets every bloody five minutes.' And 'I promise to tolerate your imperfections and varying moods as you tolerate mine, and not to use these as private justification for entering my old girlfriends' names on Google.'

There was a big cheer as the stars of the show stepped out on to the decking from the kitchen doors. Gary, now dressed for some reason as a bishop, or perhaps the Pope, calmed the crowd and reminded the guests once again what a special occasion this was. 'For earlier today, Vaughan and Maddy finally took the big step that so many of us have often thought about but never quite had the courage to do, and finally got themselves divorced.' A big drunken cheer went up from the crowd. I looked out at the swarm of benevolent faces and, swaying there in the blazing sun, felt myself sweating under my stiff hired suit.

'Now, Maddy and Vaughan appreciate that some of you came to their original wedding fifteen years ago, and brought them some lovely gifts, which they now feel morally obliged to return to you . . .'

There were a few shouts of 'Shame!' and one lone voice heckled, 'They've bought them back off eBay?'

'. . . particularly,' he continued, 'the unopened tin of pink trout roe caviar which passed its sell-by date at some point during the last millennium. Mark and Erena, it is with a heavy heart they are returning the twenty-two-piece dining set you gave them, which after one particularly fierce argument is now a ninety-two-piece dining set.' Slightly nervous laughter greeted this joke; the audience were unsure whether it was acceptable to refer to past marital difficulties at a divorce party.

'Pete and Kate – to you they are returning the set of six crystal wine glasses, which is now a set of eleven crystal wine glasses, as Maddy and Vaughan buy their petrol from the same garage as you.' This joke was enjoyed by all the people old enough to remember the cliché of petrol stations giving out free glasses, though Dillie laughed her head off along with everyone else, even if she didn't have the faintest idea what Gary was on about.

He was milking this chance to perform to a generous crowd for everything it was worth. But after a while, though I could hear the sound of his voice, I ceased to hear the actual words. Of course I smiled and chuckled along in all the right places, but my mind was taking in a hundred other things at once: the detached interest with which Jamie was observing these curious adults, the knot in one of the guy ropes holding up the marquee, the vapour stream from a jet plane heading thousands of miles away from all of this. I saw friends I had got to know all over again, other teachers from my department at school, and the next-door neighbour with the cravat whose name I feared I might never find out. And I saw Madeleine, smiling and laughing with her bouquet of roses held before her, nodding in agreement at Gary's jokes or feigning outrage at some of his humorous suggestions. And then I closed my eyes and felt the warmth of the sun on my face, the brightness burning through my eyelids, the spirals and the swirling sunspots floating me somewhere else. When suddenly it happened – a major piece of my past gatecrashed the party; an entire sequence of memories arrived in my head uninvited, as I blinked at the piercing sun, feeling dizzy and distant and now utterly distraught.

I had had an affair.

While Maddy and I were still married, I had been unfaithful to her. I had lied to her about my late nights and a weekend away in Paris. It returned to me now in every detail.

Her name was Yolande; a short, dark-haired, twenty-something French language assistant at school, who had eventually returned to France, with both of us agreeing the affair should end there. But for a month or so I had seen her secretly after work, going back to her flat and lying to Maddy about school plays or department meetings; and eventually I had been bold enough to muscle in to a school trip to Paris with Yolande, creeping into her hotel bedroom long after the other staff and students were all asleep.

And now, after everything that had happened, and standing up here with the woman I loved, I felt appalled with myself that I could have deceived and betrayed Madeleine in this way. I remembered that the affair had come at a point in our dying marriage when normal communication had utterly broken down; months after Maddy and I had ceased to have sex, when we no longer behaved as husband and wife. But if I'd felt that there had been any moral justification, why had I never told her, why had I kept this secret locked up so tightly that it was one of the very last memories to re-emerge?

I looked at Gary concluding his comic turn, explaining to the congregation the nature of these new vows that Maddy and I were about to take. I glanced across at my wife and she caught my eye and gave me a mock long-suffering smile. I looked at my daughter, clasping her hands together in delight at the hilarity and romance of her parents' party. Jamie was watching me sweating up on the impromptu stage of the decking, and gave his father a little thumbs-up.

Other details of my affair were churning over in my brain. I could recall the potent illegality of that first time. There were so many good reasons why I should not proceed to have sex with this French-language assistant, I remembered thinking. However, ranged against all the very valid and persuasive arguments was the incontrovertible fact that she was lying naked right in front of me at that very moment. In the complex balance of power within the male psyche, there are times when the collective judgement of mind, heart and soul are all overruled by penis.

I remembered the first time I had come home after having had sex with another woman, wondering if Maddy would be able to tell; whether she would see it instantly in my eyes or hear me confess in my sleep. But eye contact between us had been lost months earlier; there was too much brittle hostility in the air for Maddy's antennae to detect any suppressed contrition. Nor could I possibly tell her. She was already furious with me on so many counts and I was angry in return. If she knew, it would only make everything much worse. Whether we split up or somehow resolved to try to save the marriage, either way my actions ruined everything. But not if she didn't know.

But that was then. Standing here now in our own home, surely she had to know the truth before the two of us began our new life together? If not now, then when? Tonight when we'd said goodbye to the last of the guests and were loading up the dishwasher? 'Well, that was a lovely day, wasn't it? Oh, by the way, I had sex with a woman from school a while back.' Tomorrow morning over a cup of tea in bed? When is the best time to tell your wife you've had an affair? There really ought to be some official guidance on this. Before or after you make a set of vows in front of friends and family? 'If you immediately confessed I might just forgive you . . .' That was what she had said.

Gary had finished his speech, but before the climax of the afternoon's entertainment Maddy just wanted to say a few words. She wanted to thank all the people who had helped make today's party possible: she thanked her mother and father, Dillie and Jamie. She thanked Gary for being so entertaining and for agreeing to be today's MC. She thanked Dillie's best friend for cueing up the music. She thanked everyone who had brought some food. In fact, she was thanking so many people there was a chance the marriage would run its natural course and one of us would die before I ever had the chance to come clean.

'Gary!' I whispered, gesturing him to step back inside the kitchen. 'Gary!'

'It's all right, mate – rings are in my pocket. Just checked . . .'

'No, listen – I just remembered something.'

'How to play football?'

'Listen, this is serious. I . . .' I lowered my voice to almost inaudible. '. . . I had an affair.'

Gary grinned at me. 'Yeah, right! And it was you who smashed up the *Blue Peter* garden . . . You won't get me on a wind-up, mate – that's my specialist subject.'

'No, I swear I did. Really – a couple of years ago. It was only a month or so, but I was unfaithful to Maddy.'

Now he did step back from the decking into the relative privacy of the kitchen.

'Bloody hell, Vaughan. What the fuck are you telling me this now for?'

'I only just remembered it. I have to tell Madeleine! I have to tell her the truth before the vows!'

The two of us looked at Maddy out on the makeshift stage as she effusively thanked the neighbour who had provided one of the trestle tables for the buffet.

'Are you insane? Don't tell her now. Don't tell her ever, but especially not now. You've come so far, don't throw it all away, you idiot.'

'But it has to be before we commit. Withholding it is deception.'

'Deception is fine! Deception is normal. You should never, ever be completely open and honest with your wife. That's the worst thing you can possibly do.'

This was a decisive moment in my life and somehow I felt cheated that the only person I could turn to for advice was a pissed bloke dressed as the Pope.

'But later is too late. I have to kill the lie now. She said she'd forgive me if I told her *immediately*.'

'At least sleep on it; think it over. Don't ruin her big day. 'Cos this whole thing today, you know, it's actually a bit like a wedding,' observed Gary, as if this was a rather perceptive insight.

The applause for Maddy cut the furtive exchange short and now the moment had come for the spoof ceremony and the symbolic (and unironic) exchange of rings. I stepped back outside with Gary, who seemed slightly less assured than he had before, less relaxed in front of all these people, and he stammered and mumbled his explanation of the next section of the proceedings.

I caught Maddy's eye and she raised her eyebrows at me with a slightly coy grin. This might possibly be the last smile I ever got from her, I thought. Which was better: a happy marriage based on a lie, or the risk of no marriage because I'd told the truth? Or was that first choice really available to me? Wouldn't it only *appear* to be a good marriage but not really be happy at all, though she would never quite put her finger on what was missing? And why *did* they stop giving out free wine glasses with petrol? Was it sending the wrong message to drink-drivers?

'Maddy!' I whispered behind Gary's back.

'Ready?' she said back, unsurreptitiously.

'Maddy – there's something I have to tell you before we do this. Come into the kitchen.'

I sounded so deadly serious, it must have seemed ridiculous.

'Stop pissing about – you'll give me the giggles.'

'I'm serious. It's about before we split up. I've only just remembered it, but you have to know now.'

'Vaughan, you're freaking me out. Shut up!'

With just a gesture of my head, I indicated that we move back from the exposed stage and, looking perplexed, Maddy stepped inside.

'So what's the big deal?' she whispered.

'You know when we were barely talking and I went to Paris with the school? It wasn't just with the school. I went because there was another woman.'

Now Maddy could see that I wasn't joking, and no amount of blusher or lipstick could hide the colour draining from her face. She struggled for words for a moment, but finally half whispered, half choked a question.

'What do you mean? How . . . who is she?'

'She was a French language assistant at school. It was over in a month, and I'm not in contact. It was just a thing, when everything was going wrong, and I'm really, really sorry, but I had to be honest with you.'

'Jesus himself attended a wedding in Galilee,' read Gary from his cue cards. 'He gave the happy couple his father's blessing and some IKEA gift vouchers . . .'

'Maddy, say something. It'll never happen again, I promise. We were both so unhappy then, I think I was, like, pressing a self-destruct button.'

But Maddy had nothing to say, though her mascara was being diluted and a dark line ran down her cheek.

'So, Vaughan and Madeleine, step forward please!' demanded the unconvincing clergyman. We hovered on the other side of the open doors for a second. 'Come on, come on, don't be shy!' said Gary, ushering us back out into the open air. 'So if any person or golden retriever knows of any just impediment why this man and woman should not be disunited in unholy divorce, let them speak now or for ever hold their peace.'

I glanced at Maddy, who seemed too stunned to quite under-stand what she was doing there.

'Jack Joseph Neil Vaughan, do you take Madeleine Rose Vaughan of this parish to be your legally separated ex-wife, to live with in sin from this day forth? Will you notice when she's been to the hairdresser's and accept her choice of driving routes as a reasonable alternative?'

'I, um . . . I will.' I glanced at her; at least the crying seemed to be at a minimum. But Dillie had seen that her mother had shed tears, and though many present presumed she was moved by the emotion of the occasion, her daughter could sense that it was something else.

'And, Madeleine Rose Vaughan, do you take Jack Joseph Neil Vaughan to be your legally separated ex-husband, to live with in sin from this day forth. Will you tolerate him and humour him? Will you not use his razor for your armpits? Will you laugh at jokes you've heard a hundred times before? Will you pretend to be interested in his theories about what might have happened if Hitler had invaded Afghanistan?'

A silence followed. Jean's mother at the back saying, 'I will,' didn't count.

'She's forgotten her lines, ladies and gentlemen – it's a very big day . . .' Gary had been aware of us whispering inside and feared the worst. 'Just say, "I will",' he murmured to her. She looked down and saw her friends staring expectantly at her – almost mouthing the two words on her behalf. Gary smiled at the crowd, as if to suggest that this sort of pause was perfectly commonplace and normal service would be resumed any moment.

'She's changed her mind!' shouted a drunken heckler, whose wife then slapped him on the arm because she realized that maybe Maddy had.

'Take your time, Maddy – it's a big decision . . .' The humour had gone from Gary's voice, as if he was speaking to her sincerely now.

Finally Maddy seemed ready to speak and a wave of relief came over the crowd.

'You . . . you . . .' She was staring directly at me. 'You BAS-TARD!'

A couple of people attempted to laugh, as if this was all part of the day's ironic script, but their hearts weren't really in it. 'You complete and utter bastard!' And now she really did burst into tears as she threw her bouquet at my face. 'I never want to see you again for as long as I live.' And then she barged past Gary as she ran off the stage into the house, until the stunned crowd heard the front door slamming behind her.

Dillie's friend was supposed to cue the music the moment the ceremony was over, so at this point she nervously pressed 'Play' and the opening chorus of 'She Loves You' by the Beatles suddenly started up. I didn't know quite where to look, but ended up attempting a brave smile at my son, who was staring back at me with the fury of a child betrayed by his own father.

'Oh, fuck!' said Gary finally. 'Not again.'

Chapter 24

Apparently the party went downhill a bit after Madeleine left. The whole '*Isn't it funny that they're getting back together just as they get divorced?*' motif lost its ironic edge after the bride had thrown her bouquet in the groom's face, shouted that she had never wanted to see him ever again and stormed out in tears. Gary still tried to do one or two of his prepared jokes, but even he soon realized that perhaps the moment had gone. I eventually ran out after Maddy, but she'd grabbed the car keys and sped off as aggressively as is possible in a Honda Jazz automatic.

Her instinct had been to go and seek comfort with a friend, but after she had been driving for a minute or two she realized that all her friends were in her back garden with her adulterous partner, so she ended up in Sainsbury's car park and when the £5-car-wash man said her car was very dirty, she burst into tears again.

The party guests drifted off, mumbling embarrassed 'thank-yous' to me, and saying that most of the party had been very enjoyable. One of them took their wedding gift back home with them. Later that evening Jean came round to collect a few things of Maddy's, explaining to the children that their mummy was going to stay with her mummy for a night or two and that she would ring them later.

'If I could just talk to her for a moment,' I pleaded. 'Could you tell her that I need to talk to her?'

'She just needs a bit of *headspace* at the moment, Vaughan. Every relationship goes through this . . .'

I thought about this after she had gone and was pretty sure that every relationship did not go through this. Husband and wife split up, he has a mental breakdown resulting in total amnesia, spends an anonymous week in hospital, eventually sees his estranged wife as if for the first time, falls in love with her, bluffs his way through a court hearing, changes his mind about getting a divorce, eventually wins his wife back, then at the party to celebrate their new beginning remembers that he was unfaithful, tells her and she breaks up with him all over again. If every relationship did go through this, I would certainly like to read the self-help book or see the staged photos in the tabloid problem page featuring perplexed-looking models in their underwear.

In fact, Maddy stayed away for more than a couple of nights, and now I was the stressed single parent, getting the kids off to school, dashing on to work, then rushing back and cooking their tea and failing to be of any assistance with their maths homework. After that we'd all sit down to watch 'an hour's television' and a few hours later the kids would wake me up on the sofa and tell me they were going to bed now.

Jamie and Dillie spoke to their mum on the phone, but didn't ask any questions about what was going to happen in the long term. But passive acceptance is not the same thing as inner contentment.

'Do you want tuna pasta or sausage and mash?' I asked Jamie on the second night.

'Either,' shrugged my son.

'Well, say one. Tuna pasta?'

'Okay.'

'Or sausage and mash?'

'Okay.'

'Which one?'

'Either.'

I let out a significant sigh. 'Dillie, do you have a preference?'

Poor Dillie just wanted whatever would lighten the atmosphere and so endeavoured to be as accommodating as possible.

'I don't mind,' she said nervously.

Maddy rang Jamie's mobile every night and he grunted his few words before passing the handset to Dillie, who used up the talk-plan minutes within the first couple of days. I had texted and emailed Maddy but she couldn't bring herself to speak to me just yet.

I offered to move out if Maddy wanted to be back at the house with Dillie and Jamie, but in her anger she interpreted this as me not wanting to be responsible for the children so that I would be free to chase other young female members of staff.

Gary and Linda had me round for supper and I learned that they had tried to talk to Maddy about me, pointing out, in my defence, that I had at least told her the truth.

'Okay, it was wrong, he admits that,' Linda had said. 'But not every bloke would have owned up—'

'I wouldn't have,' Gary had chipped in brightly. But now Gary had reasons of his own to be depressed. He reported to me that he had finally decided to close down YouNews.

'Oh no – I'm sorry to hear that.'

'I thought that was the big one, man. I thought we were going to blow Murdoch out of the water.'

'Yeah, well, he is quite powerful. You know, in global media terms . . .'

'User-generated news doesn't work. People were just making stuff up.'

'What – unlike tabloid journalists?'

'I liked it,' said Linda, supportively. 'There was this really funny clip of a chimpanzee with a power hose—'

'Linda! That's not what it was for.'

'So are you no longer online?'

'Well, I posted a message saying it was closing down. But then some joker posted another message saying my message was a spoof and that YouNews had bought CNN and now everyone in the chatroom is really excited.'

'That's the trouble with the wisdom of crowds. Sometimes the crowd turns out to be really stupid.'

It felt like everything went wrong in the end. In your twenties you're full of optimism about all the things you're going to achieve; you pile up ambition and plans to be accomplished at some point in the future. In your thirties, you're so shell-shocked by babies and toddlers and moving house and working extra hard to pay for it all that you don't get a moment to glance up to see where you're going. It's only in your forties that you finally get time to catch your breath, take stock and reflect on where you are and what you've achieved. And that's when you suddenly realize that it's nowhere near what you'd hoped and lazily expected would just come to pass of its own accord. Your forties are the Decade of Disappointment.

I had a final appointment with Dr Lewington, who said she had been meaning to call me back in to monitor the progress on my amnesia. 'But here's the funny thing – I forgot!' She chuckled. 'What an intriguing organ the human brain is!' We chatted for a while, but when she asked me if I had regained any more significant memories I hesitated for a moment and then said, 'Er, no. None at all.' The curious thing that I should have shared with her was that this was the first memory I had regained and then subsequently lost again. I clearly recalled the moment it had all come back to me, but the details of Yolande and Paris were now a vague blur. It was as if my subconscious thought it was a little impolite to dwell on the whole sordid business.

I noticed the ceramic head on her desk had been broken and clumsily glued back together. Finally she announced, 'Well, I don't think there is anything else we can do for you. You can just walk out of here and get on with the rest of your life.'

I had decided that, since I was back in the hospital, I would try to locate Bernard. I had kept meaning to visit him before now, but life had been such a helter-skelter that I had never got round to it. I could already hear him chuckling, 'Better late than never!'

'Bernard?' asked Dr Lewington, blankly, when I asked where I could find him.

'You remember Bernard? Talkative bloke in the bed next to me. Had a brain tumour, but wasn't going to let it get him down.'

'Oh yes, him! No – you won't be able to visit him, I'm afraid.'

'Is he not here any more?'

'No. He died.'

Then, on the fourth day of limbo, I was surprised to receive a call from Maddy's father. Ron wanted to meet up with me and suggested the Humanities Café at the British Library at Euston. He did not say what he wanted, but I was reassured by his choice of venue. If he wanted to punch me in the face for betraying his daughter, the British Library did not seem the most obvious place to do it.

I had never been to this cultural cathedral before, and felt like a student again as I crossed the vast piazza. Gazing down upon me was a giant bronze statue. 'Isaac Newton from a drawing by William Blake'; two extraordinary brains at the other end of the scale to my unreliable piece of junk. At the top of the escalators a central pillar cased in glass revealed some of the millions of books contained within. All human knowledge was in there – a sense of quiet reverence came over me as I absorbed the echoes and hushed tones of students and academics all around me.

Ron was already waiting for me in the café when I arrived; he was seated at a booth and got up to shake my hand. He showed no hostility towards me for the trauma I had caused his daughter, even though I felt too embarrassed to look him in the eye.

'Vaughan, thank you so much for coming.'

'No problem at all. How's Maddy?'

'Well, she's been staying in her old bedroom most of the time. Her mother puts large plates of food beside her bed, then takes them away again a few hours later . . .'

'Right. So . . . this is a long way from home.'

'Yes, well, Jean doesn't like having me under her feet in the house, so I've been commuting to London to do a bit of research on your medical condition. I hope you don't mind?'

Inside I felt a pang of disappointment that this was what he had come all this way to talk to me about. I had hoped he might have a message from Maddy; that he was the junior diplomat sent to make the initial overtures in a historic rapprochement.

'I think I may have unearthed some interesting case studies,' he said. I gave a neutral nod, hoping I did not betray my private resignation that I was going to have to indulge him here. I'd already read everything there was to read on retrograde amnesia and dissociative fugues.

At the next table a young student couple were staring at one another, too in love to have separate drinks, their two straws intimately sharing the same iced mocha.

'Now I'm not saying that this definitely applies in your case, but it's something I think you should be aware of.' He indicated the pages he had photocopied from various reference books and old journals that were spread out all over the table.

'In 1957, this businessman in New York had exactly the same thing as you. He had been under great stress as a chief executive, with millions of dollars riding on his decisions and so forth, when one day he disappeared and was found a week later with no knowledge of who he was or what he did for a living.'

'Okay, well, I've not actually read about that one – but I have read about other cases like my own.'

'Yes, and just like you this gentleman gradually regained all his memories, until he reached the stage where he could return to work, and eventually the board voted to reinstate him.'

The student took his straw out of the cup and presented the foam on the end for his girlfriend to lick off.

'But at the moment when he returned to his old life, he suddenly remembered that he had defrauded the company. He was racked with guilt, confessed and resigned.'

'Sorry, Ron – but I don't quite see how that helps me now? I remembered all the worst stuff last as well. It's not much consolation to be told that there might be even worse stuff yet to come . . .'

'It's just I think this might have some bearing on your indiscretion in Paris.'

I blushed to hear the episode even mentioned, least of all by my father-in-law. 'Yeah, well, the funny thing is, I don't even remember that any more. It came back to me as clear as anything on the day of our party. But it's the first memory I've regained and then completely lost again.'

'But that's one of the symptoms!!' said Ron, excitedly. 'Look, this is the interesting bit. His company investigated his confession, and *it wasn't true*. There had been no fraud; it was a false memory!'

I had never seen Ron so animated.

'A false memory? How does that work?'

'It's all here. Deep down he was frightened of returning to the stressful challenges of his old life and subconsciously needed an excuse not to make that final leap.'

Only now did I look properly at the photocopied pages on the table.

'Where did you get all this from?'

'From books. Just books in the library here. You said you'd read everything there was to read on this?'

'On the internet, yeah.'

'Well, these examples are from years back. I suppose they were written up long before online medical journals and suchlike. But it really is amazing what you can find in the libraries when you look.'

'You mean there are others?'

'Yes – look. This was in a very interesting 1930s book about psychiatry. A local alderman in Lincoln actually confessed to killing a woman who, it transpired, was still alive.'

'I don't get it.'

'The sufferers aren't pretending to have these memories; they really do believe they did these bad things.'

I hurriedly scanned the rather dense print of the photocopied book, littered with terms I half recognized. The long-dead psychiatrist's theory was that this handful of individuals had experienced false memories for the same reason that they had suffered their original amnesia. Unable to cope with pressure or the possibility of failure, their brains had created an extreme solution: wipe all memories of the stressful life or create new memories that would make a return to that stressful life impossible.

Neither of us needed to point out that it was possible that I had imagined my affair, but I did so anyway.

'When I told a language teacher at school the reason Maddy and I had split up again, he said that Yolande never went on the Paris trip. He said she'd already left at that point. I thought he must have got it wrong.'

'Well, it seems like your brain has been playing tricks on you again.'

'Oh, Ron, this is fantastic! I feel like I've been let out of prison. I *didn't* have an affair!' I declared a little too loudly. A couple of elderly ladies were passing with a tray of tea and biscuits. 'I *wasn't* unfaithful to my wife!' I told them. 'This is incredible. Does Maddy know about this?'

'Yes, I told her last night.'

'What did she say?'

'She suggested I came and told you.'

'Right. Was she happy?'

'She was quite thoughtful. She said, "So Vaughan may not be an adulterer . . ."'

'Oh this is fantastic!'

'". . . he's just a total nutter."'

'Oh.'

Nearby there was the sudden scrape of a chair. One wrong word or gesture had clearly upset the teenage girl and she stormed off as her confused boyfriend called after her.

'Will you tell her that Yolande didn't even go to Paris? Will you tell her that I don't remember an affair any more? That proves my innocence, doesn't it? Will you tell her and get her to call me?'

'You're not really mad at all, are you? You're just mad about Maddy,' he said, with a smile. 'But then, who wouldn't be?'

A few hours later I was seated in the hall at my children's school, saving the empty seat beside me, though I had no idea whether it was likely to be filled. Jamie and Dillie were both appearing in the school production of *South Pacific*, and I had rushed there straight from the British Library. I had texted and emailed Maddy to say that I would leave her ticket at the desk, or that she could always go on her own the following night if she still didn't want to see her ex-husband. The nerves of all the children on the stage were nothing compared to those of one of the adults watching them.

The band struck up the overture, and Jamie looked as though he wished his guitar was big enough to hide him completely. All the parents were looking directly ahead except one, who kept looking round. My ability to follow the storyline was further hindered by the director's decision that the casting of the islanders and their white rulers must not be in line with the skin colour of his cast. I knew that Dillie's entrance was coming up, so now I endeavoured to concentrate on one of the show's most famous numbers. It was at that moment that a body quietly slipped in beside me and I heard Maddy whisper, 'Hi.'

I felt a surge of elation. What better time for my wonderful wife to make an appearance than during the chorus of 'There Is Nothing Like A Dame'. I turned to her in astonishment and exclaimed, 'Maddy!' so loudly that several indignant parents turned and glared at me for interrupting the song. Jamie smiled at having spotted his mother joining his dad, but immediately checked himself and focused on looking cool again. 'You haven't missed Dillie yet,' I whispered.

She said nothing else to me for most of the first act, which made me anxious and distracted throughout 'Some Enchanted Evening' and 'A Cockeyed Optimist'. The South London audience were particularly attuned to the musical's tentative racial discrimination theme and there were gasps of outrage at the use of the term 'mulatto' even though almost no one had ever heard it before. Still, it sounded racist, and that was enough for a bit of spirited hissing.

Finally, when the girl playing Emile sang 'Younger Than Springtime', I leaned across and whispered, 'So I spoke to your dad.'

I continued to stare straight ahead, but then she leaned across and whispered back. 'Yeah, he called me immediately afterwards.'

'Isn't it fantastic?'

'Fantastic? What's fantastic about it? Thanks for Saturday by the way. I had a really lovely party.'

'Sssh!' said a couple of teachers in front of us.

'Sorry!' I mouthed to them.

It's important for a couple to find time to talk to one another, I told myself, however hard the outside world seems determined to make it. I tried to establish how her father's discovery could be anything other than positive, but every time I whispered loud enough for her to hear, heads would turn and parents would glare.

'But it's great news. I imagined the whole thing – it never happened . . .'

'Can you please stop talking!' came the harsh whisper from behind us.

There was a round of applause for the end of the song, so Maddy gestured to me to come outside for a minute so we could talk. At that moment Dillie made her big entrance. Just in time to see both her parents getting up and scurrying towards the exit.

The two of us stood and talked in the school corridor, beside a noticeboard entitled 'My Inspiration', where one or two teachers had controversially *not* chosen Martin Luther King. Pausing whenever we were passed by a hurrying teacher or cast member, I tried to fathom why Maddy was still so cool with me.

'Look, I remember Yolande being at the school, but that's it. I mean, now it's like I hardly knew her. But I don't understand why you aren't pleased. I *didn't* sleep with the French-language assistant!' The group of teenage girls in grass skirts rushing down the corridor gave me a very strange look as they passed. In my euphoria I gestured to hug Maddy, but she did not accept the invitation.

'So why,' she asked accusingly, 'did you imagine you had an affair with this Yolande woman?'

'I don't know – ask the neurologist! Oh, you're not going to hold it against me that I *imagined* I had sex with another woman, are you? That's every male in the known universe . . .'

'I don't care who you imagine you have sex with.'

'Hello, Mrs Vaughan,' said one of Jamie's friends, dressed in a sailor costume.

'Hello, Danny. The first question is, did you imagine you had sex with Yolande because you fancied her?'

'Hello, Mrs Vaughan!'

'Hello, Ade. Well, did you?'

'What?! No!'

'Really?'

'This isn't fair. I've just discovered that I'm an innocent man but with a brain that's still playing tricks on me, and you're giving me a hard time because of something I didn't actually do.'

'But did you fancy Yolande the French-language assistant?'

'Yes, of course I fancied Yolande. Everyone did – she was gorgeous.'

'Thank you.'

'What's more pathetic is that my subconscious believed that a stunning young thing like Yolande would ever have an affair with an old fart like me! It's ridiculous – how could I have been so gullible as to believe my own brain?'

At that moment, the double doors of the hall burst open and the audience swept towards the school dining room where the catering students would be selling interval drinks and chunks of disintegrating pastry. Maddy and I went through with the rest of the crowd, feeling mortified when someone congratulated us on Dillie's wonderful performance.

'Very impressive set, I thought,' said Maddy, pointedly, in earshot of the head of art.

'So are you going to come home?' I demanded. 'Are we going to be a whole family again?'

'And the costumes! What a lot of effort must have gone into that.'

'Maddy – come home with me, Jamie and Dillie tonight. They've really missed you. I miss you.'

'Do you want an orange squash?'

'No, I do not want a bloody orange squash. You were all set to give our relationship another go, we made a big public thing of it, until I tried to be honest about something that had happened in the past. Well, now you've got the best of both worlds: I *wasn't* unfaithful, but you know I'd tell you if I had been.'

'It's not as simple as that.'

'It *is* as simple as that. You walked out because I had an affair. Now it turns out I didn't have an affair. So surely at that point you just come back again—'

'Didn't Dillie look fantastic up there? You must be very proud,' said a teacher I didn't recognize.

'Oh yes, she loves performing. Thank you!'

'And Jamie in the band as well! What a great night for the Vaughan family!'

'Well, let's see how it turns out . . .' I said, more pointedly than I had intended.

'It such a great musical, isn't it?' said Maddy, grateful that the teacher was still there. 'Great songs!'

'Oh yes, wonderful songs.'

'Yeah, tell me, Maddy, which number do you prefer?' I asked. '"I'm Gonna Wash That Man Right Out of My Hair" or "I'm In Love With A Wonderful Guy"?'

The teacher hovered politely to see the outcome of this interesting question.

'Oh, I'd say the best song is yet to come. "You've Got To Be Carefully Taught".'

'Good answer!' said the teacher.

Other families we half knew came and joined us, and I was frustrated that I didn't get another chance to talk with her before the second act. Madeleine seemed to be deliberately chatting with another mother as we returned to our seats, and stubbornly refused to talk about our future happiness throughout 'Happy Talk'. Finally, during the applause, I grabbed my opportunity.

'You said the *first* question is did I fancy Yolande. What was the second question?'

She was about to frame an answer when the applause stopped and she put her palm up and mouthed, 'Hang on . . .' and I had to wait until the end of the next song to get a response.

'Why did your mind need to create a false memory?' she finally said above the noise of the clapping and whistling. I was about to give my instant reaction, but the hall fell quiet again and she gestured for me to wait. So now I had time to frame a carefully judged response. I could analyse the question, think about the best answer, then floor her with my brilliantly worded reply.

'I dunno,' I said.

'Because at some deep level, you don't want to commit. Your brain invented a reason not to be with me because it doesn't want to be with me.'

'But—'

She put her fingers to her lips as the room fell quiet again. All the way through 'This Was Nearly Mine' I wanted to scream at the unfairness of it. My memory was like some random involuntary muscle: completely out of control, acting independently, wiping files, making up stuff, while I was held to account for the way it was trashing my past and future.

'But I *do* want to be with you. This is my brain talking too. I want to be with you, okay? In sickness and in mental health. Remember our wedding vows.'

'Yeah. Except we got divorced . . .'

Now Dillie was on stage again and both of us made a big show of craning our necks and making sure she could see us in the audience. We clapped loudly and I whistled and cheered, then realized I had lost my chance to reply to Maddy's killer argument.

Only at the end of the play did we really have another opportunity to talk at any length. During the standing ovation and repeated curtain calls, while we waved enthusiastically to our two children on stage, we tried to work out whether their mum and dad were going to stay together.

'I really don't know what I think,' sighed Maddy. 'I thought we had worked it all out and then you went and pulled a stunt like that.'

'You can't blame me for that. I have a neurological condition.'

'You have a psychological condition. And your psyche doesn't want you to be with me. That will manifest itself sooner or later, and I'm not going through all that again.'

'This is so unfair.' I had stopped clapping now and was just standing there looking at her. 'I want you back home, okay? Believe *me*, not my lying, broken memory banks. I want you back home, the kids want you back home, I didn't sleep with anyone else, and now you know you can trust me to tell you if I ever do. What else do I have to do?'

'Dillie's waving – wave back!'

I waved at my daughter, then gave two thumbs-ups to Jamie.

'Oh, God, I don't know,' sighed Maddy. 'I spoke to the lawyers before this false-memory stuff came up. Under the terms of the divorce, you have to vacate the house and I have to allow you access to the children every weekend. They're waiting for me to direct them to instruct you or something.'

'No, Maddy, think about it. Give us another chance.'

'Look, we can't put the kids through another break-up. I'll go back to Mum and Dad's and I'll be in touch, okay?'

That night Dillie went to bed later than normal, and I tucked her up like I used to when she was little. 'Why did you and Mum walk out just as I came on stage?'

'Oh dear, you saw that, did you? I'm very sorry we weren't there for your big debut. But it was because we were trying to sort out whether we're both going to be there all the rest of the time.'

'What did you decide?' said Jamie, standing at his sister's bedroom doorway.

'Oh, hi, Jamie. Well, we aren't sure yet. We're both going to be in your lives a lot. It's just whether we do it together or apart.'

'Can we have some crisps?'

'Look, just because you know I'm feeling guilty about missing Dillie's debut and Mum not being here and everything, you think I'm going to be a soft touch for junk food after you've both brushed your teeth. Well . . . there's a big cheese-and-onion grab bag in the cupboard.'

*

The next day the kids went to school and I called in sick. I waited for the phone, running to answer every call, then gasping for breath as I told the insurance salesman from Bangalore that I really wasn't interested. Late that night I jumped out of bed at the sound of a taxi pulling up outside, only to see Anonymous Cravat Man and his wife staggering towards their front door. I really should have taken the trouble to find out his name by now. For two days I waited for any message from Maddy. I had sent her a long email listing all the reasons why I felt that we should be together, but heard nothing back. I didn't dare leave the house in case she came round, and the stir-crazy dog barked and stared at the front door. The longer the silence went on, the more pessimistic I became.

Her response finally came in the only form I had not considered. It arrived by post. On the third day, a solitary letter landed face up on the doormat and in that moment I feared the worst. A formal letter, addressed to me, from her lawyer: that could only be an official instruction to vacate the house and adhere to the terms of the divorce.

I looked at the family shoes and coats in the hallway. One of Maddy's coats was still on the hook, and Jamie and Dillie's shoes were lined up beside their mother's. Up the stairs were framed black-and-white photos of the children: Jamie with his sister on her very first day at school, taking her hand as he led her out of the gate; the two of them a few years older standing on the beach looking sea-washed and salty; and there was Maddy holding both of them when they were tiny, one in either arm, laughing at the camera, innocently unaware that it would indeed just be her and the two kids in years to come. The optimism of this image seemed so ridiculous. I summoned up memories of Maddy and me laughing together on a rowing boat on the Serpentine; of Maddy rocking our sleeping child; now I could see her excitedly waving at me from the window of a National Express coach when she'd returned to university and I'd been waiting for her at the station.

I was not sure where exactly I wanted to be when I opened this emotional letter bomb. I took it into the kitchen, but decided I didn't want to read it there. I wandered into the lounge and then back to the hallway. I held the letter up to the light, but the envelope was too expensive to see through. And finally I ripped it open to have my fate confirmed to me.

Inside there was no letter from the lawyers. Just a tatty green postcard featuring a cartoon leprechaun saying 'Top o' the mornin' to yers!!'

Chapter 25

'She's beautiful; she's absolutely perfect!' I said, looking at the newborn baby in Maddy's arms, or possibly at Maddy, I never actually specified.

'Would you like to hold her, Vaughan?' suggested Linda, from the hospital bed, and with a nostalgic smile Madeleine passed the baby over to her partner, as Gary and Linda proudly looked on.

'Can I take a photo of her with my phone?' asked Dillie, and Linda said that was fine.

'Did you want to take a picture as well, Jamie?' I said, noticing that my son was fiddling with his mobile.

'What?'

'Did you want to take a picture of Gary and Linda's baby?'

'Not right now. I'm playing Angry Birds.'

Linda's birth plan had specified her wish to have a more traditional birthing experience, which Gary had taken as his cue to play it like a 1950s husband and remain in the pub the entire evening. He only just made it in time after a call from an extremely tetchy midwife, who, Gary claimed, had been grumpy whatever he did. 'Put that cigarette out!' she had barked at him. 'This is a hospital!'

'It's not a cigarette, it's a joint. Surely if it's a special occasion . . .'

But now, incredibly, here the new baby was. And here was Maddy with our own children, marvelling at the miracle of a whole new life.

'Isn't it amazing, Jamie? A perfect new person who will see the world with completely fresh eyes—'

'Yes!' exclaimed Jamie, enthusiastically, not looking up from his screen. 'High score!!'

I looked into the unfocused eyes of the tiny baby, feeling some sort of vague affinity with this new arrival. And Maddy smiled as she looked at the baby staring up in the direction of her newborn man. I randomly suggested that she had her mother's eyes and her father's chin. I couldn't actually discern any physical similarities in this scrunched-up little red face, but it was the sort of thing that you were supposed to say, and nobody bothered to contradict me.

'Does it take you back to when you first held our two?' said Maddy.

'God, yeah, I'll never forget that—'

'*Again* . . .' heckled Jamie, without looking up.

Linda took the baby back and went to breastfeed her, and, struggling with the etiquette of this situation, I pointedly fixed Gary directly in my gaze and asked him if he was planning to do any late-night feeds with the bottle.

'It depends whether Linda is able to express enough. We don't want to use formula milk when obviously breast is best for Baby.'

'He said "best for Baby",' I thought. No definite article. They've got him too. And soon after that an attractive nurse approached to check Linda's charts and Gary's gaze did not wander one millimetre from his wife and child.

'Shall I take Baby?' suggested Gary.

'*The* baby,' said Jamie.

'Oh, we brought you a present,' I remembered.

'You didn't need to do that . . .'

'We were going to pay for a newly discovered star to be named after her, but it turns out that's an expensive con.'

'Unless you do it the other way round and just call the baby "Beta J153259-1".'

Linda gave a little shake of the head, as if this was not one of the names they were considering. Gary ripped open the paper to reveal a specially commissioned family tree, surrounded by various photos of the baby's parents and grandparents and with an empty space for her own image right at the bottom.

'Wow – look at that! That's really kind of you!'

'Well, after all you've done for us over the past year . . .'

'Hey, forget about it. Sorry, I mean, "Don't mention it" . . . Wow, look at that – my great-great-grandfather was an internet technician as well!'

'Really?' said Linda.

'No – it says here he was a draper. How do they find out all this stuff?'

'It's all in the Public Records Office.'

'Or else they just make it all up and hope you won't check!' joked Maddy, and it occurred to me that this was, in fact, perfectly possible.

'It's a present for the whole family, really,' I continued. 'Your history is important. Where you come from, what went before . . . you know, it sort of defines who you are.'

'Look at that picture of you at college!' said Linda. 'And who's that blonde tart leaning all over you?'

'Er, and all the pictures are interchangeable,' added Maddy, quickly.

We left Gary and Linda to make the disappointing discovery that none of Baby's ancestors had gone down with the *Titanic* or been hanged for horse-stealing and we headed home.

Family life had quickly reverted to normality after Maddy had returned. The children found it slightly irritating that their parents were so obviously trying really hard to be nice to one another, and shouted, 'Get a room!' every time we so much as cuddled one another. But on a deeper level they obviously appreciated having both their father and their mother around, to remind them to get off the computer and do their homework, to tell them to tidy their rooms and clear the dinner table and walk the dog and put their clothes in the washing basket. It was just at such a profound level that the children wouldn't have realized quite how much they appreciated it.

But Madeleine and I hadn't just got back together for the sake of our kids. Maddy told me she'd realized that I was, in fact, 'the light of her life'. I was momentarily amazed to hear her being this romantic, until she added, 'Okay, so the light flickers a bit these days, and the fuses keep going, and the bulbs don't last five minutes, but frankly I can't be bothered to get another bloody light now.' I'm sure what she was trying to say was that relationships evolve, marriages ebb and flow, and you just have to keep working at them, adjusting your hopes and expectations but never taking one another for granted. As long as you try to see things from your partner's perspective occasionally, and don't forget to get her a card for your divorce anniversary, you should get by.

Despite our kids' outwardly confident and contented manner, I still worried about how much they might have been affected by our original break-up. Every self-help book and parenting guide I read alluded to the notion that, at some level, children will blame themselves for a parental split. However much her courtiers tried to reassure her, Queen Elizabeth I would still say, 'But I'm sure Dad would never have beheaded Mum if I'd been a boy . . .' I'd been particularly worried about how Jamie might react to the reunion. I was still haunted by his outburst at the swimming pool, and the look of fury that he had given me when his mother had run out in tears at our supposedly ironic divorce party.

I contrived an opportunity to walk Woody on the Common with

Jamie to give me a chance to have a grown-up talk with my half-man, half-boy.

'I won't let it ever get like it was before,' I said, sounding more apologetic than I'd intended.

'You can't promise that,' he said, like the admonishing parent.

'Well, I can promise that I've changed.'

'We'll see,' said Jamie, which is what adults always say when they don't want to agree to something. We walked on in awkward silence for a while, and I worried that my son might never forgive me for the trauma of his formative years. Then from nowhere he piped up, 'Still, at least it means we won't have to see that wanker Ralph any more.'

'Jamie! Don't use words like that in front of your father.'

'What, "Ralph"?'

'Exactly . . .'

In the distance a tractor chugged and rattled, and the delicious aroma of fresh-cut grass mingled with the smoke of the first summer barbecues as impromptu picnics spread out across the giant green tablecloth of the Common. Then Maddy and Dillie were spotted in the distance, approaching on their bicycles, my daughter all puffed and pink-cheeked from racing to catch up with us, flushed with excitement at springing this moderate surprise.

'We thought we could all go to the bandstand and get an ice-cream.'

'Great idea! Get me a coffee,' I said, as they cycled ahead, pursued by the dog.

'I don't want an ice-cream. So can I just have the money it would have cost instead?' suggested Jamie, not quite entering into the spirit of the moment.

It was just a perfectly ordinary scene, a family sitting outside a café in a London park, spooning the chocolate froth off their parents' coffee or sharing a taste of each other's cones. But as I chatted and laughed along, I felt myself detach from the unit, like some hidden social anthropologist or lab scientist gazing down in wonder at the whole incredibly unlikely scenario. How blissfully unaware this family was of the preciousness of this moment; how fragile and ethereal a thing was human happiness. This might turn out to be the best moment ever, right here, right now. I might look back in years to come and realize that that was the happiest it ever was.

Maddy was so beautiful and warm-hearted, her face showing the creases of forty years of smiling at everyone. Jamie was quiet and dignified, always so judicious when he did choose to speak. Dillie glowed with enthusiasm and unshakeable trust in the goodness of people; she wanted to agree emphatically with everyone she spoke to, and attempted to chastise the scrounging dog with a voice so gentle and loving that he thought he was being invited to climb on her lap and lick her nostrils. And there was I in the middle of them all, consciously recording this precious memory, cured from the classic paternal blindness to my own importance to my family; finally aware that I was one of the retaining toggles that held this fragile self-assembly unit together. I felt like a born-again father, an evangelical family man; I wanted to knock on doors early on Sunday morning and ask people if they had ever thought about worshipping their partners. 'For, yea, your wife did bring forth new life, and verily you did call him Wayne.'

Or maybe I had just drifted off, because Dillie was talking and I had learned to filter it out like the rest of the family. 'Dad-can-I-upgrade-my-phone-to-a-BlackBerry-so-I-can-BBM-Mum-and-my-friends-because-oh-my-cone's-finished-but-it-is-free-and-so-it-would-actually-save-money-if-you-think-about-it-ah!-look-at-Woody-he's-so-sweet-have-oh-nice-shirt-by-the-way-and-what-I-should-get-Grandma-for-her-birthday-oh-it's-*How-I-Met-Your-Mother*-tonight-can-we-watch-that-and-tape-*Glee*-to-watch-later-but-the-BlackBerry-Curve-not-the-BlackBerry-Bold-9000-which-is-for-businessmen . . .'

Jamie smiled an affectionate smile at his sister and just said,

'You're not due an upgrade till Christmas, and the timer is already set.'

Maddy had told me something remarkable about our quiet, contemplative son. During that terrifying purgatory when Madeleine had been staying with her parents in Berkshire, she had answered the front doorbell to see Jamie standing there in his school uniform. This place was an hour's train journey and another hour's walk, so Maddy was both shocked and delighted to see her son suddenly turning up at his grandparents' house, clutching the present of a chocolate orange for his mother. And while he was supposed to be in double maths, mother and son had sat on a bench in a pretty back garden in the countryside sharing his thoughtful gift.

'Anyway, me and Dillie were talking . . .' he had said.

'You *and Dillie?*'

'Yeah. I persuaded her to pay my train fare,' he said, through a mouth stuffed with chocolate. This was 'sharing' in the sense that Maddy had about two or three segments and he had the rest. 'Anyway, we just thought you should know . . . that whatever you do, it should be what you want, not what you think we want. Because what we want is what you want.'

Maddy said that was the first time she noticed his voice was breaking.

'Well, that's no bloody good,' she had told him. 'Because all I want is what you two want, so now we're completely stuck!' and she kissed the top of his head so he couldn't see that she was crying. I later noticed that Maddy kept the cardboard packaging of that chocolate orange in her bedside drawer. Every time I saw it I felt a surge of pride in my teenage son, preceded by a moment's disappointment that I hadn't stumbled over some hidden uneaten chocolate.

The day after Gary finally became a father I offered to take my old friend out for a celebratory lager or, in my case, sparkling mineral water. Gary took the last empty table, dangerously close to the dartboard, where random darts would occasionally bounce off the board and threaten to skewer us if we touched on anything personal.

'Well, here's to your new arrival!'

'I'll drink to that . . . Gazoody-baby!'

'A baby girl! Now that's two people in your home you won't understand.'

'Talking of which – how are things with Maddy?' ventured Gary, as a dart spun back off the board and landed near his foot.

'Great! Really great. I mean, it's early days, but we're both making a real effort and I think we're really happy.'

'That's good.' He took a large sip of beer. 'So she still hasn't twigged that her father forged all that false-memory bollocks?'

'What?!' My mouth hung open at the enormity of what Gary was suggesting.

'Don't give me that!' said Gary, looking slightly disgusted at my hypocrisy. 'We both know you *did* shag that French bint. I clearly remember you boasting about it to me at the time. Yeah, he did a good job, old Ron, with his phoney photocopies and made-up psychiatrists. It's quite flattering that he went to such lengths to get you two back together . . .'

Another dart bounced off the board and just missed me.

'You mean . . .? So I did commit . . .' A wave of sickness washed over me. Was everything back in flux? Would I have to tell her, or was living a lie actually the only possible option? Fortunately, this impossible dilemma never had to be faced, because a few seconds later Gary burst out laughing at my intense mortification, spraying a certain amount of lager across the table as he did so.

'I tell you one thing that has never changed over twenty years. You were gullible when I first met you, and you're just as fucking gullible now!'

'Bullseye!' came the cry from behind us.

'Ah, you should see your face!' laughed Gary. And I affected a good-natured smile, using muscles normally intended for screaming. The young darts players made way for an old man with very thick glasses, and we decided to continue our drinks standing up at the bar.

The next morning in school, I found myself wandering off the curriculum in a philosophical discussion during my last lesson with this Year 11 class. 'So all this history we've done over the past year – is it all true, do you think?'

'Yeah, 'cos if it's not true, it's not history.'

'But who's to say what's true?'

'True is what happened.'

'Or is "true" what everyone thinks happened? Tanika's letter to the *South London Press* about how her dad really died – and the big article it prompted – that's changed the official history, hasn't it, Tanika?'

'Yeah, and we're planting a tree and we're going to put a notice underneath. Will you come, sir?'

'I'd be honoured.'

Six months ago, an exchange like this would have prompted catcalls and jeers to the effect that Tanika loved Boggy Vaughan, but all that seemed to have been left behind.

'You see, it's all a question of perception. If a tree falls in the forest and no one hears it fall, does it make a sound?'

There was a pause while they thought about this.

'Has Tanika's tree fallen over already?'

'No, Dean. Try and keep up. The point is, do things just happen, or do they happen because we perceive them to happen?'

'Maybe she should have put, like, a little fence around the tree?'

'Sometimes we think we remember something, but have actually reinvented it, because the fictional memory suits us better. And the same is true in history—'

'Nah,' interjected Dean, "cos in history I never remember anything.'

'We all put our own angle on everything that happens to us, consciously and subconsciously. Governments, countries and individuals—'

'What – even Wikipedia?'

'Even, incredible as it may seem, Wikipedia.'

'So, basically, what you've been teaching us all year might be a load of old bullshit?'

'I wouldn't put it quite like that. I'm just saying that history is not what definitely happened. History is . . . well, history is just old spin.'

That evening, Maddy and I sat out on the wooden decking as the evening light gently fell away. We had banned the children from watching any more repeats of *Friends*, so instead they watched *Friends Bloopers* on YouTube. The garden was in full bloom, brimming with beautiful flowers snapped in two by Jamie's football, with the lawn now a perfect, uniform dusty brown, where children and the dog had worn away every last blade of grass. Green parakeets swooped over the rooftops, with distressed-sounding shrieks at the realization they'd somehow ended up in South London.

'Linda and Gary took the baby home today.'

'Blimey! I wonder how their marriage will cope with all the pressures that's going to bring.'

'Oh, I'm sure they'll get through it,' said Maddy. 'Gary's probably got a special app for it on his iPhone.'

'Ha! I could have used one of those. GPS technology to tell me where I'd gone wrong in my life . . .'

'I think the secret is just to find what it is that really makes you happy. And then drink a few glasses of it every evening.' She took a sip and visibly relaxed as it hit home.

'I must tell that to my Year Eleven class.'

'You seem to be enjoying school much more than you used to.'

'Yeah, we had a really interesting discussion today. About the nature of history. Quite existential, actually. They so want to be certain about what definitely happened.'

'Yeah, well, you might not be the best judge of all that . . .'

'Fair point. But having completely lost my past, it makes you realize how all that stuff can actually get in the way. Countries go to war over distorted versions of history; couples get divorced from accumulating bitterness about stuff that never quite happened the way they remember it.'

'So that's Vaughan's solution to the spiralling divorce rate? Everyone should get chronic amnesia and not recognize the person in the bed beside them?'

'You don't need amnesia for that. Just a swingers' website. No, I'm just saying that you've got *your* version of the past, and now I've got mine back, and we should each respect the differences.'

'You probably still don't remember the time you promised to do all the ironing for the rest of our marriage . . .'

'No, strangely, that memory's still not come back. But I do have a very strong recollection of you agreeing that whenever it was my turn to cook, it was fine if I just ordered a curry delivered to the front door.'

'No, I think that was another false memory.'

'Damn!'

'Chicken korma, please.'

She went to pour some wine into my empty water glass, but I covered the top of it with my hand.

'Not drinking any more – remember?'

'Oh, yeah – sorry. Old habits die hard.' But the end of the bottle somehow knocked my fingers and the glass fell and broke in two.

'Shit! Sorry.'

'No, that was me – I knocked your hand.'

'No, my fault – I thought I had it.'

'No, really . . .'

We burst out laughing at ourselves and I picked up the broken glass.

'Give it a few months and I'll remember that was definitely your fault.'

'In ten years' time, I'll say you smashed the glass. After you threw it at me in anger.'

Dillie's hysterical laugh could be heard coming from in front of the computer.

'Ten years' time! Do you think we'll still be together in ten years' time?' I asked.

'Maybe. Maybe not.' She put her bare feet up on to my lap. 'Who knows what the past will hold?'

A striking eighteen-year-old redhead walks into the Students' Union bar.

I have never seen anyone so beautiful and charismatic, and once she sits down I place myself in an empty seat nearby and hope she might notice the fellow first-year directly in her eye-line. I pull my brand-new textbook from the bookshop bag, but decide I can't just turn to page one: it will look more impressive if I open it somewhere near the final chapter. The words blur under my gaze and I can't help glancing up every few minutes to catch her eye.

'That's a very scholarly-sounding book you've got there,' she says eventually.

'This? Oh, I'm just reading this for pleasure; it's not part of my course or anything.'

'Hmm . . . Do you mind me asking, why are you starting at the back of the book?'

'Oh, er, well, that's just how I prefer to do history.' I feel myself blushing at having been caught out like this. 'You know, I can never wait to find out what happens at the end . . .'

She laughs a little at my attempt at an explanation. I glance down at the final page and exclaim, 'Oh no! The Romans win!'

'Oh, shit! Now there's no point in me reading it!'

'Sorry about that. I'm Vaughan, by the way.'

'I'm Madeleine . . . Sociology.'

'Unusual surname.'

'Yeah – Russian or something . . . Are you here for the Experimental Poetry Performance?'

'What? Er, yeah. I love that stuff. Oh, you just made that up, didn't you?'

And she grins and that is the moment I decide this is the woman I want to marry. Then a couple of Maddy's friends arrive at the table and she invites me to join them. 'This is Vaughan, everyone. He's studying history,' she explains. 'Backwards.'

Acknowledgements

This story is based on an original lunch with Mark Burton, my former TV co-writer, whose generosity with ideas and advice is quite frankly beyond careless. Enormous thanks are also due to all the other friends and professionals who read various drafts: Georgia Garrett, Bill Scott-Kerr, Sophie Wilson, Brenda Updegraff, Pete Sinclair, Jenny Landreth, John McNally, Karey Kirkpatrick, Jonathan Myerson and Tim Goffe.

I would also very much like to thank David Fitzpatrick, who himself experienced an amnesia similar to the fugue at the beginning of this book, and was kind enough to tell me all about his life since that day. For technical and legal advice I would like to thank Alex Carruthers and Tony Garment, who allowed me to put away that copy of *Divorce for Dummies* that was so worrying my mother.

Thanks are also due to the countless other friends and relations whose faulty memories tell them that it was they who came up with all those off-hand jokes and one-liners that seem to have found their way into my book. My children, Freddie and Lily, have been a wonderful source of encouragement and enthusiasm. Lily in particular was full of elaborate suggestions about the possible wording of the dedication. But most of all, it goes without saying that a book about a marriage owes an enormous amount to my wife of twenty years.

All those times I seemed to forget things, Jackie; that was just me researching this novel. Thank you. x

John O'Farrell is the author of three bestselling novels: *The Best a Man Can Get*, *This Is Your Life* and *May Contain Nuts*. His non-fiction includes the political memoir *Things Can Only Get Better* and *An Utterly Impartial History of Britain* which won the best Comedy History book at the 1815 Congress of Vienna.

As an award-winning comedy scriptwriter his name flashed passed the end of such productions as *Spitting Image, Murder Most Horrid, Chicken Run* and a few shows he'd rather forget. He is the founder of the satirical website NewsBiscuit and can occasionally be spotted on such TV shows as *Grumpy Old Men, The Review Show* and *Have I Got News for You*.

www.twitter.com/@mrjohnofarrell